Britt and Jimmy Strike Out

A Novel

By Stephan Salisbury

Alternative Book Press
2 Timber Lane
Suite 301
Marlboro, NJ 07746

www.alternativebookpress.com

Britt & Jimmy Strike Out

2018 Paperback Edition
Copyright 2018 © Stephan Salisbury
Cover Illustration by CL Smith
Book Design by Alternative Book Press

Author Photograph by Jennifer Baker
All rights reserved
Published in the United States of America by
Alternative Book Press

Originally published in electronic form in the United States by Alternative Book Press.

Publication Data
Stephan Salisbury [2018]
Britt & Jimmy Strike Out/ by Stephan Salisbury—2nd ed. Ask Publisher for Further Publication Information

ISBN 978-1-940122-42-7 Printed in the United States of America 10 9 8 7 6 5 4 3 2 1

For Mollie and Nathaniel

Presidential Log, Morning, 5/23

The President awakes at 5:16 a.m. EST.

The President lies in bed for six minutes, eyes closed.

The President makes the following remarks:

"I am at the mouth of a tunnel. The tunnel can be reached through a trap door in the laundry closet off my room. I open the door, get down on my hands and knees and enter. It is dark. As I shuffle along, the tunnel gets narrower and narrower until I find myself unable to turn around. I hear a scuffling sound ahead and decide to back out. I then hear a low growling noise behind me. I can neither go forward nor back. I try to remain calm. The scuffling sound grows louder. The tunnel then vanishes and I am lying on my bed. The skeleton man who lives below reaches up for my hand. When I see his boney finger inching over the bed sheet, I become afraid."

The President lies silently.

At 5:44 a.m., the President asks for the Overnights. He puts on his glasses. An aide, Mr. Zinc, brings in a full-size laptop computer and hands it to the President.

The President issues a request:

"How about some coffee, Zinc?"

Mr. Zinc goes to the open door and whispers to the security aide in the hallway. He then returns, standing silently near a settee along the north wall of the presidential boudoir.

The President looks at numbers from 5/22 to 5/23.

The President makes the following remark:

"Shit."

After a moment the President elaborates and issues an interrogatory:

"These suck. What the fuck?"

The President spends some time staring at the computer screen, scrolling through page after page.

At 6:22 a.m. the President sighs and delivers the following remarks, interrogatories, and directives:

"For Christ's sake. Get me that coffee. Where's Antimony? Get me Antimony."

Mr. Zinc attends to the President's requests.

At 6:31 a.m. Mr. Antimony enters the President's chamber. The President makes the following remarks and engages in a colloquy:

"What the hell, Antimony. These are terrible."

"Sir?"

"I'm talking the Overnights."

"There is a considerable variation from day to day, Sir, as we've discussed, most recently on 5/22. But looking at the trend charts, the numbers are definitely moving in the right direction, big-picturewise. Sir, if I

10

may lower the overhead screen, I can present a brief PowerPoint™ that explores the demographics, the target-audience participation rates, and, of course, your sticky message.

"Sir, your message, as delivered in the new package, is most definitely sticky."

The president tells Mr. Antimony to proceed.

At 6:48 a.m. Mr. Antimony lowers the screen and commences walking the President through the data underlying the current Presidential Marketing Campaign: *The Three Goals of The President: Excitement. Penetration. Satisfaction.*

Mr. Antimony uses his laser pointer for emphasis.

"According to Focus-Group Data from the beginning of the year through 5/1, Awareness is up to 21 percent; Desire has risen to 22 percent; Contentment is now at 20 percent; and Satiation is at 32 percent. On the whole, we believe – and I don't think this is out of the ballpark – that these numbers represent a clear overall positive."

At 6:54 a.m. the President makes the following remarks:

"That's shit, Antimony. It's right there in the data. Look at your Satiation number. Is it an outlier? Bad data? Either way spells trouble, with a capital T."

Mr. Antimony makes the following rejoinder:

"Point taken, Mr. President. But if I may, the Satiation numbers are the result of highly successful pre-present rollouts. In other words, we are talking citizen-consumers who have embraced the Presidential brand completely. They have incorporated message and product as one. They are locked in, you might say. They are, Sir, in your pocket. They want you. They need you. They love you. You are everything to them. At the least, you are not Nothing, which is the only option for them, really, as you know. Given the option of the President or Nothing, our data show that the average citizen-consumer is nearly two times as likely to select the President. Inertia? Perhaps. Sick of it all? Maybe. But they stick around and that's a fact. Most definitely a fact. We see this on Slide Six, if I may fast forward?"

The President gestures with his right hand for Mr. Antimony to continue. At the same time, the President delivers the following analysis and directive:

"Blah blah blah. Go to Six."

"Yes, Sir. Here we have Six: *Meet Joe D.: Resourceful Re-Seller, Powerful Screen Personality, Satisfied Citizen-Consumer, Green-Screener, Leisure-Activist.*"

The President makes the following comment:

"I can read."

"Yes, sir. Here are the guts of the slide, coming up now, the audio-visual component."

Whereupon Mr. Antimony adjusts the volume; the video element commences with a VO:

"Here is Joe D. in his room. The White-House-By-The-Sea stretches invitingly in the background. And here is what Joe D. has to say."

Joe D., sitting in a tall chair, his white hair ruffling in the "breeze," begins his comments without any prompting:

"I've come here, oh, I dunno, most of my life. I know every nook and cranny of this place. There's nothing they can throw at me that I haven't seen before. The holo-golf, the viscous pool, the Amethyst Grille & Lounge. It's all there. Just the way it was there for me last year and the year before that and for my dad too, I guess, and for his dad. But I wouldn't have it any other way. Because you know what? There's no place like the White-House-By-The-Sea. What ya gonna do? Go west? Ha ha ha. Yep. The President still has the best franchise anywhere. He keeps the ball moving around the bases. That's the way I see it. If you don't keep the ball moving, you're not gonna be in the game. And, hey, it's the only game in town. I'm Joe D. and don't forget it. You can find me here, with the President, as always, and at www.joedsstuff.com."

The President issues the following interrogatory:

"That's it?"

Mr. Antimony responds:

"Yes, Sir. Don't forget we're going after the Grey Ghost Solitaries, your older empty-nest peddlers. So, here is a customer who knows you through and through. He's comfortable. He understands there's nowhere 'out there.' There's no upside to walking away from the White-House-By-The-Sea and testing uncharted territories. Yet, as he says, there's nothing you can throw up at him that he hasn't seen before. No matter! You are what he wants! He's satisfied. He's full. A textbook case of Satiation. What's his response? He's back again and again. Most importantly: He piggybacks his site onto your site. He hangs on. He even throws his web address into his comments. Touching, really, don't you think, Sir? It's not that he can't get enough; rather, he doesn't want anything else that's out there. Why? Well, yes, there is nothing else out there and the poor man has to live. But what's the underlying 'feeling' exposed by our research? Need for comfort and, if not that, need for existence. Or, expressed another way, instinctual distaste for deprivation and want. The imagined or the new is untested, possibly dangerous and materially unproductive. Joe D. doesn't need that. He doesn't want that. Why? Because he knows the President delivers. The President satisfies and, more to the point, the President moves product. Play on the President's team and no one's going to take the ball and go home.

"Sir, Joe D. works his sites, sells what he's been able to acquire via the Presidential Pre-Owned Acquisition Collection System, then, at the appropriate time, he embraces his exclusive reward: the annual sojourn at the White-House-By-The-Sea. Oh and that's something, Sir. He knows nobody's going to ram a garbage barge up onto the veranda. Nobody's going to leak oil. Nobody's going to stagger in and try to cadge a quarter or blow up the room. He knows the roof is solid."

Mr. Antimony points to the ceiling of the presidential bedchamber, cocks his head, and continues.

"Plus, and this is key, Sir, Joe D. is living, breathing, animated proof that citizen-reseller product moves when lashed to the President's product. Snare a link with the President and you are wrapped in brand security, such as it is. All the fuel is the President's fuel. Ride with the President and your product moves at lightning speed, presidential speed. Ignore the President and you're left on the launch pad smelling gas, so to speak. Satiated, yes, and most definitely satisfied. Sticky, Sir, as I said."

Mr. Antimony pauses and looks expectantly at the President.

The President responds:

"Get rid of that damn screen. What you're saying is that our whole strategy is to stay afloat, totter around,

14

and not smell like shit? Do that and these people will stick with us and not starve, for god's sake. They'll drop their links on our sites. They'll try to sell their stuff through our networks. They'll look to us to carry them out of the mess we're all in. Yes. Sticky, like fly paper – we're just hanging out there by our thumbs. They're with us because there is no one else. Zippo. They stick with us because they can't get away. They're just trapped on the so-called sticky message."

"Yes, Sir, that's about it, bottomlinewise. We don't put it that way. We talk about Presidential Security, Presidential Stability, the Presidential Rewards System™, that sort of thing."

Mr. Antimony returns the screen to ceiling storage.

"If I may, Sir, that's a pretty good strategy. It's worked for centuries. Joe D. and the millions like him continue to rack up Presidential Rewards™, Sir, year in and year out. They buy space on the Presidential Home Page. They make use of the Presidential Reseller Network™. They collect product on the ground from the Presidential Pre-Owned Fill Areas™. These are loyalists, Sir, locked and loaded."

The President drinks his coffee, quietly brought in by Mr. Zinc, and places the cup on the night table.

The President comments and then poses an interrogatory:

"This Joe D. and the thousands out there like him are hanging by their thumbs like the rest of us. We're all bats in a barn. His re-sale numbers are down, year over year, if I'm not mistaken, and I just looked at the data; our numbers are down on an annual basis. Demand's declining. Product Delivery Systems are withering away. That's the reality. That's what the numbers show. Why are you spoon-feeding this blue-sky nonsense to me? Do I look like some clueless customer ripe for a shakedown? Do I look like Joe D.?"

"Absolutely not, Sir."

"Am I an apple? A mark? A sucker?"

"No, Sir. Far from it."

"A rube? A chump?"

"No, no. No way, Sir. You are the big-boat rider. The captain. You are the sharpest of the sharp."

"Then tell me, Antimony, what I am to make of these numbers? They are up in some instances, yes, but the revs streaming in are flat to down. You're suggesting a successful rollout. Unpack these numbers and what we have are on-going critical lows at all coastal franchises. We're talking a lot of franchises. We are up because we've cut costs, you damn well know that. We've lopped off practically a continent from our control. That's gonna juice our net, but it's not an answer long-term. Not in any way. Plus, the Satiation number is often used, if you recall the Smith-Macomber research, as a proxy for Boredom or, worse, Frustration. Death, I'm told, is a Satiation benchmark experience. Product does not move to listless or inert customers. Where is desire? Where is need? Where is that indefinable yearning and dreaming? Your Joe D. is our canary, I'm saying. What has he got to say about traffic built off our sites? What is he saying about redirects? What does he want, dammit?"

"He didn't mention any of that, Sir. He's just there. We're emphasizing reach and comfort in this phase of the rollout."

The President pauses.

"Do we remain able to assure findable and collectable product in the Authorized Fill Areas? Those

16

piles are picked pretty clean, I'd wager. Resellers don't leave much behind after they swarm a site."

"Yes, Sir. While it is true a considerable amount of reseller product has been extracted from pre-owned sites over previous centuries, our latest research estimates a rubble-to-product ratio of 2.37:1, which remains within the sustainable range. Joe D. has plenty to find and dish out through his reselling operation, particularly if he remains with us and maintains authorized-site access. He knows that. We know that. And the word is spreading, yet again, to everyone else, so that they know that too. You, Sir, are the Future, built on the past, what's left of the past, what's pickable, you know, for the future."

The President remains silent with a hint of a furrowed brow.

Mr. Antimony waits for what appears to be an oft-repeated directive.

The President makes the following request at 7:57 a.m.:

"Break it down. Do the math."

"Right."

Mr. Antimony pulls out his pad, scrolls through, plugs in some numbers and presents the President with the following data points:

"Okay. Frustration: 61.2. Boredom: 66."

The President winces and makes the following demand:

"Let's have the Big Enchilada."

Mr. Antimony takes a deep, sucking breath.

"Doubt: 16."

After a moment's silence, Mr. Antimony continues.

"I should add quickly here, Sir, that there is no statistically significant difference in the Boredom quotient from previous campaigns. And let's not forget, Sir, the Frustration data points could be the product of new algorithms put in place at the onset of this campaign. Research is on-going."

The President makes the following comment and request:

"Oh my god. Doubt is the issue, Antimony. You know that. The trend line is up, up. Now. Talk to me about the overnight share and distribution numbers."

"Right. All down, it's true. Down and diffusing. Each of the Omni-Time and Late Night shows built on the Presidential brand and sponsored by the Presidential Partner Networks, which are the only Networks, are down. New independent streams show a statistically insignificant, though measurable, increase."

The President and Mr. Antimony engage in the following colloquy initiated by a presidential interrogatory:

"Down?"

"Yes, Sir, down."

"What the hell is with these people? What the hell? We give them the ride of their lives and they hop off the jet. All right, Antimony. You know what to do. Our partners in the private sector are not going to be happy. When they're not happy, we're not happy."

"No, sir."

"How are the Personalized Solo Feeds working? Do we remain able to craft message-per-consumer in an acceptable way? Are we maximizing? I'm talking the hard stuff here, Antimony. Can we deliver, to each and every customer, the kind of experience, the kind of news, the kind of brand punch that keeps product moving? If they piggyback on us, are we able to carry and redirect? Are they getting measurable return? Are we jacking salability? Are we pumped?"

"Yes, sir. I'm not sugarcoating you. Our spots are hitting everyone on the tubes with something crafted just for them. Everything from news spots to reality streams. For instance, at this very moment, early as it is, we have over 11.1 million individual newsfeeds playing to specific news consumers, providing them with news messages to fit their profiles. Each citizen is receiving individualized news videos and stories generated by real-time consumer and buying data and behavior. We're talking real specificity, Sir, no guesswork."

"Good."

"These are news steams, of course. And we're delivering them all with personalized brio, if I may say so, right down to the weapons employed by Presidential forces in meeting the Eastern Threat. No one uses 'a gun,' Sir, not in our hostilities; we kill with product. Plus each audience member, by way of example, is subjected to a personalized ethnic threat analysis and an on-going, targeted campaign. We are paying close attention to providing individualized languages, dialects, and accents for news spokesmen, subjects, aggressors, aggresses, and collaterals during the course of – and at "the end" of -- the threat, etc. etc. You know the drill, sir. Whatever is happening, we insure people hear what they want to hear in a way we know they want to hear it. They see what they want to see, determined by our MIT-designed news-relationship algorithms. In a total way, Sir, they want what we want them to want. Why? Because we are right there with them. We know them. It's all in the data. And, I might add, Sir, they know us. We deliver.

"We are particularly keen on our Focus Group Work here, sir. We have sussed out the general, overall threat factors, including fear of the street. We have particularized sector threats. And here is the real meat: Using the research findings, we have drilled down and teased out what each of our consumers most fears. They may be Satiated, but when they enter the threat vortex, they cleave to you, Sir, like barnacles. We are particularly pleased with the results of this package."

The President interjects with an interrogatory:

"What about placements? Are we providing tactically adequate placements for partner product?"

"Indeed, Sir. No question. I've mentioned the weapons placements already. There can be no question what weapons we favor, based on strategic visuals and news-reader vocalizations. We're casting a wide net, brandwise – hardening products and outlets; water brands; safe zones; quake riders; daily nutrients and leisure-meals. Everything from what people ingest to what they excrete – we are right there placing partner product. We individualize content; we provide interactability allowing product to move based on anticipation of consumer needs and desires. In other words, Sir, to use Joe D.'s phraseology, the ball is moving."

The President makes an analytical comment:

"Yes. Yes. Not enough. Somebody's dropped that damn ball. These numbers are not satisfactory. We're talking change here. Something has changed. Why aren't we out in front on this? Now it's too late to make the anticipatory play. We have to retool strategy."

"Sir?" Mr. Antimony responded.

"Doubt," the President says, snapping his computer shut. "The Doubt Index is troublesome. More than troublesome. Lest we forget: Fear Trumps Doubt."

"Yes, Sir. But it's a new day with a new citizen-consumer. They balk at new threats, and I would say, just for emphasis, that our traditional threat generators are more than enough to sustain underlying anxiety. Our consumers are queasy, but not too queasy. They know the presidential threat barriers will keep them safe. And the threats they fear are the good old threats, branded threats – the Eastern Bloc, the Street Marauders, etc.etc. Bottomlinewise, in the vernacular, they believe their butts won't get kicked if they stick with the President. They know the President knows how to deal with these familiar threats, which we've been throwing at them for ages, Sir. And our partners are staunchly with us, as always. We've had several Presidential Network Relationship Officers congratulate us, by way of example, Sir, on our subtle use of defense products in the Eastern Threat videos and message environments. Our customers enjoy the threat because they know the threat. It's basic threat branding, Sir."

A thoughtful President is silent.

At 8:27 a.m. he issues an interrogatory:

"Antimony, what are the relationships between anxiety and frustration and malaise and doubt?"

"Sir?"

"That's right. You have no answer. You're even surprised there's a question. Listen up: There is no difference, or rather, we are talking a continuum. A frustrated consumer is an unpredictable consumer. A frustrated consumer is anxious and gravitates to others who share the frustration. Whining begins. Doubt is seeded. Before you know it, you have a mass, a grumbling mass, a mass unhappy with the smooth functioning of the system. Where we see smooth, they see rough, or, worse, nothing at all. The public space becomes filled with cacophonous voices. The wrong consumers begin to shout. They cannot be silenced with the usual bromides. Language fractures into epithets. In a word, Antimony, frustration is a step away from disgruntled anarchy. We don't want that."

"No, Sir, we certainly don't. But, if I may, I think we are light years away from anything of the sort. And, if I may, Sir, all of our research shows that even comforting fear that drives your consumer into comforting arms only moves so much product. Some product, yes, to be sure. Most product, no. Fear, Sir, needs careful calibration. It needs to be tended and nurtured and pruned. Too much fear will disrupt our predictabilities. That's why we stick with the old fears, the tried and true. Those are fears we can work with."

The President pauses for several moments, his hand covering his eyes. Mr. Antimony remains silent.

At 8:39 a.m. the President breaks his silence:

"Who am I, Antimony?"

"You are the President, Sir."

"What does that mean?"

"It means you have the most difficult job in the world. You have an awesome responsibility. You are the most powerful leader of the most powerful nation. Nothing happens unless you authorize it. You have the biggest network, the most franchises, the greatest access. When the President speaks, all other voices recede. You gather us all up and protect us and help us. You are a magnet. You pull us in and launch us on our way. You make life possible, Sir, in these difficult times. As I said, awesome."

"Antimony, I have no power. I have nothing. I am a lone figure."

"Sir?"

The President closes his eyes and again falls into silence.

At 8:52 a.m. the President resumes, eyes closed:

"There is a towerlike structure in the midst of a field. It is night. I can hear their angry voices and I can see the lights of their flickering torches. They are getting closer. No matter how fast I run, they are gaining. Perhaps I can escape into the tower. I push open the flimsy door at its base and climb the stairs. Their voices and shouts seem everywhere outside. I emerge onto a small deck high over the countryside. Looking down, I see hundreds of them gathered, looking up. They are shouting and yelling. All have torches. They begin to throw them through the open door at the bottom of the tower. I wave my arms. They are ants. They are nothing. But the flames begin to shoot up the walls and the smoke billows everywhere."

Mr. Antimony listens quietly. He remains silent for a few moments after the conclusion of the presidential remarks.

Mr. Antimony makes the following comments:

"Sir, the numbers are simply at the high end of the channel. We expect them to drop. If I may, Sir, your predecessor topped the 61 Frustration rate several times, according to our database research. You, yourself, have played in the 60 area repeatedly during past campaigns. Doubt at 16 is nowhere near the record high. We are not in a burning tower with angry citizen-consumers swarming at the base."

The President responds at 9:11 a.m.:

"You're not listening, Antimony. I'm not simply talking villagers here, although god bless Joe D. I am talking no place to go. I have no power except the power to persuade, the power to sell, the power to bully-pulpit the marketplace. And I have that power not because of Joe D., but because of our proud private partners. Where would we be as a nation without them?"

"I can't say, Sir."

"Try looking at the bottom of the barrel. Without those partners we'd have no juice."

"I think 61.2 Frustration is hardly cause for alarm, Sir. We've seen worse. Maybe our customers are frustrated. Maybe they've had their fill. But they are passive, Sir, passive! We see no evidence of any move to alternative product. We supply, they consume. Alternative product is a nonstarter. Of course, there is no alternative product, nor do we allow it. No alternatives out there, Sir, except those that are pale reflections of our own robust product."

The President issues the following interrogatory:

"Who is going to move them away from the base of the tower if we don't?"

"Sir, again, I don't believe we are atop a tower. But your perception, Sir, is what counts. We can tweak."

At 9:33 a.m. the President issues the following directive:

"Show me the feeds."

"Yes, Sir."

Mr. Antinomy proceeds to rotate the east wall of the presidential boudoir. A bank of screens appears, each showing different representative street and home scenes captured by the Individual National Feed System (INFS) and used by the President "to get a feel" – as he likes to say – for citizen-consumers across the land mass. A separate smaller group of screens displays different rooms within the Signature White-House-By-The-Sea complex. Those screens, a recent addition, were mounted during the President's GiveBack Initiative™: "Here for you – yesterday, today, and tomorrow."

At 9:39 a.m. the President issues the following interrogatories, as the screens settle into viewing position:

"What am I doing now? What are we broadcasting? Is that it, Screen L45?"

"Affirmative, Sir," Mr. Antimony answers. "And others."

Mr. Antimony pauses and then proceeds: "In L45, as you can see, Sir, you are engaged in sexual intercourse with the First Lady. She is wearing an attractive, high fashion top from NaughtyGal, those are Sof-Tee sheets on the presidential bed, Baby Dolls, I believe. You recall, Sir, we partnered with Sof-Tee last year after their robust contribution to the GiveBack Initiative™. And I see we have, right now, a growing number of watchers interested in the presidential tumescence."

The President makes the following remark:

"We don't do it like that, Antimony. I've told you that before. You're going to lose morning share if my producers continue to push that same old, same old on our citizen-viewers first thing in the day."

"Sir, I'd interject here that robust displays of presidential eroticism are consistently our most powerful tools, so to speak. What can distract those consumers from surrounding the tower and burning it down?

25

Presidential intercourse. Who would miss it? The one consistent response we've had in all Focus Groups, across all marketing segments, refers to the awesomeness of the presidential performance. When the President and First Lady retire, the audience pays attention. Product moves once the President has had his way and the First Lady signals Completion and Fulfillment."

The President remains silent for a moment. The President remarks:

"I can't do that 24/7."

"Sir, our live Presidential Feeds suggest otherwise. Your performance boosts the White-House-By-The-Sea. It entices our partners in the private sector to jump in bed with you, if I may. It draws secondary citizen-retailers to cross link. In a very real way, Sir, it says, 'Ride with the President and get what you need to get.' All segments respond, Sir, but none responds with as much enthusiasm as the Aging Faithers, your theocratic retailers, particularly those in outer districts. You recall we targeted that demographic group several campaigns ago."

Mr. Antimony waits for a moment, apparently expecting a response. Receiving none, he continues:

"As I suggested, our private partners are very satisfied with product movement during shows exploring presidential intimacy. You might want to consider, Sir, the relationship between Orgasmic Release and our broader Satiation numbers. It could be break-through market research. What if Satiation is directly correlated to masturbatory satisfaction?"

Mr. Antimony makes some notes regarding new research initiatives.

The President remains silent, eyes closed. The President makes the following remarks at 10:33 a.m.:

"I am lying in my bed, sound asleep. I feel something warm and wet. My penis is distended. I open my eyes and see a strange woman with my penis in her mouth. Who are you? I want to ask. But words die before forming. I cannot make a sound. I cannot move. I lie on my back as this person continues to fellate me. I ejaculate involuntarily and she looks up at my face, my juices dripping from her mouth. I realize this is my Mother. I try to move. I cannot move. I try to scream. I cannot scream. I am silent."

The President ends his monologue and appears to ruminate. The President then makes the following statement:

"We cannot suggest anything like that to our partners, Antimony. They will back away very fast. They do not want to associate with presidential incest. We are not going to continue to fuck ourselves."

"No, Sir. Although there is older research suggesting ambiguity on that point, at the least, in some demographic areas. I'd want to analyze a bit more before blanket-statementing it, if I may."

"Is my P-Chat™ up and running?"

"24/7, Sir. The President never tires of conducting his P-Chat™, crafted personally, of course. You are speaking to, let me see here, 7.2, no, 7.3 million followers at this very moment."

"Good."

The President pauses and then continues with an interrogatory:

"We are not ignoring those of Faith? Are we exploring their adherence to traditional ritual or have we cast them aside with orgasmic enthusiasm?"

Mr. Antimony responds with a grimace.

"No, Sir, most emphatically not. You can see, on Screens A-6 through B-2, that representative examples of your personal daily devotions are now taking place in the White-House-By-The-Sea Templette. Sir, you are solemn and reverent. Multiple Faith Promotions are also being conducted in the C Section feeds and feeds sprinkled through D, F, and G. Of course, we also have feeds X and Z for those who eschew all practices and beliefs or are devotees of outlying creeds."

The President responds:

"Yes. That is good."

At 10:59 a.m. the President makes the follow statement:

"Alright Antimony. We will ramp up Threat suggestions in the South and in neighborhood subsectors. We will reach across all channels with an announcement of presidential appearances on Key Partner Networks addressing the "rumors" of dislocations and disruptions. We will allude to multiple partner offerings in the presidential statement – security supplies, vehicle alarms, clothing and uniform designers, rations and dining, luxury safe zones, etc. We will suggest acquisition of appropriate product – that's your territory Antimony – and provide appropriate links for the aroused and anxious consumer. Dig into those Satiation numbers. Widecast reminders of atmospheric and geologic instability. Don't forget: the streets are dangerous. We need to keep them at their screens. Perhaps a crisis is in order. Have Systems take a look."

The President pauses. Mr. Antimony takes the opportunity to interject:

"We must be careful, if I may, Sir, in our exploitation of the Fear matrices. Overwhelming

28

amounts of research data going back centuries conclusively show that broad product sectors suffer when fear becomes too widespread, even if not all encompassing. Other activities ensue, as you know. Some elements of the marketplace thrive, of course, under such difficult conditions; but others tend to lag."

The President considers this remark and makes the following statement:

"Yes. Fear is an unpredictable wind. We want predictability. We want the warm breeze, not the gusts from all directions."

At 11:27 a.m., Mr. Antimony says: "Yes sir, no gusts."

The President thinks for a few more moments.

At 11:36 a.m. the President makes the following remarks:

"Ramping up the threat does enhance unpredictability, it is true. But we are then able to cull the herd, as you know, removing those elements that tend to degrade or disrupt the system. Ultimately, we return to a level of quiescent and purposeful citizenship. The marketplace stabilizes. Product moves. Brand is enhanced.

"Build the Threat, and prepare a presidential appearance on all Networks."

Mr. Antimony makes notes.

At 11:41 a.m. Mr. Antimony inquires:

"Partner Networks will be notified. Should they be prepared for presidential delivery of personal content, Sir? Remarks?"

At 11:42 a.m. the President responds:

"What is called for, yes."

The President pauses and delivers his analysis:

"Leadership, Antimony. They want leadership. We will defeat this Threat. We will face the foe and emerge even stronger. We will rid ourselves of those who despise us for what we believe, whatever it is. This is the only answer for those of us looking to the bright future together."

"Yes, Sir."

At 11:50 a.m., after some thought, Mr. Antimony makes the following statement:

"I'll get on this immediately, Sir. I will pull together the Campaign Team. All will be up and running within hours. Your remarks, Sir, will be delivered from the White-House-By-The-Sea Library. Should we stoke the fireplace, Sir, prior to commencement of remarks?"

The President responds:

"Whatever. No out-there threats, Antimony. Do you understand? We want them to recognize what will wreck their lives – but the President stands tall and firm to protect and guide. A pillar of trust and resolve. An example. Run a Meta-Search through the Behavioral Data Files to locate appropriate images. We will lock arms and proceed as one to meet adversity."

"Understood."

Mr. Antimony concludes:

"We will Green-Screen the appearance and other elements as quickly as possible. By the end of the day, we should begin to see some results, if past campaigns are a guide. If I may, Sir, you are certainly the Captain of the Ship and we are all grateful for your service."

At 11:54 a.m. Mr. Antimony departs the presidential suite.

The President lies silently for a few moments.

At 11:59 a.m. the President closes his eyes and makes the following remarks:

"I am alone. My eyebrows are gone and a large red spot has spread across my tongue and around the stud riveted through its fleshy tip. Could it be the blood of cherries? When I open my mouth, I seem to invite vermin."

Chapter One

My name is Britt, and this is my account of the disruption as it happens, okay, that I'm telling because no one knows it like I do, having been disrupted and a disruptor and a flailer on the swirling sea.

Okay. Okay. There's no swirling sea, like literally. And no, I don't kill anybody or anything like that. Not even close, although there're tons of killings, which I'll get to – disruptions are kinda nasty, if you don't know. What I'm telling is what's happening, not anything more or less, featuring me and Jimmy as we move through it all. Don't go, Oh let's tie it all together and explain it like they did back in the day. Let's all ruminate. Let's chew it over.

Forget it. Nobody really cares. They say so what, or frack that, or that's all just rumors or a lot of fiction; get to the good parts, they say.

Get to the good parts?

Look, what I know for sure is some of what comes through my eyes and what I can touch and what's inside my head, and I don't even know all of that except that it's in there somewhere all at once.

This morning's where I'm beginning because it's like the beginning, although the actual beginning goes back quite a ways. What's a beginning? It's where you start, but you may have started someplace else and my beginning may be your middle or the beginning of your end or the actual end or after that, and what happens then? A story is like a ride. You get on, but the bus or whatever has probably been traveling for a long time before you even see it, let alone get on it, you know what I mean? And it's filled with who knows who headed off to who knows where or it's empty of what once was and where's the beginning or end of that?

Insider info: I've never been on a bus.

Or a story's like one of Brute's vids. You plug into his stream and he's standing there with somebody or other, and Plato666 is jiggling the cam so stuff's all jerky and the falling ash and grey light makes it hard to see and – boom! – some geezer comes wheeling round the corner through the haze and whacks Brute on the head with a bag of plugs and pulls his pants down. Unless the whacker is somebody you know from on screen, you're like, whoa!

Those are some of the issues with Brute's vids and with bus rides.

You don't know what you're getting into if you've never been in it before.

I need to get up now, but I'm lying on my back in bed here, cam rolling in the corner, like always. My eyes are shut. You can probably see me, if you're there.

Hi!

I don't want to open my eyes, truth be told.

What am I going to see that I haven't seen a gazillion times? My bed with the Miss Olga Baby Dolls? The whitish wall with the studio cam plopped on its platform? Stacked stuff? The screens for all my feeds? My windows with the blackouts? Slumped geezers out on the sidewalk? The gutted place with the crooked TWISTERS sign across the street?

All that stuff is the eternal part of the scene, what's always littered around the Hood now and forever. It's like, so what? But there's a close-to-the-bone problem this morning, way too boney, way too close, like right here in my rooms, like with me, and it's whooshing out of control like one of those dust whirls out west.

I think my audience is drying up big time.

I keep my eyes shut super tight.

I really, really don't want to see that. Give me a geezer slumped over on the walk any time.

Usually there are tons of comments and questions waiting in my inbox when I get up and I can kick right off and set the day's message and really get behind it. When I'm on, when things are smooth and humming, a lot of people pick it up and pass it on and pretty soon I'm mostly fixed for the whole day. Revs stream in. An ad or two. Orders. Ka-ching! I do Ten Retro Hip Ties, Hip Nibblers?, Six Hip Tops You Can Wear Anywhere Outside the Zone, Four Hip Corners You Can Text Out, Ripped and Hip, and Hip But Not Banged. That's me.

I'm Hip, okay? You don't think Britt without thinking Hip. Vice versa also as well. That's the whole point. I am totally branded. Even so, as much as it's cringy to say it, maybe you are so completely outside of all of this, so completely unsure of who you are yourself and where you are in the great chain, that you haven't worked up your brand or even know that you need to have one.

Listen up: How can a system hum without adequate brand density – that's the question you need to ask yourself.

Okay, there are probably some hits and stuff waiting for me in the inbox and on the site right now: That's awesome! Where can I find some of those shoes? And: You really got it, you nailed it, u r so beautiful!

Well, okay, I like that.

But still something's not right. I'm flagging and kind of wobbly. Maybe I'm shrinking. I've lost some regulars, I sense it, and I can see it in the numbers. Where did they go? Plus, all that foot gear I picked up at Bernie's Throwaways & Castoffs? Not moving. I need that stuff out the door. I'm getting that feeling, like something gnawing away inside. Actually, it's more than that. It's not just the numbers that are down. Where's Deb? Where's Brute? Where's Melinda? A lot seems to be vanishing – more than usual. It's kinda comforting that I can see myself on my screen inserts. Dozens of tiny squares filled with little skinny Britts with their thin arms and sharp shoulders. So I'm still here – I can see myself on my screens. But Deb and Brute? Where are they? It's like they've dissolved and now maybe I'm on my way to dissolving too, shrinking fan by fan and down and down and down and maybe you can't even see me anymore or maybe you're not even there watching, which is worse. Maybe I'm the only one watching myself. If I'm the only one who's watching me am I here? Oh gosh.

Lemme just lie here a sec, forget the overnights, forget the metrics, forget the reach.

Okay.

I can't.

I think yesterday and the day before that and maybe some more days, a lot of days actually, it seems like there weren't so many hits and no orders and I'm wondering where this is all heading and whether I've wandered off message.

What if it's down big again today? What if nobody buys? What if nobody buys in? What if nobody says they want to be me? When nobody says they want to be you, are you you?

Like I said, gnawing away.

Jimmy always says you have to stay focused, that's the key, otherwise people become confused in their heads about who you are, and your audience begins to drift and you get all empty. You shrivel and blow away off the screen and out of the picture. Which is true. You lose friends and admirers. When they go, they take a bite of you with them. It hurts. Hurts your pocketbook too – then what? Let's be practical here. I need the ads; I need the revs; I need the orders, the fans, the followers, the customers. I love all my friends, I surely do. Their hits are like life. What else is there? I need to be seen.

Here's some inside dope, not for publication, alright? I'm not just a star on screen, though that's the main thing. Really. I scavenge. I barter. I trade. I haggle. When the last word drops, when the fridge is stale and the Veet is gone – whatever it takes. I'm maybe roughly about 22, give or take, you know, and this is what I'm made for, what we're all made for, as you guys know.

By the way, since you're here or might be here, how do you like the hair? I'm doing that cerulean and burnt sienna thing, color by KlawDia? I talked about it last week, I think it was – a half 'n' half with a flat press over the ears? Kinda mussy at the moment. Actually kind of faded, too.

But mussy's Hip and Hip is where I'm at. For fulfillment. Okay, I'll be totally straight, for the ads and the orders. There're revs in Hip. People want to see it. They want to be it. They want to buy it. There's only one place, and one place only for all that. Right here. With me. On the site.

Yeah, my site – oh man, that's where my action has to be. That's where it all flows together and comes to life! If something happens in my room, which is not infrequent, as you may know, and the cam picks it up? That's when everything becomes so real! I want you to see that! Like my segs with Mike? I know you've seen them. I like Mike, plus he drops the reds on me, you know? Then we always go to bed for fun, so I want you here, watching – and you should be here experiencing it all! The site's where I am and what I am and who I am and all that stuff everybody knows so well, or should want to know.

So what I'm thinking here, anxiety percolating, cam rolling, aqua SleepyGirl top just peeking from the sheets (you can check out SleepyGirl on my Nite-Nite page): Have I sucked it all dry? Am I looking at a rebranding issue? Do I need a redo? Is there anything worse?

Build the brand, Jimmy says, and you build the life. To brand is to be. Thing is, you can get everything working like you want it to, you are who you seem, and it goes okay for awhile, and even then your followers start to wander off. What do you do then? What if you come up with wrong solutions?

Like with Deb, she got totally messed up, and her fans didn't just drift away, they went over a cliff. Oh Deb! Where is Deb? That's part of the hollowness here, a part of the gnawing I'm feeling. A big part, if you want to know. Days now it's been, I think, since I've seen her here or since she updated. Where are you Deb? Your screen is dead. Your site is a like a tomb.

She's the President's Girl, right? Really worked at this awesome video where she's with the President and all on the beach. Jimmy did the tech stuff. I set up the location. Here's a big secret: It wasn't really on the beach. There's no beach around here. We went out to the dunes shifting near the Ville and used them – I thought of that! – and then Jimmy slapped in the waves and stuff and if you look real close, you can see the seams in the images and the color's just a bit off. Not Jimmy's best. It worked though and then Deb wrote the lyrics and we sibeliused the instruments so she sounds all musical, not all pounding and bassy:

> Hey, Mr. President,
> I've got some sand in my hand
> and I'm gonna take a stand,
> come on and lie on me.
> Let's grow, we can make it change,
> make it big on the range.
>
> Life is no beach, we know.
> You gotta reach, we know.
> We can do it together, all together.

We did it on the Excellon Dunes, too! They still haven't picked up on that, the corps haven't, which is good, because we'd get a cease-and-desist and maybe even a little visit if they did. The corps are like dogs on a rabbit.

Greetings: The Excellon Dunes™ are a registered wholly owned Mobile Land Mass (MLM). Excellon Corp and its subsidiaries, directors, and shareholders consider any unauthorized use of the Excellon Dunes™ -- no matter their location at any given time – to be a violation of certain inalienable rights constituting an irreparable loss punishable... etc. etc. etc.

Stay out, they're saying.

Jimmy says, Blah, blah, blah. They don't know as much as you think they know. Yeah, he says, the dunes are pretty dangerous – what do you expect with all that extraction activity Excellon's been up to? Now they're just trying to keep away from liability issues – that sand can open up faster than a Nutri recycling chute and you are gone, sucked right down the gullet into the dry hole of what used to be down there underneath all of this collapsing, whirling shit up here. Stay on the road, or what's left of it, if you can find it on the car screens. That's the way I see it, he says.

Thanks for the insight, I say.

It's like a control thing too, he says, with the corps. Keep you stuck in the Ville where they can wrap you in stuff. Wrap you in their stuff from their sites and their outlets. But everybody already figures there's no place to go anyway – why'd you bother going anywhere when there isn't anyplace to go? So they just sit around popping yellow jax and reds and following their shows and working their sites.

That's what Jimmy says. The corps don't want anyone messing with their dirt. They don't want anyone exiting the Ville, even if there's no place to go and nobody cares anyway. They don't want this, they don't want that. The corps just want, and they want you to want what they want you to want.

All I can say is so far so good. No cease-and-desists. No greetings. And no visits – at least not that I know of.

Jimmy knows a bunch, I'm telling you. He's been in the Zone. He goes down to the removal sector, aka the pits. He's been outside the Ville, which is how we got to

the darn Excellon Dunes™ in the first place. That may
have been my idea, but I'd never done it on my own. But
he found one of those old EcoCars, a SmithVerber, which
can do about 75 a pop (no, I do not know where it came
from – he told me I don't want to know), and Deb and me
got in with all the tech gear and we drove out through the
back way Jimmy knows, out of the Hood, out of the Ville
and into the Dry Restricted Area (DRA) to the northwest.

Okay, I was kind of scared, I admit it. I'd never
seen it.

Watch out for that pile of rocks, Jimmy! I'm
shouting like every two minutes it seems.

And he says, I'm not even driving – these babies
drive themselves.

So true. I'm embarrassed. The SmithVee can
sense a collapse or a sinkhole like seconds before you're
on it. Heading out of the Hood and the Ville there's a lot
to avoid, too – one pile of rubble after another, is what I
see on the SmithVee monitors. I love those Smithers!
They surround you with screens that show what seems to
be outside in such sharp detail! We watch piles of bricks
and rocks and cement streaming past all around us, and
then we're out of the Ville! You can see the towering
spires of the West Ville gates beamed in through the
Smither roof feed. They are all corroded and flaking,
jagged at the pinnacles. So old! What a show! They flash
by and we are out onto what looks like flattish ground
with acres of crumbly cement and brown powdery stuff
dribbled over the ground. The screen on my side shows
more rubble, long heaps straggling out over the land like
great jaggy beasts, lumpy and enervated, dry as bleached
gristle. Same on Deb's side.

Let me tell you, you don't see this kind of stuff on
Mindy's Loft Party or any of the other Zoner-wannabe
shows, mostly because Mindy's always home, in her
rooms, fucking somebody or other and pouring in the

reds. Who cares about the land out here anyway when your head's full of reds and you're a star on screen?

We reach the Dry Restricted Area, bumping along some old hi-tech road. The collapsed rock piles finally give way to simple heaving sand. I'm talking dry. The dunes rumble off, all tossing and roiling, like somebody sick. It is unbearably bright. Here and there you see rebar piercing up from underground. Those metal pikes don't move in the wind. Needley sand zings everywhere in your face.

Jimmy, what if we get spotted? I ask, after we've stopped the car. I'm looking at the screens.

Jimmy says, Not a problem.

Deb doesn't say anything. I look at her. She's staring at a screen full of sand, working her performance out in her head, immobile in desiccated thought.

I say to Jimmy, We're shooting in the dunes. They're all owned, like everything else. We're not supposed to be here. There's all the Private Security, and it's all on cam, cams everywhere – dustcams, motecams, sandcams, and the sats, too. Besides nobody is supposed to even think about the dunes and here we're putting them dead center. So how do we get around all that, Mr. TechnoWizard? (He hates it when I call him that.)

And he goes, Nobody will know it's the dunes, Miss Mumble, because when this vid goes up, it'll show an ocean resort, it'll be the White-House-By-The-Sea, the flagship of the President's franchise. It'll be Happyville. It'll be LeisureTime. It feeds into the President's brand. It's not gonna be a question.

And I couldn't argue with that. Nobody has a bigger, more powerful brand than the President. The President sells. Simple as that: You can do your part, he says. Support the President and we will move forward together.

That's what Nutri and Excellon say too.

And really, when you get right down to it, the President's a part of all of us. So when he sells, he's selling us. The corps like that. It's made for them, you might say. He's made for them. And so are we.

Jimmy shouts, Deb, let's go!

I point towards an ochre wave of sand with no piles of cement or spikes of rebar. That's where I want to set up. Deb heads over, walking in that languid way she has sometimes. Jimmy shoots.

We are done in less time than it takes to swallow a plug. Perfecto.

So with Deb, like I'm saying, the President's Girl vid goes up and millions pick up on it and shoot it around. It turns viral. It's more than viral. It's a friggin pandemic. The President's Girl. I can't get it out of my head:

I got some sand in my hand and I'm gonna take a stand come on and lie on me ... da da da da.

Everybody loves the President and Deb linked right into that. We're all happy for her. Micros swamp her inbox. Ka-ching! It's pretty spectacular. And on her site she talks about how she's the President's Girl and that she's pretty viral and she thanks all of us, like with our names, including me and Jimmy, mostly.

We photoshop a lot of images, a lot. Debbie and the President on a ski lift. That's my favorite, and he's smiling and has his arm around her, like he has his arm around all of us, and they're riding high up over the tree tops, heading up the mountain slope. Deb has Coombs Combacks dangling from her feet. She doesn't know a ski from a waffle iron. But that doesn't matter because she's there, on that mountain, ready to shush down with the President! His wavy hair is riffling in the wind, his arm's around her shoulder, his eyes bathe her with light.

I don't think there are any mountains with snow anymore, are there? Doesn't matter. Nobody really knows anyway and the comments she inspires are outstanding. Deb set up a micro mart for photos and autographs, she starts to work up ideas for the P-Girl line of balms and glosses, suits and sandwear, and the clicks and micros and ad revs just keep coming.

This is so awesome, everybody says, one after another: awesome, awesome, awesome!

Which is what you want to hear as the star, and it's sure what you want your advertisers and sponsors to hear and see. She picked up the high end and some of the middle. Coombs, of course. OndadeMar and BeachBunny. Royal River Resorts. Cold Fusion. They love her. Slap her with ads. Everybody re-posts and embeds their own stuff in her stream and it all goes around and around. What a resource. Deb's a breeder. Everybody uses Deb for their thing and the micros just whizz in from all over. That's the system – all that awesome and desire transformed into micros. A humming system. Oh that is the grail for us all.

Then the President's site actually links to the President's Girl! My oh my oh my. Just knowing Deb and watching her reach extend is monster big. You can't do better. No way. And I'm the President's Girl's Friend. It just gives me a glow that everyone can see and feel, almost anyway, and I link to her and lay in some Hip embeds and draw a lot of traffic. What a ride. I pick up

Cold Fusion too. And SeaBots, Submaureen, and Connie's Cool Tops – see what I mean? Ka-ching!

But more than that, spiritualwise, I pick up the intangibles. Everybody looks to me for something they don't have but think they should. It's superfine, and I have it, no matter what.

So are you ready for this? After the President's Girl launch, Deb gets a Zone pass! How rare is that? Gives me chills and prickle-pear arms.

She takes Jimmy and me to one of those places past the checkpoints, and even Security and Sentry recognize her. We still have to do the body scan though, but they're all friendly about it. And before you know it, we are right there in the Zone – the HQ, the Sweet Spot, the Center of it All. Who knows what we might see.

Oh my gosh, we shuttled right past Antoine's Meat Palace, with its noisy animatronic cow – Moo! Moo! – what a trip. The eyes light up too, just like I think the real ones do. The cow's right out front of a plexi-enclosed plaza with a Totally Controlled Environment (TCE), very cool. The meat is outstanding too, I hear, no Plugs or Nuggets, and it comes strictly from actual Nutri animals.

Okay, I know, it may be that a lot in the Zone is sort of faux – building fronts with incised windows, streets with LiquilLite people all flashing and bustling and squishing along. But, hey, you have your Antoine's and Wheezy's and Papa's and all those places that are so familiar on the screens and there are Zoner types using them. It's all there, behind security.

At Antoine's there're even special live feeds from the P's White-House-By-The-Sea cams. That's what I heard on our visit, although I'm just telling you what I heard. You can see what's what with the P in every room.

His shows are great, too. Even the sleep shows. Maybe we didn't actually see him, but we sure saw the outside of Antoine's, and you don't think of the Zone without Antoine's and its landmark cow. I don't know how they do it, what with animals all so gone. But I don't think it's just lab magic. Nope. I hear from Jimmy, and he may really know, that the President has special reserves in the north for his good friends at Nutri, somewhere near the camps.

Okay, here's a super hot tidbit: after the shuttle, we're sitting there in Wheezy's Skittle Café just talking and looking around, soaking it all in, and in walks Matt D and his Bruisers! The waiters are all over them with Mr. D, your table, Sir, and the Bruisers line up near the door, all in their black jackets and hairy wrists. They just watch behind those shades. (Mr. D's Eyewear – his own personal line, of course.) Yes. Matt D. He has his own cam crew too, streaming it all for you guys watching Zoneratti and we can see it all on our pads and there we are too – I can see us in the Zone. I am there!

I remember when I first really got to know Matt. That was awhile ago – thanks to Deb. She was studying him, trying to unravel his sorcery, like a scholar studies some scholarly stuff or something. Matt was doing Zoneratti, of course, and I never missed an update thanks to her studies, not once. We watched Zoneratti like it seemed all day on every screen in my place. We were surrounded and submerged, even when Matt and his beloved Mizz D had their words and there was the plum-pudding incident. Everybody seemed so annoyed and switched out of Matt's stream, but me and Deb, we hung on. Then we were there when the Mizz held Matt's hand at the hospital and he forgave her and all. That's when she introduced Mizz D's I-Color, with Matt looking on from his bed, a little grin on his face, a nod and a squeeze. It was so tender. I-Color is too much, too, and I was there for the launch. I saw it!

Anyway, here we are in Wheezy's and he's sitting right there! I am not making this up. The D-ster looks at me and I feel his eyes on my neck, ruffling up to my ear. He doesn't come over though, and he doesn't eat much – but he loves it all, I can tell. He loves using his mouth.

There's some blond girl with a real sparkly diamond in her nose with him. Who is she? What happened to Mizz D? Is there some shocking news? So I look at him aslant as he's whispering to the Mystery Blond. There is something going on there. Oh! He has the whitest teeth, and lips thin as blades. The Mystery Blond keeps rubbing his ankle with her Madam Bleus (the strap-ons) like she's some kind of kitten.

D wants me to notice those Madam Bleus. His cams zoom in. He wants me to notice the ankle play. The image is fixed on multiple screens around Wheezy's. Everyone stares (except for the Bruisers). I should be jealous, he's saying with his eyes and those unzipped white teeth. He laughs now and then and tilts his head. There's a glitter around Matt, I swear, something regular people don't have, but want. That's one of the reasons he's Matt and that's why we all are reaching to him and watching him and following him on Zoneratti. That's why Deb was studying him night and day. He's a star, with Nutri totally behind him, and not just with the occasional ad. They've swaddled him. Which gives him an aethery power. The biggest of the corps – and Matt. He's endorsed, certified, bona fide, sanctified. He works with them to smooth everything out, to hone the message, to move in the same direction. He is who he is, swathed in everything they do. His brand. Their brand. What's the difference?

How many times have you gazed on a Nutri Plug or seen a digi-poster of a country road with corn and plants and stuff growing for miles and dreamed of Matt? Be honest. All the time it happens. It's crazy. He's become like the fields and the trees and the good people at Nutri protecting what's left of it all. That's powerful stuff, you know? Matt D and the corps and the P keep us going, keep us striving to achieve our dreams and to be all we can be and have all we can have.

He looks towards me again with those clear blue eyes. Or are they hazel? Who knows what they really are and that doesn't matter because they are all over me. Oh, they are everywhere.

I don't mind saying that I shot the whole visit, captured all of it on the pad, gave Matt D my own star turn, wiped out the check points, gussied up the Bruisers, erased his personal cam guys, redid the menus, sharpened up the Niblets, and turned it into a Matt's Four Hippest Bistros in the Zone post and show.

I piggy-backed it all onto Deb's President's Girl page, tapping into all that yearning – even though nobody can really get into the Zone without a timed pass and security stuff. But everybody wants to and they want to know what they'll do when they get there and how great it is and all. Secret: It's pretty cool – everybody's always watching you and there are more cams than back in the Hood. (I go to pee and I open the stall and I'm sitting there reading the door, about the new Sassy Girl AromaView unit, which seems pretty awesome, and then I look up and there's a pinhole! I mean, come on guys, in the bathroom? It's not all that interesting, even if it is me. I'd better not see that on Vinnie's Vids either!)

Then I did a post on the Mystery Blond and the romance and where is Mizz D? Did Matt dump her for the MB? She must be back at the D-Nest, crying and crying. She feels so deeply. How is she going to treat Matt when he gets back home? Maybe the Mizz knows the Mystery Blond. Maybe the Mystery Blond is her friend and is pulling a doublecross? The possibilities! Or there's something else going on. Maybe that wasn't Matt! What do *you* think?

That went up on my personal blog, Britt's Hip Bitts. Got a lot of hits – The Shocking Tragedy of Mizz D Revealed: EXCLUSIVE!

Typical comment, at random, more or less:

Thank you Britt for showing us who he really is and how he really is when he's away from the crowds and his dearest Loved Ones. Bless you, Mr. Arcade.

Thanks Mr. Arcade!

And Madam Bleus dropped one on me, which put some serious change into my account. Madam Bleus – the shoes for the blues. I added that little joke in an Update, which annoyed them, which led their External Affairs and Relationships Manager to reach out to me and share their displeasure, which was out of line from my point of view.

No, I'm not going to take it down.

He says, Our message at Madam Bleus is more inclusive and upbeat. It's not about the blues. The blues are a sign of sorrow and sorrow is foreign to Madam Bleus.

Which is ridiculous. Why back the Mystery Blond's appearance?

What a derp. I don't care. Back and forth – and they yanked it. I lost micros on principle. But you know what? You can't realign just because some Madam Bleus brand guy is worried about message taint. That's the meaning of free speech. They were into squashing the marketplace of ideas.

Oh yes, the President's Girl's quite a ride, but all rides kind of slow down and end and so you've got to keep thinking and refueling. You've got to build on the awesome stuff, not wipe it out or fuzz it up. You've got to maintain focus. So Deb comes up with the next one, which is probably the wrong thing. She's The Boy's Lost Girl.

Did I say probably the wrong thing? Let me make a major clarification: Big Mistake. You don't go from being the President's Girl to being somebody alone in a boy fantasy, I don't care how good the fantasy is.

Jimmy had serious doubts about the vid.

He says, Deb, this may be going in the wrong direction brandwise. Why not The President's Girl: Blowin' It Out? Or even the President's Girl II? Why have Lost anything? Nobody wants to glom onto Lost. There's too much Lost around already.

And Deb's like, That's the point – we can reach everybody with this and everybody will understand. Even the President's Girl misses the boat sometimes and goes astray. People will worry for her. This will tie them to her. It's human, like us, like everybody. Then we can come back in the next episode with the President – he intervenes and helps her, like he helps everybody. We'll pick up the high end and the mass stuff too. Plus we'll show how the P keeps things humming and on track. We'll expand the franchise.

And Jimmy goes, Is the President on board?

Deb pauses and says, Sure.

And Jimmy looks at her for a sec and then says, Okay, but I hope you've got a Plan B.

This is the vid, which maybe you've seen: Deb's in bed and she has this furrowed look – oh she is beautiful! – and wonders where he's gone, the boy, that is, and then you get her walking and running down these hallways and there are transparent outlines of this guy (Jimmy did the layering) and she thinks she sees his back and there are hands reaching out through the walls trying to grab her. And he's a fade out. And she fades in and out, like you can see through her. It's supposed to be dreamy, okay? Lots of cuts and syncopation. And Deb's lyrics are, I guess you'd say, kinda stark?

> Where am I when you don't show?
> What am I when you don't show?
> That's what I want to know.
>
> When you're not here with me to see,
> I don't know where here might be.
> I can't hear what might be.
> What might be I can't see.
>
> What's the cost of lost?
> What's the cost of lost?

And then it shows her out on the street with all the crap out there, the rusted out hulks and boarded up buildings and bricks spilling out on the sidewalk and some old guy slumped over on the cement. A geezer on the walk! She stumbles around him and there's nobody else out there, of course. She looks wild. Totally in need of rescue.

> Where can I be when you're not with me?
> Am I me if you can't see?

Huge mistake. Way off the tracks. The comments after it went up on The President's Girl site said it all:

WTF?

Go back to wherever it is and don't get found again.

Forget the boy. Hes runnin from u cuz u don't know shit.

Why did I ever follow you? I need a GPS to get out of here!!

Nobody wants to be out there on the damn street! What r u doing? Bodies on the walk? Rusted cars? Mess? Collapse? Broken brick? Where are the mountains and the beaches? Zero out the street!! Yech!!

lost is right, grrl, and runnin scared, get off the damn street for starters and get yourself a head screwed on strait. u need a doctor, not the p

It was like unremitting. Deb was destroyed. She was sooo upset. She went from being the President's Girl to some whacko on the street in about a nanosec. Plan B, whatever it was, down the tubes. How could the P ever be on board with this even if he did know about it? Oh man. She was just like the rest of us, that's for sure – scrabbling. No more lunches in the Zone, no more Zone, period. BeachBunny goes bye bye. The bots drop all these ads on her for on-street clean-up services from Nutri subsids like Corpus Remotionem, Defuser, Pox Away, and the worst, Waste Removal & Medical Systems, WRMS. It was death staring you in the face. Click here. Oh my god.

Deb is so sweet, innocentlike. People made her some kind of crazy person or something, some loopy attenuated loon. That's what happens. They turn on you so fast. One minute you're on a mountain slope with the President, a virgin sheet of snow stretching before you and a party waiting to burble in the lodge; the next you're hurtling down an endless incinerator shaft thick with black gook. Like there's no time to come back from the brink or anything. She fuzzed the brand. No. Let's be honest. She didn't fuzz the brand, she stomped it and left it like one of those geezers on the sidewalk.

Here's the thing: she broadcast that she's not what they thought she was or whom they thought they saw the last time.

Her fans scattered pronto, like pigeons from a square. It's almost like she blew herself up deliberately, you know?

And we went along with it, that's the thing. We let her do it. Me and Jimmy kind of saw her as the President's Girl and this was a sequel, a twist in an adventure tale, or a segment in a magic series, and she'd miraculously return with the climactic third part of the trilogy, The P Saves the Girl. That wasn't right, though. Not only was she creating a whole new image each time, but in the teeny tiny Hood, where we are, and in the whole other-worldly world of the corps and the P and Matt D and Zoneratti in the Zone, and out in the Ville, the dark sprawl surrounding us all, lost has the taint of an infection, the power of a supreme glitch spewing gunk everywhere. Lost is where stuff goes haywire. Lost is what nobody wants to touch. Lost is what is off the screens.

A complete mess up and I have to admit to you that I feel responsible, and so does Jimmy. Dumb. Dumb. Dumb.

Lose your brand, you lose your self. And vice versa also as well. That's the way it works.

It gets worse. She's wandering around in the wake of that disaster and goes to Mike. I'll never forget it. She goes to Mike's place, which I didn't know she was going to do, okay, and she comes here that afternoon, right through the sun, and rings the buzzer, and I open the door, and there she is. I can't believe it.

What the heck did you do? Don't move, I tell her.

She's tearing up and I grab my pad and begin shooting. Tears are streaming down her sweet, smudged face. Mike's inked her shoulder, right above the BeachBunny logo on her arm – that one's pretty cool, I have to say, nets about 50 a month, too – right there on her left shoulder, Mike stenciled YOUR AD COULD BE HERE! I am not kidding. In red and blue Century Bold.

I say, Deb, what are you doing? That is so tacky. You don't advertise your space. Everybody knows it's available.

And she says, Britt, I had to get Mike to do it. My micros are gone. I've got to eat and I've got nothing but the BeachBunny people behind me and I got this text that said they are re-evaluating their priorities and looking at different directions and they want to conference with me. What a mess.

I say, When you're lost you're all alone.

And she says, I hit a speed bump on the expressway to your heart.

I've got the key to the highway, I say. And we laugh a little.

What a great scene. I got it all on the pad cam.

Poor Deb. Maybe she isn't The President's Girl. Is she the Boy's Lost Girl? Who is she? She doesn't know. Or maybe she does; maybe that's the issue. She does

54

know and it scares her, like it might scare all of us if we looked inside.

She settles in though and we upload the vid from my pad – the latest episode in the life of the President's Girl who's now the Boy's Lost Girl who is, well, okay, just Lost. Will she find her way back? Will she find the boy? Tragedy on the Stoop!

Goes onto her site and she picks up a lot of traffic – everyone wants to see someone else crash, burn, and cry. It's the oldest in the book and it never fails – but no ads beyond those darn geezer clean-up ops, WRMS and Corpus Remotionem, and such.

And I think: what's a bigger sign of failure than a slumped body on the sidewalk being swept into a robo-canister?

I want to be clear. Deb and I are like sisters. Her business *is* my business. It's *our* business. We are together. We are with each other, and Jimmy, too. I've got to remember that and remember how far back we go, way before the President's Girl.

Like we both heard the collapse of the General Merchandise Mart. Felt it is more accurate. That monster had been boarded up since before time began, and it fell in a heap with an incredible ka-boom! Petticoats of dust yelped into the air. The whole Hood staggered with the crash. And oh, the rubble! Nobody would go near the place – who knew what was gonna come down next? But I was hungry and Deb was too and it was right down the street, you know, you couldn't avoid the heap if you wanted to get anywhere in the Hood. Basically that collapse was one more reason to stay off the street for everybody. Not for me, though, and not for Deb. You have to seize opportunity – that's the entrepreneurial spirit! We both hit the rubble.

Oh yes, Deb and I go all the way back, like maybe three years, or two, since I graduated from camp. We sort of knew each other from bumping up on different sites with chat and comments and stuff, but the Mart collapse was like a bonding experience, like in the flesh. She was working up something called Debrity, and I was working my way to Hip. She was shooting her trek to the Mart, and I started shooting her – she looked so great clambering over the rock piles in her torn green fatigues – and we cross-posted and started to hang. She could talk about anything and make it sing. What a mind!

Like the Hood is not huge, as you know, or maybe you don't, those of you who don't go out much. Small, but it's got a big heart. So it's not surprising we hitched. The Hood's where you go when you're starting out and need a place and the rest of the Ville could care less and the Zone is just Dreamland. At night in the Hood you can hear the noise of the Zone to the east, like caws across the Ville's dark sea. You can hear the drums, the whines, the blares, the thwackas – all the stuff that makes up Zoneratti, which is much closer, of course, because Zoneratti is everywhere, on every screen across the Zone and the Ville and into the Hood and all that stretches to the west and south, past the sands and dust and everything that doesn't blow away.

Knowing the Zone is right there makes the P seem so close too, at the heart of all our blacked-out rooms, where no one wants to see in or out but where everyone has a screen for multiple views. Think about it. I do, and I get all shivery. He's right there! The President makes all of this hum and click; he oils the systems, gives a boost, deploys Sentry and shout outs, pumps the corps, sells the best of the best. He's the guy we all look to, or should. Oh, listen to the P and you're entranced by a lilting flute. You are still as a fallen limb as he winds and coils and delivers his message directly to your every cell. Makes you shiver just to think of the P gathering you in and giving so much of himself to you. Just to you. So delicious.

The quality of caring and of democracy – that's the P.

Enough!

I sit up. I move from my bed. I look at my numbers and I am not happy. Shit. This is like armageddon. Hits are down. Reach is down. Six Hip Nutri Sandals fell through the sub-basement. I mean, nobody liked it. Nobody shared it. Did I mention no orders? I am screwed.

Doesn't anyone want vintage Nutri sandals anymore? On the blog – the one where I wrote about how Matt and the Mystery Blond are nuzzling ankles – hoover32 wrote: Matt don't need no dumb shit from OCD suede punks.

Plus not one ad.

This is what I need first thing in the morning. Zilch on the rev front and some jerk calling me an OCD suede punk. This Hoover is such a doofus. OCD? This is the Hood! Rubble. Rats (mostly mutants). A building here. A building there. Lots of stuff fallen down. More fallen every day. Crap everywhere. People behind their blacked out windows working their sites. Drone deliveries. Drone cleaners. Drone security. Flexi-cams on plexi-poles. Geezers on the walks. My kind of place – there's value in abandoned, if not in Lost.

But this Hoover twerp? I am outraged! Mostly I am bummed. This is not good. I feel queasy and crumbly on the inside, like a dry drained ditch.

This is it.

My inner screen has fuzzed.

I pull up Jimmy on the pad and punch in.

Hi Britt, he says, looking over my shoulder toward the back of the room, like there's something there he hasn't seen. His straight brown hair is falling over his eyes, like always; his face is as angular as broken brick, though not as dusty.

I tell him, I want to talk to you. I want you here, now, please. Because I feel something needs to be done.

He says, What is it? What's the matter? Hits trending down? Some kind of threat? Gotta job? Stuff disappearing? Like where's Deb? What is it?

I say, Stop. Stop. I haven't seen Deb. I haven't seen her!

Oh. And?

I say, Okay, this may sound creepy dumb. It feels like we're in a black alley and there's a brick wall ahead and I don't know what to do. You can't go back because there's nothing but more crumbled brick and WRMS bots trolling the walks on contract. Hits are in the tank. I need to see you.

Jimmy isn't particularly impressed. He shakes his head and kind of snorts. He tells me that he's got to green-screen some stuff for the flower-pot people. He's got to feed the pigeons on the street. He's got to help his mom.

And I tell him, Your mom is dead. There are no pigeons.

And he says, Yeah, but the audience doesn't know that. She's a prop.

He's got to finish helping her gather food and secure the windows. Today he's going to help Mom and show everybody how he goes down the pits I mentioned, opposite end from the Zone, the ones where all the waste is off-loaded for sorting and removal? You get there around dawn and you can pick up all kinds of building junk and bistro throwaways – if you're lucky. It's not so easy because WRMS drones are programmed to skim and siphon off any reusables – food you can process, stuff to deal and trade. Stuff, stuff, stuff. If you're nimble, you can grab and survive.

In the olden days, you'd say Jimmy's dumpster diving; now he's doing entrepreneurial mining.

WRMS isn't happy about the competition, even though it seems small, so you gotta be quick on your feet, like cats used to be. I've never seen the pits, actually, only Jimmy has, so all my info comes from him. Just so you know.

Yeah, Jimmy runs a how to site for life in the Hood – Jimmy's Alley: Life, Liberty, Bricks, & Mom – kind of practical matters and such. He doesn't try to ride Matt D or famous types like the rest of us cause he says there is something to be said for the day-to-day world. He doesn't go for the big-time splash, like the President's Girl. He doesn't try to drum up the right kind of daily infatuation, like with Zoneratti. He stays his course. He listens to what we say we need.

Besides, he says, the niche is wide open. He says you can live in his niche like 24/7. I say we are all niches. We need more. That's what I feel now. The secure window thing? I admit, everybody needs tight windows in the Hood. Since Sentry pulled back to cover the Zone, everybody fortifies for themselves. Jimmy will show how you can put razor edges in the sills and jambs, even the grills, if you want. You can set up an open circuit and the dude comes through, grabs onto your setter plate –

Jimmy prefers a molybdenum alloy, helps your creep strengths, he says – and it's fry time.

If you want to know – and why wouldn't you? – I use them here. Just as a precaution; adds a level of uncertainty when you put that little yellow WARNING! sticker with the lightening bolt and the exploding body at the bottom of your window gard.

Here's something else I'll let you in on backstagewise: I've never had a hassle.

But nobody wants to hear this kind of thing. Who wants to think about all that crap on the street? Who wants to think about the dumps and break-ins and where your next bite is gonna come from? Or how you're gonna live without a job or a site. Or what you're gonna do about your mummified mom. Or how you're gonna survive the next building collapse.

Jimmy says, lots do, Britt, masses of them.

And do you know what? He's right.

Chapter Two

While I wait for Jimmy I go and get a packet of Blossom Beads (a soother – maybe not as sweet as the tabs Mike drops off, but not a bad little buzz) and my last bottle of Aqua Veet.

This just won't do.

Okay, I'm worried, alright? What the heck is Deb up to? Does she even know? I have the weirdest feeling that something has torn away from me and we are going down. She hasn't updated in cons. I check her site again and all I see is her bouncing ball.

President. Boy. Lost. Girl.

Deb's got a nice plug in where you can go and ask questions and you get a personal response, like a chat. Alright, another insider tidbit: It's all stuff that Jimmy worked up for her and it's really just Lucy, aka IntelliWord. You're chatting with software. Deb plugged in a list of questions and then gave her own on-cam answers and the program absorbs all that like a parrot and then squawks it back at you, embellished. I mean, it paints a whole portrait of her, kind of.

She isn't even there.

Polly, aka IntelliDupe, I call it. She doesn't think that's funny.

I'm here! she says. Okay.

Q. How did you meet the President?

A. The President saw my vid about the Hood and how sort of happy we all are and how pretty strong we could be all together and he looked at me and said to himself, this is someone I am all about. This is someone who gets it. I reached out and touched him and his message came in like a chunk of rock right through the blackouts. The next thing you know we're building things together.

Q. What kind of guy is the President?

A. The President is caring and concerned about all of us. He likes to fix things so they hum even more than they hum already. He wants us to know what it is we want. He wants us to have what we want to have. He's all about smart choices. That's his job. That's his dream. Whether it's Coombs Combacks or BeachBunny or a week at the White-House-By-The-Sea, the President is all for it and he wants me to get the word out. The President loves Nutri Plugs™, too, and thinks everyone should enjoy them because they make life better. Just keep cool with the good stuff! He says I'm the one who lets him know what people say and helps them know what they want to want by spreading the word. He says it's not just his circle that matters, his producers, and the corps – it's me, and you guys too. And don't forget those BeachBunny two-piecers. You can find them on the President's Girl in the Sun page.

Q. Does the President eat out often?

A. The President believes it's awesome to be with his friends, his people, his family. That's us. So he's out in the Zone almost every night. Sometimes you can see the rotating lights and the spotter planes from the Hood! We are so close to him! He enjoys Antoine's, Mary's House of Cheese, Dine-O-Mat, Papa's – you know, regular places. That's the President. Most of all he wants me to bring him even closer to everybody. He wants everyone to tap into his streams and absorb his message of strength. That's why he takes my message wherever he goes. My message leads to his message. We are all interindependent, he says, like linked.

He was out in the Post-Forest-Latitude Area (PFLA) in the west, you know, past the sands, where the thermo-readings are up there? And now the President says to all these guys stopping by his site, he says: Hey, this is where you really need SeaBreeze Netwear – the coating breathes naturally, just like my girl says. Click through this page and you're right in the thick of the coolest dune suits ever!

My girl. That's me. Thanks Mr. P!

Q. What is your message?

A. My message is that we are all here together. The President is too, even when you can't actually see him or see the lights in the sky that show he's there, or might be there. That's why I'm his girl. You can hear me 24/7. Here we are now, together, just you and me! He sets the direction and keeps the micros flowing and I'm here to say, Wow! Look at that flow!

That's why you always click for him in the decennial P-Poll™ – he gets the job done! Now here's the real deal: The P's totally big picture. He can see things we cannot see and hear things we cannot hear and the stuff he doesn't think we need to know, we can get along without! And the stuff we know, he knows, and if he thinks there's a problem, why, he lets us know and helps dead-end it. That's why I always listen to everything he says and pay no attention to what he doesn't say. I don't need what isn't there. The P wants to protect and serve and stay on track! I can show you how. Start by scrolling down.

Q. Who is the President, really?

A. The President is the emblem of who we are! He's like my dad and my brother and my bff and camp counselor all rolled into one. Plus he knows so much and if you have a real problem he knows how to fix it and where to go and what to buy. Like once my mom needed a new set of teeth – I know, so back in the day. But there were lots of people around back then too and those that are left, well, they still have to eat, even though Nutri's out with a new injectable LiquiTuber™. Okay, so I mentioned it, just sort of in passing, and boom! the P hits up Meta-Dentier, Inc. and soon everybody in Ville-O-Care is chewing away, not just my mom – everyone! The President has the connections. Every needy soul at Ville-O-Care has the MD Model 10 – The Cruncher, A Senior's Best Friend. Each received the first two sets free and then it's four percent off each additional set, excluding options, servicing and taxes. Not every grey person's a geezer on the street, and my mom is beyond happy now when they wheel her out for supper. Thank you Mr. P! The offer's so great, the P reworked it and now he's extended it to the entire Ville – with a TornadoRagg™ thrown in for free! You can go to the landing page for more details.

I look and listen and shake my head. Thing is, Deb's mom's dead too. And I'll bet she exited with all her teeth. Nutri owns Meta-Dentier, if I'm not mistaken, and I don't think I am. Those Nutri guys know how to get you coming and going. What market wizardry! Meta-D dropped a nice spot on the P Girl site too. Oh Deb! She's so tied into the President, she's put her whole self there (and now her late mom) and nothing's left for the Lost Girl except waste-removal ads. Can't help but notice

WRMS and Corpus Remotionem have muscled out Meta-Dentier.

I'm tempted to open up a session and chat.

Q. Where are we going?

A. I'm really glad you asked that question. We are all heading toward greater strength, harmony, and most importantly, greater share. It's that simple. Just follow the P. We don't need to pay any attention to where he is not. You know why? Where he is not is not there or is already over and done with. It's that simple. Where he is leading is a harmonious land filled with the unforgettable! Our dream lies there. Just watch this page.

Q. How can we all achieve greater share at the same time?

A. When you grow together, there's more for all. Everyone gets their share! That's more.

Q. What is wrong with that reasoning?

A. Nothing! The President is so right! He grows and we grow too. From each according to his needs to each according to his wants. The P is a fixer and a hummer and a rebalancer on the high wires of the Zone!

Q. What is the President gonna do about all the bodies out on the street?

A. The President is concerned about vermin, just like you and me, and he's implemented a program of waste pick up that will clean and sanitize the public environment. He's solicited bids from Corpus Remotionem, Pox Away, WRMS, and Liquesce LLP, for expedited removal (ER), disposal, and cleanup. He has reached out to his many partners in the private sector who share his concern and has received an overwhelmingly positive response. I can share with you his statement, which just arrived in my inbox:

Unobstructed thoroughfares inside the Ville and around the Hood are key to achieving the quality environment we all should enjoy. A fragrant street is a functioning street. If we all work together we can achieve this laudable goal. Discount services are now available from a list of vendors on my site, www.thepresident.gov/freedom/youcanhelp. Let's all lock arms and share the burden and the opportunity of this important project. Please give generously.

Q. Where is the Girl?

A. I am here.

Well that says a lot, doesn't it? I look at my screen. There is Deb, head cocked to the side, curls falling away, waiting expectantly, like I have something to ask that can readily be answered. She doesn't blink. Where is here? Is that Deb? All I know is that this stuff with the President is painful. When you run it through the chat, it comes out nowhere. I'm looking at a whisper, an echo, a ghost.

I am here.

Poor Deb. No way. The P looked at that camera sweeping over the dude sprawled on the sidewalk in the Boy's Lost Girl vid; he looked at the dumped bricks and the planked-up windows and skeletal cars and no scrims and no color and just a great world of broken and his producers told him something real basic: Get out now. If you don't, it'll really screw up the whole presidential message; it'll spill over into the White-House-By-The-Sea brand. None of the corps will go for it. They want that unblemished Mr. P, the dreams of blue horizons, the warm waters made real on the screen – for everyone.

Yeah, the President is something he's built and polished a long, long time, like all the Ps going back and back and back.

Gems, they are.

My HipCam's always rolling, I should tell you, in case you're wondering. I have one in the back room here. I used to have another one in front because you can never show people too much. But the front one's boring, just me sitting, usually hunched over my pad or staring at my blackouts or some of the other screens. Sure, I think people want to see everything, particularly the sex stuff and cheesy stuff you do and how you do your lips and all, so I keep the back room rolling – that's where I've got the bed and the dressing table. What I do is whatever I do – it's all part of being a star on screen, you know. Like I want you to see that I wear a taupe pullover from Highly Contagious when I go to bed, even if I'm alone. Stuff like that.

But then I'm talking to Jimmy over at his place a little while ago. (Where the heck is he now?) He doesn't have a proper cam set up.

I say, Jimmy, nobody can follow what you do. How can you tell if who you are is who you are if nobody is watching to let you know? It's hard to be a star if no one can tune into you whenever.

He says, Britt, you are right. There are some things you don't want them to know. Besides, I'm not a star. I'm just working the system, like behind the screens.

Jimmy, I say, what can you not want them to know? You want them to know everything! You want

67

them to consume your product. You are your product. That *is* the system. No hiding!

He says, I don't know, that's the problem. Remember Brutus11?

Of course.

You seen him lately?

No. So?

Brute's a piece of work, says Jimmy. He has his PalCam on all the time. He has his channel and his site up. He's chatting doing dishes. He's streaming on the can. I draw the line there. Too much info! And then he's over here the other day and he's shooting from his pad and watching himself watching his own place on my screen.

I look at him and I say, Brute, you are self-absorbed.

And he's like, What's wrong with that?

And I say, Look around you.

And he glances around and he says, Yeah, that's why I'm checking out my own place.

I point out to him that there's nobody at his place, he being at my place. And he hears a creak and a snap and he sees a shadow in his own room streaming on the screen and the cam goes down.

Brute says, What the fuck? What's with your connections, Jimmy?

I show him there's nothing wrong, I can pick up the street feeds, the building feeds, even your feed, Britt, on multiple screens. And he shuts down and restarts and there's a long wait and then the PalCam feed is back up again, nothing different.

Jimmy stops and shakes his head and looks at me.

So? I say.

Where is Brute? he asks. Did you wonder about that? Brute leaves my place after awhile and says he's going back to his place and says he's gonna invite some Pals over to mess around. He says, There's nothing like conviviality.

And I tell him, You got to retool that Brute because Pals are problematic. You got to have Associates™ if you're gonna live in this world. You can't have just any old Pal, you've got to know what they're up to, and you don't know. What if they have associations? You don't have to worry about that with Associates™. Associates™ don't have associations. They're vetted; they're branded.

And he's like, You don't vet your Pals, that's the whole point. There's something to be said for chance and coincidence.

And I'm like, Yeah, but in this world, you've got to vet. Forget coincidence. I saw that group thing you and flowergurl had. What do you know about flowergurl? Because I've heard she's pretty loose with words, among other things. And we won't even go into the whole cloaking scene. Flowergurl couldn't cloak a closet.

Brute got all PO'd.

Where'd you hear that? he says.

I have to tell him I get a lot of stuff from talking to Pluto and people down the pits.

Brute says, That's the problem with your information, Jimmy, it comes from talking to the near dead at waste removal. That's like the end of the line.

That's where you go when there's nothing left to say or do. That's where a Pal don't mean a thing.

Jimmy looks at me very serious. He says, Waste removal is where you get everything. That's where it's all boiled down to basics – bone, raw chips, metal on a stick, stuff about who's really up to what, info stripped of all the fat the corps throw at you.

It's the bottom line, not the end of the line, Jimmy says.

I laugh and say, What's the big deal? Brute isn't here because he went to the Zone, that's what I heard. As far away from the pits as he could get. It's all over the tubes – I saw it on like four Pal sites. I can show you what they're saying. He picked up a gig and I don't think he's Brute anymore, Jimmy – he rebranded. But I don't know. Here's the way I see it: A lot of people head to the Zone, you know that. It's like gated. It's for the stars, the corps, the P. It's Matt and Zoneratti and everything. It keeps the Ville together, like with the screens and stuff humming, everything on track. It's where the corps cook stuff up and the P figures out how we move forward together. The Ville's this big mushy place where they sit in their loungers and watch gazillions of shows, which hum, oh man, do they hum – thanks to the Zone. And here we are, squatting in the Hood, making show after show after show. We can almost make it to the Zone. We can hear it. Our dream, right? Why wouldn't Brute go for it?

No, Jimmy says. I don't think so. That's a mythological, the never-ending myth of the Zone. The Zone is about itself. It's all scripts and screens and scrims.

That is everything, I laugh. What else is there? The Zone is what we all strive for, the Land of the Makers and Doers, even when we can't quite get there. Besides, those Zone scrims are pretty awesome.

It wasn't Brute's dream, Jimmy says. He didn't want to make it to the Zone, at least he never said that to me. He always talked about the crazy stuff on the street. How it's more empty and threatening every day. How the geezers are slumping all over. How more and more walls are coming down. How WRMS drones are sweeping up everything. He was a guy who was curious, you know? He was curious about how he fit into this, this whatever it is we have here.

It's funny, now that I think of it, Jimmy says, the more he showed in his street vids, the less there was actually to see out there. It's like a spreading emptiness. He says, When more's not there, there's more to see.

I used to think, what is he talking about? Now guess what – I'm thinking Brute just disappeared like everything else. His cam goes down. And he disappears. Why? Jimmy asks. That's not fantasy. That's not heard on the tubes. That's the actuality of the sequence of events. So you tell me, Miss Mumble, why there isn't a connection? Online, offline, vanished. That's what it looks like from where I sit.

Well, let me tell you, I've heard about this kind of thing. Okay, we all vanish when we're off screen, you know? That's like obvious and it's not what Jimmy's saying. When the micros dry up, people take on a different focus, a different brand. That's a vanishing too. So Jimmy is saying there's maybe something else? You ask me, I say when you lose your focus and the audience drifts, you either double down or rebrand. That's what happened with Brute and I tell that to Jimmy: Brute rebranded. He moved on.

Jimmy snorts. Moved on is a way of putting it, he says.

Jimmy, I say, look at what Brute was up to, look at who Brute was. Brute was working an old brand. It wasn't like retro. It was old and used up. He didn't keep on top of his image. The screens moved on. His micros vanished because the PalCam was crappy, and his daily updates didn't deliver any deets anybody wanted. It was all about Brute's Buds and whatnot out on the street and over at somebody's place and there was nothing about what you ought to have or who you ought to be or how you were gonna get some micros and move forward. It was kind of about the opposite of all that.

Remember when he pulled in one of the geezers, I say to Jimmy, and the guy started talking about where to go on the street at dusk? And FaviusFootwear says, That's essential information, and Brute just laughs.

The geezer stands there staring at him until one of those bots turns the corner and starts to troll for trash and the geezer scurries away, kind of like a spider himself, snatching the Veet right out of Brute's hand? Remember? Like what's with that? He streams it live!

I continue: Or the time he was headed to a PalFest and there's this street dude in a blue cap holding a bag, shouting, Get your loosey goosey! I got em all! Loosey goosey! Best prices! Guaranteed. Loosey goosey! And Brute stops and says, Hey, what's a loosey goosey?' And the guy whacks him in the face with the bag. Whoa! A showstopper for sure.

That's what I tell Jimmy.

Jimmy says, That's not Zone stuff and it won't get you there, Mumble Pegs. Brute's an innovator, he continues. Self absorbed, yeah; flakey and careless, yeah; but an innovator. He was going places they didn't want him to go. He was showing what there was to show. On the street. They don't want people to know the street for some reason. It distracts, I guess. It makes you wonder. It makes you doubt. Maybe everything isn't exactly humming. Maybe there's no way out.

No way out. That can't be true, whatever it might mean, which I don't think is anything. I think about Brute and his antics on the street here in the Hood. It's not that there's no way out; maybe it's there's no place to go so no reason to leave.

I say to Jimmy: There was the time he strapped a cam to Melinda. Remember that, Jimmy? Brute says to her, This is an experiment. He says that to Melinda! The MealyCam he decides to call it. Something new. She's lost everything and lives in some dark, spacey place, and Brute wants to experiment with her like she's another rat from back in the day. He wants to send her out in the dark. That's innovation?

Jimmy says, You need somebody like Melinda to make those kinds of runs if you want to show what's out there, or not. Who would go around like that at night? She was fearless, in her way.

What's the story on the streets at night? I say. Everybody hears it's a mess out there. You never know what's gonna come out of nowhere and take you down. You even get that from the P-cast anchor guys.

Jimmy says, That's what they say. I don't make night runs.

I sure remember Melinda's run, I say.

Oh?

I say to Jimmy: Brute calls her in, points, and out she goes. I'm right there with her, MealyCam wrapped in her headband. We move down the street. Just black. So late at night; so silent the mic picks up nothing but our footsteps. We weave back and forth and stop and kneel down and I don't know what we're looking at and then I figure out we're bending over into an old storm sewer. What's with that?

A shout: Billy, Billy! And I cringe. I'm really startled. Are we going to crawl into a crumbling storm sewer? What's under there anyway? Who's Billy? Do I want to know?

Then I hear: Go away Mealy. Get out of here.

Billy, come up!

No. Go away. Nobody home. Not hungry. This line not in service.

It's just a voice coming out of blackness beneath the pavement. Shit. We stand up and look around and head down the street. It's so quiet, so dark, not even a sodium buzz. A little black ash drifting down – you can hardly see it, but you can feel it brushing your cheek, like a thousand dark wings. Then we turn the corner, must have been around Edger Street, or something like that the sign said, and there's an old street lamp up and functioning and we stop in front of a beat up wooden house, brown paint cracked and grayish door closed, naturally. Remember that? We look up at the windows. Nothing there. Is that a faint light in the second floor front room? Is something leaking from beneath the blackouts? And then I see our hand on the door knob, turning. We open the door.

Jimmy says, Yeah, I didn't actually see that. I don't remember personally. But I heard about it from one of Brute's Pals. They were so excited. It was better than anyone hoped. Nobody could believe it was so quiet. Nobody could believe she roused that storm sewer dude – they never come out, I mean, are they really down there? Maybe not. I'll tell you this, no one, but no one, could believe there was an open door. Nobody has open doors. If you're out there in a house or a room, you fortify. The streets are dangerous at night.

Jimmy shakes his head.

With Mealy, that night, we are where we never are, I say.

We're in the house now, an ordinary house, I guess, and it's very quiet, I continue, looking at Jimmy.

I think, Holy shit, are we gonna rifle through drawers and closets and steal silver like back in the day? I can't imagine there's any silver in there anyway.

We look around the downstairs room. There's a couch and a chair and an empty bottle of Veet on a table – the usual, not much. I can almost smell the must and dry rot. Nobody's here, I think. We turn around. Are we leaving? No. We stop and turn and look at the stairs. Little, narrow stairs. We look up.

I say, No! We are not doing that!

But up we go, one step at a time. At the landing there's an open door. The room inside has a dull light, one of those old LEDs plugged to the baseboard? There's a woman lying on a bed, asleep, and she's not alone. She has a baby there. I am not kidding. I am not making this up. I am beside myself.

No. No. No!

We head in. And for the longest time, we stand by the bed just looking at the woman. She's young, with short red hair and one arm thrown back and the other around the baby. Nobody has babies around, you know? But there it is. We're just looking and then the baby opens its eyes and sees us. It doesn't make a sound, it just looks at us, or through us, or whatever babies do.

We reach down.

No!

I am talking to the screen. I can't help myself.

No!

We pick the baby up. The woman opens her eyes at the movement and sees us. She is frozen for just a moment and then she screams!

Keep quiet! Keep quiet! Nothing is wrong. I'm just borrowing this.

She sits up and stops screaming and just gasps with this look of revulsion and plain fear. And we turn around and there's a chair and we sit. The woman is dumb, frozen, hand stuck on face. We look down at the baby in our arms. It looks back. And we free our breast and offer it to the baby, its little hand grasps one side and its lips close around the nipple. We sigh. The woman in the bed has both hands in front of her mouth now and says nothing, the breath has been punched out of her by an invasion in the middle of the night. The baby begins to suck with these squishy sounds and I can almost smell its sourness. It sucks, but there is nothing but dry nipple. We have lied to this baby. We have bamboozled it. We start to laugh. That's when the woman really starts to scream, a piercing wail of NO!

The baby rejects the nipple and begins to cry. This quiet space is churning with noise. The baby turns its head away, bangs at one breast and kicks at the other. It shrieks. The MealyCam turns full on the woman. She is now out of the bed so fast! Her eyes are filled with fear and purpose. We just sit there. She grabs the baby away and we don't fight her. We let the crying baby go.

Please. Please. I need it, is all we say.

Get out, she screams at us, boiling now. Get out of here!

We get up from the chair slowly. We are looking at the woman full on. She has her arms wrapped around the baby and her back is against the wall. I am afraid we are going to hit her. Or maybe she is going to hit us. But no. We turn toward a window. There is whimpering. The woman is whimpering. Or are we? Turn around again. There's the hallway and we make our way to the stairs and down and out the open front door to the empty street. But it's not so quiet anymore. There are shouts coming from inside the house. We turn back toward the open door, now it seems like a threatening hole, and then we turn again and head down Edger through the flakes of ashy darkness drifting all around. Brute's infrared shows empty street, planked building fronts, cascading concrete. Where are the outsiders, the outlaws, the marauders? I don't know. The shouts grow faint as we move further away, until they are gone.

Wow, Jimmy says. He doesn't call himself Brute for nothing. You know, in point of fact Britt, maybe his dailies laid out too many deets. Brute gave us a kind of street diary, a ledger, an entry or so a day. Maybe we just don't know how to read it. Now they've picked him up, whoever they are, and maybe he's teaching them the language. Who knows what kind of deets he's delivering now, even as we speak.

Picked him up?

Jimmy says, You heard correctly. Picked him up. Why not? Case in point: the MealyCam out on the street. Second case in point: Melinda – where is she? Because I haven't seen her in a long time. Third case in point: felony b&e, kidnapping, assault. You name it. Plus trying to get a rise from a storm drain. Who's down there, if anybody, you know? Melinda seemed to know. Somehow, she knew that was an entry point or an exit or a window or something. And the baby? I don't know. What's with babies out there?

Jimmy stops again and brushes his floppy straight hair out of his eyes.

Yeah, picked up, he says again. Or maybe he just walked in to them and said here I am. They want info. They want names, dates, sites, data, whatever. He says, Here I am. Ask away.

Oh come on. What's to know, I say. That's like an old stalker show. They? That's just rumor. That's nonsense. Picked up? That doesn't happen. Have you even looked at Brute's site? All he does is talk to his Pals, for the most part, and pop reds and bag girls. We've got our own issues. Stuff's flagging. We need micros.

And Jimmy drops this: So where is Mealy? Where is Brute?

And I can't answer that. I still can't.

Anxiety thickens this room like pulp. My blackouts, of course, are always in place, so nothing gets out and nothing gets in. When the front cam went down awhile ago, I didn't do anything about it. I told you, it's boring – no sex stuff or anything. There's more now, though. The room has become private space. Can you imagine it? Everybody watching, everyone hungering to be watched, everyone linked, and a space opens up where you can disappear in your own place. Maybe that's what Brute did. Or Melinda. Or Deb. They disappeared into themselves. Or what was left of themselves that they could find.

It seems like I've been up for hours, frazzled like this the whole time, but finally there's a bang on the door, a buzz from outside, my visitor sensor flashes yellowy.

Britt! Open up!

Jimmy slides in and sits himself down at the table, right here in my invisible front room. Finally. I look at his sharp face, his cheekbones out of some geometry book, his sparkly eyes; he looks at me. I wonder if he notices my cerulean, burnt-sienna hair thing. I wonder what he sees when he looks at my thin face and my thin arms and my old khaki shirt with the ripped out arm patches. I feel like a stick.

You hear anything from Deb? I ask.

No, but she's around somewhere, he says.

Look, there is something wrong, I say. I don't feel right in myself and this thing with Deb and the P and such has me strung out. Where're my fans? Where'd they go?

Now Jimmy is my best friend, as you no doubt guessed, just as much as Deb, and I say stuff to him that I wouldn't say to anyone else. It's like vice versa as well too.

I think you are right, Britt, he says. In fact, I know you are right. There is something wrong. I know that my street feeds show some strange dudes hanging for the last few days and there're weird nanoclouds on the street, like motes. Could be watching. I could be tracked, but I don't know exactly who would bother. Maybe WRMS – they don't like me in the pits. The P has no interest, I don't think, and if he did, we'd never figure that out. But why should he? Real threats they take down and jam – the guys who posted from inside the corps in the Zone, stuff like that. Or the guys who had the vids of the pre-grad camps. I never saw those, but I heard about them. I know a guy down the pits who said he had a friend who saw them. But he hasn't seen the friend in awhile.

I am kind of shocked to hear this. Jimmy is always so even and on top of it.

Watched.

We're all watched all the time, okay? We watch each other. We go out of our way to be watched. We live to be watched. We want to tell all and the more of all the better.

Here I am getting prepped for my breast slits. Here I am with my wrist tagged. Procedures are great for micros, I have to say. I've got lots of running items: Ten Hipped-Out ERs, Seven ORs Flipped from Hip, Eleven Top Docs from HeebyJeebyLand. I like that last one. So many of these guys are creeps.

They watch you in the Zone, like intensely. Here, not so much. But the potential is there. Let's be real – this is the stuff that lies beneath the micros, you know. If something comes along to roil the waters – whether it's a Brute sending a spacey Melinda out to wander the streets and steal a baby, or, now that I'm thinking along these lines, a Deb-with-glam out in the Hood stepping over bodies – you have to do something to still the sloshing waves, the upset and nerves. You've got quell it all so that the hum can return and the micros can resume their regular soothing flows to the corps and Mr. P and back to us, if we're lucky. Which seems less and less the case.

Doubt is what the corps and the P don't want, I guess. That's what it amounts to. Doubt about how it all works and flows and how great it all is. They like the blacked out windows. They don't like weirdos stealing Veet on the street. They adore the screens. They don't adore loosey goosey. Screens are everything. We all want them. We need them. We want them to surround us and coffinate us.

We are lucky, right? We have all these free feeds and cams, all these connections slinking out from node to node around the Ville and the Hood and all over; we really get into what's on the screen! It pulls you in, as all you guys know. There is nothing like an afternoon of Zoneratti with Matt, brought to you by Nutri and, yes, Excellon. They back Weekend with Missy, too, and I love that because it's all about Missy, who's just like me and you, and her husband Bart, who is so understanding! She has so many quirks and stuff and he puts up with it. Like she has a fear of heights and open places so it's hard to get her out of the house. That's okay. Where would they go anyway and how would they get there? So she's always planning parties and stuff and she has a fear of crowds. But she comes up with great ideas, I'm telling you. She did a whole running thing on how all the girls need to have one shiny nipple ring, one that flashes, like on and off. But Bart was really down on that idea.

And he tells her, No, that's like a stop sign.

And she says, Oh, Bart, honey, it's really the thing for girls trying to keep abreast.

I swear. She's great. Missy's been in the Zone for at least a couple of seasons. Decorating her nips brought in Connie's Cool Tops big time too. Ka-ching!

Jimmy is saying something to me.

He says, There're a lot of anxious guys down at the pits nowadays.

Which doesn't surprise me, I tell him. They're always anxious, I say. They're living on the edge – out at the end of the world, where everything goes to die like Brute says. Who wouldn't be anxious?

Jimmy says, No, not everything. You are way wrong, Britt, just like Brute was wrong. The pits are where you can pick up so much, you know that. They just dump it all and WRMS trolls for the reusables. Those bots are there for a reason – there are a lot of reusables. A lot. It all gets dumped in the pits, that's where everybody goes, including me. I was talking to Pluto down there and he told me there's a push on from the P to clean up a lot of outlying areas, you know, the geezers, the marauders, the threats. There's more, too.

Pluto is always there, you know. He knows the pits like some undiscovered country. He knows what leads up to them and everything leading away, and a lot more. He heard from somebody else that they're sanitizing the streets and the tubes. Some kind of kink in the works. Muck or nonsense or something's hit the tubes and he says they are cleaning it all up. They want to close the system and let it find a new level. The hum balances out, he says. It's happened before.

I tell Jimmy that makes sense to me; you jigger and harmonize the flow.

And he says, Well, yeah, that's the problem. Me and you and Deb and everyone else, we are the points. Pluto says they're cleaning the pipes by shutting down points and re-stitching around them. Like they are closing the points down. Hello! He says there's been too much discombobulation in the Ville and on the streets and in and around the Hood. And I start thinking right away, Jimmy says, about Brute and the Pal thing. Like Brute was in the streets and we saw a lot of what was out there, more than I see even when I come over here or go to the pits. Like I don't like to go out at night – day's bad enough.

What we see mostly is stuff that's not there, I say. We see nothing. That's what Brute's showing. He's showing nothing.

The guy in the storm drain? Jimmy says. The baby? And that's another thing – there are a lot of guys who don't come to the pits anymore and I wonder why and I was wondering even before this and so I asked Pluto. There was one guy, Oppy, who said he was looking for yellow cake mix to blow up for his birthday party. I ask about him and Pluto says he hasn't been around for like weeks and he hasn't been back at his place or any place else, far as Pluto can tell. Birthday's come and gone. No cake. No Oppy. I think there's something wrong and they can't fix it. Are they just eliminating what they decide are problem spots?

When he finishes this Jimmy stops for a second.

It's like they think there's leakage that needs to be plugged, stress that needs relief, Jimmy says. Disequilibrium. I don't know.

I have never seen Jimmy in a state of uncertainty, I have to tell you. He always seems to know exactly what's going on. He's like so competent. His site is so straight-forward. Useful, too. Many times I've watched him hammer together gards or toss up a decent dinner from old plugs or cobble together a way around a glitch in the tubes or patch a vid player. Like what doesn't he know? I mean, I know a lot too. I know about how to get by and what's useful and how I can make up myself and what you may want to get out of me that I'm willing to give. He's the same way, of course. You have to be, in order to hum.

So, I say, what's different about all this? It doesn't sound like anything other than what they always do when things start to slosh around or slide away. They clean it up, or switch it off and then back on and then everything begins to run smoothly again and we can all be who we are and check each other out and get back to what we have to do, which is get in each other's faces.

I don't know, he says. Ever since we hit the dunes putting together the President's Girl vid, I've felt things veering, Jimmy says. Maybe they can't get it right. There's bleeding, something draining.

We pretty much aren't supposed to go out there in the dunes, I point out. Plus, there's the car thing. I don't know where that car came from, and I'll be straight Jimmy, it has me worried too.

Well, yeah. I got a line on that from Pluto and a girl down the pits, like I told you at the time, if you remember.

Yeah. You said I don't want to know.

Maybe they just don't want us out there, he says. Who knows what we might be up to? Maybe there's more of a containment thing now. They don't want anyone leaving the Hood or the Ville, even by the back. They don't want anyone navigating through those shifting dunes. They want it all closed. Even the dunes, if you can believe that.

Jimmy talking like this makes me extremely nervous. This is not what I want to hear. This is not what Hip is all about.

When you're Hip, you just deal with coaxing the corps, enticing fans, stiffing cranks – the usual. Micros come in, more or less. Now we're into stuff that's way beyond that. And around it and under it. This is not the they-don't-know-as-much-as-you-think-they-know Jimmy. Maybe they do know as much, and more. Maybe they know a lot and they don't like what they know or what we know or might wonder about. Who is they anyway? They is nobody. Not here. Not me. Nothing.

So I guess I'm not all that surprised when – yeah, that's right – there's a sharp knock at the door.

I should say right up front that I'm not even startled. Neither's Jimmy. Even though no one much hits the streets at that hour of the day anymore and my approach sensor didn't even glow. Like Jimmy says, he feels he's being watched. He feels he's being tracked. Or maybe it's me. Maybe I'm being watched, and not in the way that brings me anything but hard times. Trouble in mind.

I guess we were somehow expecting the knock, deep inside.

There could be a bug in here too, of course. We'd never find it if we looked for hours. Nothing as crude as those pinhole cams they use for obvious watching everywhere. An audio bug can be as tiny as a cell, as flat as a stain.

Chapter Three

How they got in here is a pretty good question. I can't figure it out.

Jimmy and I were in the front, so it must have been through the back, although the knock was in the front and later I couldn't find anything wrong with my back door or windows. Setter plates were charged. Locks were fine. It doesn't matter much anyway when you get right down to it. There was a knock and then, Presto! They were inside, and that's the main thing – we couldn't keep them out, no matter what.

So they walked into the front room, and the big guy, who was wearing an open Oxford button-down, blue, a browny Harris tweed jacket (must've been warm!), and old black Chuckies, says, Excuse me, there's a problem with the line feeds. The signals are being disturbed, he says.

Like, as you might expect, I ask him who the frack he is and how did he walk into my place like the walls were made of butter?

He laughs at that.

Did you hear that, Morrie? he asks his bud, who's a small guy, very natty, wearing old Florsheims, oxbloods, and chinos with cuff rolls. She wants to know who we are.

Yeah, yeah, I heard, Morrie says, and he starts picking up stuff on my counter-top, which is mostly junk, like electrics, an old Timex™ (wrist watch), my squiggly purple straw, an angle edge (nice one, a Bocchi), one of Jimmy's micrometers and his straight edge, ragged books and zines (yeah, I got em, stiff and crackly yellow), empty bottles and cups, an old lamp filled with colored liquid that oozes in shapes and shifting colors. (What a find! Thank you old Merchandise Mart!) Lots and lots of beads in little porcelain dishes. (I like the feel of their roundness, their unexpected colors, vermillion, paisley blues, swirly lime; when you hold them, they click and rattle, like teeth.)

Jimmy is just sitting there, his mouth open, speechless, looking at these two dudes.

We're taking a look at feed static, says the first one, eyeing me. We traced it back to here. You having any issues, miss?

I say, I've got lots of issues, but the feeds aren't among them. There's no problem with the feeds here.

Are you sure? he asks, and looks over at Morrie. Our tests say otherwise. Our tests show pulse disruption coming from this location. A damping down, a confusion.

Well, that's news to me, I say. Didn't I ask how you got in here?

It's our job, miss, he says. We are trained to track down and eliminate any signal disorders. The training is very extensive and includes a number of what they used to call classified techniques. What's this? he asks, picking up one of my router chipsets, an old one Jimmy fished from the pits one day.

Meanwhile Morrie is holding a ripply Mexicana glass up to the light, its dark blue could hold the night, but all it has inside is some stale AV, colorless as plexi. He dumps it out and looks over.

It looks like an old chipset, Jewell, very retro, Morrie says. Look at the size of that thing! Hip-O-Matic! Hubba hubba. Ha ha ha!

It's an old set, I say, frowning. This is exasperating.

Jimmy finally gathers himself in and says, There are no feed problems at this location. There have never been any feed problems. Do you have any identification?

He puts that out there and I'm thinking, Whoa! Ease up. I don't want any trouble, but, you know, I want to see those IDs too.

Jewell says, Sure.

He pulls a card from his pocket and holds it out. All I catch is Brand Remediation and Control, which is enough. What would *any* kind of control op want with me or Jimmy? I'm only uncontrolled in myself at this point and that's only because I can't seem to establish elasticity. I can't stretch the brand and maintain focus – okay, maybe they could help there – and my personal friend has gone out somewhere and hasn't come back and I can't figure out where she is or what to do about her or me or our general malaise. I guess that needs attention, but nothing an agency would be interested in, or should be. That's just marketplace noise and interaction and flagging micros. Personal issues don't require regulation or anything, in my book. The brand thing is the usual; it happens.

Jimmy says, That's a pretty lame pretext, feed disruption. I mean, our feeds are strong, is all I'm saying. No issues. Is that why you're here? Or is there something else we can help you with?

Jewell looks right at him and says, Are you questioning me?

I keep quiet. I don't think I'd want to question him, personally speaking.

Not at all, says Jimmy, sinking back into himself, or seeming to.

Jewell says, That's good to hear. Who did you say you are, speaking of IDs?

And Jimmy says he is James J. Jones, a fan.

Well Mr. James J. Jones, a fan, says Jewell, you look mighty familiar to me, yes you do. You look like somebody who's been out in the sun and you have ash stains on those dungarees. (Boy aren't we observant?)

Didn't I see you down at Waste Removal about 6:42 yesterday evening? Jewell continues, scrutinizing Jimmy with a scrunched eye.

And again at 6:37 this morning? he goes on. Yes. Yes. I'm sure of it. Weren't you the one scuttling away with the large bag culled from Pit C, Bistro North? Wearing a flasher cap with 360° LumaLites? You look very much like that fellow. Very much like a fellow who might skip the authorized Presidential Pre-Owned Fill Areas™ and illegally remove trash and waste from the pits, return it to the Ville, and distribute it in the Hood in some manner. Would you be that kind of guy? Would you be the kind of guy who counseled others to do the same and showed them the best routes to the Waste Removal Area? And how to avoid the WRMS drones? And when each Waste Sector disposed of the day's collections?

I don't think so, I mean, no, that's not on my schedule, Jimmy says, not too convincingly.

Jewell says, Do you know that waste is private property, Mr. Jones?

Really? says Jimmy.

Waste is waste for a reason, says Jewell. It's discarded. Something used and discarded and carted to the pits. But here's the thing: Ownership is retained. Ownership never ends. Once owned, always owned, unless formally transferred and on the record. And even then, ownership continues, just in a different direction. Ownership is like elemental mass. It can't be eliminated. That's just plain physics. You can look it up.

No, no need for that, Jimmy says. I sort of know most of the regs and try to follow them as best I'm able. I'm just a guy, says Jimmy. I do my thing, help people out. Sort of like a utility worker or a yard guy. Show people stuff, you know. A handyman sort of type. Sometimes people need a little assistance, particularly now that Sentry has pulled back to the Zone pretty much and most everybody is stressed by that. I mean, people ask for assistance in filling in unnoticed gaps and stuff.

Jewell ponders this for a second and I can see that he is dubious and that Jimmy has opened his mouth maybe when he shouldn't? Jewell seems to make some kind of decision, standing up a little straighter and fiddling with a very old fragment of embroidery that's at the top of a pile near the counter. He turns back toward Jimmy.

Stuff? says Jewell. Show people stuff? That sounds very helpful. Does that stuff include showing people what lies out on the streets or in the Ville or, gawd help us, please, outside the Ville? I'm sure you wouldn't want to go that route, would you? Kind of nasty out there. Ask some of the Pals, you don't believe me.

I hear you are right about that, says Jimmy, but I wouldn't know from personal experience. Some Pals have

90

told me about what they've heard goes on in those parts. No need to check myself.

I listen to this and I'm thinking, huh-oh – we are gonna get fracked for that President's Girl dune run for sure.

Very nasty thereabouts out there, Jewell says, shaking his head and looking around at the rest of the mess in the front room. Okay, it is a mess, you might as well know it. Get away from the cam and it's like walking into another solar system, an attic stuffed to the sky. It's got mounds of old clothes and gear, including some of my favorites – the Fabio's knockoffs, the boxes of eye wear, the black stuff, nylons (very hard to find), the drum pads, the huge box stuffed with those unwanted Nutri sandals, the Guatemalan fabrics (they threaded in pictures of themselves doing stuff in villages, little huts with animals and old people all together; they needled it right onto the cloth!), the little notebooks with lists in tiny writing – cheetos (pre-plugs), hot pockets (?), green salsa (?), snickers (candy, I think), and other retro eatables, the old dishware with birds and flowers and little houses in blue, the Mexicanaware – all that, a lot (and much more!) found in the rubble of the General Merchandise Mart or in rooms of potential squats nearby in the Hood. Oh I've got stuff here. Stuff in the basement. Stuff in the back. Stuff is what makes stuff hum. Which is the point. And, of course, I've got screens aplenty, wrapping their way around the room, all waiting to show stuff and track stuff and tantalize and satisfy via stuff. Those screens are, amazingly, off at the moment.

Very nasty in the Ville and beyond, Jewell says again to Jimmy. Not cozy at all, the streets. No indeedy.

Yes, Mr. P has spoken often of the threat on the streets, Jimmy says. He says Sentry shields us all. And I know that's a fact because I've even seen Sentry show up now and again here in the Hood. I've watched the street feeds and seen those lines of buglike security dudes stalking past the fronts of our empty buildings. And the VO tells you the patrols have great success eliminating the threat. Who's gonna argue with that? You can see there's no threat around those guys.

Are you suggesting, Mr. James J. Jones, a fan, that the P warns of a threat that is not there?

No! Absolutely not! The opposite! Jimmy exclaims. The P has all of us in his heart. He wraps us with his cloak and you can see that in the Sentry patrols wrapping around us and needling through us right here. That's all I'm saying. The successful patrols, I'm saying. Keeping the threat at bay.

I listen to Jimmy and wish he would, at this point, shut up. Now that you mention it, I never knew Jimmy's name was James J. Jones, I want that out there right away. All the years I've known him, I never knew that. You think you know someone, but you only have a hint, I'm trying to say, a tiny glimpse, which may be refracted even, like light through a really old window. It shines through and breaks up into all different colors. Light is invisible, you know, but it's full of every color you can think of. Maybe that's the way we are. Deb is. Me? Jimmy? You contain everything and disappear.

It's easy to break you up, I think, but maybe the devil to bring you back.

Jimmy blinks at Jewell and stops talking. He tells me later that sometimes it's best to keep your mouth completely closed, particularly when you don't know what direction a conversation with weird authority types is taking. He confesses he must've been startled.

Which I might have once said was impossible – Jimmy startled? – but not any more, not after these guys materializing, not after Deb and Brute and all the rest that I'm relating here for you as it happens.

You might want to think that over, those treks to waste removal, Jewell is saying. It's not just the persistence of ownership rights, although lawyers can be expensive if charges are ever brought, and what a mess! My goodness! Courtrooms with judges and piles of paper, endless piles of paper. They still do it that way. They still dot every eye and cross every tee. People used to write books about that kind of stuff, I've heard, though not anymore, what with the paper situation. All and all, we think this legal merry-go-round is an extraordinary waste, especially in these perilous times, but there you are. And that's just a part of it.

The main thing you want to remember, Jewell says, is that things are here and there for a reason, as I was saying. What is discarded or no longer retained for immediate use is discarded or disused for a reason. I guess you can think of the pits as kind of holding and sorting ports. Plus, you know, a lot of hard work and effort goes into maintaining the stability and balance of the whole system. Start messing with one part and something up the line begins to wobble, even something in advance of discard. That's just more simple physics again, thermodynamics and biomechanics. When somebody starts mucking with stuff, do you have any idea what it costs the good folks who manage the reuse systems? Or the rest of us here in the Ville? Talk about re-harmonizing! It's ruination in some cases.

For us, Jewell says, if there's a glitch, well, we have to fix it. You can see that. And what could cause a glitch?

Jimmy stares at him blankly.

Jewell turns around and looks at Morrie. What do you think? he asks.

Morrie's been listening with a sad, sort of droopy look.

I dunno, he shrugs. Maybe infrastructure problems; maybe personnel; mistakes of one sort or another; bad gear; improper input; faulty analysis; bile. A glitch is a glitch, though – it disrupts things for everyone.

He sighs and says to Jewell, You'd think, what with all the good the corps and the President do, all the assistance, all the help with collection, all the ad dough and shout outs, all the marketing, and all the thought going into it, you'd think that everybody would pull together.

It's a shame, Morrie says, finally putting down the Mexicana glass, that people aren't willing to let waste rest. That people try to go their own way. And not only that! They tell other people to do the same, to strike out into the wilderness or stray from the path.

You know Jewell, he says, shaking his head, it's like one of those old mythologicals you hear about. People going off alone. They strike out on their own, you might say, yes, and they seek success and security and, get this, a different future! It never happened that way. Never will. Not only that, Jewell, did you know there was never even any wilderness? What is wilderness? It's something not known and not explored, and that has never been the case here. Never. What I may not know, you may; where you haven't gone, why, I may be coming back from that very spot. Everything's been mucked with.

And what other future? What? What future is there when you go off on your own? On your own, you can collapse, or worse, and there's no one there, emptiness stretches out cold in front of you, all around you. You just disappear. The future is something shared, just like the present, something where you're in it together and can talk about it, like we're talking now from our different perspectives. Sheesh. But I'm digressing. I apologize. A glitch needs to be fixed, that's all.

After a moment Morrie sputters up again.

Part of the problem may be software related, he says. Sometimes content can degrade the machinery, like acid in a pot. Content can corrode the works and mess everything up. Boy, that can be a challenge.

He picks up the Mexicana glass again. This is nice, Morrie says. Where'd it come from?

I don't know, I say. It just is. I think I found it at Greta's Classix.

You do this very well, he says, looking around. You see, we're fans, right Jewell?

Right, says Jewell, still looking at Jimmy.

At first I am kind of stunned, to be honest, and then I think, well of course, why not? Everybody wants Hip. I have followers all over. Though fewer, I admit, than I had this time a while ago.

Morrie turns from Jewell and casts his eye over my bags of netwear in the corner, the ancient bike parts by the back counter, the stacks of old cam pads in different colors, the mountain of ripped, blue dungarees.

Oh yes, fans we are, he says, looking back at me. Hey, check out these Florsheims!

He lifts his right leg up to show off his old shoe.

Nice, I say. I want to get along. That seems about right, given the situation, don't you think? I want them out of here with minimal fuss.

Speaking just for myself, Morrie says, I don't understand the stuff about the street. I don't understand how that fits into the message. Huggers, Scuffers, NaughtyGirl, Britt's Hip Bitts – none of that has anything to do with the street, which is out there, hard and crumbly and unsightly. You see, it confuses me. I don't like confusion. That's not what I'm about.

I look at him and just listen because what else can I do? So I say, I never do anything about the street. I avoid the street. I use drones. I'm in my rooms.

Morrie ignores this.

My Aunt Rita was all about health, Morrie says, like remembering from his own personal past. And then she started picking up on the strangest things, like where to find fresh food – he did a little quote thingy with his fingers when he said fresh food – and how some things are tainted – (quote thingy again) – by how they are made or what they are made from. And that led her out onto the street and feeds that showed the most gawdawful stuff. All those hits from folks just looking for straight-up nutritious meals with Nutri-brand ingredients and from Nutri-Buckets™ – why, all of a sudden they find themselves in live streams heading off to the pits and then the next thing you know they're looking at what seem to be carcasses of something or other. Her channel started to feel like some old fiction movie. And sometimes she used microcams to follow plugs and such as they made their way through internal personal space and even through the Nutri recycling chutes and down into the pits, and after. That was really revolting to her old health fans. It made them dizzy. And the fact is, they didn't know what they're looking at.

Poor Aunt Rita, Morrie says. Here she is working with plugs, working with Nutri-brand, working with the system, helping her fellow men and women, helping the President and the corps. She's a caring woman. And then she steers herself into all kinds of wrong-headed questions like where and how stuff gets made. And what it all means.

Like she can know that kind of thing from wandering around the street and down the pits? Morrie says. Once she starts down that road, she veers off course. Almost inevitable. Hell's bells – it *is* inevitable. She's in the pits and watching the loads come in and streaming and dodging WRMS drones. Live streams from her FoodCam – all these muddy, jerky pictures. Like what did they mean? They didn't mean anything. It sickened lots of people, just looking. I know because we were talking about it in the family. Doubt and confusion, that's what we're saying, you know, that's what Auntie Rita communicated to us.

I don't say this to Morrie or Jewell, but I'm thinking this Auntie Rita has some balls even if she was a little screwy.

Morrie continues his story. She started picking up other kinds of fans, he says, fans from out and about, from who knows where, fans not interested in nutrition, it seemed to us, fans more interested in gumming up the works, fans more interested in wrong-headed questions: Like how can we go on this way? Like what kind of system is this? Ridiculous questions with unfathomable answers. They shot her stuff around all over the place. Her stream ricocheted across the continent and pretty soon she's known as the Queen of the Pits. My Auntie Rita!

Finally, one day, I'll never forget, she's streaming from down in the pits – actually in the pits! – and one of the Nutri-Waste chutes opens up and masses of plugs come hurtling all around, a load showers down like brackish hail. It overwhelmed her, knocked her silly, and her vidstream gets jumpy and frazzly and then blotchy and then nothing. Dark.

They never found her, he says. Not WRMS, not Sentry, no one. And for what? For what did she do it?

I don't know, I say. For her site? For her fans? Revs?

Sheesh, Morrie says. Her site? Her revs? Here's what: she lost her focus, she lost her fans, she even lost her feed, her micros, and she lost her whole self. And we lost Aunt Rita. All we had left was her jerky final stream, which we buried in our own plot, with services and all. Buried images of Auntie Rita buried in a looping shower of digested plugs – that's all that was left for us. There was upset in the family. Upset for all who followed her. It was a long time before all that subsided, before the perplexities washed away, and there are still questions that come into Central about it. Poor Aunt Rita. And it was all so unnecessary.

Morrie falls silent at last.

Terrible, says Jewell. I never knew that story.

Yes, it was a tragedy.

I say, That is awful. So why did she do that?

That's the thing I'm saying, says Morrie. She didn't have to. It was a misplaced sense of whom she was and what she needed to know. It was confusion. It was doubt. First off, she was straight-up health. And everyone following her was straight-up health. Nutrition by the numbers. What does it take? How many plugs? What can you do with leftovers? How do you properly age a plug? Fun kind of stuff. But she started asking herself, well, what is health? That led to larger, silly questions. What does it mean? Where does all this come from? How is it made? How does it get to us and where does it go? And the next thing you know, she's headed for the pits. She got some bad information or something, about how things fit together or don't, and the next thing you know, she's covered with used-up plugs flushed through the Nutri chutes.

That is a sad and instructive story and I am so sorry to hear of your loss, says Jewell.

Thank you, says Morrie.

There are a couple things you need to keep in mind, Jewell says to us as he heads for the back room. Hey Morrie, he calls, fire up the HipCam. Morrie flips open a pad.

Anything going on, Jewell shouts.

I've got it right here, says Morrie, looking at his pad. Nothing doing, just the bed and whatever.

Okay, says Jewell, who is then stepping right into the picture. Check this out, he says. Jewell looks right into the cam and Morrie shows us his screen.

So, Jewell says to us, and to everyone tapping into the stream, I want to send everyone the best regards of the President, who is, as we speak, right now, headed to Greta's Classix to check out the best collection of retro glassware anywhere in the Ville. He just needs to have the cups and tableware that Britt loves, and just about the only place left in the world you can find them is at Greta's, the Hippest slot in the Hood for such. Now you may be too late to get down and see him – this was something he only decided to do like minutes ago, and the P moves fast as all of you are aware – but you can still pick up some really out-there stuff by going to gretasclassix.com. The finest in older accessories, like Britt says. Greta is more than vintage. She delivers the whole experience. She gives and you get. Tell her Britt sent you, or enter coupon code PSDAMAN, for *an additional discount* courtesy of the P.

He winks into the cam and comes back out to the front room.

Jewell continues, That's like one thing. The President wants us all to work together and stay at our screens and on our respective messages and he will help. He cares. He is focused on all of us. Morrie's poor Aunt Rita! She really hopped the track. She didn't reach out to the P. She just dropped the bucket. Everything spilled out and left her empty-handed, and not only that, it slopped over everybody up and down the line – right to the corps and the P. Stay on message, the President firmly believes, and the bucket will be passed. Whether it's Hip or celebs or Matt D or the President himself, if you are screwed tight into the message, everything will flow freely. Go off message, though, and this is number two, you can cause some serious disruptions and even pain. Doubt leaks out and spreads. Oh no, can't have that. No slopping over.

For one thing, Jewell continues, you confuse people about who you are, and if you confuse them about who you are, they get confused about who they are. That's one area where we come in. We help keep the flow moving. Discord is what concerns us. Confusion and muddle are what concern us and the corps and the President. When people are upset about who they are and what their place is, then they get upset about other things as well and before you know it, the tubes are all over the place, micros are flying around, not running smoothly up the line, people fret, brands get blotchy as a pox, and springs start flying from the wheels of our every-day lives that we live. We're talking doubt, almost anarchy, or at least a serious blooey in the works. Can't have that. You don't want that. Plus poor Aunt Rita! Think of her. She lost everything and her real fans lost her. We need reliability. That's why the President is what he is. That's what the corps are all about. We stay on message and we help others stay on message. We help people be seen the way people are used to seeing them. We fix the glitches.

Jewell looks from Jimmy to me and back again, brow expectantly puckered – like do we get it? I'd say so. But I don't utter a word. I just look up at him in his blue Oxford and browny wool. I notice there is not a single dribble of sweat on his face, all round and pale and full of heart-felt concern. His yellow hair is swept up in a pouf, eyes are cloudy beads of Depression glass pulled from a box. I see he has a little silver chipset hair comb almost hidden in his billows of dry straw, and a single Victrola charm dangling from his left ear. Not bad.

Morrie has been listening. So, he says, are you familiar with the President's Girl?

Geez. I feel a sourness inside, but I do not show it. I am straight and calm. We seem to be getting to the point here, now that we've dispensed with the tragedy of Aunt Rita.

Why yes, I say. That would be my fan Debbie who has done such a wonderful job crafting herself that the President personally, it seems, has linked to her and chatted with her. She is aligned completely. She is an open book. She is what you see on her site, like we all are.

Really? says Morrie. Do you know where we might find her? You see, there are disruptions emanating from her nodal point as well. We want to fiddle with the glitch and help her embrace her message and show herself. Maybe you could help us find her because her feed is frozen and her studio is empty and the President is concerned that something may have hopped the tracks when he was focused somewhere else. We can't see her. She has not shown anyone anything about herself in quite awhile. That spells trouble. Perhaps she's ill and needs medical attention? Perhaps not. Our suspicion is that a bucket has been dropped and tracks have been hopped and slopping over is imminent. So naturally we thought you might have some ideas.

Why no, I answer, I can't say I know exactly where she is at the moment. She's not on a leash or anything.

No, no, no, says Morrie. We're just concerned. Usually we can locate and ease disruptions very quickly, and without assistance. We're having a little problem here, though. We thought Mr. Jones, for one, might be able to help us out, since he's been so forthcoming with transportation for the President's Girl and since he seems to spend so much time on the street. Why do you spend so much time on the street, Mr. Jones?

Jimmy doesn't hesitate.

I don't. I mean I need to get from one place to another, he says, to help with stuff. I need to see Britt so she can stay tuned into her fans. How do I see Britt without hitting the street to get here? That's about it. I don't spend time on the street. All I did for the President's Girl, Debbie, of whom I am also a fan of and have saved numerously and tune into all the time, is to help her with the technicalities of making a video and building an attractive, focused screen presence, a site. I think that's pretty acceptable, for the most part?

Morrie seems to consider this question for a moment. And he says, The President, I've heard, is worried about Debbie. He saw her reeling around on the street prior to a sanitization effort. She posted a vid and seemed to think she was some kind of lost. He is concerned now, in a personal way. The President doesn't want anyone lost on his watch. Or thinking they're lost. Or encouraging others to lose themselves. Or streaming the idea. He says, That's not my girl. Who is that?

You see, says Jewell, confusion.

Well, I respond, I think she hoped Mr. P might become more actively engaged. She's hoping he can seal the deal. Like swoop in for a rescue. Show her fans how fast moving he is and how much he cares. It's part of the show.

I'm thinking we are so fracked.

Morrie looks at me and says, The President is very caring. He cares about the Zone and the Ville and the Hood and all the lands to the west and north and all the other directions. He absorbs masses of live streams. He manages numerous franchises. He has his own streams he wants everyone to embrace and the corps he needs to consider.

Absolutely! I say. The P has to cover so much!

Even so, even with all that, he is deeply concerned with every one of us, Morrie says. Believe me, he cares deeply. That's why we've stopped by.

Here, Morrie says, I want to give you my numbers and I want you to contact us if there is any indication of where she might be. She is still thinking lost, you know, as far as the President is concerned in his mind, and he wants to find her and bring her back into the fold, which, of course, she has never left in the first place, like the P says. There is no lost. Not here. Not now. Not to mention, bringing her back into the fold with the P would make a heckuva episode. The President gathers her in at the last minute, and all. He'd consider that classic twist, I believe, particularly if she's off the street and showing us who she is at all times, hewing to the track, carrying her bucket. He wants to see her, you know? He wants His Girl. Otherwise, we may have to take remedial nodal action, which really is a last resort. We don't like to do that if we can avoid it. Every nodal point is important to us. Precious, really. So find her and bring her on home. That is, get her up and streaming. A nodal disruption in the Hood can be very insalubrious. That's why we're reaching out and sharing this now. We want to help. We want to gather her in, fix her glitch, and get her ship shape!

He turns back to my counter and picks up the Mexicanaware.

Listen, says Morrie, do you need this glass? It would be great if I could have it. How much is it?

Take it, I say, pausing a moment, it's yours for 13.

Thank you, he says. He shoots some micros from his pad into my reader. I accept gracefully.

We'll be going now, says Morrie. I'll leave our contact info right here on your counter, next to the chipset pile. Remember, contact us right away if you encounter any future problems and without question if you hear from your wandering fan. Mr. Jones, stay off the street unless you're visiting someone like Britt, who is well worth listening to, that's my advice. Why don't you take it? And consider the many opportunities and rewards offered through the Presidential Pre-Owned Acquisition Collection System. Authorized Fill is Fill you can believe in, and so can we.

Yes sir, says Jimmy.

Call me Morrie.

We'll leave by the front, says Jewell who has just been quietly listening to Morrie – and minutely examining my little stuffed room with those murky, adamantine eyes.

Jewell unlatches the door and they slide out quickly.

Jimmy and I are alone and I realize that my heart is racing. It is pumping so fast I feel like I've just missed being sucked into a street-cleaning bot.

Jimmy, I start to say, and he shakes his head. He doesn't want me to say anything, and I realize that he's afraid now to speak in the room, afraid of bugs, afraid of motecams. I realize that if there are motes we can't communicate in any way. We can't speak, they'll hear; we can't write, they'll see. They've warned us to keep off the street. Let's review for a nanosecond. Yep, this folksy visit was all about warnings and restrictions and consequences – all kind of vague, but not too vague. Containment.

We can't plan. We can't do location work. They know about the SmithVerber. They know about the dune trek and shoot. They know about Deb's issues. They know we worked up her vids. A deeper conclusion: They understand everything. And then they turn around and hand us that gift endorsement, that presidential pitch for Britt and Greta and retro stuff. The perfection of it is stunning.

No question but I'm having branding issues. I mean that's what started this whole business today, on a practical level. Remediation could be useful and Mr. P can do wonders. Oh my gosh. I see that we have been beautifully bound and wrapped for Christmas.

Check out my site, I say to Jimmy, who looks as though he's been having similar thoughts. He powers up and I immediately see the paybox is jammed with micros, a teeny slice of everyone hitting Greta's.

I should be ecstatic. Followers! Fans! I should be thrilled. But I am not. All the anxiety about declining hits and waning viewtime and slumping revs – all erased by one simple nod from the P. Thanks Mr. P! That's what Deb said after he gave her that Seabreeze Netwear shout out.

I don't feel so much like thanks. I feel trapped.

Yet, I don't know. Maybe I should reconfigure a bit? Maybe I should work up some partnering solutions? If the P can do this so casually, what else can he do? Let him coil around me.

Oh I have been bribed!

Jimmy gets up and heads to the back, kills the setter plate, unlocks the door. I follow. We step outside and find a dead rat on the back stoop. It's just there, mouth open to nothing. Great. Jimmy kicks it aside. Like there are only rats out here now, mostly dead. They live off each other. That carcass won't even be there in an hour.

We stand on the stoop, shaded by the backs of the boarded buildings all round, and by my back wall. It is as though we are standing at the bottom of a wide, brick shaft. The grey light filtering down barely reaches us.

Jimmy says real low, so low his words are like rustling paper: We've got to get out of here. They can see us now, I'm not sure how, but I know they can see us, and I just hope to shit they can't hear too well.

His eyes are flicking back and forth, looking for motes. I don't see any. Just a little ash floating down. Maybe they're working ash with cams too? I would not be surprised.

Jimmy says, Drain those micros and let's go. We've got to find Deb. We owe her that. We owe her herself. We are off their tracks already. They see us as wanderers and doubters and we can never get past that. We are listed. I surely am. And it seems to me you may be too. They are mining everything about us. You think they didn't know what I told them or you told them already? Of course they did! That's like the first thing. You ask what you already know. They are going to remediate, the only question is in what way.

I don't know what to think. I mean, part of me is grateful to the President for the Greta's pop. I was down to my last AV, my last Blossom Beads, my last cache of Soi Bar deliveries. Plus, I have no ideas for Hip anything at the moment. What the heck is Hip anyway? That plug with Greta's was a gift from gawd, though, I tell you. And I say that to Jimmy.

I say, I am all about Hip and I don't have a clue about Hip at the moment.

And he says, Let's just take it. Pull the micros right away and then head for Pluto at the pits. Pluto hears every cast off rumor, every bit of discarded info, all the talk that's curled up and blown away. Pluto knows what's going down.

I don't know, I say.

Fact is, I'm super worried on multiple fronts. I don't want to stream this. I don't want anyone to see it.

I say, What about poor Aunt Rita?

Geez, Britt! She was buried in plugs in the pits! What does that tell you? What happened then? Was it an accident? Where is she? The family and mourners buried her stream!

Jimmy says all of this in a voice so low, it's like something slithering over dirt. Of course it was an accident, I'm thinking, what else could it be?

I may not have another chance on the streets, Jimmy says. I may not be able to get from point A to point B. What will happen then? My whole life is navigating the street from place to place, mining the pits, building up defenses, fixing flows and hardware, working locations. When you get right down to it, I clean up after these guys. Authorized Fill? No way. I fill in the blanks. They fracking need me, only they don't see it that way, obviously.

We need to hit the pits, Jimmy says. Forget the Authorized Fill that everybody else has. The pits? That's where everything ends up, you know, before it's fished out. They fish it out. We fish it out. If it's used, it's consumable; if it's consumable, it's used. That's where everything goes, the pits. It's not the end; it's the beginning. We should be there. No question in my mind. That's where information collects. What else is there but information now?

I have issues with this idea, I say to him. They are obviously watching the pits and they are obviously watching you. They even had exact times. They are playing with you.

He says, Of course they're watching the pits. Everybody knows that. They always watch the pits. But we either do that, or they are going to move in here for heavier remediation. This is what Pluto's talking about like I told you. They are sanitizing the streets. They are eliminating disruption. They may be cleansing the pits, too. That's what Pluto says. We have to speak with him. He'll probably have important rumors about Deb.

I say, We should go inside, we've been out here for ten minutes already.

I look around. There is no exit or entrance from this shaft of brick. The backs of buildings, windows boarded, wrap around this little space of dirt and weed and rat. This is the back end of Hip. This is where Brand Remediation enters. How can you make an entrance through something so wasted, blank, and locked up?

We go back inside and I flip on Zoneratti and Matt D. We need the company. You need family in times of stress, and I say that to Jimmy. He doesn't say anything; he's just staring at Zoneratti. I look and see that Matt is at Papa's (thank gawd his groupie Ralphy is nowhere to be seen; what a derp in his Fandango blouse). Matt is hunkered low at the bar, okay, but then what really grabs me is the crawl:

SHOCKING NEWS P-GIRL! SHOCKING NEWS! P-GIRL VIDS! EXCLUSIVE! SHOCKING!

This is too much. I say, Deb!

The screen switches and I see Deb, collapsed on the street. She is lying on the street! I fire up the SituScreens and the street is all around in my little room.

Jimmy! Oh my god!

P-GIRL STAR ENJOYS NIGHT ON TOWN! NIGHT ON TOWN ENDS WTH GIRL DOWN!

Jimmy says, Wait. And looks closer.

Deb lifts her face from the crud and looks around. Her hair is a scraggle. Her face is empty of Deb. I can see spotlights in the distance. A faint thwacka fills the air, something present but far away.

Jimmy says, She's in the Zone – check out those lights. They have her in the Zone. He looks even closer at poor, dazed Deb. She has a cold look, like she's been frozen in a truck and dumped out like a bad plug.

SHOCKING! NEWS! P-GIRL! SHOCKING! crawls around us, floats in the air, curls around the room like smoke.

Jimmy is quiet and finally says, I don't know. I don't know. Is that Deb? Is that her?

Of course it is, I answer. Who else would it be? They've dragged her to the Zone and dumped her.

Who? he says. Who would do that? And why? I mean, we just got a visit from some of the President's men. They're looking for her. And then the next thing is she's all over the tubes plain as day in the middle of the street in the Zone? It could be coming from Zoneratti producers – they may want hype and mess and hassle, that kind of thing. The corps? The ad guys? They want conflict and intrigue?

I don't think that's Deb, he finally says. Get off this Zone rumor board and go to the President's Girl.

The President's Girl site is simply a scene of flecked white fizz like an old field of muddy ice.

Access Denied, Code 634-CROPPER flashes around us. The server must be off line or something. Highly unusual these days. Jimmy tries a back-door kind of gizmo and, Voila! The screen explodes with action. It is humming. Her fans are all over like hatched bugs:

I told you bozos what this was all about. She is just a slut. Now she's lost on the street herself. Maybe Sentry'll finally get a whiff and clean up her act for the rest of us!! Good riddance. I want to see it go down! Maxwell in a Can.

@Maxwell in a Can You are one dumb frack Anon.

Deb we know there is something wrong and our hearts go out to you and your loved ones. If there is anything we can do, let us know. Please reach out. Barb and Bob (in the west).

I don't get it. I gave everything to you, and now this? Is this what I have waiting? I wanted you. How could you do this to me? I have been with you all the way. And you are on the street and who knows where else. What about the P?? I am so sorry for him. He brought you in and now you turn around and stab him in the back! You've stabbed me too! How could you turn on me like this? What did I do? What do I have now? Where can I go? The President's Girl is gone. The President's Girl is lost. The President's Girl's a lie! Sal, who used to love you but now doesn't.

Told you not to frack with the P. P rules! PFan3202

@PFan3202 You don't have a clue. What this Deb does she is only to herself in blame. Mr. Teatime

What is with all of you? What's going on? What is all this about? Mineola of the Ville

@Mineola of the Ville: Do your homework!! Anon

The constantly moving screen now shows an embed of a robocanister rolling down the street sucking in trash. Another vid, a loop of blackish and lumpy yellow water spilling into a storm sewer, bubbles up. I have yellow water running through my room!

Jimmy, turn off the Holo. This is gross.

He switches off and now there is just plain screen. Another embed pops up. It's Deb! Oh her limp, clear sadness just hangs before us. She's wearing the Fabio's and the jangly copper wrist wraps she made famous on her site. Oh they are fantastic! What style! Now she's standing in some room, blank wall behind, just staring, empty.

Deb, how can you stream this to your own site at such an unstable time? I ask. Where are you? Silence.

I want to reach out and pull her into my room. Wait. Is that Deb? Could it be? So blank. She reaches down and holds up a printed sign.

There is no sound. No President's Girl theme song. No da da da da. No VO.

I read, I AM NOW. She puts the sign down and tears off the jangly wrist band. I AM NOW. Next the Fabio's go. The screen dissolves into a sparkly grey shower and returns. Her hair has been ripped off. It is now short, like bristles, and black. Her face has been wiped. She is no longer Deb. This is not Deb! She is someone else, someone else exuding an ocean of sadness. Tee shirt. Jeans. I AM NOW HERE. The screen begins to disassemble again. The sign animates. I AM NOWHERE.

Jimmy looks away and heads into the front room. I follow. What possible good could this do the screens or Zoneratti or Matt D or any of the super-nova stars? How could they? Why would they? People are now very upset on that board and it seems like the upset could slop over. Isn't this the kind of thing Morrie and Jewell were talking about? I don't understand.

It's like they are creating this as some kind of excuse. They are sowing doubt and discord in order to quash it? We have to find Deb. There is no question. This is not even open for discussion. I look at Jimmy and nod. I don't know where nowhere is, but here has vanished for me.

Chapter Four

There is a way, I tell Jimmy.

Zoneratti is spewing a comforting blare from several of my screens. My room, my building, my block brims with Matt and Matt's plugs and Matt's groupies; stuffed to gagging. My stacked chipsets rattle on the countertop.

You know, that's okay because I am so stupefied by Matt decked out in Noblesse huggers that the racket on my counter barely registers. What a placement for those Nobleepers! Right in the middle of Zoneratti! Everything that Noblesse puts out there has West Ville Boys all over it and when Matt swaggers around in that stuff, he looks like he should have daisies in his ears! Wrap him in a taco! Kebob him! Anything. It makes me angry. Why would the Noblessers do that to him? And why would he let them? Some things you just don't do for micros.

I should put it out there. Matt, baby, keep your mouth shut, take your pants off, and come home to mama. Somebody has to set him straight! Absolutely he'd be PO'd. He has a temper. I've seen it go wild and it hurts to see the Mizz get so bent she forces his pills on him.

They were both soused one night, I remember, Matt's weaving down the street, with his beloved Mizz D, little bottle in hand, hot on his tail.

You come here! she shouts. You take this!

He looks at me and says, Get her away from me now!

And I want to, but the Mizz is right there and she grabs him by the back of the neck like a Rottweiler and dumps the pills down his throat. He's thrashing there on the street, in the middle of my room, legs kicking in the air, and she has him down and is sitting on his chest! What a night. He chills after awhile and apologizes to her. She tells him he's so gentle, like a lamb in the countryside, like a great big beetle bear.

Anyway, I say to Jimmy, We can do this.

I don't say exactly what the this is, he knows I'm talking about a way to get out of here sort of unseen or at least kind of quietly. There's a particularly rambunctious uproar on Zoneratti, my stacked chipsets teeter, and I see that Matt now has a cut on his nose and he's having angry words with some guy with a camera.

Get out of my face, Matt spits out. I'm trying to have a quiet conversation here and you're in my face with that thing.

He pushes the guy away! And the guy nearly falls flat on his back but somebody catches him at the last moment and keeps him from hitting the floor. What is going on?

Did you see that? the guy says. He attacked me. He assaulted me.

Matt says, Bug off. Where's Papa? Get this insect out of here.

Everyone just stares. There're at least three people recording it all. Oh this is going to be a shocking and shameful feed across the tubes!

Jimmy has been watching and tugs on my sleeve and we head out back again. The rat is gone. There is a jerking, skittley thrashing in the shriveled weeds over toward the old Blatstone Brothers building wall.

We can't keep coming out here, I say real low.

Wait. Listen, he says. If you have a way, tell me now, quietly, and then when it's time, after dark, we'll take it.

Ash sifts down.

I say, Sure. In the back room, off camera, there's a closet with a walled-in portal behind a pile of all my best Wingers, the cotton ones? You can tug back on a drywall patch and it leads down into the basement. I opened it up a long time ago – I store old Hip stuff down there, you know, stuff that might come back from the past, like those solar mice? So you go down there and there's actually a sub-basement – like, you go through this kind of trap door and once you hit the bottom, you can go from building to building, I'm pretty sure, and come up over where the canal used to be or around there.

It's how they off-loaded workers back in the day, I say. Or moved them and marched them underground. Right here. All these buildings are interconnected deep down.

What? Jimmy replies, a look of complete perplexity on his face.

That's like so old, nobody remembers, I say. I just found the old patched hole in the closet by accident myself – the panel started to disintegrate after one of those long, really dry spells, you know, and I tried to fix it up and it came away like pancake flour. What a mess. And there was this opening and I was curious, so I poked in and thought, storage space! You can never have too much storage space in this business. And I went down there – there's a spiral staircase – right into the dry empty dark. Perfect.

Then I was browsing around later on the old Hood website – the one the squatters used to run? Before that server went off-line? – and Donny K's Hood-Loom was still up and he talks about the olden times and the workers and stuff. He said it was all rumor, though, because all the old papers and records have been lost or carted away or something. He heard it from this old guy who used to live over by the Yards, or what they used to call the Yards. Guy's long dead now. That guy heard it from some geezer on the street long before that who got it from another geezer leftover from even further back in the day. I don't know how many geezers back, but a lot. They're all gone now. Come to think of it, Donny K's gone too. Anyhow, this is like geezer lore, going way back. Donny K was talking about how the workers came in underground right to and from their work sites. There were work sites all over here. Seems crazy, you know? Like what could they be working on other than themselves? Maybe they worked on each other? I don't know. Stuff?

No, Jimmy says, kind of stunned.

Yes, I say. And after I read Donny K, I went back to the basement and found a trapdoor to the sub-b, like all the way down. I looked around down there and found a square brick section and powdery mortar and I started poking and scraping at it – just curious – and it kind of fell apart, which worried me: what if the whole damn building comes down like so much other stuff? It didn't, obviously, and I looked through the hole and son of a gun I could see a tunnel and another wall and partial opening and I knew that Donny K's rumors and stories were more than rumors and stories and geezer lore. How about that?

I absolutely did not know that, says Jimmy.

That pleases me, to impress him with something I know about the outside or the underside. That's his turf, and it always stresses me and everyone else I can think of to even talk about it, let alone explore it. You don't want to go out there and get in the sun or miss the best sale hours on the screen or episodes with Matt in a dither or any of the important stuff. Plus, you know, there are all the threats and marauders and stuff they're always talking about on the screens and in the crawls. Outside's creepy as heck.

Wait until dark, Jimmy says. It's kind of weird to travel then, but better to fend off the unexpected than to deal with whoever might be out there now for security. Brand Control monitoring the street.

I say, You can make fun of it or dump on it but that's like the only thing that matters – brand control. You yourself, you own your niche and can get by no matter what, it seems; for the rest of us, how we control ourselves matters – a little brand security would not be a bad thing, I'm saying, not necessarily. Look at Deb, and now I've lost my feel for Hip. Do I need a focus group? Do I need to reposition? Where can I pick up fans? Where'd the old ones go? Where's my growth? What's my weed barrier? Where did it break down? Where's Deb?

Britt, Jimmy says, what were you before Hip?

Jimmy, I wasn't anything, I say. There's nothing before. You know that. Deb and I were fooling around for awhile after the big Mart fell and she was playing with the idea for Debrity. Remember that theme she worked up? – Wanna be me! Wanna be me! Me me me me! Oh oh Debrity! Thumpa thumpa thumpa! – I loved that bass. The whole thing was great. When you're talking being seen or getting people to see you the way they should? Nobody's sharper than Deb. Thumpa thumpa thumpa! Wanna be me! Oh oh Debrity!

Yeah, I continue, she was way ahead of me. I hadn't put an actual name on what I was doing. I was still mooshing. My first roll out – that's when I became me.

We have to go inside, now, I say.

I remember that roll out, Jimmy says, as we walk into the front, camless room. But I don't think I ever knew what came before, or even considered that there was a before. So that was when you became you. Wow. Remember that black brim and the knee boots and the line about how nobody looked right in the Hood anymore, we were all like polymethyl bots? I liked that. Because nobody did look right, nothing was really working right, and polymethyl was everywhere. That was when the outer parts of the Ville were getting hit by those big Excellon extractions and the dunes were shifting around and everybody was freaking out because of the collapses and disappearances. It wasn't just the Mart that came down, remember?

We all thought sinkholes were opening up everywhere, Jimmy says, sucking everyone down.

He pauses in a reverie of collapse. Great for his business.

The P said we need to all lock arms and hold together – nothing can defeat a purposeful citizenry, or something like that, Jimmy says. You and I talked about that. Remember? The P says we are in this together and the solution is to go to www.presidentlocksarms.gov/dustbusters/store for strategic purchases and advice on best practices.

I do remember that, obviously, I think to myself. The accelerated extractions. The topside cracking like a plate. Houses and buildings sliding into holes opening up, or so they say. That was all on the screens, though the

Mart came down right here in the Hood. I remember the P hitting the screens telling us it's all rumors put out by waves of hackers and marauders in the streets.

If you listen to these rumors, the P says in his big chat, the marauders have won. Stay in your rooms and go about your business, visit with Matt, visit with Bart and Missy, work your sites, broadcast your stuff, and acquire the stuff of the stars. That's the way we pull together. That's what Nutri's all about, Excellon, too. We are all here together and we must put shoulder to shoulder, arms locked, as they say. You can do your part by visiting with me at my DustBusters compound. God bless the Ville and God bless you.

That's how the P put it, smoothing the disturbance and dislocation, giving a shout out for a return to a humming system.

Jimmy says, I started getting all kinds of hits after that. Here in the Hood, nobody can even think about acquiring luxe stuff from the P like high-density strutwork to prop a dwelling, or hiring off-duty Sentry for the marauders and threat, that kind of thing. We're talking mucho micros. So people come to me. Somehow they think I have some magic words or something that will hold up a roof or keep out a crawler or block a jumper – at a discount. All I can do is help try and make it from day to day without complete disaster.

Jimmy stops and looks around, afraid he may be going on too much. Fine with me. I want Jimmy to talk to me, you know? But I don't want to hear cave ins, sitting as I am above two black crumbly holes, the basement and the sub-basement, dug into the heart of the Hood who knows when so long ago.

I turn up Zoneratti even louder. Sentry is on the scene and the guy with the camera is screaming at Matt and his circle of bruisers:

Just wait! Just wait! You transparent phony!

Matt now seems calm.

He says, This man attacked me. He sought unauthorized videos and stills of a branded image, me. That, of course, is a felony. He's a simple thief.

The guy is shouting: He beat on me! He assaulted me! He's supposed to be my friend? You know who I am? I'm Myles2go! I'm not some crazy guy on the street! I'm not some geezer off a truck! I take pictures. I share!

One tall officer says simply, Sir, come with me, and bearhugs Myles and hauls him out of Papa's.

There are cheers. All the cameras disappear as soon as Matt starts talking brand theft and felony. No one in the Zone wants to be associated with the word unauthorized. If you're certified unauthorized by the corps or their subsids, or the P or his subsids, or Sentry and its subsids, forget it. You're back in the Ville or the Hood like yesterday. One mark on that eternal record is a sentence to a lifetime of banishment. You can't lose that dream of the Zone, at least a lot of people think. You just can't.

Jimmy fiddles with the jiggling chipset on the counter and I watch Zoneratti some more.

My mind feels totally wasted, like the western lands. I'm not really seeing what I'm looking at, if you know what I mean. My eyes are wet and burn like an old oil field. Zoneratti goes on and on, but I'm not listening, not really. I feel used up. Where did everything go? Even my rooms are vanishing. The light flickers from the screen; it flickers from the Zone. Nothing catches the light here. Hip is gone. It just disassembled. It dissolved in my own inner mind! Is this like it was before Hip? Before I was set goalwise? Before I had my niche fixed? Before I was me? Back then, at least I knew there was an answer. I knew there was a me waiting. The answer was the niche. Everybody has one. You find yours and theirs and use them. I am my niche. All that has shifted.

My head is hurting.

I pop a red and let it wash through me. This is a river.

Time decants moment by moment until Jimmy stops fiddling, looks up from the chipset, does a little eye toss, and we head into the back room, past the cam, into the closet and down the dark spiral stairs.

I can hear Matt say: Just make sure he shows up in court. I want it in triplicate.

Yes sir, yes sir, Mr. D.

Jimmy's grabbed a Lumalite so we can see. I wonder if anyone is watching my dying cam the moment two ghosts pass by.

There are boxes of boots and about 50 orange shirts with different color vertical stripes in the first basement. Orange and Stripes are *It!* (Old ones were for awhile, you guys may remember, thanks to Britt's Hip Bitts.) There's a whole wall with bicycles leaning against each other – can you believe it? I am so amazed I found them all just around the Hood, though a lot of them don't have all their parts. We could use them if we could cannibalize them and then go from point to point to point, and not be like now where we're stuck wherever we are whenever we're there, for the most part. We need to bring places together somehow, the places that are left. At least that's my opinion. You just don't want to move around much without a way to move besides your feet. It's something I'm thinking about, but haven't branded yet, you know? Just an idea.

Over in the corner are bags of buttons and beads and pins, crates of windup cat bots I got from the Mart rubble, large boxes of pre-hyperspecs with black-and-brown mottled frames. A while ago, I thought pre-hypers might be worth pushing because they're so lame – you can only read the weather with them, which you're already in to begin with, so what's the real point? Lame can be very Hip, though, like the little triangular flags stuck to sticks on the back of those bikes? (Ha ha! I've got a duffle of them down here too!) Then I figured nobody wants to know the weather anyway because it's always worse than you think, and so I dumped them all in these great boxes and stashed them down here. Maybe someday? I have other boxes jammed with old electronic gear – chipsets, transistors, even big-assed tubes – sitting over in a far corner. Lots of that used to go inside heavy-duty consoles and cabinets, some even made with wood. I've got some of those cabinets, empty, guts torn out, on the other side. I even have boxes of old tools, pretty rusty.

Jimmy picks up a double-head hammer and then shines his light on the tubes and wires and capacitors and whatnot.

Wow! he says. This is like a gold mine. I had no idea you collected all this stuff.

I tell him I don't collect. I save for future use and retailing.

He says, Why didn't you tell me? I really could use some of this. Just last week I was greenscreening for the flower pot people – you know, the guys with the hats – and could've used some of these chipsets and even part of a bike – would've saved me a lot of phony build-outs of stuff.

It's stuff I have, I say. You could've asked.

I tell him to move the crate – it covers the way down. He shoves it over, exposing a metal plate pocked with rust. I lift the trap and we look into the black hole, down where the workers once slogged, the workers mentioned by Donny K in his old collection of geezer lore. Must wafts up.

Britt, Jimmy says, looking up, anything can be Hip, that's what I'm seeing around your space here.

As I look down into the sub-b I see those old workers or whatever they were. Stolen from somewhere maybe, marched somewhere else, used, encased, forgotten for sure. What's that about? What if Donny K had never talked to that old geezer at the Yard and then written his Hood-Loom post? What if one old geezer hadn't talked to another old geezer going back and further back? There was activity here, until it all wasted away, like water from a desiccated streambed. You can't see any of what was, now; but it was here, right here! Who even knows all that went on here way back? I look up at Jimmy – no, he doesn't know – and pull away from my own thought. Nobody remembers anything.

Everything's in how you brand, I say, lapsing into comfortable talk. How you brand is how you see; no, more than that – it's your whole mind. Like, you see a capacitor and a greenscreen set up; I see a console with funny pictures and a retro world. You see an empty black sub-basement and a way to the pits. I see a black hole with echoing workers on the march. It's all in the spin and in the forgetting, really, particularly the forgetting. We're good at that.

He says, That's true for everybody. A lot of people say the more you forget, the more real you become. You continuously re-create. That's why there are so many neighborhoods in Zoneratti. Infinite niches. Bored? Forget it and move on. You can go to the main square, you can check in with Matt. You can check in with Mizz. It's a village, you know, you're welcome anywhere, hitch onto to anything, if you can. You get caught up in it and it becomes part of you, maybe more. You can go to Papa's and get into the action there, or you can even hang with Ralphy, if you want. You can go over to Lauren and Ron's and see what's up with Baby Dawn and Ron. Jr. Ron Sr. just got canned, I hear. Should turn up dead soon. They have lots of new stuff, though, and they just did their place over, and Lauren's got a nanny now. Or maybe you want to go down to Big Bill the Butler's place and hang while he gets sloshed and disses everybody in the building. You know, they got a whole world there. You can plug into any place at anytime, whatever fits. You can piggyback your stuff and move it around, use whatever niche is best at whatever time. A community. What was there before? Probably nothing. And nobody cares because it's always something new and different every moment. You see, Britt, there is no before, not one that matters.

Yeah, I say. What's your point, Mr. TechnoWizard? Everything's made and remade and remade again there. That's the Zone with mountains of micros, the corps, and the President wrapped around it all, and this is the Hood on the far side of the Ville. Baby Dawn and all those guys are cradled by the corps. Zoneratti is a haven for the corps. The P watches over all. He even pops in, now and again. Here, this is where we scramble and yearn for all that, for Matt and Matt's micros. There's no village here, no micros, only this big-assed black hole down to where they forced workers to march back in the day. Or so Donny K. says.

This is the Hood. Like where's Deb? Okay? The only available niche at the moment is down. Hang on to that hammer.

We go down.

The air is dry and brittle. I lead Jimmy over to the wall where I opened up a hole and we step through. There is nothing but dust and darkness here as we move along the snaky tunnel into the next building and the next and the next. Most openings from one sub-b to the next are still walled off, although the seals are crumbling. I never tried to map it or anything and never went very far, so this is all new to me. Jimmy runs the light over this new old world. The walls are mostly brick. They used that a lot back in the day. That's why so much stuff crumbles, I think. Not built to last or withstand the extractions or weather or the endless sun and trembling, the winds. As we move from one building to the next, the air fills with fusty tangs. Is it my imagination? Here is sweat. Here is dead. Here is the must of long absence. Empty. We don't talk.

The seals – just crude cement or something – basically fall apart with a hammer tap as we pass through. I see some stairs still intact in a few places, but we're interested in distance, we don't want to go exploring. Despite having to bang through those seals, it takes hardly any time to hit the end point – the far street where the great SupraSteel storm drains block everything like prison barriers. The road stops here. There is no further.

What's that sound?

Shhh, I whisper.

There is a murmur coming from somewhere. It's like a ruffling of papers or the rattle of broken crockery or maybe like – this is hard to believe – distant voices? We listen. The sound is very low and seems to come from everywhere beyond the tunnel. No way. I look at Jimmy who is listening very intently. He holds his finger up to his lips and softly says one questioning word: Melinda? What

125

a horror! Billy, the storm sewer guy? We listen closely, but the sound never rises above the level of fluttering, an audible quaver beyond the storm drain, beyond the brick, beyond us. Walking through the absolute bottom of the Hood, we are surrounded by the sounds of the absent, what we cannot see.

This is a passageway for the disappeared, I say to Jimmy.

He gives me a quizzical look. We've crossed over into something, it feels like, but I don't know what, he says.

Great, I say.

He says, You are the one with the knowledge of this place. Where are we?

Think again, I say. This is from long ago. Who the heck knows long ago? I don't know where any of this comes from or why it's here or what it was. All I've got is Donny K, and all of his old posts have been taken down or have tech problems or the servers are dead, supposedly. No access anymore. Seems nobody much cared about them anyway.

We head up these rickety steps off to the right and then, from there, up another spiral stair (sort of like mine), hit a seal, bash a hole, find some stairs, go up until the steps end in another trap.

Jimmy pulls out a combo-tool, jiggers and kicks, and the trap gives with a shotlike crack! The whole Hood must've heard that. Oh boy. But we emerge, like two teeny ants, on a low rooftop outside, not all that far from my place. The night air hangs hot, long after sunset. The old canal, probably was a river way back in the day, stretches like a long depression behind us. We wait.

I can see someone leaning in a shadowed doorway of a boarded building way down the street, across from my place, only shoes visible. They are Florsheims, I am sure. A cloud of dust hovers above an intersection.

We should head the other direction, Jimmy says. They may be tracking us, but we may have dodged the sats, at least for a bit, by moving so far underground. Would've shown up as glowworms, not people, he says. Maybe wouldn't have shown up at all. The pads, nothing we can do about them.

I check my screen, its faint glow shows zero hits. Nothing on the back cam. No micros on those sandals. What a waste. Damn. Nothing more from Greta's. I'm keeping my pad on, you know. I have to, don't you think? Why would anyone even bother with us, really? Turning it off doesn't do anything anyway. It's always on for the sats to track.

I look out at the empty street. I have never been here before, way up on a nighttime rooftop looking out at the Hood in all its sorry nothingness. There were people here once, I know from reading Donny K, maybe some of those old workers, or their sons and daughters, maybe people that came from somewhere else, attracted to this place because of – why? Why would anyone seek out this snarl of frayed streets? What was the bait? How was it sold? What did those people think they'd find? Chunks and fields of cement and spreading collapse are what they got.

No workers trudging out there now; only people in their rooms, working their sites, selling what they can get their hands on, mostly from the bland authorized fill network, pushing it out into the sphere. No time for streets. No time for anything but screens and cams and showing your goods, whether it's yourself or your stuff – if there's a difference, I mean. Ghosts we are, all

127

translucent – until we hit the screens in all their incandescent flatness. Ah! There's life! Sublime. We are full of color for everyone!

But out here? We're only us. Spectral, emaciated.

Far to the east, the spots shine from the Zone, hitting the thick billow of Plaxo-Cloud that blocks the sun and the UVs. Those Plaxos look almost like old pictures I've seen of the real McCoy, puffy gobs of white and gray in the sky.

Between the Zone and here, on this roof, is mostly black, a maw of darkness. Here and there a faint glow, either from a window with tattered blackouts or from an old sodium light still buzzing over a street. I'm rarely in the open at this time of night and it seems strange, as though we're living inside a melanoid machine about to disassemble itself. Prickles the skin.

There's a rat-tat-tat-tat, a sharp, gritty noise, Zoneward. What the heck is that? And from the other direction, to the west, there is nothing, not even a faint glow. I hear a scream, for sure, it sounds like. Another. A whole series of them.

Jimmy, I gotta say I'm kinda scared.

We're okay up here, he says.

I can tell he's nervous. We've moved from our niches, from our spaces – to what? We've gone underground through the forgotten tunnels and come out on a building top. We are now outside in a world where there is no outside and no life outside. I was born outside, I think, although I don't really know, it's just a feeling. I don't remember. But outside is never a place I want to be. No one would want that. It's where you came in from, it's the place you fled, the place you've been that no one else knows, the place where you cannot share and cannot work together because no one else is there on the team.

128

When I was little at camp, they never let us alone outside. They taught us to hold hands and stick close and do as we're told.

Use your inner resources to find your niches together, all snug and secure, kindly Mrs. Petri droned to us.

You are in a beehive that you all build together! You are busy bees who all work adding to the hive! Guess what, she'd say. It's Sally's hive and Billy's hive and Angelina's and Urethra's hive, too. And remember that you are never bored and you never lose if you use your inner resources. Working together, you will get the most honey and the sweetest.

Ha! What a crock I think now. Most of it is boring, let's face it, and none of it is sweet. You use your inner resources to find your niche, set your brand, style your site, and get the micros flowing, because they are not, repeat, not, going to flow on their own. And if you screw around with your niche, then remediation is necessary. That's a lesson in life I am learning real fast.

Let me tell you right here: there are no niches outside, zip; no micros out here; no way to build a system and sell yourself. Nothing to broadcast. Nothing to share. No one to share with. Here's the rub, though, that I just thought of: all niches on the inside are in a state of continuous disintegration. Buff them up and right away they begin to dull and blur and fall apart. Think Deb. The outside is secure in its dilapidation. Geez. I need another red.

Deb, oh Deb! We will find you! We have to, for ourselves, for you, for each other.

The screams stop – What was that? Was it even alive? Sounded kind of mechanical – and it's quiet for a long time. We sit with our backs against the low wall that runs around the roof and let the blackness enter us and surround us and we feel the machinery slowly grinding. Finally Jimmy says we should climb down and head around the corner. The Florsheims seem to be gone – when did they leave? – but the dust cloud is as thick as ever, shrouding the street.

We clamber down the wall on the other side, across from the boarded up Disco-Bra warehouse – Auctions! it says on a faded sign – move slowly along the walk, cross the street, and head south. There is still not the slightest breeze and the street is very dark. Anything could happen, anyone could spring from anywhere. A herd of rats skirrs in front of us from curb to curb. I can just make out their bulbous grey, a gang of trotting polyps.

I stop and lean against a wall. It has INK OUR LOOD looping in silver spray paint across the yellow stucco. The street is totally empty now.

I stop.

Jimmy, I want to go back, I say. I want to go back to my place and try to sell myself. I want to be on camera. I want my brand back. I want to be visible! Maybe those guys, Morrie and Jewell, can really do something, you know?

A frantic siren sounds in the distance, of course. Why not? Why not everything bad you can think of out here? Why not roving packs of – what? I can't even imagine. Roving packs of the disappeared. I see great holes opening up and Jimmy and me falling in, leaving the here, exiting the hive. Isn't that what's happening anyway? Our streams and our sites will show nothing. White screens of showering snow. Access denied. Code 634-CROPPER. We will be swallowed up. We will vanish. Remember Britt? Who? Who was she? I don't know.

Jimmy stops and looks back at me. He arches a brow.

It's so dark, I can't see in this muck, he says.

Isn't that great. Just great. Thanks. He seems to me doomed. Or maybe we're both doomed, like the Ville and the Hood and the rest of this vanishing place. Maybe it's all doomed. Oh my god. I shake my head. I can't believe that I'm in the middle of a nighttime street, crying. The tears run down my face. I am completely outside and the inside is bubbling up like lava.

I shake my head. Deb. What about Deb? I go rigid and breathe slowly. In and out.

Jimmy, I say, we have to get to the pits. Pluto'll have info. We need info. Deb.

He looks in my direction. Is that concern in his eyes? I can't tell.

Right, Jimmy says.

He heads down the dark sidewalk past a bank of boarded buildings crumbling like decayed teeth. I follow. There is no one on the street, not on the walk, not in the shadowy recesses, not in the dank empty lots that suck out all light between the building wrecks. How did Melinda wander so much that she knew where to find an occupied house in this empty confusion? Where is Ledger Street from here? It's not here. It's over toward Jimmy's. No. It's past where the old Mart once was. I don't know. Did someone befriend Mealy at some point? Did someone take her in? Was it luck or chance? These buildings all look like slag heaps. There aren't any sounds, not centipedal scratches, not bubbling cries. Nothing except some metallic tinkling I hear faintly. It sounds like chicks must have sounded when they were hungry and no food was coming, again.

Cheepie! Cheepie!

No chicks on this street or anywhere else.

What is that? I say.

Jimmy hears it too. The night is a skein of faint sounds and nothing but abandoned black.

I don't know, he says.

The cheepies gradually grow louder as we move slowly down the street, past the tumbled stone and old boards, the crushed brick, the thickets of shredded plastic, the dead trees here and there. The sounds begin to morph into something else after awhile and I realize that we are hearing the faint strains of music. Music? In the middle of the night, in the midst of the teetering Hood and depopulated Ville, we are hearing music and it is getting louder. I hear brass and a snare drum now. I hear it!

We round the corner, where something called the HORN AND ART used to be, or at least that's what the broken up sign says, and midway down the block we see them. And maybe even more importantly, they see us.

There are about half a dozen boys, really, I don't think you could call them men. One kid stands in front of a snare drum and bangs away; the fingers of another fly up and down the intestinal twist of a saxophone; there are two tall players of old silver trumpets, the bells pitted and dinged. Street musicians! But the most striking member of the group is their, I guess you'd call him their front man. He's laid out flat on a gurney, legless, armless, an old sheet thrown across his back and a bucket-like micro-reader hung from his neck.

A sign on the gurney says, Give What You Can. Can What You Give.

He is singing an old song and I wonder how he can gather so much sound lying flat on his belly with a weight around his neck that should be dragging him to the depths of a heaving rasp. But he is singing:

> After the ball is over,
> After the break of morn –
> After the dancers' leaving;
> After the stars are gone;
> Many a heart is aching,
> If you could read them all;
> Many the hopes that have vanished
> After the ball.

The trumpets pierce, the sax moans, a tambourine shakes like a rattler.
WTF?

You see, the boy on the gurney says to me as we approach and listen, I sought the kiss of my sweetheart and she sought the kiss of everyone else. There were no embraces for me at the ball, and I vowed never to forget. Everything crumbled away, after the ball.

Now she has gone, the ball has too, and I'm left without limbs, please give a micro or two.

The players around and behind him offer up a tremendous trill, a soaring crescendo that ricochets down the alleyways and off the boarded windows, a clattering, keening, winding sheet of sound. They abruptly stop and all look at Jimmy and me.

Well, I say, that is very sad. I actually don't have any micros.

Jimmy is excited. He says, That is beautiful and tragic.

He reaches into his pocket for his pad and pops a few micros through the dropbucket reader around the gurney boy's neck.

I think I could never do that.

Jimmy regards the boy, who has eyes dark as any alleyway and a head smooth as a melon, regards him for a moment and says, I've never seen you before.

And the boy says, You hear that fellas? Never seen us before. Jajajajajajaja!

They all laugh.

Never seen us! Jajajajajajaja!

Let me tell you mister – what did you say your name was?

Jimmy.

Mr. Jimmy. Let me tell you we are here most every night. We pass the night here and entertain. Those that pass by stop and shed a tear, often they dance and often they share the fruits of their labors with us. Sometimes they tell us their stories, if they're of interest. They share what it's like – after the ball. It's a beautiful thing. Right fellas?

Oh yeah. Oh yeah.

One of the trumpeters soars off on a flight, the saxophonist follows, the chase is on. Their notes flap out high into the night, like bats.

The gurney boy shouts, Hold it. Hold it! And then turns his head to us.

And where are you folks headed at this time of night? No reason to be out here now. You might run into something. I hear it's not safe.

134

We are headed to the pits, says Jimmy.

I thought so, says the legless boy. That's where it all goes, that's where I lost it all. I needed something there, maybe it was my sweetheart. She left the ball. I went back to the pits and this is what happened. He gestures with his head toward a few of his stumps.

Right fellas? he says to his ensemble.

Tell it, someone shouts. Tell it!

List to the story, I'll tell it all:
I lost myself after the ball.

The horns and drums strike up that melancholy tune. I pull out my pad and the gurney boy nods. He wants the vid. I power up.

Bright lights were flashing in the grand ballroom,
Softly the music playing sweet tunes.
There came my sweetheart, my love, my own:
She wanted a brand, she wanted a home.

I looked round the ball, nothing was there,
Nothing available, niches were bare.
I looked back at her with my hands upraised –
What did I have that would kindle her praise?

Long years have passed, child, I have never wed,
True to my lost love who turned round and fled;
She dinnint try to tell me, dinnint try to splain –
She couldn't speak; to hear was a strain.

That's why I'm lonely, no home at all –
My sweetheart has gone and taken it all.
I have no brand, no home, no ball.
The pits end it all, it all, it all.

After the ball is over,
After the break of morn –
After the dancers' leaving;
After the stars are gone;
Many a heart is aching,
If you could read them all;
Many the hopes that have vanished
After the ball.

The trumpets and funereal sax slow and with a mild flourish and a tap on the snare, the song ends. The tambourine settles.

Jimmy sniffles a bit and slips some more of our micros through the reader. The gurney boy nods again. He says, Thanks Mr. Jimmy, you are a gentleman of the old school.

Turning toward me, he says, Miss, and pauses.

Britt, I tell him.

Miss Britt, will you show me the video?

I hold it up for him to see. The whole scene plays out again. You can almost see the mournful notes melt across the street.

Not a bad rendering, he says. I need more work with my diaphragm. When you're my age, you need to pay attention to the details of your body. I ask you not to send it out on the tubes, out of respect.

What do you mean, I say. This is beautiful and a poster for the life in us all, I say, a bit floridly. I guess I'm caught up in the temper of his song.

Besides, I say, this will be you for everyone. Everyone will know you. It will make you real. It will make your brand, after the ball.

Jajajajajajajaja! he laughs.

Jajajajajajajajajajaja! laugh the others.

Oh Miss Britt, that's rich. Real! I think I'll take a rain check on real, he says. I'll pass. Count me out. Let it be. Jajajajajajajaja! I'll tell you, Miss, I've got real enough real right here on Chestnut Street. People come by, maybe not a lot at night and fewer and fewer, it's true, but they are real enough for us. Right boys? And the drones. The drones come along, make us all hot steppers.

Oh yeah!

Sure enough!

That's the man!

Drones beat it!

Our patrons have legs, the gurney boy continues when the band quiets down. Not like me. Arms. We encounter them. We entertain them. We challenge them. They share in return. We don't want anything bouncing around out there in the tubes to ring the wrong bells. Sweetheart, you are off the reservation – that's what they say. Off the reservation. Off the rez. Off the track.

So, Miss Britt, save your moving pictures for yourself. I've got them in my head now.

Okay, I say, concerned that I've somehow offended him. But until a few minutes ago, he didn't even exist as far as I know and that doesn't seem right, don't you think?

Why do you want to go to the pits? he asks.

Jimmy steps in and says, I go down the pits all the time. We need to see somebody there.

Jajajajajajajajaja!

137

Wrong answer, says the gurney boy.

The horns blare. The drum bangs a chaotic beat.

We need to see someone and talk, Jimmy says.

More blaring. Someone – the tambourine man? – blows a raspberry. The gurney boy closes his eyes and shakes his head.

No, no, no, no, no. Stay away from the pits, he says. Bad juju. Can't let that happen. Lost my baby there. Lost most everything. Sun never gonna shine my backdoor down there.

Are the pits after the ball? I ask myself.

He is quiet for a moment and then says, You know, I am the white child of a black man.

What does that mean, I wonder. Night time and day time? Vice versa? People?

Oh? says Jimmy.

I say, I've read about that kind of thing back in the day, I think.

Indeed, the gurney boy continues. I am a wingless bird, but you can see I fly to heaven.

I wonder where his memories might take him; he seems to have them.

Jimmy says, The music, yes.

The gurney boy sighs.

I render mourning tears in pupils that see me, even when there is no cause for mourning.

How could that be – no cause? wonders Jimmy,

snuffling. I wonder the same thing – there is so much to mourn.

When I am born, I begin to disappear, the gurney boy says.

I look at his delimited torso. He is vanishing, slowly, like so much else.

Smoke, says Jimmy.

Bingo! says the gurney boy.

The band instantly sirens a hallelujah! The trumpets lead. Hallelujah! The street is filled with a joyous welcome in the blackest nighttime. Hallelujah! Hallelujah!

That is it, oh yeah! says one of the musicians.

Go! says another.

Yeah! Brother Rat!

Congratulations! You have solved the riddle! Keep to the path south, past the old Orpheum Theater, says the gurney boy, and hit the pits just before dawn.

The group parts to let us pass.

Remember: they are watching now, more than ever, the gurney boys says. The ball is over. I know because I hear everything, right here, every night. Here is where all words come to rest and are resurrected in song and story and riddle. We are the Nighttime Echoes. Tell your friends to come by and pay us a visit. You are travelers now. Jajajajajajajajaja!

Jajajajajajajajajajaja! they all break out.

Jajajajajajajajaja!

Hit it!

Go my man!

Yowza!

The drummer starts a beat. The sax and trumpets rev up and a tune forms from the noise, a tune I know but can't quite place. I've heard it in the long ago. We walk around the band as the gurney boy begins a new song:

The night was mighty dark so you could hardly see

For the moon refused to shine ....

We are around the corner heading down 18th Street and I don't hear the rest, but I imagine it's a sad tune. We are travelers on a moonless night.

Jimmy, I say, have you seen them before.

Never, he says. But I got to tell you Britt, I've never gone the pits this way before. Everything's so broken up now, if you don't know a part of the Hood or the Ville, it's like entering a foreign country or something. I sometimes think we don't even speak the same language. You meet someone in a strange part of the Ville and you wonder if there is any way to communicate at all.

I start to say something about the gurney boy, how he seems a goner and has turned it all around somehow. Somehow he has ventured outside and created something I've never seen. How could he be out here like that? How could he take those vanished limbs and broken words and fit them back together? His song fills me; it is like our song or what it would be if we had one.

Jimmy says, All that for a few micros, and shakes

his head. I don't get it. Not even a vid. I could make that vid sing! I could build a universe around it! What a site!

I don't say anything. Jimmy's eyes are shining, but he doesn't seem to understand that we are venturing outside and the outside has taken the gurney boy away from sites and into its fold. The gurney boy has lost his arms, lost his legs, and discovered a voice here, after the ball.

What did he mean, I say to Jimmy, he lost it all at the pits?

Jimmy shakes his head. WRMS, I guess, he says, and doesn't say anything more.

Oh my god. What is there for us? What waits? I shed the thought, beat it down. Down.

Where is that theater? I wonder out loud, and Jimmy says, I have no idea. I think it's south of here – that's what he said.

We continue to walk, away from the Echoes, and the murmurs begin again, all along the street, murmurs barely heard, and I wonder if the gurney boy's sweetheart knew Auntie Rita.

Chapter Five

This must be it, I say, looking up at the blackish face of a desiccated ziggurat, the Orpheum. Not much else around here – a few broken buildings, emptiness, the usual debris. We are standing in an open square, surrounded by neat piles of collapse, a teetering stony column at the center, fenced-off lots here and there on the perimeter.

It seems like we've spent hours slowly walking. Not talking much, just kind of feeling our way along in this old, unknown world. My pad has been buzzing constantly – since the Echoes, really – but I haven't opened up. Jimmy warns that it's a tracking maneuver, although I don't understand that. The darn thing pings all the time anyway, it broadcasts me into the air and around the world every 0.02 seconds no matter what, and the sats home right in through wave frequencies and pingulation. Sats are picking up a lot of the work street feeds used to do, Jimmy says. So many of those feeds are down and it's too much hassle to bring them back and coordinate the info, he says. Sats do the job, and more.

I don't get it, I say to Jimmy. What's the point of trying to make contact? Who's calling anyways?

Jimmy says, You mean the buzzing? They want to see you. They want to smell you and everything around you.

How do you figure that? I ask. Who?

It's not just knowing where you are but where you're going and what you're planning, he replies. That's the way I figure it. You can open up and find out.

We're standing near the Orpheum in all its dark squatness. Everything around here seems so forgotten – the fringe of the Ville, so outside the Hood. Seems more spread out, more openly broken than our close little neighborhood of scraggly piles. The Hood seems far away now, though we haven't gone all that far, I don't think. Hard to say with this walking.

Jimmy looks around. He looks way up toward the blank roof tops and toward the teetering central column. He spins on his heal. Nothing.

I mean, this is what I think they want to do, he says. First off is they want to talk you back to Zoneratti and the Hood, get you off the streets. Okay, you're contacted, you flip open, and they see exactly where you are through the two-way and they process your demeanor. Heart beats, breath, blood pressure, you know, biometrics. They get behind your eyes. They see into you. Oh, they know what you see and what you do with what you see, all right.

And then they entice, he says. They take it all in and sweeten it and talk you back to base: Come to us Britt. We can show you micros. We can optimize your site. We can bring you Deb. We can deck you out. We can fill you with whatever your little heart desires. Green shorts? We got em. Bike parts? Sure. Boys? Not a problem. You will overflow. Come back, little Britt.

Jimmy laughs, a dry hacking laugh, like a cut stalk.

Geez. Who?

The corps? Jimmy says. The P? The producers? The humming-system guys? All of them. I don't know.

143

Why don't they just shower us with dust? I say. They'd get everything. Those nanomotes sprayed over the street can broadcast details of every cruddy weed dead on the block. Why bother? Why would they care? We're not worth the effort, and Deb's already off somewhere or down a hole. She's not in the picture.

Every human life is precious? He laughs again. That's what they used to say, back in the day, according to Brute, anyway. Really, I don't know. Maybe they think we're questioning them or something. They don't like stuff flying around outside that they can't control. They don't want us walking around. They don't want volatility. They just want everything humming. They see us as sowing uncertainty and confusion – that's what Morrie and Jewell made clear, you know? You can understand their point. They probably didn't mean for us to really go out and look for Deb. They probably already know where she is, don't you think? Maybe they wanted to see if they could goad us.

Okay, I say. I'm goaded, I guess. Nothing's gonna keep me from finding Deb. It never occurred to me that they might know already, that they're using her. Deb! How could they do that? I didn't understand how much I want her in my life. That's their handiwork – they're showing me me.

Jimmy looks around again, and I can see a pain – or is it something else? – on his face. Like he's acknowledging something he sees as inevitable – a retreat back to the Hood? Remediation? Failure? I look around myself. What the frack is here? Nothing, I have to admit. But this is just a place on the way. Does he see that? We are on our way to Deb; we're not headed here, we're not headed to nothing. Nothing is not the goal – it's what you have to get through.

No matter what, Jimmy says, you can't keep out of Fat Boy, that's what all this says, all this screw up.

Every move is funneled into Fat Boy. They didn't come to you about Deb on a hunch. Every stupid thing on the tubes is gathered in. Every breath you take. All your cam action. Walks, eating, calls, sex, Brute on the can. Sat images. Street feeds. Conversations. Watching the screens. You name it, Fat Boy's digesting it. He sucks you in, all of you, and gets bigger and bigger as you get smaller and smaller and skinnier and skinnier. He's a like carnival mirror, that's what I hear – your emaciated self reflected as yourself stuffed to bursting. You know, Fat Boy?

Yeah, I say, stuff about us, all those blips packed away out past the Dry Restricted Area, deep beneath the extractions even. Fat Boy lies under everything, under the mines, under the drill holes, under the collapses, way, way down. That's what Mrs. Petri used to say at camp. She loved him. He drives the micros and keeps the dreck out of the system. That's what we were always taught. That's what she said: Fat Boy's what the P uses when the ship begins to list. Fat Boy rebuilds it all. Fat Boy's more precious than anything, I guess. Holds us up as we sink. Each and every one of us.

Nothing's dreck to Fat Boy, says Jimmy. Nothing's wasted. Fat Boy's so full of you they can model a new Britt tonight, I bet, from what you've left behind. They can build you up, bend you in and out, change whatever, pull you out of a can, and set you on a shelf. More you than you.

Right, I say.

Jimmy's into it, that's for sure. I hadn't quite realized that. He exudes a whiff of admiration.

They can read your future better than any software reader from the olden days, he says. They know what you're sure to do, what you won't do, what you're capable of and what you're not. They probably already know we're headed for the pits. They probably know why

145

and what we'll find there. Open your pad and confirm it for them.

I think I'll just let them ask the new Britt they're cooking up, I say. She'll know better than me. When they find out where I'm going, maybe they'll let me know.

It's like a great game for them, he says. Absorb everything about everyone, determine what will happen next, and then do whatever is necessary, or not, depending on what the action-response software comes up with. Then everybody huddles over the results. The new, improved Britt!

He laughs, that dry humorless laugh.

They probably want to dig at Deb, probe her, he says, take her apart, see where and how she deviated, tinker with the malfunction, displace the doubt. They want everyone on board, right? When someone jumps ship, they want to know why. They'll tickle her insides and come up with an answer, run it all by the analysts, re-jigger, focus, and re-launch. They get her through us. We're part of her — necessary for the re-do.

Okay. Why? I ask. What's the point here? Look into that olden crystal ball and answer that Mr. T-wizard.

Keep us in our rooms with our screens and our fans and Matt D and the Mizz and all the other shows for company? Jimmy says. Good for business. Theirs, and mine, really, now that you mention it. No business out here. No President's Girl. Lots of lost, though.

He laughs that raspy laugh yet again.

Jimmy pauses and looks up at those rooftops. He's thinking. The rooftops are as silent as nowhere. Ash falls, lightly.

What if everybody started going for the unexpected and ignoring no trespassing signs and no-go zones and all that? he finally says. Like Brute on the street. Like Mealy with the MealyCam and the baby. What if everybody started wandering around the streets at night, cams stitched in their caps? Too much uncontrolled street activity or something. Or maybe too much curiosity. You'd see too much? I've been thinking about it as we've walked along here. Doubt's what they're after. They want us to embrace everything. What if you questioned who and what's okay? Is that Pal a Pal? Does that Associate have other associations? What's with the P? What does he do? What about the corps? How do we know everything? How do we know anything? What do we know that doesn't come off the screens? What's with the food? What's with Auntie Rita? The extractions? The collapses? The dislocations? What happens to stuff that disappears? I don't know. I don't know. Everybody's suspect, I guess.

He shakes his head.

Everybody's suspect? I'm pained. I don't like this. Am I suspect? Suspected of what? I never heard Jimmy talk like this.

Suspect of what? I ask him. Of what?

I don't know, he shakes his head again. Asking questions? Looking for Deb? Knowing Deb? Knowing Brute? Being you? I'm just thinking, that's all. What do they see? What do they want? What do you want? And me? A system needs to hum, but maybe it's on the blink.

We're standing near the Orpheum looking across the open square at some other smaller blank buildings.

Got a micro or a plug? A plug for an old man with one leg? A spare micro? Come on, gimme a hand. Ay!

The scratchy voice seems to come from nowhere and catches me out and I flinch.

Aww. Can't you lend some help?

We look around and see a form on the walk deep in a recess of the Orpheum foyer. One leg sticks out into the fuzzy glow on the street, the glow bouncing from the Plaxos. The spots shoot up from the Zone, hit the Plaxo clouds, and then diffuse faintly down through these narrow streets and dreary squares. No moon. There's never a moon anymore.

Jimmy stares, but I move forward a little and see a geezer hunched against the stony wall. He has a doughy face with a greenish tinge, a few lumps like Brussels sprouts on his cheeks and neck, a tee shirt that says Plug It!, and an oily old coat, kind of grey, looks like beleaguered fleece. His boot has lost a heel and sports a big hole dead center of the sole. Definitely could use a make over.

I don't have any plugs, mister, I say. My friend here has some micros. Jimmy, shoot him some micros.

Jimmy pops some micros into a box reader lying beside the old guy and asks him if this pile is the Orpheum.

The guy says, This thing here? He jerks his thumb. Sure enough.

And the pits? Jimmy follows up.

Ho ho ho – right down there. The guy gestures to the south.

What are you doing here? I ask him. I feel a sudden concern after being startled by such a helpless figure. Shouldn't you be home or wherever off the street?

There is no off the street, he says. Lost my leg somewhere. Lost my building. So I live out here on plugs and rats and micros. Keepin it simple.

Okay. I don't know what to say to this.

Naw, he continues. Just kidding you. It ain't simple, it's heavy. Whatcha gonna do? Enough people come by. I got a crutch. I can get around most of the time, though I gotta tell you, it's getting harder. My leg's all itchy and getting that funny feeling, numb I think.

Your one leg that you have left? Jimmy asks.

Yeah. Numbnuts! Other one's fine. Har! Just kidding. Lost it awhile ago, down the pits you're so interested in. Was down the pits cause nobody wanted to watch me no more and I didn't have nothing else to sell. You're out here, you probably know what that means – nothing left to sell and the music stops; it's hit the road, Jack. Down to the pits to scavenge. Har!

Jimmy says, We're out for a walk down to the pits. You say south?

Yeah, I say south, the geezer says, peering up. Oh, I know you, he says. I've seen you hundreds of times limping along here.

I've never been down this way before, says Jimmy.

Don't be so fucking literal, the old guy says. I'm talking what I see, damny! You know the drill. I've seen you. I've seen lots of yous.

What drill? Jimmy says.

149

Everybody wants a part of you, right, and they want you to see them, that's the way it is. That's the way it's always been. If they can't get off on you and your site, or you become a turn off, they split and find somebody else to get off on. Kind of like a circle jerk, I'd say, one great intercontinental circle jerk, complete with electronics and cameras and lights and conveyances to drive you to the ball. You can't get it off, you split. Har! So poor old you, you're left alone; you head for the pits.

His snorts are bitter.

Nobody gets it off on me, says Jimmy. I'm not about any of that stuff. We're on a search. We're looking for somebody.

Okay, big guy, the geezer says. But watch your self.

He seems to turn a bit reflective, like someone pondering a pool of regrets.

One of them bots in the pits took the leg, he says.

Even after the gurney boy, this startles me totally. What?

He pretty much ignores me.

You know, back in the olden days, I used to be the Cancer Dude. What do you think of that?

The Cancer Dude? I say.

You wouldn't guess it now, the way I am here, he says. Back then, we had everything going for us. We had cancer – what could be better? – we had the President, we had one of the biggest things ever to hit the electrosphere – the Tumorthon! It shot everywhere like prions in a pigsty. I was bigger than Pred-Trak! Bigger than Vinnie!

The geezer kind of loses it at that point, maybe remembering those olden days. He drifts away, looking into the gloom. I never heard of the Tumorthon, and I'll be honest, it sounds like something I wouldn't want to see or be a part of, you know. But I give the old guy an encouraging smile anyway and wait. Jimmy is standing next to me, fumbling around with something, and doesn't say anything.

Everybody was into it, the Tumorthon, the geezer finally says, seems like the whole planet. And they should have been, damn it! Should still be. We had the Kid with the Tumor in His Brain right there with us. Everybody loved him, and I found him, me, and I brought him to the Ville and the Zone and I put him up there for everyone to fall in love with. I was a matchmaker, you might say. Matchmaker to the planet. I had ads and micros pouring in from everywhere, and comments and vids and recordings and casts of all kinds. Thousands!

I tell you though, he says, in a whispered, confidential tone, that kid was a dumb little fuck. Didn't matter — I was MC with all these sick kids and grief mongers and tears and money flowing everywhere. Jerry the MC.

The geezer, Jerry the MC, falls silent again, lost in what must have been a reverie of disease back in the day. He's just hunched there by a column. Must have been awhile since anybody's come by. What are those green things on his neck, I wonder. Probably something he picked up out here.

We were with the kid when Dr. Wenceslaus described the surgery to him, Jerry the MC says at last, breaking back to the present and me and Jimmy. He looks at us and smacks his lips.

It was all part of the show. Oh that kid was stoic, I tell you. Positively stoic.

You going into my brain? the kid asks.

The doctor, I'll never forget, takes his glasses off and looks right into that little guy's eyes – bluey they were.

Son, he says, that's where the disease lives. We're going in there after it.

And the kid, with the sensitivity of a brick and a flair for showbiz, not to mention the tumor in his brain, says, Let's roll!

Don't you just love that? Let's roll! What a trooper. The fans loved him. He'd been any smarter woulda wrecked everything. He had a mother, but we took care of her. So many micros flowing, she gladly, gladly took the dough and gave the painful interviews and wrung her hands and wept and egged on her stoic little boy and patted his stoic little head. Yeah, go for it, she said. Go for it!

So we did. Everybody followed us. We were completely sponsored by Nutri, of course. They paid for the pop-up counseling – and we all needed it because we were all part of the little guy's family. It wasn't just his mama. We all did stress relief and deep-breath work, all that shit. We had operators online 24/7 to chat with people struggling with their emotional dislocations. Our WeepLine was hopping like a thousand and one frogs.

But when we were in the operating room? he says, the Grief Center was as still as a ruin and the line was as quiet as a rat's bones. We all held our breath. Doc W spent, I don't know, maybe six hours drilling through the little guy's skull and sticking in that Laz-O-Grip to yank out the growth – seemed as big as a basketball to me. Popped it in the can, patched the head all back up. All like pulling a tooth to him. Not much blood for the most part, just spritzed the kid off now and again.

Course, he could've dissolved the sucker, the tumor, that is; but no nasty Laz-O-Grip with that mean-looking claw means no visuals, you know? Drill was a monster, too, with a wild growl when you flipped it on and went inside the head. We had awesome drama on the screens! Disgusting! Mesmerizing! Doc W knew how to perform!

Jerry the MC is excited again. He is telling his story, just like the olden days.

Every hour that passed on the show, Jerry remembers, you could feel the hope and expectation pumping up until it filled the studio, even the Ville – a bloated parade balloon floating high over our heads, an emblem of our faith and caring. That's what it was. Faith and caring.

We got it all! Doc W announces when he walks out of the OR. Every last millicell. We got it all. He breaks into a great smile, holds up the Laz-O-Grip with that goddamn tumor in its teeth and showed it to the world, a gangly mass of gunk – coulda come from something squashed on the street. Then he plops it back in the can and snaps the lid.

I am enthralled by Jerry's story. Imagine!

What a trophy! Jerry says. What a fish! We all exhaled at once. The expectation hissed all over the Ville. This was it! There was a torrential downpour of micros after Doc W's Miracle, right after the operation. It was a sight to behold, micros tumbling in like monsoon season. It was like the blessings of old.

We only sliced off a little over 35-40 percent of the gross for administration and a bit more for other costs, fees, and cap expenses. The rest went right to Nutri for charitable distribution, less their own administrative and counseling expenditures, security, grief work, marketing, and advertising, of course. It made my heart glow. It was a wonder.

What a story, I think to myself as Jerry the MC takes a breath. Saving a whole kid with everybody on board. That's really what it's all about.

Kid died anyway, Jerry continues after a moment.

Oh no! I exclaim. How? What happened? That's awful.

Little fuck just up and died – personally I think he choked on a plug, Jerry says. How didn't matter to us. Dead's dead. So naturally we wanted a big takeout for the show, a show of shows, a celebration of how deeply we all cared and would continue to care, despite the setback. A streaming portrait of our full hearts.

We had Die Toten playing the gig. They came in from somewhere special, I don't remember, set up with their dancers and backups. And do you know what? I'll tell you: Nobody gave a shit! It was like this kid was dead and there was nothing left for him, no more entertainment beyond the takeout fest, nothing left for me, no more micros. Turned on me before I could come up with a new Dying Kid, that's what they did, and for amusement? They got plenty out of Vinnie and Pred-Trak. They trashed me on Pred-Trak! That is low. Nothing for cancer and everything for some dude milking nine year olds on camera. Oh I was a mess, the life tanked. Oh humanity!

He sighs a deep and heavy sigh.

So the admin expenses lasted me a bit, I'll admit, but everybody started to think of me as the Guy who let the Kid with the Tumor in His Brain Die. Some of them were angry, more treated it like it was all a rip off – that's what it became, that's what people said. A rip off! We saved that dumbo's life! We gave him the opportunity to go out in style, more famous than he had a right to hope for. He was viral for days! And still it all turned sour. Overnight I was like an untouchable, and now I am one. Can't believe you never heard of me.

Maybe I did, I say. I kind of remember.

But do you know what? he asks.

What? I say.

Jerry the MC gathers a bit of dignity, or as much as a man with one leg lying in the street can gather, and says, I wouldn't have it any other way.

But you're out here on the pavement, says Jimmy. You went from the very top to lying against a wall in the middle of the night with one holey boot.

Yes, he says, that's true, that's true, that's all very true. But I don't have to worry about being fucked with. I don't have to sell nothing. I don't care what anybody thinks or sees. Just gimme a plug and a warm place to shit, like the poet says, and I'm a happy camper, if you'll pardon the expression. Could use a new boot, but I can get by.

That's when I first hear the rumble growing louder and louder.

Jerry the MC cocks his head.

Drones, he says. That's the one thing that I can't get away from. Those damn clean-up drones. Nutri and that lackey, the P, send em out to clear the streets. Debris, they say. Fucking with me, I say. Can't get rid of all the debris until you get rid of everything making debris, ya understand? I'm debris. Har!

I don't know about any of that. I think Jerry the MC is entitled to his opinion and all, though – that's what makes the P and the Zone and all this so special.

The rumble is quite loud now. Jimmy and I look down the street just as a pack of WRMS robocanisters careen around the corner, sweeping up castoffs and debris. I've never seen so many working a street. There's even a Mega Whisk, the kind Corpus Remotionem uses in bulk contract work for removal of large objects like, I realize, defunct geezers.

We should get moving, I say to the old man. They won't touch anything that's warm and moves.

Sure, missy miss. Sure. He tries to get up. Where's that damn crutch?

The drones are sucking up everything on the street and the big one is bearing down on us, on our little group in front of the Orpheum.

Where's my damn crutch, Jerry says, casting about. I hear a boom from far off toward the Zone, a boom so loud dust sifts down all around.

Jimmy says, Here, let me help you up.

No, no. All I need is my crutch, says Jerry. He looks around some more, patting the cement. The Mega is targeting now, heading right for us and picking up speed.

Jimmy sees the sealed entrance to the Orpheum and runs over to try and break in. The drones are strictly for outdoor use and if we can get the geezer inside we should all be okay. Jimmy's movement confuses the Mega and the drone slows with a whirr. The Orpheum seal won't budge. Jimmy stops pushing and begins to unpack and work the door lock with his combo-tool. Jerry is still kind of thrashing on the pavement looking for his crutch, which I don't see either. He seems like an upturned roach or a broken pinwheel.

Uh-oh.

Broken mechanicals, even moving ones, are fair game, although I don't remember the drone specs and restrictions exactly, such as they are, and the Mega begins to accelerate for our area again. Jerry's become a pinwheel to this machine, an edible compadre. The smaller drones fan out, forming a battery of suction cleaners rolling down this dumb street that nobody cares about at all. Who cares if it's got trash? The buildings are all goners anyway. No businesses around here. Nobody lives anywhere except on the street, which the bots are programmed to depurate, denude, and disinfect.

The drones are organized now, sucking in paper and scattered stones, fallen bricks, a dead rat, a hub cap, an old plasma screen, a rotted and frayed rattan chair seat, one black shoe.

The loudspeakers on the units blare away into the empty street:

Please lift your feet! Please excuse the intrusion! This is an authorized street and district sanitization activity. Please remove all wanted items. Repeat, Please remove all wanted items from the sanitization zone. Thank you for your cooperation.

And on and on, every metallic syllable bouncing off the brick and stone facades facing the square.

The Mega Whisk stops whirring and focuses on Jerry the MC. It moves toward the Orpheum foyer.

Jimmy, I yell, head up the street and crouch down! Jimmy bolts a few yards and hits the deck. I do the same. Again confused, the canister stops, reconfigures, and starts toward Jimmy's still form. Jimmy gets up and runs across the way. The canister stops and tracks him. I'm already on the pavement, still as a burned hulk. It spins again and heads in my direction, befuddled by the alternating movement and stillness and body heat.

Jerry the MC yells out, Go fuck yourself! as the Mega moves on me. I get up and trot off and it stops. Jimmy is immobile again, watching in a frozen hunch. The Mega spins around. I'm quiet, watching. It spins again. Jimmy hops up and squats. It spins.

Then I realize that Jerry the MC has yet to find his fracking crutch and the Mega has danced itself perilously close to Jerry's aged, flailing body. It zeros in. I get up and run, waving my arms, and slump down right behind that rolling compactor. It has odd orange symbols ringing its top, a series of interlocking circles wrapped like a glowing headband.

Oh, we are in trouble. The Mega now has a Cadaver Lock on. It powers up with a great Whoosh! Jerry has nothing to hold onto, not even a crutch or a stick or a fallen board. He is being pulled along the cement, leg first. His micro reader and plug bucket crash and bang along the pavement. His hands and arms are thrown back, dragging above his head, his Plug It! tee and oily fleece are scrunched up and ripped toward his chest. And then he is gone, sucked directly down the Mega's shiny oval intake chute, burnished from a night of removals. I stand in the middle of the street with my mouth open. Where Jerry the MC once lay is nothing, not even a drop of blood or a sliver of bone. Not even the crutch. Or the bucket or the micro-reader.

The Mega suctions off, spins around, focuses on me until I take a step, and then it continues along the wall of the Orpheum, smaller canisters rolling behind it. They all disappear around the corner; only the rumble lasts awhile.

I just stand in the middle of the street looking at what is now nothing. Jimmy comes over. We are both there in the pale half-light.

I got it, Jimmy says. I got all of it.

What are you talking about, I say. I realize I am shaking.

That was a person, I say. A geezer, yeah, but a person who was talking to us, just having a conversation, telling us his story. I never heard a story like that before.

That's what I'm saying, Jimmy says. I got it all. I got the story and the removal.

He holds up his pad.

I am amazed.

I got his story and the removal right here, he says, waving the pad like a flag.

Jimmy, I say, I have to sit down.

We walk slowly to the Orpheum foyer, not more than five feet from where Jerry the MC used to be. I feel his absence. I feel a heavy fog. I'm still trembling.

Why did that happen? It's just supposed to be debris that's swept up, part of the P's Fragrant Streets program. They clean up so we don't have to worry about it, so we can keep the focus on a smooth system and the untroubled flow of micros. How does sucking in Jerry the MC help a smooth system? It wasn't an accident. It couldn't have been an accident. That Mega had a Cadaver

159

Lock on and moved straight in. Jerry never even had a chance to find his crutch. He was kicking around like something drowning.

Jimmy and I sit and lean against the Orpheum's rough old stone.

Should I upload this? says Jimmy. He has his pad out ready to go. I don't say anything. I can't even think beyond why. I can't get beyond that one word. I was talking to this guy and then he got sucked up and compacted.

What do you think, Britt?

This is worse, I think, far, far worse than the corps re-thinking their priorities and demanding that you erase a branding tattoo or something. It's worse than getting locked out of the Zone. Oh my god. I am stricken with fear and uncertainty and doubt. So this is what it's like.

Jimmy, do you think, like, Deb? She was down on the street. She was in the frackin gutter. She was confused, like too many reds or yellow jackets or something. You can flatline on that stuff for hours. Like into the night, and it was already night, or dark, when we saw that vid of her face in the muck.

That's what I was wondering, Jimmy says. I don't think so. Do they even use those drones in the Zone? I guess they do. But the P can't risk losing somebody there, I mean, that thing moved in very fast. Can you imagine if Matt or somebody zoned out and got swept into a Mega? The whole system would go kerflooey. Matt D vacuumed up like a dust bunny under the bed?

Yeah, but what I'm saying is that, from the sound of it, Jerry the MC was Matt D back in the day. Everybody wanted a part of Jerry the MC, until they didn't. He

160

owned the Zone. He talked. He conversed. We were interacting just now. He was a person!

So what do you think? Jimmy asks.

I look at him and wonder.

About what?

The upload, he says.

Why did you shoot it? You never shoot. You don't do vids of stuff that just like happens to you. Like arguments or dinner or somebody coming over. You don't do your self.

Jimmy turns away. This is different, he says. This is not the usual. This is on the street near the pits on the fringe of the Ville. Jerry the MC gave his life for a clean street, you know. In all the years, I never talked to a geezer before, he says. Never once. They're usually bent over or sprawled out waiting removal. Hoping for it, maybe. So I wanted to get that down, and then the bots, you never see them work in formation like that, not around me or anything. So I kept shooting. It was like some kind of organized hunting mode – for trash? And when the Mcga moved on the old guy, well, I couldn't stop. I have it all now, beginning, middle, and end. A total story. An episode. People need to know what's out here.

Will they care? I am lost, I think. Deb is lost. Hip is lost. Jerry's lost. Smooth running is lost. Now Jimmy's documenting it all like we were back in our rooms in the Hood. And he never documents. He fixes and tweaks.

Sure, I say, go ahead.

Jimmy flips open his pad.

I'll shoot it to Zoneratti! he says, suddenly excited. I'll embed it for Matt and the gang right at the top of Matt's Wabbit feed.

He starts the upload.

Jimmy, what about Deb?

Deb's all right, he says again, with certainty. We saw her. Pluto will give us the word once we get to the pits. Everything funnels to Pluto, eventually.

How can he be certain?

The upload is complete.

Let's keep going, Jimmy says. We can't be too far now.

I don't want to move, I think. I am in a vat of glue, and there is that scratching noise again, and the murmurs – the ones we heard in the tunnels, the ones we heard after the Echoes. Now, here, again. They seem to be following us, stuff barely heard, like skittering bugs. Or are those tinkling notes? I strain to listen.

Jimmy says, You hear that? It's coming from inside, behind the seal, inside the Orpheum.

He gets up and moves toward the door, or what used to be the door. Hello! Anybody there? Hello!

The murmuring stops. Was it music?

Hello! Jimmy shouts. I know you're in there. We hear you. Open up. Let us in. A guy just got mopped up out here. A guy. Maybe you know him? Jerry the MC? Hello!

He stops and listens for a bit and bangs again on the seal.

After a pause, a voice shouts from inside:

Go away! We don't want what you're selling. Get out of here or we'll run you off, you with your friend there. There's nobody here. You don't know where you are. This is the big empty. You hear nothing. There's nobody home.

A moment's silence, and then hastily, This is a recording.

Jimmy bangs some more. Nothing.

There must be people all over, I say. Somehow they just leaked away and now they're in these buildings or under the street. That's the only thing that makes sense, if anything does. They come up to die or hold their babies in the night or something. They don't want us. They don't need us. They are completely outside. Melinda must have known them, or maybe she was one of them. Brute must have known them too. Why else send Melinda to the street with the MealyCam? He wanted to document it. For entertainment? For amusement?

I know there've been rumors for a long time. That's all there's been, rumors. The P says forget the rumors. Nothing's disappeared. Nothing's vanished. Nothing's lost. Forget the rumors. Forget. Who are these people?

Jimmy says, I know those rumors. They make us out like we're sailing on an ocean of what's unseen. I've gotta tell you, Britt, I've never, never seen anyone coming up or going down below the streets. I've never seen anyone coming out of these closed up hulks or heading into a drain. Never.

He looks at the blank and boarded buildings.

Rumors, he says, are rumors.

Jimmy, we came out on a roof not more than a few hours ago. We traveled underneath in the tunnels and came out above ground and all the while we were down there, we heard the whispers.

Yeah.

He knocks on the Orpheum seal and gets no response. No more murmurs either.

I lean against the wall, deep into finality or futility or whatever. That's it for Jerry the MC. He's dead in a trolling Mega. Gift boxed. Where will he end up? One thing for sure: no more entertaining – except the vid Jimmy launched!

That should make for one last star turn, an exit with a difference, a last spin under the lights with everybody rapt on closing night! Maybe somebody will see it and remember. Yes! Jerry the MC! The Tumorthon! That's real, anyway, right? Kinda what the Kid with the Tumor in His Brain got in the end. Morrie told us they buried Aunt Rita's final stream too, her last vid. With full rites. All the dead are really streaming.

Memory's all that's left of what was, don't you think? It's what we gather in and save. In the end, that's what we have. But what if the memory goes or if it's never gathered in? What then, I wonder. Oh we're so locked in the now. So locked into the streams. Streams are our memory. What is memory in a world without what was, a world that doesn't even know that there was a was? Jerry is circling all around. Auntie Rita is looping eternally

What if there's a monumental glitch? What if the streams are erased? What about that? How can you learn what you are, if you don't know what you were? Memory is lighter than daybreak. It lifts your head up; it raises you higher and higher until you can see the dim cracked land all the way out, beyond the horizon, past everything, out to your past self, your own outlying territories. Memory is what we all float on. And the land is sinking.

Jimmy, what happens when we die?

I startle myself with the question, and I really startle him, and I don't even know what I mean. Or why I'm saying that.

Nothing, he says. Streams go on and on.

So there's no end to it?

Are you kidding? There's never an end, you know?

But like the flesh?

Calcium phosphates, old bone, he says, grey grit. There's nothing else. You end and go on, that's it. We're loops, I guess.

No, I say. No. I mean everything has a place it goes. Like, where is your mom? Did you scatter her? Plant her? Shoot her off? She could be on a boat to the moon, just about. That would be something. You could look up and imagine she was there when you could see the moon, if you could ever see it. Somehow we need to remember, is what I'm saying, we need to remember what was in order to know what we are. That's what Jerry says to me. All we do, though, is see what's right in front on the screens, you know?

Jimmy grunts.

We're just locked in, I say.

I don't know what happened with my mom, Jimmy finally says. They never told me and I never asked. Didn't occur to me. She just wasn't there anymore. Disappeared, you know. Sentry comes to our room and says your mom's gone and we are here to help you. They got me some stuff in a bag and we left. I wondered sometimes, but she wasn't anywhere, you know? She never was – that's what I remember. I remember just the not being there. She didn't leave any vids or streams or anything real.

The same thing happened to me, I say. I mean, I was way little. I don't know what happened with her. Did you do grief work?

No grief work, he says. Didn't want any talk. Just went to the Bulb Center for a little while, sat around and listened to them rattle on, and then to camp, and after awhile, I left. They sent me off with full honors, such as they were.

I went to camp too, I say. It was huge and went on and on and they kept us so close inside with team play and all that stuff; we never thought about what was not there and where it might be.

Yeah?

They said we had everything a girl could want and more! Plus we got a boost from the P and a slew of credits when we graduated. After awhile you don't remember anything from before, or care. Sally Kamaski – you know, Miss Diva on Balloons in the Ballroom, Bubbles in the Bed? – she was everybody's best friend.

Oh? says Jimmy, I know her; she's always working multiple streams.

You know what? I say, thinking about Sally for a sec, she was a funnel of information. They got everything from her, and so did we, and if it was about something not authorized, you could get tossed, no matter what. Pre-Graduation Exit, they called it, PGE – peegee. You got peegeed right out the door to the pre-grad camps, probably, if there really are pre-grad camps, that is. Sally picked up a lot of transferred credits that way.

I'll bet she did, says Jimmy. She was working the system, whether she knew it or not. Still is. We all are.

You know I don't know how many got peegeed, and I never saw any of them again, I say. But I've seen more than I'd ever want to see of Miss Diva. And the thing is, she wasn't really malicious. She wanted to, no, she needed to tell everything and show everything because she thought everyone would want to know all there was to know about her. She saw the credits she picked up as a reward for putting on good daily shows and being so sparkly.

She was right, I continue. We all wanted to know everything about everybody because then we'd tell about ourselves, which everybody wanted to hear too. Right? But Sally K. was nonstop. She told about what was told to her. And what she said back.

She told about what she thought Carrie was doing down by the back kitchen. Like Carrie never went to the back kitchen, I know, because I did and I told Carrie about what was going on there and she was wide-eyed. It was a revelation to her about all the gorging. Sally got it in her head, or maybe somebody said something and it got all changed around, and suddenly it was Carrie by the back kitchen with Googie and they were going through the Nutri boxes for themselves, and then playing with each other, among other things. And Sally watched it all, she says, which she didn't, but must've thought she did. That was it for Carrie and Googie – peegeed right out the door. Then we got a long session on team play. Mrs. Petri, our camp teacher, never mentioned Carrie again. But I remember that. I do remember.

So you vanish, you disappear, you die, you're gone, you're post-present, I say. Our lives are like sinkholes opening up, you know? Oh my god. How do you hold on to what is vaguely drifting away out of your head? How do you remember what you remember? How

167

do you keep it from dissolving? Maybe they'll remember Jerry, spiraling out now in invisible waves through the sphere. Does anyone remember Die Toten playing for the Boy with the Tumor in His Brain? What about Aunt Rita? Say something to me Jimmy. Speak to me. Speak. Please.

Jimmy doesn't say anything. Why doesn't he answer? I need him to answer, but he just has a puzzled look, like I'm speaking one of those foreign languages from weird parts of the Ville. Like he doesn't understand.

Finally he says, I don't know.

My pad starts to buzz incessantly. I decide to open it up.

Britt, Britt – what the hell are you doing?

Oh Christ. It's Morrie. I see he's taken his jacket off. He's in my front room!

Get out of there! I shout at him. What are you doing in my place when I'm not there? How dare you. Get out!

Britt, he says, very calm. You know why I'm here. I'm looking for your friend Deb. So much can go wrong out there. It can be dangerous, even. The P can't shield everyone. He just can't do it. He wants to. He wants to spread his wing. He sympathizes. But that won't help much when trouble comes trolling around the corner on the outskirts of where we all are. I think it's best if you and your fan Mr. Jones just come on back here. We can have a little chat, maybe move you to nicer digs with more secure storage, that kind of thing. Maybe closer to the Zone? How are things down there by the Orpheum? Best not stay there too long, I hear there are some problems on the street. Come on back.

Where's Deb, I say. Where is she? What has happened to her? What have you done with her?

Morrie gets a wounded and pained expression on his face. He looks like he's about to tear up. What an actor.

I'd like to help, he says. I'm trying to help. I haven't done anything with her. She was in the street, you know. Looked awful from what Jewell tells me – he's monitoring the tubes. Now there's some kind of disruption in the Zone. Did you hear those booms? It never rains but it pours. That's what I said to Jewell. Do you know what he says back? After a storm, a calm. Ha ha ha. Sheesh. So come on back, Britt, and let's do the calm part.

Get out of my place, I say, and slam the pad closed.

We're not far, Jimmy says. The pits can't be far, and we want to get there by daybreak. He was starting to get to you, wasn't he? Storage? Deb? Calm? They drill right into you.

No, they don't. They only think they do.

We crumple down near the Orpheum and whatever it contains within and the absence of Jerry spilling everywhere in front. I have to think, and I am so tired, and parts of me from long ago are drifting away, even as I finally realize they were once there.

Chapter Six

First off, for those of you still with me here, I'd like to apologize for what happened with Jerry.

I'm really, really sorry. I failed. We failed.

I mean, I've never seen anything like that and, you know, it happened so fast, it was like I couldn't recalibrate. It was right there in front of me and Jimmy and we did the only things we could think of when something that's not ever happened before happens. We stood still and stared. Can you imagine? Of course you can.

We should've done something more. But all we could do, when you get right down to it, was mesmerize ourselves. That's all we ever do. We stare. We sit in our niches. We lure others into watching us do pretty much what they're doing. That's what I know. What else is there?

But now we're out here who knows where, I sure don't. The Orpheum? We've launched our actual selves, not just pix and texts and scrambled collages, mashups of this and that. We are moving! We are here and heading to points south! Geez.

We never move. We are never off the tracks. We never leave the authorized frequencies. That's where we've been forever, our whole lives – that's where we're supposed to be, and there are so many frequencies, so many choices, why go anywhere else? We have all the freedom we need in our little teetering rooms. Plus who would be around if we veered off the legit spectrum?

Nobody, that's who. Like what Morrie and Jewell said: no future if nobody's there to share it. Same with kindly Mrs. Petri with her pinched little mouth and her rat eyes.

Where are you if no one tunes in? she used to ask.

You looked at Mrs. Petri, scrunched your nose, and said, Nowhere?

We need each other and our screens or we'll all disappear, she'd say.

When you're alone, you have nothing, we said back, arrayed around her in a circle.

No one, she said, can see you if you're off the screens. Where are you if no one can see you?

Nowhere.

She pounded that in like a ball peen hammer.

You know what? I knew it was dumb or something. I knew somewhere in my own head that I was there, inside myself where my blood runs and my heart beats and where no one else can see or feel. I'm there now; I was there as a kid. It's where Deb is, too. She tried to tell us:

Whatcha whatcha whatcha wannabe
Whatcha whatcha whatcha wannabe

Thumpa thumpa thumpa thumpa thumpa
Oh, oh Debrity! Oh, oh Debrity!
Wannabe me, wannabe me, wannabe me!
Me me me me me

Thumpa thumpa thumpa thumpa thumpa

Oh, oh Debrity!
Oh, oh Debrity!

Her very first theme. She called it Debrity.
Wannabe me? Right. The Deb she put out there? She
never really wanted the weight of all those fans hanging
on her like she's a bus to Bangladore or someplace. That's
Matt's world. That's Matt.

She thought she could hold on to herself and be
everything for everybody else at the same time. All those
fans. Deb thought she could create Debrity and remain
Deb somewhere.

Careful, Jimmy says to her. They will claw you
like crabs. They will want to take you apart.

They will be into me, whatever they think I am
at any given moment, she says. That's the point. But
inside where I live, where the clear light is, nobody's
going there. That's the best place anyway. That's where I
can hang secretly and where they'll lose themselves if they
try to follow. Inside, I am me, and there is no way to get
from the outside in. It's a maze. Besides, they'll get
sidetracked by the ads.

Oh Deb, Deb, Deb! Do we have any secrets,
really? Can anything be hidden? When you are there,
when they all are pulling at you, when they are tugging at
your name and absorbing your feeds, there is no you.
There's only them and what they want to see and hear.

She wanted a hidden me in a me-less world, a
girl with a secret garden inside, and she walked away
from Debrity before it even launched.

I'm gonna hold onto me, she says.

172

Where is my secret garden? We're not supposed to have any darn secret gardens. You know what? They don't want you inside yourself, thinking up your own stuff totally unmonitored and unmentored.

Successful thought leadership, Mrs. Petri says, looking at each of us in turn, comes from group brainstorming and sharing in a structured environment. I want the team to open screens now. Let's share!

Mrs. Petri didn't believe that buildings and even people, whatever, were outside the Zone and the Ville. Nothing existed beyond the right now of our little world and our team streams. She didn't want to hear about me. She didn't want to hear about my mom, whom I couldn't even remember and still can't. And I'd ask. I'd ask Mrs. Petri.

What about before? What about my mom? What happened with that? What was that all about? What was it?

And Mrs. Petri would say, We are all pulling in the same direction. We're all building what we're building now, together, and what matters is here, and what doesn't matter is what isn't here, just like the P says, and he is mentor to us all. He is setting the stroke, and we are in synch.

And Mrs. Petri absolutely never mentioned anything like collapses or sinkholes or post-animation or body removal. No way. That was out of the frequency range, no trespassing, owned and gated, like the Zone. Inside the Zone is collective fame and desire – heaven; outside the Ville is isolated obscurity and need – hell.

I wondered, when I was small and skimmed through our screen set-ups and watched everybody do what they do every day, and laughed with Chrystal and

Billie7 and Frazzle, I wondered, why don't I know what's out there? Will I remember Chrystal's stories about her mom, the P's emissary, and life on the island? She tells me late one night how her mom fell into a ditch and was swallowed by a great toothed plant. Right in front of her eyes! She tells me. And how she watched her mom dissolve like Blossom Beads in a glass of Veet. Chrystal watched, just like we watched Jerry.

Oh, I do remember her telling. Now I think what she saw was on a screen. That's what I think. Chrystal's mom was never any emissary. There are no big toothy plants. Chrystal's no island girl. It's easy to get mixed up.

I'll say one thing about the screens – they have no yesterday.

Everything is always right there in front of you. There's nothing else. That's the fun, Mrs. Petri explained in her twitchy way.

You don't have to worry about yesterday because now is always now and tomorrow is not even happening, she'd say.

I didn't want to upset Mrs. Petri, for anything. She anchored my day. I didn't want to confuse her, or myself. So it was always, Yes, Mrs. Petri.

Anyway, it's hard for a kid even to think about a solo life or life beyond where you are. I mean, you can think about being alone and exploring, but you can't imagine how you do stuff or how you get along without your friends – so they've got to come along, which would be fun. But how is that gonna happen? How is your underwear going to get clean? What do you do about fixing dinner plugs or how do you get the little people in the screens to come out and go with you on an adventure?

Alone's scary, too, inside the brain scary – even though alone is the most natural state of all. How can you learn to be if you never learn alone? But it doesn't help keep the system humming, does it?

Like most everybody else, I held on to Mrs. Petri. With every hole left by one of my peegeed campmates, I held on to the here and the now – the yes, Mrs. Petri. When Carrie and Googie were selected for Pre-Graduation Exit and disappeared, yes and yes. Now I am outside the bandwidth, outside the frequencies, outside the Hood and the Zone and (almost) the Ville, and I am alone with Jimmy, and I am sorry, sorry, sorry about Jerry, who was unconnected, okay, but was just as real as those screams or whatever I heard on the roof top a few hours ago. Maybe more real? More real than Chrystal's made-up mom on a made-up island.

Jerry the MC is just as much a part of our great life as Jimmy or Matt or Morris or me. He's no failure! I just didn't know about him and now I do and I have his story and his life in my own head. And I am memorializing him, making him a real memory, for sharing beyond the horizon. What do you think of that Mrs. Petri? I am offering a blessing to Jerry, a geezer on the street who once was the Cancer Dude and is now dancing through the sphere like the aurora borealis, thanks to Jimmy. This is a prayer for the past, mine and ours.

I see I need forgiveness. I need to explain why we failed to save Jerry. But I can't. I can't really explain it. I couldn't act. I don't have the inner resources. My inner resources, the ones that are mine and mine alone – not the mentored ones – have been sucked away, I think, by some great sanitizing bot I can't even see. I'm wiped clean.

When Jimmy shot the vid in the middle of that chaos? I really wondered. Didn't you? What's with that?

He's always gone his own way and shooting the scene with Jerry overwhelmed and consumed by the Mega Whisk was something I didn't even think of, and I always shoot stuff. Jimmy used the system. We saw a guy sucked in by a mechanized environmental sanitizer and now zillions are seeing it roll by on Matt's Wabbit feed – while we're left standing near the Orpheum with what's in our heads. Shooting something out into the sphere produces nothing, makes nothing – it only inspires more shooting around the sphere. What was, is not here; its image is everywhere else. We're left on this grungy street with the afterlife of what went down. That's okay. I can say that. Yes, I can remember.

I can tell you one thing, the corps and the P are going to be on us so fast for that vid! They will attribute motive, and I don't even know the motive, other than the motive to get the message out. Oh, they will not be happy. But isn't that what we've been taught to do? Live on the screens? Play there? Everything?

I can imagine the Jerry crawls:

WHISK SUCKS FLAILING GEEZER! WOOPS!

SHOCKING! WHISK BOMB!

WHISKED AWAY!!

CAUGHT BY A WHISKER!

The corps or somebody's on our case already, and now an embed of a thrashing geezer removed by a bot with a Cadaver Lock on max? By a wandering clerk and a rogue handyman? We are so in trouble, we are so unauthorized. Plus Jimmy back-doored Zoneratti with the Wabbit gambit. We will have to address this sometime real soon, I'm sure. We will be proscribed. We will be peegeed right out of here. Peegeed forever.

Okay, maybe you never heard of Jerry the MC. But you know what? That doesn't matter to me because now you know right from me. I saw him, I saw him clearer than Matt at Wheezy's Skittle Café, that time with Deb and Jimmy, and Matt was with the Mystery Blond in the Madame Bleus?

You know, Matt was there, but only because he had to be there to be seen on the screens. Right? He was there for the screens, for the vids, for the revs, for the Madam Bleus placement. He did everything the Matt way that we all know about and he didn't care about anything around him or anybody else.

Jerry? Jerry was there because he had to be there too. But he didn't want to be seen, he just wanted to tell his story, cadge a plug and a couple of micros – like the Echoes. Jerry and the Echoes and those whispering specters in the Orpheum are what aren't seen. They aren't heard, either, not in the authorized frequencies. The sphere hears and sees only what it wants to hear and see, and only what is authorized and approved and broadcast clear as a glass of Veet. Everything else is removed or erased.

Yes, I'm sorry, so, so sorry. We just didn't know what to do. We are near helpless, it seems.

I'm gonna open up the inside a little more and lay it out for you. What have I got to worry about now, you know? So if I confess one more thing, it doesn't really matter a whole lot, and I want to tell you. I want you to know what I was thinking, okay?

There I was, listening to Jerry, and, okay, I was making mental notes about his style, about his tee and fleece and crappy boot. I admit it.

Forgive me.

Jimmy was shooting the vid, which I didn't, and I was looking at Jerry and thinking this could be a Hip post. This could be a cautionary tale. What happens when you let everything go. This is why the streets are messed up. 16 Ways Not to Look. I was composing it for BHB (that's Britt's Hip Bitts for those of you with short-term issues). The guilt is heavy on me and I'm even starting to feel a little ashamed. I was so wrong.

Jerry didn't let anything go, you see. Not that he had a lot of options. He followed the script. He stayed on the tracks. He was the Cancer Dude for gads sake. He was everywhere. And the same thing happened to him that happens to just about everybody, and is still happening.

The brand fuzzed.

They turned on him. They walked away. Usually they don't even bother with a reason. They just call you a dumb fuck, a suede punk, a twit, and check out. Did any of that stop Jerry? Heck no! He rebooted, so to speak. He made his way outside. And it wasn't easy, but when is it easy?

From the whole array of choices, that was the choice left for him, the only plug left on the tray. They always leave at least one plug.

Now I'm thinking that Jerry was made for us in heaven. He was there for all of us, me and Jimmy, and you too. We could've taken Jerry the MC and made a great return. If only we'd snookered that Mega Whisk over a crevice or into a ditch, spinning rollers and all. Or if only we'd dumped a bucket of glop on it. If. If. If.

We could've taken Jerry in and worked him up and decked him out. Duds! We could've carved out a whole new niche: Up from the Street! To the Street and Back! Jerry reloaded and rebranded as the Peg-Legged

178

Voice of Wisdom, the Truth-Telling Dude; the guy who went to the apex and fell to the nadir and rose again. He could give some heft to the sphere, tie it back to bricks and stones and streets and stuff. He made it out of the cave alive and has come back to tell us all.

He could broadcast something to believe in outside of Mrs. Petri and the P and the screens. Something beyond today. He maybe could be the guy who put butts on the seats of those bikes in my basement, or what used to be my basement. One man's true tale. He could bring people back into the world. He could give us a place to be. Jerry the MC could remake the world! That would be the goal. Save us! Why the heck not?

Jerry's dead. Long live Jerry!

Looking around here, that's a goal that would have been tough to achieve, okay, I understand that. More than tough. This is a dead place. No, it's beyond dead. It gives me the creeps, for sure – all the empty spaces, the boarded windows, the fallen stones, the grey weeds, the ash, the dust, the ooze coming up from cracks in the cement. What is that ooze? And the voices from down below. A tough sell. The street.

We need Jerry! We need an army of Jerry's!

Listen, I had rooms in a building. It was on a street and it was in the Hood in the Ville. What did I know about the street? Do you know what I'm saying? It didn't exist for me, not really. It was a hostile space you moved through. There were a few people I needed to see, just for my personal life and information. Like Deb and Jimmy. But where did I really live, you know? I was studying Matt and Hip and enriching the niche, working on my self. The screens.

And my fans. Oh, my fans:

Britt says this is the only place to be!

We love you Britt!

Britt if I get the red bird one, is that just as good as the lavender?

Britt I need to get my bf out of my place, he's eating everything and won't talk cause all he does is pant over the Mizz and I have had it! But I don't want to lose him! I know you are the one to help me do this! I need advice!

Britt I can't afford to drop any micros for those jeans with the cuffs? Code SS-47? Can you save one in small till next month? I am trying to sell my BL33???

Yes! Sell that BL33! I will save 4 u. Dump the bf! Who needs the bf?? Red's best! Go with red! Check out BHB for my latest! Luvya!

On the big days they fell on me like confetti. I was waving to everyone right from the back room without moving an inch. I was floating in my self. I was in the screen. That's where we all live: a flat, internal world, featureless, even with VR and holos and all the other bright stuff we have to mimic what isn't there.

So much is not there. Mrs. Petri, did you hear that? No real voices are there, no real voices from the likes of Deb. No real past like the True History of the Cancer Dude, who now floats back from the dead.

Oh Deb, where are you? Debbie! I have you on my pad. I have you in my mind. I want you close to me. When you're lost you're all alone. On the expressway to your heart. Where is the key to the highway? Deb. Deb. O Deb.

I'm beginning to understand.

I look at these buildings, or what's left of them, and think they used to be more than hulks looming over the crumbling street. They used to be more than obstacles and hiding places and things you had to hurry past to avoid collapses and serious personal injury. There used to be people inside and they spilled out and bumped into each other and talked. They liked that. They liked sitting in the sun and eating bread or whatever together.

That was way back, described in a lot of old Donny K's Hood-Loom posts, which are no longer available – Access Denied! Server Unavailable! Error 404 – and there's no going back, not now.

Nobody would probably want to anyway. Why go back to scrabbling on the street and getting scabs and tumors scraped off your nose and your neck? Coughing from the dust. Tramping through tunnels. Fighting the wind in the west. Why go there when you can be part of everyone and show everybody your true self on your own show and your own show is on all the time and you can remake your true self any way you want, like daily, if necessary? Who would relinquish that freedom?

That's why we need Jerry. Jerry and Deb, they live in themselves. They have stories and secrets and questions inside. They speak to what was, whatever it was; they could remember and imagine and shine. That could kill the screens. Kill this world we've woven so beautifully for ourselves, from the P and the corps all the way down to us lil numbers in the Hood.

How have we created something so contrary to what we are? And given it such power?

I see that Jimmy has not only blasted his vid around the world, but he has his pad out to check

181

locations. That's pretty iffy. For one thing, the locater doesn't work very well, it throws out false information. It tells you what's there isn't there or what isn't is or it points you away from whatever it is you're looking for, depending.

Like with the extraction problem? Stuff that was there not too long ago – like maybe yesterday – isn't there anymore. They don't really want you to know that what's been there isn't there. And they don't want you going anywhere at all, as you know. I know what I'm talking about here.

Once I heard Brute describing about being on the street, the walk all crumbly and the street riven with broken ravines and fissures, and he wants to go to the old Memorial Hall, the one in the park? He uses the locator and it just doesn't load. So Brute says he navigates by smell.

Huh? I say.

And he says, You sniff the wind and follow your instincts.

Okay, I say, thinking Brute really needs to lay off the reds for awhile. Then he says he gets there, or what he thought was there and there's just a pile of stone and weeds and a hole big enough to drive a SmithVerber EcoTruck into. You could disappear in those holes. There's no place there anymore.

You get out into those western zones – like beyond where we did the President's Girl shoot? – and locations are constantly confused. You lose any idea of where you are and the locator maps are worthless or they lead you there and then let you go, like you're a kid abandoned. Plenty of witches and dwarves around, but where are the breadcrumbs laid down to find the way out?

So Jimmy, I ask, what's with the pad and the locator?

It doesn't show the pits, he says, but I know there's that intersection of Jefferson and Washington pretty near them, so if I can find that, I can find the pits. But the sats seem to be down or something, because all I'm getting is a search signal. Can't even find myself.

There we are, standing in the middle of this street, blank buildings all around, north looks just like south, and we can't even find ourselves with a sat locator. Here and lost, lost, lost.

I walk back over to the Orpheum foyer and look at the sealed entrance. There is a shower of ash, a thin silt drifting down. Must be more fires in the canyons outside the Ville, although they keep saying the fires are out for the season. Seems to me the seasons are getting longer and longer as it gets hotter and hotter and the ash flurries down all the time, or close to it.

They must be loading it all with noncoms. That's really how they see everything and hear everything. They burn stuff up to keep track of what's left.

The sealed doorway for the Orpheum has not even the slightest crack. There is no break in that grey, dirty polyslab anywhere. No murmurs from within.

I bang. I hit the door with my fist. I kick it. I butt it with my head.

Please, I say, we are so lost. Can you help us?

There is no help.

Can you tell us the right way to the pits?

There is no response.

Are the pits to the south? Or the north? And what's the difference because, you know, one damn boarded up building looks like the next one.

No response.

Okay. Thanks. Thank you very much.

I remember Mrs. Petri drilling and drilling about our inner resources and the team working together and now I feel completely locked out and bad alone on the street. Me and Jimmy are standing around and he's pecking at his pad and punching in numbers or something and I am cold and the ash is sifting down and Jerry has been sucked away and there is nothing but silence and vague light. I want to be in! I want to be inside the Orpheum, behind the seal, away from this broken street.

Please. Please.

Nothing.

There is another boom from the direction of the Zone. What the heck is that?

Wait! At least we can use it to feel out direction. We can head away from it. When the sats are down, rely on your inner resources.

There've been no more murmurs or whispers and no more wild screams from off somewhere else. The street, in the hazy light, leads away from the Orpheum, the direction the bots took, and that seems right to me. South, according to the Echoes. It's time to continue south. But Jimmy is just standing there looking at his pad.

When I first met him, when he fanned me, I remember reading his message (see I do remember stuff). Something like, You are on to it Britt. You have identified exactly my feelings about things now. There is definitely something wrong and you have described it so perfectly! Polymethyl is everywhere – it's in the sky and on the ground and in our cranial substrata. It doesn't matter – the buildings are still falling and geezers are still on the walks. Hey, I've got some ideas about how to sweeten your site. One of the things I do. We should hang. Jimmy.

Oh, I wasn't so sure about that. Who was this guy? Was Jimmy even a guy? All I'd done is say people seem like polymethyl droids. It was a kind of joke. I gave him a shot, though – you get a feel after awhile on the screens, you get a feel for legit.

Sure, I say, I'm pretty new at laying myself out, so I guess maybe we could work up some ideas. You know, Hip's how you think and how you see.

And he says, Everything's about how you think and see. And we're all seeing what's going on out there out to the west and in the Dry Restricted Area, at least we see it if we look on the right screens. Nobody talks about that. Think about it.

It's true. Collapses were accelerating right then and the P was just like, Whatever.

Like it doesn't matter? He seemed to be spending all his time at the White-House-By-the-Sea, with all those babes from the Zone and he's shooting off one text after another about how he's consulting, and his producers are reporting on all his advisors and what they're saying:

Gryph11 argues light blots collapse answer
Steel shore ups neck sez Mizz Poltroon

Get umbrellas 1st counters T1
Sun no more ok per P
No need 4 tarp: D2
No agree
No
N

Remember? All those sub-50 character pops? That was brilliant. *So* Mr. P. Nobody had time to get tired of it and you could absorb it before anything crashed down on you. 50 characters, the short answer. What was the question?

So that was okay. But it took hours in that time of crisis before the P announced the Piles of Power for the Zone and the Ville.

We must draw the line and drive it home, the P says. One of his most famous appearances. Everybody shot it around.

He's out in the Zone, spots X-ing through the sky – you could see them from the Hood, if you lifted your blackouts – hands reaching for him. He let himself be touched and crowded and jostled!

(Jimmy says he recognized lots of people in the crowd – they're the P's entourage, like from Zoneratti. Or at least they look like it and that looks like the P, says Jimmy, but you can't be sure. You can't quite tell. Is that the P? I tell Jimmy that I'm sure it is because of the hair. And Jimmy says, Hair's easy, the merge of crowd and P and his expressions and their grasping, grasping hands – that's hard.)

Anyway, I remember that appearance really well with the President up on the loading dock behind Papa's, his ruffled hair, the slashing spots shredding the night. Plus, no ash, thanks to the Plax clouds. The P looks out over all those people. Rumors of extractions and collapses and disappearances had been swirling for minutes or hours. Doesn't matter to the P. He just seems so, well, persuasive.

We must draw the line and drive it home, he shouts to the crowd. They grow silent as an empty box.

What falls has fallen, and what has not fallen remains upright. Nutri, Excellon and all of their subsidiaries, and all of their personalities, and all of their affiliated entities and co-entities and producers and associates and online presences stand with me and with you. We are doers, not undoers; we are engineers of the soul, which you can't even see; we will continue to create a world complete with life and with possible life. We will build with the power of our messages. Message upon message, power upon power, self upon self. Build the piles! Drive the piles! Do not step away from this terrific challenge. It is on your screens and in your hearts. If you care about your times, if you care about your selves, care about how you're seen, about how you project, about, yes, the now and even the post-present for your President and for yourselves, and for our fans and for the corps, and for all the brands and all that they promise, we must join hands. We must pull together. We are blessed with the freedom to choose and the freedom to do so in a broad area. We must keep our eyes on the lookout for the shimmering dream. It is there, we all know it, and it is calling us to our better natures. Do not delay. Act now. Time is limited. Please visit www.presidentialthoughts.gov/holesintheground and learn more about what can be done in this exciting time.

There goes my pad again. I've been ignoring it — I sure don't want to see Morris or Jewell, even though I'm sure they're watching me now.

Hey guys! Glad to have you aboard! Which way to the P's Bargain Bin Oval Office Sell-a-thon? I shout it,

187

just for the hell of it. After shooting Jerry round the Ville and beyond, what else can I do? The buzz buzz buzz continues. So I look and sure enough, it's Morris.

Hey Jimmy, I shout, Morris's on the pad again. Should I open up?

Sure, says Jimmy. Ask him if we're headed in the right direction.

I open up and see that Morrie is not in my place.

At least you're not trespassing anymore, I say to him right off.

Britt, what is trespassing? There is no such thing in the Ville and certainly not in the Hood. You guys have some really outdated ideas. Look, that video you shot and uploaded? Not a good move. Not good at all. We stripped it out of Zoneratti, oh yes we did, mopped up instantly. No one heading into Zoneratti has the slightest idea about that poor geezer and his unfortunate accident. So don't worry.

Why would I worry? It's a video, I say. That's what we do, you know. We show ourselves and what is happening right now. We sell it.

Yes, I am well aware, says Morrie. That's what you should be doing, but something like your geezer shoot is not helpful. It doesn't do anybody's brand any good to let your self get hacked to bits like that. Now, in the interest of candor and truth, because I want you to remember that we are on the same side, I will tell you that the geezer vid was captured by pirate software and there are doctored versions already up on mirror sites out in the sphere. Those of course are unauthorized. So many problems!

We are putting together an answering vid that shows what really happened, all taken from your captured stream – the poor geezer, the evacuation team, the Ekto-Med Techs who worked so hard and so fast to scoop him up and chopper him to Ville Med Center next to Villo-O-Care. Really a valiant effort to get him out of there so fast.

Morrie is enthusiastic. I have no idea what he is talking about.

The eVac was really flawless, he goes on, but I don't know if he can be saved. Whether he is or not, the P has to be commended for the farsighted action he took with evacuation funding and procedures. I don't know why you would want to send out a phony vid to Zoneratti, Morrie says. Now he is pained, hurt, even.

It seems so unlike you, Britt, bogus, actually. Why didn't you use your eVac response team images? Of course there are accidents, particularly with geezers, but we work damn hard to make sure accidents don't turn into tragedies. So you really didn't have to patch something like that together.

What are you talking about? What eVac? What team? What bogus?

Morrie gives me a quizzical look. You mean you've really been hacked, he says. Dimmit! I knew something like this would happen. I told Jewell. Jewell, I said, they are leaving a trail a child could track, if only the little tyke had the inclination.

So he says, That's what makes the obvious so difficult to follow.

The ruckus they're making, I say, would attract outlaws of the deafest sort.

The deaf have eyes, he says, and the blind have ears.

Britt, you really need to come in and rethink this whole thing. Someone has plugged into your feeds. Someone is sending out provocations. One thing the P has difficulty with is deliberate disruptions of the system.

I am utterly at a loss about this, I say. We just saw a guy, a man, okay, an old man, sucked into a robotic cleaner. He's dead! And he wasn't any old geezer slumped in a pile, he was Jerry the MC. Jerry the MC who was on top of the game and had it all taken away by an unfortunate turn of events. But he was just out here and we were talking to him and then he was sucked away to gad knows where, inside a machine, a Nutri-contracted machine.

Jimmy is now zeroing in on this interaction.

Britt, he says, ask him which way to the pits. Speaking very quietly in my ear, he says, We have to get out of here, they are going to move in soon. Count on it.

Morrie says, What malarkey. We have a line on Deb, but I can't speak to you about it over this link. The Zone is frantic. People saw that hacked video and they are fleeing in the streets. They are scrambling out of Papa's and Antoine's and everywhere else. They want to know what the P plans. There's a rumor sweeping everywhere that Mega Whisks are sucking up everything that moves and that the P and the corps are just letting it all happen. Some are even saying the P and the corps are behind it!

That is the worst kind of paranoid rumor, he says. Britt, this is simply not true. No, no, no. Not true. Sentry has had to pour its resources into blocking messages and slingshots of your vid. Some, I'm told, already say Jerry the MC was an important guy and he was eradicated.

Oh? And he wasn't? I say.

Britt, we don't do this kind of thing. Morrie is plaintive now.

That is so old, he says. We work hard to get everyone pulling together in the same direction. We don't suck people up into vacuum cleaners on the streets. That's ridiculous. We are only interested in finding Deb and getting you guys back on track.

Now there are sonic flash bombs in the Zone, he says. Where they're coming from, I don't know. But we'll find them and we will muffle them. And Matt has scheduled an appearance at the Excellon Center for tomorrow night and the producers are scrambling to find out what that's all about. They're afraid he's gonna skip too. They say he's had it with being touched and being watched and being photographed taking a shit. Well that hasn't happened! Who wants to watch Matt D taking a shit? We're talking serious disruption. These rumors are worse than the extraction rumors, and the solutions are far more difficult. We're talking about cracks at the very heart of our system! We are proud of that system. The P is proud of what he's been able to accomplish over time. So come in and we can work together to find Deb, get you set up again, and move on. Life on the screens is life. You know that.

Ask him which way to the pits, Jimmy urges again.

Still looking for the pits, Mr. Jones, Morrie says. Your little Orpheum encounter isn't enough? You've got to be kidding. Not a chance I can tell you how to get to the pits, even if you continue south.

Britt, Morrie says, turning toward me, do not listen to your fan. Listen to your loved ones, Jewell, myself, and the P. We want you back.

Chapter Seven

Look at this, Britt, Jimmy says.

He's standing near the south façade of the
Orpheum holding his pad and staring at its glowing
screen. The light licks his face. Brown hair sags over his
forehead like withered grass. Jimmy is frozen in a field of
incandescence, a brilliant square so bright I can't see
anything except skin of red and blue and green
shimmering shadow. The light frays the darkness; it spills
over him in blotches. I have to blink hard. Beautiful
blotches.

What?

Just look.

I walk over and look.

Oh geez. There's a scene of people running!
BREAKING! the crawl says. DISRUPTION!

What's going on? I ask.

Jimmy kind of shrugs. I have no idea, he says.
How would I know? We're out of the loop, you could say.

The view is from a street feed high up over a
square. Where is that? There are a few grey buildings
here and there around a broad open space blocked in by
night. A yellow lamp buzzes above the scene.

Across the square a huge sign atop a building
pulses: Plug! Me! Up!

Above the blazing letters, a massive grinning
woman with bobbed blond hair looks on, chewing. Some
sign. No wonder people are stampeding, I think. And they

are, like really.

Dozens of people are running, aimlessly, it seems, galloping and trotting across the open space. One guy trips on a small pile of cracked stones and somebody else's foot and several more people bang up behind him, a flock of turkeys following each other into a wall. They all tumble, but I don't see any serious damage – no one hurt, no one concerned, everyone up quickly and loping out of the square and off the screen.

BREAKING! DISRUPTION!

This seems to be happening right now. I hear nothing around us. No shouts. We haven't heard screams for hours. There is an occasional boom coming from far off, Zoneward – those sonic flash bombs Morrie was talking about? But nothing here. I don't know how far northeast the Zone is now, and we are well out of the Hood. The Orpheum seems to sit in a blank sector at the fringe of the Ville, the area that's always a smudge on the sat maps. They must be able to pick up the streets here, those sats, but our locater is sporadic, always searching, searching, searching, network unavailable, like Jimmy said.

A single man comes running into view, looks all around the square and then heads back the way he came, panic springing from his emuish legs. I think I've seen him before. What show was it?

What was his show, Jimmy? I can't remember. Was it the one about the chicks and the bros and they pop all these reds and get into their own issues and hang in bed and do sex?

Jimmy says, Dunno. Yeah. Gotta be, right?

The scene of aimless runners begins again.

Okay, it's a loop. I get it.

They all pile up again. The giant billboard woman chews and grins away. She seems so content to chew and chew and chew some more. A slow, steady rhythm. The man again enters, looks around, skids and turns, holding onto his hat, a boater no less. I hadn't noticed that the first time. Cool. I could use one of those.

Now an announcer is seeking to explain the confused distress. I have to admit, I haven't seen anything like this really since the rash of collapses and the hot days of the Mobile Land Masses and the dunes. Back then, they wanted everyone to stay put and not frack around. Like right. There were loops of running crowds, wildebeests scampering everywhere. You saw that DISRUPTION crawl all the time.

The announcer says, as the loop begins yet again: Zone denizens have been struck with a kind of mass delusion, suddenly fearful of ordinary sanitation.

That is one authoritative-sounding VO, I think.

Probably a machine, do you think, Jimmy?

Could be, Jimmy says. They could be running Lucy, aka IntelliWord, through a reader scan, like Deb does. Most of these casts are on auto, I've heard, or sourced to software ops somewhere.

The announcer continues in full basso profundo:

The incident was sparked by an unauthorized mockumentary that appeared briefly in Zoneratti tonight. The bogus clip, placed as a prank, unexpectedly incited an all-too-familiar rumor surge, and denizens, fresh from dismantling their pointless fire shelters, are now fleeing nonexistent death machines supposedly raking the streets of the Zone. People, there are no death machines in the Zone.

What's this about fire shelters? I say to Jimmy. What's he talking about? I don't know that rumor.

Oh yeah, Jimmy replies, eyes still stuck on the screen, hands still caressing the pad. There was a huge rumor that Excellon's FireBack Safe-T kit was laced with an accelerant, not a retardant. You set up your kit and instead of blocking the fire and protecting, you're engulfed in flame. That was the rumor during the last fire season.

I got a lot of queries about that, he says. But I didn't take any jobs and I didn't make any posts. It seemed everything was stoking bad rumors, and I didn't want to pile on. I just stayed out of it. Stick with the good rumors.

I look back at the screen. Now we've got a woman inside a Sentry station. (Near that big square maybe?) VICTIM'S NEIGHBOR flashes at the bottom of the screen; it's replaced quickly by WITNESS TO TERROR. That changes to VICTIM WITNESS.

She says right into the cam:

Well, Marie just banged on my door and screamed at me something about street cleaners of death! I sure didn't think I heard that right, you know. I was watching Matt and chatting with another friend of mine, she lives down somewhere outside the Zone. But near, definitely near. On the other side? She was telling me about this girl who's become quite the star on a ballroom stream, Waltz Right In, where you're out on the floor and notes are piped in and there are waiters and multi-glow balls and tables for some kind of audience and everybody bets on who's got the best footwork and the best matching outfits – that kind of thing. Do you know it? We were talking and watching the waltz stream and watching Matt too. So I didn't think I heard Marie correctly, because this girl on the show was pulling way out in front with a half step she worked out to a metronome. Like I was distracted what with all I was doing. Then I have my own stream and I was up and running with that. Lots happening like always, if you know what I mean.

Marie's neighbor looks a little nervous as I watch, like she doesn't feel comfortable appearing on somebody else's show in somebody else's setup. She's wearing a sack floral print dress and holds a handkerchief, kind of balling it up in her hands. Oh my gad, what a mess she is! Jerry looked better.

Marie's neighbor continues her account:

I yelled to Marie, What? And she shouted, No time! No time! Get out!

What the heck? I think. All I have is time anymore, you know? But I thought about it and I kept hearing these thumps and bangs outside. It was messing up my audio too. So I decided, well, what do I know? So I pulled open the door and looked out and there were all these runners. They were just tearing away real fast. Down the corridor and then out the exit gate. So I ran too. I just left the room door open – I'm worried about that, you know, any outsider could walk right in, sit right down and take over my feed! I left my door open, like I said, and ran.

She stops and looks kinda thoughtful for a sec.

Now I wonder, she says, why did I leave my room to go running in the street to get away from killer street cleaners? Shouldn't it be the other way around? I guess it doesn't make any sense, you know. No accounting for what you do when you act on everybody's impulses. See they all panicked too. But what are you gonna do? You see everybody running like crazy? Maybe they know something. They probably'd heard a lot! You know what I mean? I hightailed it out of there, which isn't exactly easy at my age. Marie showed the way down the hall and out the gate and into the field. Now I'm worried about my door. Do you think I can get back to my room? Is it safe? Is it safe out here?

There you have it, folks, says an announcer, who now appears on screen, a bearded dude wearing a heavy flak jacket and a helmet. He seems to be in a

196

makeshift studio on a street somewhere.

We now have this in, he says, and reads something: The International Times/Zone Edition has contacted the President, who says that the inflammatory video was a misguided effort, a fantastic reworking of actual scenes recorded during a successful presidentially ordered life-saving rescue op in the Ville just hours ago. One lone bogus vid has now spawned powerful rumors – as you just heard from our reporter at the center of the disturbance – of street sweepers run amok.

This is a completely ersatz video, placed by unauthorized hackers, the P explains. There is no issue with sanitization or the smooth working of the mechanized cleaning system (MCS), in place and functioning flawlessly for many years. The President's Fragrant Streets program is a complete unmitigated success, according to the P's close aides and producers.

People should settle down – that's a direct quote from the P – and pull together. Check your rumors at the door. Rumors are just that, rumors. What matters is what is authorized by the P. You can find accurate and up to date information at www.presidentexplains.gov/ justthefacts/maam.

Disturbances? Ersatz?

The actual video, the announcer continues, referred to by the P and showing an accidentally injured denizen assisted by one of the P's Ekto-Med squads, can be seen at www.presidentexplains.gov/justthefacts/ savior. We will take you there now.

I am amazed by all of this. Does it have anything to do with us? I look at the screen. Jimmy holds it as still as a sacred stone.

The scene, already described by Morrie (as I related to you, a moment ago), unfolds now on the screen just the way Morrie portrayed it. There we are, me and Jimmy, near the Orpheum.

Oh my god Jimmy!

He says nothing, just stares.

There's the Mega stopped in the middle of the street, smaller bots arrayed around it in a semi-circle.

There is what looks to be Jerry the MC, stretched out near me by the wall.

There is a pounding thwacka! thwacka! and I hold my hands over my ears while half a dozen techies race into the frame carrying satchels and wheeling a gurney and an eVak-U-Rig with tubes and clips and I don't know what. They swarm over Jerry, completely blocking him from the cam view. Lots of indecipherable shouts, lots of visceral urgency. One guy looks up and signals to someone off screen. A split second later another tech runs into view holding a green canvas case. He passes it over. A few seconds later, they hoist Jerry onto the gurney and run him out of view.

A quick, blistering thwack! and a cloud of dust and ash swirls all over us. Jimmy looks up as though he is following something flying through the air. My hands fall to my sides and I say something I can't hear to Jimmy. The scene dissolves.

How can this be? I ask. What are they talking about? What are they showing? How can this be us? Is that us?

Jimmy says, Yes, that's us.

But that's not what you put out there.

No.

It's what Morrie described.

Yes.

It's not what happened.

I guess not.

So where did it come from?

I'm not sure. I have no idea. The P's people? The smooth-system guys?

Go to Zoneratti, I say. I look inside myself for the memory of Jerry the MC, devoured. I reach for that awful moment and try to hold on to it. It's inside me. It's mine.

Jimmy heads over to the Z-spot and we are in Matt's living space, looks like his dining area? Not sure. There are voices off-cam – Ridiculous! I hear someone growling – and then Matt shows up through the rear archway. He's followed by a Megette whirring away, sucking up all the household dust and grime and empty containers.

Ridiculous and completely unacceptable, Matt is saying to somebody. But his voice is almost inaudible.

What is riling Matt? I wonder as we watch. He's stomping around, trailed by his dust bot. Without warning Matt disappears and a curtain screen drops down – an ad completely blotting the scene. In exceptionally crisp white script it reads:

Corpus Remotionem! The only player at the end of the game!

A vid then unwinds showing a dark street with a Mega Whisk and a fleet of smaller bots heading through haze and shadows toward a couple of figures in front of a grey dilapidated building.

When you are looking for serious removal, an announcer intones – what gravitas! – consider the options. There are none. Corpus Remotionem Pro Whisk II. The final word.

Hey, I say, wait a minute.

I watch the Pro Whisk II, so called, move toward the figures. I recognize the Whisk with its tiara of orange circles. I recognize Jimmy. I see myself. We are hunched over a body keeled over near the building. We look up at the Whisk, look at each other, and then back away. I bow slightly and point to the body. The Whisk moves in silently before its suction mechanism whooshes! into action. What a whirr! Jimmy and I back away from the body as the Pro II moves in, Cadaver Lock on, and cleans it up. The body, which may have been a lumpy man or a large misshapen dog, simply vanishes into the machine. The Whisk ejects billows of StreetSweet.

Something big in the way? the announcer says, No problem for the Corpus Remotionem Pro Whisk II. Intelligent. Sensitive. Clean. And it leaves you smelling like a spring flower.

The Whisk moves on down the street and around the corner followed by the smaller bots, a mother and her chicks. Jimmy and I look at each other and smile.

What is this? Where did this one come from? This is the same darn thing, I say to Jimmy.

Yes it is, he says. That vid I shot out was like a mother lode. I blasted it out there thinking this is the real deal. I guess it was. Kind of like raw material for everyone else. Really something.

I hold Jerry tighter inside. I won't let go, Jerry!

Jimmy has not stopped looking at the pad. He holds it cupped in his hands like an offering.

The screen curtain has zapped away now, and Matt is pacing back and forth.

What the fuck is going on with this show? Matt demands. He looks at the screen, looks right at us. How can you even consider fucking body removal? What the fuck? I will not have that on my show, in my life, in my damn living room!

I flinch at the accusation.

Hey, you, I didn't do anything! I shout. What

are you talking about? I'm nowhere near you! Do you hear? We didn't dump anything on you! We just lost Jerry the MC!

He stomps wall to wall, hand to forehead. Mizz comes in from the front.

What's the matter? she asks. What's the problem?

The problem? The problem? Oh there's no problem, no problem at all, Matt says, turning toward her and working up a good one.

We have the fucking removal services all over our case, he says. Everybody but Zap! That's the problem.

This is Zoncratti! he says. This is the crème de la crème, you know. This is the top of the line. The most ultra. Do I want to take a piss brought to you by Pox Away? Oh I really want this. This is the fucking Zone! If those assholes in the Hood want to lie out on the street and get vacuumed by death machines, fine, let em, good riddance. But not on my show! Not here! They're like the rankest of dead meat, they attract flies everywhere, those Hoodlums. We are covered with them already. I have flies up my ass. They ride with me wherever I go. Their fucking pix. Their fucking vids. They scratch and scramble just to be around me and drain my micros and drink my fame and fortune and essence. Fuck them. I tell you, I am sick to death of it. This is my life, not anybody else's!

Settle down, she says. Worry somewhere else.

I think this does not look good. I think, whoa!

There is no somewhere else, Matt says. This is it.

He looks at the Mizz for a long time.

Where the fuck did you come from? he finally spits out with that thin curled-lip voice.

I built this baby up with my own angst, my own majesty, my own openness, my own issues. Me. Me. Me. That's what they all want. They want to see me, and then they want to ride me as far as they can. Where did you come from? They stuck you in for the demographics. You're just another epiphyte sitting on my root. This place was nothing when I came in. It was just another waste zone, but I worked with Nutri. I worked with Excellon. Got the P on board. I worked with all of them and we gave this dump a tone. It was from me. It's because everyone is interested in me. What I think. What I do. Where I go. Who I'm with. There was no place around here. Nothing. We built the whole bloody thing. It's my basic back lot, bigger than any of the mythical old-time back lots. This is about a whole human being – me. How I spend my time. Who I hang with. What I think, when I have a thought! This is all my studio. These are all my extras. It's a whole fucking world. It's bigger than the Ville. It's bigger than the western lands where the dust is so thick you can't even see a screen. And then they stuck you in it. You're an extra too. Now you act like some kind of cop or shrink or star or something. No. I will not have this on my show!

This doesn't seem right to me. The Zone has always been there, isn't that what you've heard? Mrs. Petri, my super-duper teacher who I thought knew everything, said the Zone is a shining place, way up high, sort of – a vision, a dream, the vessel for all our wants, which stick up, you know, out of the top, like sticks. Matt is rattling on. Oh he is agitated!

I will not have geezers and cadavers and removals and riots dropped into my friggin show, he says. The Mizz just lets him go on.

Unless I give the okay! he says, Period! I will not be brought to you by Corpus Remotionem!

Jimmy and I are speechless. We just watch. I think that Matt has just made his situation worse. One of my rules, when I'm on: never open your mouth without having some idea of what's going to come out.

Maybe Matt follows that rule too. Maybe he wants out.

I can't even imagine that – he has no clue what it means. He's never even heard of Jerry the MC, I'll bet. Matt could end up in a Corpus Remotionem vid himself. Could Matt make it on the street? What a joke that would be. He'd be meat for that Pro Whisk II faster than you could say dust buster. Faster than you could say Plug It! Then Matt's removal would become an ad supporting his own show from which he has just been Whisked Away. Cradle to grave.

The thing is, he's right. Zoneratti is a universe now. I don't know how it began or where it came from, not really, Mrs. Petri was vague on that point, but it is something vast, something that grows and absorbs and ejects and continues on. It's been here forever, don't you think? It is an everywhere. Zoneratti viventem in aeternum, as they used to say. It extends way beyond Matt.

For every one who visits, there's a different Zoneratti, like Jimmy said. Matt has a big space, sure. But you know what? There are spaces all over the place, some are filled, and some of them have been empty so long, that's what they are, empty places.

I mean, all they have to do is move the cams and Matt and his room vanish. Mizz is her own world. Mizz is Papa's and Antoine's too. Matt vanishes and you're left with a forlorn Mizz, there's a concept! What does she wear in her grief? Where does she go? How does she fill the holes in her life? There are so many holes. Do they spread? Lots of placement opportunities there. Grief isn't Hip, but why couldn't she change all that? She could begin a whole new trend! The New Look of Loss!

Shouts come from off-screen. I snap back and look around. Those shouts are coming from the darkness around us. There is a banging and a big boom. I shudder.

Mizz says nothing and leaves the room. The scene starts to jiggle in Jimmy's hands. The booms are from the pad speakers, I realize, not from down the block or around the corner from the Orpheum foyer. Matt follows Mizz off cam. More shouts. Then a looming quiet everywhere.

Go to the Community Room, I say to Jimmy. See who's shooting pool or chit-chatting. We need some insight. We need some info.

The CR is alive. There are voices jostling everywhere:

Sentry has laid down the Grid of Graphene and nobody can go from Antoine's to Papa's or anywhere, I hear. P-Luv101

they are watching Member32047

@P-Luv101 A grid? Why? There's nothing. P says there's nothing. Rumors. More friggin rumors. Matt just flipped out though. He sez he wants to level the Hood. People running scared. Artless in Gauze

@member32047 they r always watching. what's yr point? u got s/t 2 hide? if u got something 2 hide then u got some kinda worry. if not, not. P-Luv101

@P-Luv101 I got nothing 2 hide, but I got a mount of worry. How u know what 2 hide or not 2 hide or whether 2 hide? member32047

@Artless in Gauze: no Matt wants to wipe out EVERYTHING! He is insane. Im not Matts backlit. Im not his extra, his roadie, his techie, his groupie, his bruiser, his fan, his portapotty, nothing. P trying to put stop to it. I think Matts been drinking the water. Mizz iz on yellowjax or something. They are a copula a ass$ %#&s. Andy S.

@Andy S. They both drinking. Now i can't find a/b @ home. all rooms empty. looked @Papa's feed and n/b there either. Street feeds are down. @Antoines down. No moo. Not even the butler's home drinking the nite away. Whats w/ that street body anyhow, ya know? Artless in Gauza

Get those ad bots out of here. I can't believe that Reply spider got through the blocking gates. Mort_in_West_Ville

Matt wants to level Hood! XXOO4U

Matt wants to level Hood P says!! AnonAnon

Hood fucked – Matt AnonAnonAnon1

Matt will blitz hood MATTHONEYPIE

What? What? What? Street body? Matt? MattFanboy66

Matts got a killer machine in the room! 3LUV

@3LUV I saw that. He wants a killer machine, he wants lots of killer machines, the works. Level the rest of us, okay? That's the word. The word, dude. Yep. RicardoMonteyBond007

Look, I nudge Jimmy, there's a street feed embed right there on the screen. Kind of unusual to see real-time feeds in the CR chatterbox.

The feed shows two people, a boy and a girl, standing by a building, looking at a bright pad of light. The girl, wearing an old khaki shirt with ripped off patches, is so thin she almost disappears. She is pointing to the screen. The boy is hunched, hair hiding his face, his two hands wrapped around the light. It radiates through his fingers, a consecrated gift almost, something heavenly. They seem so tiny and immaterial and frail in the gloom.

Hey! We are right there in the middle of the Zoneratti CR, I say. How can that be?

I don't know, says Jimmy. They are on us, that's for sure. Impressive.

He closes the pad quickly.

Let's go south, Jimmy says. Like now. This is beyond us.

He has a kinda wild look that I've never seen before. It makes me uneasy for him.

Wait a minute, I say. I look around and then see the cam on the wall across from the Orpheum. Let's just move around this corner here.

We walk over, away from the street cam. I look up. Okay, it's gloomy, but there is obviously another cam stuck on a wrought iron balcony jutting from the second floor. I didn't think this fringy part of the Ville was so well covered on the streets, not with the sats operational, anyway.

Hey Jimmy, look at these street cams.

He looks up and says, Whoa! Those are old ones.

He reopens his pad, and sure enough there we

are – the second cam picked us up and is streaming us right into the Community Room, right into the middle of all that gabble that is, right now, being viewed by probably gazillions.

The comments begin to roll in:

Isnt that the hip chik? I thought she disappeared. Sherlock221

Who? and who's the dude with the weird hair? Is that Matt's bro? MGUY

@MGUY Matt dont have no bro, bro. He do bros. Chiks slik, I give u that. I think they about to get mopped up. Sherlock221

Hey Sher, u hear those booms? See anything? Loved your last show, btw. When you riffed on the P and dealt off those green thingacombobbers. Great stuff!! Outnabout_in_lalaland

Lovely with a publish! I worked out that a lot of intimate details. If I have to say, I will have it, not only for me, and leave the responsibility to respect, but you have more fans and please follow all of the time, you know. This is my new way of thinking is not only causing me, I'm looking forward to your future contributions will inform me about what to do, but I think a great success. Thank you! AnonA

Okay. But check these guys out. They are going down. Sher

Jimmy shuts the pad again. Nothing we can do about it, he says.

A lot of this stuff they're using out here, these old square cams, it's stuff I thought had gone to seed like everything else that could be invisiblized, I say. You can see an old street cam just the way it can see you.

Yeah, Jimmy says. They don't use them around like they used to, I guess.

That's what I'm saying, I tell him. They get away from stuff that looks like what it does. Sats, specs, cams, motes, mics, micros, plugs. You don't even know what stuff is anymore.

I'm thinking now, why should you? The only thing that matters is the image gathered in and funneled wherever. The image rides the air, it slips through walls and rocks and dirt, it travels without a sound. It's all around us here, but you can't see it, and then it's gone and you don't know where and then it's happening somewhere else. All invisible to us, though they bank the image forever. Are they banking Jerry?

Jimmy, you can't hold onto anything anymore, I say. But they can. They can hold anything you can't see. They can take anything and you don't know it's even gone. You don't know, you can't remember. But they do.

Jimmy doesn't say anything. He holds his pad. He's uncomfortable. Is it me? Is it Matt's flip out? I'll just ask him. He needs to open up a little, I think. Why not? I ask if he's upset about something.

I dunno, Jimmy says. This is new territory. Lots of unknowns, I guess. Lots of variables. Takes some getting used to.

I look around, up the street past the Orpheum. Down the other way. No wonder everybody uses blackouts at night, I think. Nobody wants to see what's outside and they sure don't want what's outside to see in. Everybody's invisible!

Except us, right here. I can see.

Jimmy's put the pad on a ledge and is leaning. I notice he has really old clods on – they even have zips! In his own way, Jimmy knows how to present.

When you get right down to it, I say, they let all these empty streets fall into themselves. Why do you think?

Maybe, says Jimmy, it just is; it's what's here now. Does it matter why?

All that's outside is gone, it's lost, I say. Nobody even sees it anymore or wants to. That's the amazing part. Everybody can move without moving, and you don't even really need to go anywhere. Why bother with outside upkeep?

I live off people not wanting their buildings to be houses or living spaces or just plain rooms, Jimmy says. It's just a given.

Yeah, I say, and?

They want them to be stages, he goes on. They want them to display the most spectacular lives! The dramas! The beauty! The comedy! Shit. They're still buildings; they hold stuff all the same, need to be fortified and hardened and propped up. They have to be weaponized. Why? That's what people want. That's what they've heard they need.

So, I say, you're a security guy when it gets right down to it? Ha ha! You build frilly penitentiaries, lock downs and lock ups? You turn roomers into wardens or warders?

No! Obviously not, Jimmy says.

I think I've offended him. I didn't mean to.

Why would you even say that? he says. I facilitate, that's all I do. People want it. I give people what they want, or what they believe they want. There's bad stuff out there on the street, too, believe it or not.

Are we bad stuff out there on the street? Jimmy's not into analytics. He's not a digger. Doesn't have to be. He knows the territory. But not this territory, where we are now, on the street headed into blank wilderness; we don't know shit.

I say, All I'm saying is nothing does what you think it does. Nothing is ever there, even when it's all around you. And I guess you don't do what you think you do.

Jimmy says, I know this: everybody wants things to stay the way things are – from the P and the corps to the flower-pot guys, and I guess that's what we've wanted too. The whole point is to show everything and say everything. That's the desire. Use desire to build desire, right? That's what the P wants, and what the P wants is what we want. We show everything; they sit back and watch. And what they don't watch, they just take – and we don't even know or care.

That's about it, I say.

How else can we live? It makes me want to cry. And I do. I just start sobbing.

That cam has stolen everything and left nothing. It's all nothing. Jimmy puts his arm around me and I shake a bit, but calm down. Deb! I need Deb. I need Jimmy.

What about the voices, I say. What about the whispers?

I don't know.

Why doesn't he know? Why doesn't he speculate even? Oh Jimmy! We need to range far and wide.

Maybe loops, I say. Or echoes, or notes, or what we think of as echoes. What you can't hear, like normally, when you're doing stuff. Ghosts?

Mealy's no echo, he says. She was a true believer in her show, Brute told me once. Can you believe that? She lived the life. She was up and running at all times. She wanted everyone to know everything. Hard to imagine, like she's so wasted.

Maybe something happened with her, I say. Now she's in touch with the voices? Maybe there's some connection between her and those sounds, or what seemed to be sounds.

Maybe, says Jimmy. You could ask her, if we run into her somewhere, which seems unlikely.

I've calmed down a bit. I'm sorry I lost it there. Maybe those voices are recordings of the way we were – loops, endless loops. They claimed to be recordings, didn't they? Seems kind of unknowable, you know? Now I just feel dead myself. I mean, I was in my room. I was in my bed and I just felt things were a little off. Hits were down. Deb wasn't posting. Ideas were all fracked up. Just stuff seemed off. Now I'm in some kind of wild place talking about ghosts and echoes and invisible stuff and the P's guys are on my case and probably the corps too and Jimmy has his arm around me like I'm some kind of geezer myself and I'm crying.

I need to be held. I need to be touched.

We should get going, Jimmy says. We can pull them up on the pad and talk, but we don't want them on us, I think. And they're going to be, I just feel it. We are some kind of threat – they've just decided that, regardless. Some kind of threat.

What difference does it make? I say. Hold me tighter. You never hold me. All this time. Hold me. What difference does it make now if they come down here, swoop in, screech to a stop, surround us, whatever. What are they going to find? A couple of ghosts on an empty street. We don't even know where we are.

They know, he says.

We can ask! he says, brightening.

What the heck are you saying? I am genuinely startled. Why would we do that?

Look, he says, they know where we are better

than we do.

I don't like this idea, I say. Too many unknowables. I think we need something else. We have nothing.

I am at a loss, but then it hits me.

Vids! I say. Vids! We have to use what we know!

Jimmy looks at me, a cloud of disbelief crossing his face.

We can tell them we're going to shoot this entire journey, I say. That should make them stop and think.

He shakes his head – no, no, no – which kinda reminds me of Mrs. Petri when we didn't quite answer correctly and together.

Are you kidding me? he says. They will laugh. Look what they did with that vid I made of Jerry the MC. It was like raw material for them. They took it and molded it, added and subtracted, made it into pr and ad copy. Post a video of a guy sucked to his death by a district cleaner and they turn it into an ad for more district cleaners and for the P's program for a cleaner Ville and geezer rescue. They do that with everything. Everything is imageable; image is everything.

Jimmy says, The difference between fact and the world is in the telling.

Geez, I think. I am so out of my depth. I just want to find Deb.

Chapter Eight

We've been walking for a little while, away from the Orpheum, down what I think is Adams Street – dams Street is what the signs actually say, but I don't think that's right because they're all rotted and washed out the same way. Crappy old stencils for the caps, I guess, which makes it a lot harder to find your way around. Maybe it's deliberate? Like the malfunctioning locator sat maps? Am I on ton or Eton, roadway or Broadway, here or There?

My pad is buzzing, of course, but I haven't laid any demands on Morrie. I know this is him again. Why bother? What would I say? What's he going to say? He's just going to wheedle and coddle and bill and coo and try to bring me in. When you're off the tracks they try to lever you back on, like Jimmy said. Maybe Morrie's right, though – maybe we should let them reel us in. Maybe we should just bite at their worms, go limp and let them drag us through this muck back to shore. But I can't deal with it right now, not when Deb seems so far away she's vanishing too and we've come so far ourselves and there's a whole ocean of rot out there and we're nosing into the middle of it.

To heck with Morrie. We walk.

I've noticed that the buildings are beginning to change in this sector.

They were all neatly boarded up closer to the Orpheum, kind of tidy in a disheveled way. So many abandoned and crumbling walls. But the mounding flakes of paint, the crusty globs of stucco, the tumbles of brick, the shards, the splinters and timbers, the garbage and waste seemed sort of neatened up. All'd been swept and sealed and bound. But here, as we move further from the Zone, further from the Hood, down this grey road on the far outskirts of the Ville, even the boards and seals are falling apart, opening hungry mouths in the facades. Come here my pretties, they say. There's something you ought to see. It won't take but a moment. Come inside.

There is no inside there.

Backs of buildings have fallen in on themselves. Empty lots and rear yards are filled with debris. Plastic bags, shredded, flutter from spiky bare branches and from razor pikes atop walls. Lots of dead trees angle up from rooftops and out from masonry – forests around and above us. Beyond the lattice of dead branches, bleached remnants of old signs haunt the walls.

The grim light sifts down from the clouds. There are no street lamps. Everything seems darker the further we go. I don't think I could back track now. This is a shrouded place called deeper.

Still that feeble light is enough to make out faded letters and images high on building sides. They're telling us to stop a moment, listen, let's speak. Everything seeks to engage us here, out in the midst of nothing – nothing speaks.

Jimmy. I nudge him. He's holding his closed pad.

Take a look at these walls, I say. They've got old messages on them. Like there.

I point toward the top of a low, powdering brick façade.

See, I tell him, those are eyes there, like pearls over the brick. You can trace their outline and they have a luster. It's a face, rotting away. There's a whisper of

smiling lips, a shadow of nose – see? – a hand holding
something, a can? I can just make out some words
underneath:

something ... something ... JAX FOAMING
LEAN RIG DOWN THE RAIN

Yeah, I see. Over there too, he says, nodding
toward the other side. I look across the street. The arc of
an elongated, tubelike machine on wheels is vaguely
outlined on the wall, orange paint scabbing and bubbling
off. It looks like a decrepit missile, something you might
wheel into battle. I make out a few words:

I WISH I ... something ... A ... something ... CAR
... something ...WI NE

What the heck? Underneath it reads:

YELL ... something.

Some kind of old car, Jimmy says.

I puzzle over it. It seems like we should be able
to decipher these messages and figure out the images. It
seems like they may have something to say about how
people lived, and maybe how we might be able to live
again, out in the world. This orange missile on wheels,
which looks to be cradled on a thin, yellow cushion, must
be a sign for cars, or a warning about cars, or perhaps
they made cars in this building, back in the day. Nobody
makes anything there now, that's for sure. You can see –
it's just a wall; the rest of the building has come down into
a backyard mole hill. There aren't even moles anymore.

Hey, there's another one, I point.
A huge graphic of a building capped by a white
tower or crown covers an enormous tottering red-brick
wall across the street. You can see real bricks right
through the drawing of brick, and it's pretty clear to me
that what was once there had been rendered in

215

meticulous detail. A brick building painted on a brick building. Why would anyone do that? Across the top there's some kind of lettering:

MO   HIS   MILE

And underneath that:

AM   TARTS HER

What's with that? Sex? What's a building on a building got to do with sex? Maybe an erotopark run by Mo? Who's Mo? Did they have sex parks back in the day?

There's another one, I point up to a ragged pile:

EAT and HOME OF THE GIANT

And look, there's a whole string of them over there:

OOL THE MIRACLE OO BEST BY ... something ... ICE. WOO. WOO. WOO.

Sounds religious, I say. There could have been cults here. Or is it more sex stuff? Signs for sex cults? No, or maybe. Drool? Wool? Cool and magical water?

I dunno, Jimmy says.

These are strange and beautiful, I think. Like they're speaking to us, but we don't know the language. It's a code. Maybe we could crack it, open up that lost world.

They are affecting me and I feel like standing in this nowhere for a moment listening to the incomprehensible past.

EE   LIGHT   EE   LOVE   EE   SOTO

A sex and religious cult district? I don't know anything about religion, except that it had something to do with weird rumors that a bunch of people pushed on other people who pushed back with their own rumors. Kind of like now, except our rumors are true, I guess, because they're now.

Looking at these walls, I want to consider the enigma. I want to let the mystery enfold me. This is a place that has something to say. We just can't quite hear it or grasp it or understand it. But it is speaking to us. It is flagging us down. We know nothing. Speak nothing.

Jimmy is quiet. He holds my hand and I like that, you know. I like that he's holding my hand, and he squeezes it. Okay, he has his pad in the other hand, but my hand is more important, I think. It's solid and warm.

The unspoken spreads between us and around us. We are out in the far territories headed toward the edge of the flat world. What else do we have? We share our loss of Deb. We share our loss of house, of site, of certainty and predictable uncertainty. We have the edge. Hold my hand Jimmy! Hold on tight!

He turns and looks at me, face to face, right into my eyes. What does he see there?

Britt, he says. And he brushes my hair away from my face and slowly leans forward and gives me a small kiss. We are in the middle of the walk, in the emptiness, and he gives me a quick kiss. I close my eyes. I savor that first slight, brief touch. He turns away, looking surprised, and we begin to move down the street again, tracking the decay and its vanishing markers.

Oh! A pack of rats scampers across the street, the first ones we've seen for quite awhile. They stop in the middle and all crowd around something – a cabal, nosing and eating, and passing secrets. By the time we're at the spot, there's nothing there, just more blank. There's a slight curve in the road ahead and when we reach it, I see a faint light spilling out on the walk maybe a hundred meters further down. It creates a yellowy grey stain. Looks like a store front?

No way.

Jimmy, that's a friggin storefront. It's like an actual store! Can you believe it?

I don't think so, says Jimmy, as we stop and look ahead.

What would a store be doing here? And even if it was, what's it doing open in the middle of the night? There's nothing here. There's even more nothing than a while ago.

Do you think we should check it out? I ask, dubious.

I don't think so, he says, shaking his head. It could be dangerous or weird or something we can't even figure out.

He looks around. Maybe we can find a shortcut to the pits, he says. Or a shortcut back.

Back? I'm not even going to consider that. No back.

Just in case, he says quickly. If we need to know.

Something about that light up there gives me the creeps, I say. My skin is all prickly. Probably a lot could go bad in there. I don't know.

I turn it over for a minute. What could be more bad, really, than where we are now? It's just a store, like Greta's. Maybe we could get some directions. Maybe they sell food or drinks or something. I could use that. Maybe it's nothing. It's pretty quiet.

I say, Okay, let's check it out, but be careful, be ready to get out.

Jimmy is definitely reluctant. He clutches his pad. But I tug on his arm and he starts walking, slowly, with me. He's looking everywhere.

Hey, did you notice? I say.

What, Jimmy says.

No old street cams. I haven't seen any at all for a while. I've looked on the poles and on the buildings, checked the corners and the ledges, even the trees. Nothing.

Yeah, says Jimmy, I noticed that too, aways back. This area must be covered by sats or maybe pinholes. It has to be. The locater is still down, though, and I can't see where we are.

He doesn't open his pad to check again as we walk warily down the street toward the little island of light, but he holds it ready in his hand. I think of asking him to check Zoneratti – are we still on? What's happening in the world? But this is too tense and out there for that. I don't care at the moment. This is the world right here. I'll ask later.

It is definitely a store!

As we approach, I see this is a block of what used to be all stores, the building fronts have rotten boards covering what must have been display windows – windows that showed stuff to people who passed by, displays that sought to entice. Imagine that. It's hard, I know, to imagine people walking down a street and seeing something in a store window so appetizing, so intriguing, so full of touch me, hold me, smell me, squeeze me, try me that it draws them in just like that! But they did.

You'd go in, full of imagination, full of what you would do if only, and try it on. Someone would be there to help and to comment on how well you look today, miss, and that skirt is just the thing! If you like it, you can have it tailored at no extra cost! We have seamstresses waiting just for that! And I do say, miss, if I can be so bold, navy is a wonderful color on you. It matches your hair and your nails at the same time and also highlights the blue sparkles on your lips and nose perfectly. If it suits, we can wrap it up right now and tie it with some string.

You could buy it, simply buy it, and then walk out with it tucked under your arm, or even wear it. Just like that! That's the kind of thing I learned with Hip. In the olden days, according to Donny K, mind you, there was stuff you could buy and choices you could make up and down the streets, every step of the way. Do I want this or that? Red or blue? Sweet or not so sweet? Something to wear? Something to eat? You could actually hold stuff, feel it, smell it. And people were in the stores, they worked there, and they would try and help you or direct you one way or another. They'd talk to you! You'd think about what you actually wanted. Then they'd try and transform what they had to fit into your imagination of yourself. Seems backwards.

No wonder these buildings are empty now. Who would want to do all that? Who would come here? Even though it's not so different now, really – you just don't have to go any place outside and no one cares what you want, they tell you what you want right out, push it right into your inbox. Which is okay, because you don't have to think about it at all. Or try and explain anything to anyone. What do I want? Yes, I want that. And that. Or maybe that. Oh heck, I'll take it all. And since Nutri and Excellon are everything, they know what you want before you even know you want it. Voilá! Relationship management.

But here. These streets, this life meant something! Oh so many buildings. There must have been a lot of people or something. So real. I mention this to Jimmy.

I don't know, he says, tense.

There's more buzzing on my pad, but I ignore it. We are nearing the pool of light and I see that it really is a storefront with two great panes of glass flanking the recessed entrance. We are walking more and more slowly as we get closer and closer, and I can see jumbles of stuff piled up in the windows.

There is a poster of a woman on a street taped to the inside of the glass in one of the windows. She's wearing a dress, white as a sun-bleached clam, that billows up around her from a wheeze of air coming through a grate set in the walk. The dress forms a nimbus floating up, even as she bends to hold it down. It has gossamer wings sweeping out and she is poised to take off into the surrounding night. What a dress! Curls of golden hair wreath her face. Inviting, open lips almost form a smile – almost, but not quite. One hand touches an ear. She hears something that we can't hear. She's looking out at something we can't fathom. Oh, I think, she wants that image of herself, but she doesn't. She wants to feel the warm blast of air pouting her dress, but she doesn't. There's something else she senses. She's caught between two worlds – dress up, dress down. On camera, off camera. Airborne, earthborn.

Jimmy, look at that picture.

She is beautiful, he says. That's really an old image. It looks vaguely familiar.

He looks some more. I don't know, he says finally. They used to make lots of posters like that. I've seen a lot of them here and there.

Keep your hands right where they are, a voice says.

I am not startled, but I can't figure out where the voice is coming from. It is somewhere in the windows, which hold bulging cardboard boxes, stacked in teetering towers. There are clothes and what look like rags thrown over some of the boxes. In one corner are long sticks with little rings in them and crank handles holding spools of thread. There's a collapsed pile of what I am sure is petrified plug; lots of little boxes – wooden? – are stacked haphazardly next to it. Some kind of netting covers the boxes. A number of iron pots are strewn next to a manikin with nothing on, just a bare and featureless torso impaled on a black metal rod. A smooth head sits next to it, staring at us with no eyes.

Do not move yet, the voice says again. It is definitely coming from the windows. All I can think of now is, oh no, not again. Please, not another Jerry, not another geezer in distress.

Okay move very slowly toward the center of the window. I want to get a clear look at you.

We walk a few steps and he comes into view, sitting on a chair in the recessed entrance, a stick over his lap.

Hold it, he says, hefting the stick, which I see now is some kind of old weapon, a long rifle or something.

We aren't a threat or anything, Jimmy says. I can tell he's nervous and watching the stick very carefully.

We were just walking down the street, Jimmy continues after a sec, coming down from up toward the Orpheum, and saw the light from your windows. That was a surprise. We thought maybe you were an open store.

Sure you did, says the man.

He is small and pluggish, an old hydrant, I see, with a square head, and his face bristles with grey whiskers, some patches wilder than others. A great lump bulges from his cheek and his neck is sprinkled with flaring maroon pimples. An ashen wart snakes from the side of his nose. Oh man. He spits into a bucket next to the chair. And the street rings with pi-tang!

Sure you did, he says again, looking back at us carefully. And I'm sitting here waiting for the start of my annual white sale. Ha ha ha. Fifty percent off selected items. Ha ha ha. Start with the fossilized shit. Ha ha ha! You can have it for next to nothing, young fell.

I look at the store windows again. There is an old wicker basket filled with rusty nails. A box holds loops of electrical wire tangled like distended worms. I can see them coiling and uncoiling. Some kind of red war flag hangs on a hook. Over the man's shoulder, the store recedes into murk.

Now maybe I am a store, he says. And if I am a store maybe I'm open. And if I'm open maybe I could sell you something. And maybe you might want to buy. That's a lot of maybes, you understand.

He looks from me to Jimmy and back again.

Move closer together in the light, he says, where I can see you better.

Wait a minute, Jimmy says. We're not doing anything to you. If you're a store, fine. If you have any food or something to drink, that would be great. We'd definitely be interested. But you can't tell us to do this and that. We're just walking down the road here. If you don't have what we're looking for, we'll be on our way.

Jimmy starts to turn and walk away, and so do I, when the man says, Hold on there, pardner. No need to get all riled up. No need to get huffy. You sit out here on the front lines night after night, week after week, year in and year out, you learn to be a little cautious. A lot of bull gets peddled on the street. A lot of bull.

He leans the stick up against the door jam and pushes his thick mass up out of the chair.

Welcome to Mr. Briggs's Elemental General Store and Topiary Survival Shop, he says.

I'm Briggs, at your service.

Hi, I say. Jimmy doesn't say anything.

Yes, says Briggs, you learn to be mighty cautious, mighty cautious.

He's wearing old blue overalls, the kind with the shoulder straps? And, this may be hard to believe, hobnail boots. You don't see those very often these days. Probably worth a fortune at the Hip mart.

The other night, Briggs says, thick stumpy arms folded, I'm sitting here, tending to business, and three fellows come down the street carrying a box. Not just any box, mind you, but one, if you pardon me, miss, you could use to bury a man in. They were huffing and puffin away, right up to my place. Soon as I saw em I knew this was trouble. You learn to smell it. This one was pretty easy, thinking back.

They say, Hey pop! We're lookin for some bananas.

Are you kidding me? I say. Bananas? This is the Ville bud. No bananas. No oranges. Get a grip. You want a nail? I got nails. You want screws, I got them too. I got a big picture of a banana. You want that? It's up on the top

224

floor; it'll take awhile to dig it out. A popular item back in the day. That would be before you were around looking for bananas in a land with no bananas.

The lead guy, thin guy with a thin mustache and thin hair, says, Hey don't bother yourself.

I say, No bother at all. That's what I'm here for. Picture's better than nothin.

He says, No. We don't want a picture. We need like actual bananas.

I ask him, I say, What you need bananas for pardner? Why would you even think of bananas? Are you from around here? Or did you just ride in from Planet X? Ha ha ha.

He says, You got a hammer?

I say, Sure. Right here.

I always have a hammer near the door – you never know what might need banging, Briggs says.

So I show it to him, Briggs goes on with the story. He takes the hammer and goes over to the box and starts to pry the top off with the claw. There's a stink coming from that box and I'm getting just a little uneasy.

Wait a minute bud, I say to the guy.

Just a sec, he says, won't be more than a sec. You got a crowbar? That would speed things up a bit.

I make sure my gun is right there and I say, Hold it. I don't want no dead bodies dumped at my door. You get my drift? Don't want em. I sell stuff. I may take defoliation contracts, okay. Bodies I don't do, I say.

Hold on pop, the guy says. Forget the crowbar, I'm almost done.

He yanks out the final nail, starts to pry the top off. Now I'm getting real nervous. What the? Then the top pops – bang! – and jabbering monkeys come tumbling out! I never seen a monkey before. They start tearing into the store, like real fast, screeching like you never heard!

Monkeys? Jimmy says, a puzzled look on his face.

That's what I said, says Briggs. Monkeys. Yapping and hopping into the store and down the street. You see just about everything out here, he continues. You see stops and collapses, pickups and sweeps. You name it. Once I swear I seen the devil all decked out in a blue dress blowing a saxophone. But I never seen monkeys before.

No way, I say.

Briggs continues, savoring the story.

I say to the guy, I've never seen a live monkey in my life.

These are out of control. What a racket they make! Can't hear myself. One crashes right into my crock-pot display. I've got dozens of crock-pots, more than any store in the Ville, probably more than any store in the world. And I need monkeys knocking em all the hell and back?

Get those monkeys out of my store! I tell him. What are they doing?

Well now, that's the thing, says Briggs. These guys are clever. Those weren't live monkeys either. They're remotes, old ones too. Pretty damn clever. All covered with hair. One of em has a drum around his waist and bangs away at it. Another one wears a frock. I had to laugh at that. It took a second for me to realize they're toys, cause my first thought is that monkeys eat bananas and that's why these guys want bananas. You understand?

I think so, says Jimmy, looking perplexed.

But they're toys, which is even richer, says Briggs. They careened down the aisles like I said and knocked into more cases and boxes. They screeched! They were a whole jungle chorus. I'm watching and chuckling, but kinda angry, too, particularly after they crack into my crock-pots. I turn around to tell the guy he really put one over, when I see that he's gone. His friends is gone. Their box is gone. And most of my Freeter Crates and chipset sacks is missing! Plus my hammer. Can you beat that? Outfoxed by a bunch of fake monkeys and a guy with a pencil mustache and a coffin.

Can you beat that? I ask you now.

I don't think so, says Jimmy.

Didn't think so, says Briggs.

So, I say, peering into the store and back to Briggs, they took your crates of whatever. What about the monkeys? You got a whole box of monkeys in return. That's not so bad. There could be a run on remote monkeys. Then you'd be in fat city. Ha ha. That's a joke, I say. Jimmy laughs.

I understand, says Briggs. Yeah, I got a load of monkeys for sure. No bananas. Don't ask me for no bananas. You want a monkey?

Maybe, Jimmy says.

I didn't have any place to put em, Briggs says. And I don't have controls for em. So what do you do with a pack of gibbering jabbering monkeys run on remotes? I had to round em up, one at a time, and closet em. There were 12 – 12 monkeys. I put em in the back storeroom. Wanna take a look?

Sure, says Jimmy.

I don't know, I say. I'm wondering if you've got any Veet or packaged plugs. We could use something to eat and drink. We can pay, of course.

No problem, says Briggs. We got all that and more. Come on inside, take a look at my critters and I can pack you up victuals and drink.

Briggs turns around and we follow him into the store. It's filled, floor to ceiling, with stuff. There are boxes of light bulbs, marked used; boxes of plates, marked damaged; boxes of what look like table legs; boxes of wire springs; boxes of figurines, marked chipped. There are piles of cloth with intricate designs – flower traceries, geometric shapes, blue and gold and red piping. I linger and savor them. In one far corner is a table piled with mechanical parts, complicated iron objects fitted together with tubes and hoses, wheels strapped to other wheels, wheels with cogs fitted into other wheels with even more cogs. Black grease everywhere.

A glass case is labeled seeds, and that's what seems to be in it. Toward the ceiling, on shelves that run around the store are dead animals, stuffed, I guess. There are birds, large and small, some with curved beaks, others with long needlelike beaks that seem about to pierce their neighbors. There are animals covered with fur. Some look fierce, with yellow teeth poised the moment before a kill. Others are more benign. I recognize several rabbits. A kitten. There are no rats in here, at least not stuffed. The animals all stare out with hard black eyes.

Walls are covered with what seem to be vinyl placemats, pictures stamped on them – a guy in a broad-brimmed hat and a checkered kerchief around his neck; a flat vista, like a desert, with a red sunset on the horizon;

heads of dogs and cats; a naked albino man with one huge hand hanging down and the other holding what looks like a strap over his shoulder; another white man struggling to rip his way out of a block of stone; a deep green forest covered with snow; a little cottage sitting in a woodsy clearing with red and white and green sparkly decorations all over its brown walls and roof and chimney.

This store is like what a museum used to be, a dump for the past, I think, a graveyard. People used to save this kind of stuff to look at and chortle over. But all this in Briggs's store isn't here for show, it's here in the middle of nowhere, tucked away. Is it some kind of compulsive gathering? A distraction? Is it all for sale? What's with this Briggs? I wonder.

Jimmy walks over to the table covered with mechanical parts. He picks up an iron grinder-type instrument.

This has some heft, he says. Seems to be iron, it's so heavy.

Briggs lopes over. Yeah, he says. That's a grinder. You need weight with a grinder.

I can see, says Jimmy. What's it for?

Food, says Briggs.

Food?

Yeah. You put food in the top here and turn this here crank and it all gets mashed and comes out through here. He points to a toothed opening in the side.

Where'd you get all this, Jimmy asks. He has a glow in his eyes and in his voice.

Well, now, says Briggs. You know the Ville is a place that is constantly shedding. A man or – he looks at me – a woman with an eye can pick up interesting things most anywhere. These are all things I've acquired from the surrounding former residences. He twirls his hand over his head, as if to show us all the thriving homes in the neighborhood.

Seems almost like people just walked away from it all, Briggs says. One day, just up and left. Left their tables. Left their plates on their tables. Left knives and forks. Left clothes in the closets. Like there was a volcano eruption or an earthquake or the threat of one. You know as well as I do there ain't no volcanoes around here and there haven't been any quakes to speak of since I can't remember. It was like the people fled, though, escaped, maybe.

What about the animals and the birds, I ask. You didn't find those in any house around here.

No, ma'am, I didn't. You're quite right. Those came from a big-assed old building on the other side of the Ville. Empty now, but not that long ago it was filled with critters, some of em so huge you couldn't get em through the door, not unless you knocked down a wall. Huge they were, with teeth, some of em, and long alligator tails. I think those were just made up, you know, like art. These ones here in the store, well, they're all critters that was around here once upon a time. I thought, why not? If I don't grab these, somebody else surely will. So I gathered up what I could and brought em to the store. Maybe there's a market for em. Till there is, course, they're good company in the night.

I can see Jimmy listening very closely to this. He has that intense puzzle-solving look in his eyes, the same way he looked when he was working on Deb's President's Girl roll out. There is something that bothers him.

That's pretty interesting, Mr. Briggs, he says, looking from the beady-eyed loons high on a shelf above to the short little man with the wart on his nose. I've never seen anything like this. Where was that big building?

Over beyond the old crik, says Briggs, past Storyville and Chinatown, other side of town. Can't miss it.

I've never been over that way, says Jimmy. I've never heard of those parts of town, either.

That so? says Briggs.

We just walked all the way from the Orpheum, Jimmy says. Walked right down the main strip, Dams Street, and we never saw another person. Never heard anything. Did not have one encounter with anyone.

Really?

Yes, really. And you sit out here, and tell us that there are people carrying coffins filled with monkeys, that you ramble around and poach stuffed animals from big buildings, that you have a store here open in the middle of the night, and from the sound of it, every night.

Yes sir, that's the case. It's not much of a living, but it's what I like to do. I'm here in my oasis, I like to think, catering to thirsty travelers and those in need of seeing a stuffed bird. Maybe you're not travelers? In that case, not much here for you. Not much.

And you don't know what happened around here or where anybody went?

Nope, can't say I do.

And you don't know why we didn't see anyone, hear anyone, encounter a single being this whole way?

I couldn't tell you, Briggs says. But I'll tell you one thing, stranger, I can't say as I like your drift. I can't say that at all. It sounds to me like you're suggesting I'm prevaricating with you, that I am leading you on with a passel of tall tales. Why would I do that? What would be the point, mister?

I don't know, says Jimmy. Why don't you tell me.

Briggs looks hard at him for what seems like a minute. I'm thinking, I don't like the way this is going at all.

Mr. Briggs, I say, I don't think Jimmy is suggesting that you are not telling the truth at all. I think he's just trying to fit together our experience with yours, you know. Line them up, like pieces of a broken pot, like what's in your boxes over there.

Briggs turns his hard eyes on me and I think there's something in them that reminds me of those stuffed animals he's got up on the high shelves, something black and dangerous and not from this common world. Something old. Something from before these times. His stick is toward the front of the store and I'm thinking in my mind, can I cut him off from it, can I get an angle on this little piece of bad?

But he surprises me and breaks into a big smile.

Miss, says Briggs, I can understand that all too well. Perhaps – Jimmy is it? – perhaps Jimmy would like to feast his eyes on 12, count em, 12 monkeys?

Jimmy says, That would be incredible.

Come back here, Briggs says to us and threads his way through a path meandering between stacks of round, black discs the size of dinner plates and racks of leather seats with hornlike protuberances. The discs zag up like ragged columns toward the ceiling gloom.

Briggs skitters ahead, jerks his thumb toward the leather seats.

Saddles, he says. I got boxes of bridles, too. Used to drive animals back in the day, or something, dress em up fancy and drive em. Lotsa animals back then. I understand why you might be wondering about all this. World throws off a passel of stuff over the eons. Never can be too cautious, like I was telling you. And what's true for me is true for you. So I understand all that.

We come to a door and stop. Jimmy steps over next to Briggs who points and simply says, In there.

I cock an ear toward the door. I don't hear anything.

I thought they made a lot of noise, I say.

They do, he says, oh they really do, but only when there's a little, uh, stimulation. They need a bit of activity, monkeys do, motion or light or something, to crank em up. I don't quite understand the mechanicals. Take a look.

He puts his hand on the door handle and Jimmy moves forward.

Now, says Briggs, don't get em all riled up and hissy fittin around. Can't stand the racket. Let me open this slowly and you can peek in.

Okay, says Jimmy.

Briggs opens the door very slowly and Jimmy leans forward. I can see only that the room inside is dark and still. There is nothing.

I can't see a thing, says Jimmy.

I hear that doubting edge in his voice. He moves a little further, leaning through the slightly open door.

I can't see anything at all.

Briggs moves quickly. He rams Jimmy with his shoulder catapulting him into the darkness. The door slams shut. Briggs grabs the key in the lock, turns it, pulls it out.

You will, he says, pivoting back to me and pocketing the key. Oh you will.

I expected something, but not this.

A great shrieking breaks over the room like a roiling cloud, a yammering cacophony that obliterates everything else. It is noise, sheer noise raining down and boiling up, and I slap my hands to my ears.

Something, isn't it, says Briggs.

He leans back against the door. The yowls continue.

Jimmy! Jimmy! I finally shriek, motionless, stuck. I've got to gather myself. Briggs, leaning, reaches into his other pocket and extracts a small, shiny silver pistol and points it right at me. That little gun is huge and ugly and full of more menace than I can bear.

Okay, miss, Briggs says. He exudes calm malevolence. He is one of those open-mouthed creatures on the shelves, yellow teeth filed to points. He is charged and lethal, a stalking predatory moment.

Who are you working for?

I'm astonished. And then I start to laugh.

Working for? Ha ha ha. Who are we working for? Ha ha ha. You twisted moron. What are you, some troll sucked out of the tubes? Who are we working for? Oh my god! Ha ha ha!

I can't help myself. I'm hysterical. I'm terrified. I'm infuriated.

Ha ha ha Briggs! You've got me now. What are you gonna do? Plug me? Ha ha ha.

Watch what you say to a man with a gun.

Oh you need a gun, all right, I say. How else are you going to fend off two half starved outcasts trying to cadge a bottle of Veet? You know what Briggs? You've spent too long on the fringe. Let my friend out of there. Do you hear me? Let him out!

The chee-chee-chee continues behind the door. There is rattling and thumping, and then Jimmy shouts, Open up Briggs or I'll smash everyone of these little hairy jumpers!

Shut up, Briggs shouts and turns back to me.

Let's have it, miss. I want it all. Right now. Who are you working for and what do they want? I haven't got a lot of time, so get to it.

This is ridiculous, I say. Put the gun down. We aren't working for anybody. We're looking for our friend, you've probably heard of her – Deb, the President's Girl, the Lost Girl? You probably don't know Debrity, but she's that too. She's missing and we don't know where she is. We saw a guy vacuumed up off the street. We saw Jerry the MC vanish down the gullet of a Mega. Right in front of us. We've reached the limits! You can let Jimmy out now. Like now.

I never heard of this Debrity, says Briggs. Must mean she's so famous everyone wants to be her. Jerry the MC? Sure you saw him. Everybody sees Jerry the MC. I'm a chump, right? That what you think? Is it? Move back or I'll rip your ears off and stuff em in the pickling jar yonder.

235

He waves the gun and I start moving backward. Geez, that is a jar full of ears, I think. This is out of control.

Now start talking, he demands. I haven't got all night. Who sent you? Are you just a couple of goons? Are you freelancing? Who's your pappy? Who's your boss, your big dawg – not that it makes a difference. What do they want?

We don't want anything, I say. Please, just let Jimmy out of that room and we'll go. I swear. I don't know who you think we are or what we are. I don't know what you're talking about, but whatever, we'll just leave. We'll be gone. You have us mixed up with somebody else or something.

Nobody just waltzes in here by chance, says Briggs. Nobody. Someone sent you.

No, I say. That's not true. We were leaving and you stopped us and invited us into this loony bin.

I'm still backing up and he's still moving toward me. I've never had a pistol pointed at me before. I am shaking. I want to cry. I want to hide. There's a wobbly stack of those black discs to my right. If I can get behind them, I'll disappear. Maybe I can scrabble from there to those crates marked This Side Up Not For Export.

I step back.

Hold it! Briggs shouts. The jabbering from the storeroom ratchets up.

Briggs! Jimmy shouts. There's a crash. That's one down! 11 to go! Jimmy screams through the door. Briggs looks quickly over his shoulder, and that's my chance. I dive toward the crates. My foot grazes the tower of discs. They start to buckle toward the wall.

I see Briggs turn and try to find me with those black eyes. But there is so much welter, the ordinary welter of his store, he's momentarily confused. The top of the disc tower topples toward the highest shelf and crashes into it. I look up and see a gangly bird, labeled STORK, tip over and begin to plummet. It hurtles down, beak first, just as Briggs looks up. He has no chance. The stork nails him right through the arm.

Briggs shouts in pain, Eeee-yowww!

He drops the pistol and falls to the floor. The stork's beak drives into a board and Briggs is caught, rammed into his own floorboards by that needle beak. He's pinned like a specimen.

I watch as this unfolds, for hours it seems. Briggs squeals, the monkeys squeal, Jimmy shouts. And then I am up on my feet. I run over and grab the gun. Briggs is tossing and hollering, stuck fast. I reach into his pocket before he can focus, grab the storeroom key, run over and slide it in.

Jimmy, I shout, I've unlocked the door.

Before I can even finish, he bursts out, a pair of monkeys bounding after him, bouncing and screeching. We slam the door shut before more can escape.

Goddamn Briggs! Jimmy says, his eyes raking the store. Where is that little weasel? I'm going to hang him by the whiskers. I'm going to cover him with grease and shake screws all over him and kick him out of here.

Then his eyes settle on Briggs, flat on his back, a bird sticking from his arm. Nailed by a dead bird.

Ha! Jimmy walks over. Do you know how ridiculous you look? he says. The back end of the bird obscures Briggs's head.

Jimmy, are you all right? I ask. I touch his chest. His face is flushed. His eyes are glittering. Those are amazing monkeys! he says.

Help, says Briggs. Help me if you can.

Jimmy looks down for a long moment and sighs.

All right, this will probably be painful.

He grabs the body of the stork, puts a foot on Briggs's hand, yanks, and the beak pulls from the floor and slides free from Briggs.

It's quiet. Even the storeroom is quiet. Who knows where the two freed monkeys have gone. They've careened from the store and are headed on down the road, I suspect, looking for some action.

Briggs is holding his arm.

We just wanted some Veet and something to eat, I repeat.

I help him up. His eyes don't have quite the threat laced through them anymore. He's not even bleeding, so it can't be that bad.

I've got some Veet and food over here he says, turning away. I decide to hold on to the pistol, though I can't imagine using it and I don't know how it works.

I guess you folks are really hungry, Briggs says, rolling from side to side as he moves between stacks of this and stacks of that. He's very bowlegged.

Sorry about the monkeys and the gun. I guess you are who you say you are.

Who else could we be? I ask.

Chapter Nine

That's the question, says Briggs as we reach the front of the store. Who else could you be?

I look out the window and see the street is still as empty as any untraveled road. Briggs's stick is still where he left it. I pick it up and discover it's heavy, a leaden limb. Who could we be? We are only ourselves, unattached, like that limb, like Jerry's lost leg, like any itchy absence. Things that once were. Jerry. I remember.

All this stuff, what are you expecting? Jimmy asks, eyes darting around. You've got this weaponry like I've never seen. I mean, I understand marauders in the Hood – I made a life out of them, though to be honest, they were never all that big a deal. They used to promo them on the tubes though, Scat! ads all over the outer channels:

When your needs are tough, protect your stuff – Scat!

Remember those, Britt? Guy with an angry blade cutting through window bars? People'd get all panicky and come to me, an indy operator. It's a living. Down here? I don't see it. I haven't seen it. Looks to me like your biggest threat is yourself.

Briggs hunches his shoulders and then lists his way behind a counter at the front. He's no longer holding his arm, like there's no injury or anything – this with a guy who just got nailed to the floor by a stuffed stork. What happened to the menace, I wonder. Where is his bristling threat? Where's the hurt?

You think so? Briggs says, kind of defensive. No threat? You've got no clue, do you? What do you know about threat?

I'll tell you one thing, Jimmy replies. You're gonna blow your own foot off, or knock the head off one of those birds up there with these guns, they're blunderbusses, you ask me.

Oh, pshaw! Briggs snorts. They aren't even loaded. Got some six shooters over here too. He reaches down behind the counter and pulls out another pistol, waving it around. I'm alarmed and begin to duck. He pulls the trigger and produces a click.

See what I mean? says Briggs. Ha ha ha. Got some good ole bullets around somewhere, if necessary. You folks aren't a necessary, just a curiosity, or so it would seem for the moment. Y'all need to understand, we've got some serious issues out here. When you set up shop in the Flats you got to be prepared. I'm not talking outside marauders here, pardner. I'm talking contract players, boys sent out here to scarify the settlers, shoo em back to the Hood and the Ville, like strays.

They're good at it, too, mighty good, he says. Come in here with their black hats and their black shirts and their body armor and goggles. Mantises, they remind me of. Packs of mantises. We spray em for the most part, but they keep on coming back – pesky and effective. Greenhorns get a-feared and pick up and head back to what they think is the safety of the Ville. No law and order out here, they say. The Ville is a model for that, I tell em, specially if you can make it all the way into the Zone. You got lots of law and order there. Ha ha ha. Just don't ask any questions.

Jimmy looks real skeptical. Nobody waltzes into the Zone, he says. Settlers? I don't think so. Nobody's around here. The only things you've got to worry about are dead birds falling from the sky. That's the way it looks to me. Must be the only birds in the Ville, too.

Really? says Briggs. He looks at us with what I take to be pity. But it might be part of his act.

241

Yep. We learned that tonight, Jimmy says.

Come over here into the office, Briggs says, turning around.

Oh no, we've been down that road already, I say. No way are we going anywhere near any of your doors.

Suit yourself, but I've got some grub for you in there – Veet, plugs, you name it. But don't get your hopes up – there's nothing much else beyond them. Ha ha ha! Don't believe me, you can look yourself. I won't come near you. All on the house, too. Have a sit and eat your fill. We can jaw awhile.

There's a door behind the counter.

Open it, I say, and move away.

He does. The door swings silently onto an empty room with a wooden desk and a few hard chairs. An old fridge stands against the far wall, buzzing. Nothing else but for some yellowed paper in stacks on the floor. A dry, brittle odor spreads from the office.

Go in and sit in the far chair, I say. He does and as he plops himself down, I bang the door closed and slam the deadbolt.

Hey, says Briggs. Hey! Open up. What're you doing? Lemme out of here! Hey, you little turnips!

Quiet, I hiss back at him, or we'll fill the room with monkeys and steam it.

Sheet, he says, and I hear him bang his feet onto the desk.

Jimmy, are you all right? Are you hurt? What's with those monkeys anyway?

He shrugs. Nothing. They're toys, he says with a faint smile, like Briggs said. Real noisy toys. Jumped around a lot, bounced off the walls, knocked brooms all over, toppled some shelves of cans and baskets of screws. One of them banged my hand. One of them just kept screeching, We're the monkeys, yeah! We're the monkeys, yeah! And jumping up and down. Couldn't even think!

He has this pensive look on his face now, kind of sheepish, kind of pale. I realize in myself that I am concerned about Jimmy in a way I haven't been before. He seems drained. He seems lost inside. I want him to be okay. I need him to be okay.

Jimmy, we've got to get some Veet and figure out how to get from this place to the pits. I'm sure Morrie is tracking us. My pad's been buzzing constantly, even in here. I keep hearing it over and over.

Jimmy slumps against the counter. His eyes roam over the top shelves of the store, over the birds and animals. He shakes his head.

I don't know, he says. We are off the charts as far as I can tell. There's something going on. We haven't just found our way out of the Ville, we've stumbled into something near the outer limits. Mantises? Briggs was expecting somebody, or prepared for somebody or something. But there's nobody here. We haven't seen anyone. It's all empty space. We are walking through empty space. He's filling it with gangs? It's all in his head. Maybe we ought to go back the way we came. We've been wandering into nothing since the Echoes. What do we want here?

I am stunned.

We want Deb, I say.

A look of despair pools across Jimmy's face from deep behind his dark eyes. I move close to him and put my hands up on his shoulders.

The Flats, Briggs called them, Jimmy says. Never heard that before. Never heard of any place in the Ville called the Flats. Shantyville? Chinatown? We're someplace else, someplace that I didn't even know existed. Does it? Is this place really here? The locater doesn't function. I can't seem to get a track. I don't get it. This is nowhere near where I used to go when I went to the pits. That was a straight shot down Westway. Now we've circled into someplace else. I'm not sure where we are. I don't recognize anything.

We have to figure a route, I whisper into his ear. The Echoes and Jerry gave us the direction – south. I need you Jimmy. I can't do this myself. I want to do it with you. For Deb. For Deb.

I put my arms around him and just hold him. He places his hand on the back of my head and we just stand there for a moment, a statuary spectacle for all the birds in stasis staring from high up through the half light.

Look at your pad, he says finally, I can feel it vibrating myself.

I can't look at it in here, I say, it seems wrong somehow. It doesn't belong here. We've gone beyond the Hood and beyond the Zone, completely outside.

The pad is like an alien artifact to me.

Yeah, that may be what you think, but is it what Morrie and the boys think? he says. They are yanking. They've got us on strings.

Jimmy pulls my pad from my pocket and I feel myself clench inside as he holds it and slowly opens it.

Well, it's about time. And we have Mr. James J. Jones, a fan.

Oh my god, I think. Morrie for sure.

Mr. Jones, you and your mistress, that would be the incomparable Mme. Britt, are being more than a little difficult, you are causing a major headache, worse than Aunt Rita. But we persevere here. We are simply trying to right the ship and keep all the passengers on board. You realize Mr. Jones the water is cold and the ocean is vast. We don't want to capsize. Too many passengers for that, don't you think?

I am not anybody's mistress, I say. Not anybody's. Tell him that! Tell him he can stay in his boat. We're going to shore. Tell him. Tell him we can't hear him. Tell him we are heading off the frequencies. Tell him we are finding our way out. Tell him to think on that.

Jimmy gets that staring look again, like he's eyed by a snake. The pad glows.

Morrie says, Where the heck are you? We've got you on the screens, but you're out into sat land, just green dots on a dark ground. Lots of static, too, lots of noise on the screens. Can't seem to zero in like we should.

Jimmy doesn't say anything, just looks at the pad. Does he believe what he's hearing? I don't. I don't believe anything anymore that isn't right in front of me, that I can't hold and touch. That you can see, really see. Jimmy. Me. Briggs. That friggin stork.

I look at the screen. Morrie seems to be in some kind of command center. There are screens behind him showing scenes of screens showing something I can't quite make out. People hurry back and forth in the background. A woman with straight blond hair, outlandish purple beads around her neck, and a wire in her ear darts into the picture and whispers something to Morrie. He nods and looks out at us.

What's that room? asks Morrie, almost pushing his head right through the screen to look. What's all that junk? You're not in an oasis store are you? Oh for god's sake. What are you doing in a hole like that? Those places are havens for crazy people. You are in the midst of chaos. There is no order there. There is no good or bad, right or wrong, safe or endangered, secure or insecure, rough or smooth. If I were you, and I thank the dear P I am not, I would exit that joint pronto. They are subject to attacks of all kinds. Don't you two know anything? Those places are hit by black flag bug gangs, they are subject to marauding clowns in gassed up clown cars, they are daily festivals for rats, there may be flying things about. The whole place is outside the system. Chaos, James J. Jones, like every night practically. Who knows what moves in looking for kills and crumbs and anything that's not nailed down. My god.

Jimmy just stares. I think he has a puzzled look. Puzzled about what? Morrie is just spewing gibberish to hold our attention. Now I think Jimmy may be intrigued. I reach out and touch his arm, warm. A body. Jimmy.

Chaos is absence, you know, Morrie says. Your brain rushes in to fill the vacuum any which way. I don't even want to contemplate what you might conjure up. But that's my job, you might say. I imagine what you imagine. I'm here to save you from your inner lives. I'm not going to get philosophical with you, though. Is Britt there? Put her on. I want to see that she's safe.

I shake my head, no, no, but Jimmy hands me the pad anyway. He seems drained now and worried. He just wants away from Morrie.

Britt, says Morrie, what are you doing? You've got to get out of there. Look, I know you are upset about your friend, and we are working on it, we are trying to

246

track her down. She was last in the Zone, but with the heavy disruptions, the damage to the cam system and all that, the unauthorized disappearances, the fleeing mobs, the darkness, etc. etc., we are uncertain of her current location. She ditched her pad, too. One thing I can tell you, though: You need to get out of that fantasy land and back to just plain folks. Real people. Real places.

You're not trying to find her, I say, you're trying to track me; you want to deflect us, me and Jimmy. Why? Why would you do that? Who cares about us so much?

No, no, no, he says. I see you right where you are. You are in the midst of somebody's tricked out fairyland. I see the outlandish flora and the fauna, the chimeras, the delusional stacks of old debris. That's right, debris. I'm here to tell you, and I hope you are listening, that you and Mr. Jones have made a terrible error, that's what we all think, and we want you back. We want you out of wonderland. Okay? We can't afford any more tears in the fabric. And I'll tell you, we will do what it takes to mend things and sew up the seams, believe me.

I don't like the sound of that, I say. My seams don't need mending. I need Deb front and center.

Look, Morrie says, ignoring my need, I have someone who really would like to speak with you. She came all the way to the P's Zone HQ, we tracked her down at Elder Fields and Elysian Lounger – you know, We Put the Care into Careful and Yanked the Age from Wreckage? – and told her that you were off the tracks.

She was very upset, yes she was, and demanded to come here and speak with you right away. I told her there's no need. We were smoothing your return. But she's a volcano, no holding her back. She was just overflowing with the need to reach out and share. Gushing, even. That's why I've been trying so hard to reach out myself. Okay, I'm persistent too. We need persistence and patience to win the day.

What? I say. Who? What are you talking about? I am in high alarm now.

Morrie looks off to the side and says, Okay, come on over, it's time. We have her on the screen now.

I hear a shuffling walk and a wheezing and then an aged face sticks its way right into the center of my screen. A familiar face, a shriveled dried pear topped by swirls of white hair – a sno-cone above and a gaunt neck with flaps of withered skin below. Who is it? Then it hits me. I don't believe this.

Angelina, she says, Angelina, what are you doing? You should be home in your rooms working your brand! Analyzing metrics! Dear, dear, dear. This is such a tragedy.

Mrs. Petri, my name is Britt, not Angelina. Angelina is someone else.

Was Mrs. Petri so sour looking when we were in camp? Pinched, yes. Twitching, of course. But now she looks as though she's been moldering in a vat for decades.

Angelina is indeed someone else, says Mrs. Petri, her lips pursed in a scowl; they're twitching the way they always did. Oh my god. She exudes indignation. I am seven years old looking at my shoes. Sally Kamaski is whispering off to the right. I am about to be schooled again.

No! I don't want to be schooled like this! Fill me with the old nostrums, not this again! Bring them on, the leeches, please. Bleed me. Anything but kindly Mrs. Petri. Anything but all this. Pour the Angostura right down my gullet. Open me up and let Lydia Pinkham's rain down and soothe all my cares away.

Those are the magic potions, those are what I learned about reading Donny K's Hood-Loom stories way back, the ones where he passes on the rumors of workers in the tunnels and the ordinary stuff people did to make things better in their heads. Those were the rumors passed down and passed down and passed down until Donny K wrote them down and shot them out into the electrosphere. Now they exist somewhere where no one can see them – Access Denied. Error 404. Oops! We're sorry. Page Not Available.

Maybe I'm the only one who ever saw that stuff. Maybe I'm the only one who keeps them filed away inside my head. My head, the rumor vault. I remember.

Mrs. Petri has her own remedies. Boy do I know that.

What I need are screens and reds and meds and lots of them, she tells me when I'm a kid. Oh, I heard that again and again. I hear it now, rattling around this oasis in the dry midst of nowhere.

I need a little soothing and correction. That's what she tells anyone who hops the tracks and veers off course and needs some system toning or maybe just needs to disappear entirely. And here she is, ready to cure whatever ails my troubled soul and steady my erratic behavior. I thought she was dead. I had hoped, if you want to know. I'm not ashamed of that.

Angelina would not be off the tracks out in the middle of who knows where, Mrs. Petri says, cranking it up. Angelina would not be distracting the P from the important business of smoothing the system. Angelina would not be undermining all that we depend on and work for. Angelina is a girl who fits in, lives in the now, and pulls together. She is not someone who waffles and wobbles, who hops the tracks, who sends out false and defaming videos, who stages personal disruptions and scares the daylights out of everyone in the Zone. Not my Angelina.

I am shocked. This is too far.

My name is Britt, Mrs. Petri, as you well know. Angelina is some little girl who came from somewhere else and lives with you somewhere in the long ago.

Angelina knows what is what, says Mrs. Petri. She knows what she has to do. If you work for the man, ride for his brand. She understands that. She understands all my efforts to help her. All the years we put in together. She follows the straight and true. She takes a red and goes to bed. Oh Angelina! She dances her way through camp! She doesn't skulk around like some low extinct animal. She doesn't crawl into a bunker! She is here, under the lights, on screen! What are all those, those things around you? She purses her whole body in sour distaste.

Fuck.

Morrie, how could you do this? I say. Oh I am angry.

Mrs. Petri, with all due respect, you don't understand what's going on here. I haven't disrupted or manipulated or destroyed anything. I'm trying to find my friend who has vanished into that well-oiled system, and your minder, Morrie there, is responsible for her disappearance and maybe even her death. She may be dead Mrs. Petri! Dead! You know, post-animate? And I think it is awful that now this Morrie, or whoever he is, actually went out, consciously, of his own free will, such as we have, and dragged you into this. I thought you knew me, but you don't even know my name.

Tears are now falling hard and I feel an old sadness grab hold of me, an old shame. I am so outside. I don't want to cry, but admit I can't help it!

Well, says Mrs. Petri, a little taken aback, it's hard to keep up.

Morrie, please, take Mrs. Petri home, I say. Mrs. Petri, don't believe everything you hear.

Mrs. Petri says, That's not a winning attitude Angelina.

I slam the pad shut.

Why are they bothering with us? I ask Jimmy, wiping my face with a black cloth that has a skull stamped on it (Briggs has a lot of them stacked around). Why don't they just pull in Deb? Why are they on our case?

Jimmy looks at me. Angelina? he says.

What of it? I say. They called me Angelina until I discovered who I was, until I started building my brand. I'm Britt, not Angelina. Nobody is going to tag me with something that's not me, and that's not me. I branded a long time ago, you know that. They slapped Angelina on me, but I've always been Britt. What do they know about me?

Of course, he says. Retooling, retrofitting, reworking, reconfiguring. I learned all that stuff too. Angelina. Can I call you Angelina? I mean, we're outside now. We are on the outside.

Please, just Britt. I think of asking Jimmy who else he is, but I decide not to. You are who you are, okay? He can see me. He can see my face. He can feel my hands, touch my body. He can hold me too. Completely. But he doesn't. He doesn't grab me and pull me in. I want him to.

Jimmy opens his own pad now, set to Zoneratti. A full screen blasts out at us:

EMERGENCY ALERT! EMERGENCY ALERT!
MATT D VANISHES! MATT D VANISHES!

Geez, says Jimmy. Holy shit!

He heads immediately to the Community Room where the first thing up is a screaming vid:

DARING DUO SEEK MATT! NEW VID! REAL TIME!!

Britt get over here. Look at this – it's beyond anything I've seen, like ever.

I look.

There's a huge embedded stream of Jimmy and me walking down one of those black streets. No VO, just the two of us, walking. We are little bugs in that empty street. A light ash is falling. The buildings on either side are blurry, but you can see blank spaces now and again, vacant parcels holding their own against the crush of tottering structures around them.

Is that us? I wonder. Where could that section of the street be? You can't see any of the vanishing wall codes, none of the old language and images, none of what was there and what we saw just hours ago. Only the two of us passing beneath the cam and then receding into the distance. We're picked up by another cam and the same thing happens.

Jimmy do you recognize this?

I think it's after the Orpheum? he says. When we were walking down that first street? There were still cams, at least a few.

Yeah, but where? What's this Daring Duo stuff?

Dunno.

We see ourselves from behind now, receding into the distance again. A general fuzz and splatter hits the screen. It becomes dark green and there are two bright green splotches moving along. We've become images picked up by the sats. I watch for a moment. The splotches slow their movement and then stop. They move slowly again and stop again.

REAL TIME! REAL TIME! REAL TIME!

We must be around Briggs's store here, I say.

Yeah.

And then the image clears again and Jimmy and I are seen from the front, standing at the entrance of the store, a look of determination mixed with anxiety is on Jimmy's angular face. I'm apprehensive right behind him. We move inside. The cam pans. Briggs is nowhere.

I have good intel that they're holding him in here, a girl's voice, my voice, says. Be careful, you don't know what they might do and we have to protect Matt at all costs.

I'm ready, the boy, Jimmy, says. His eyes narrow to slits and he moves slowly to the wall. Careful – watch the right, I'll take the left.

That's you, I say. Somehow that's you. They've put us on the trail of Matt. Maybe he's been kidnapped and we're seeking to rescue him. I watch.

We are in danger, we are so in danger.

Does she say that? Did I? Did I think it? I feel my head bleeding all around from the inside out. I am transfixed.

I know, he replies. We'd better get out of here.

Not until they give up Matt.

Who is saying these things, I wonder. Is it me? Jimmy? Is that me? I watch myself edge into Briggs's store. I pull some kind of weapon out of my waistband. Jimmy has his out already. Am I in danger? Are they in danger? Is it all in danger?

The store is as quiet as a vacuum tube. We creep along the walls. I can see teetering stacks of boxes at the fringes of the screen. A quiet VO begins whispering. I watch my every move; commentators and reporters interpret it all, lending narrative to some kind of incident. The tension is almost unbearable.

They are proceeding with extreme caution, the announcer murmurs. This is apparently a hideout for a band of unknown and ruthless outsiders, those who have likely stolen Matt D; they are the possible disrupters of the system, blasting rumors of rampaging machines and imminent peril all around the world. The P's secret operatives, inserted into this sector, are closing in. Let's watch quietly.

There is a stillness, a hint of taut music. An outsider threat theme? We inch our way along the wall. I am sweating. I can feel droplets running down the side of my face.

254

We are hunting ourselves.

There is a crash from off screen. Both of us whirl around. I take my weapon and fire continuous pulses. Jimmy goes down.

I'm all right! he shouts. I'm all right!

The screen is close on my face. I can see the fear and confusion in my eyes. How am I going to get out of this? Where did that fire come from? Where's the enemy?

INCOMING! INCOMING! INCOMING! flashes across the screen. Jimmy is quickly up beside me.

CentOp just alerted, he says, holding his arm. A pulse of light crashes into the wall behind us.

Move. Move. Move. Move! I yell, and we run for the door, bursting out into the dark street. More pulses slam into walls and posts around us. Run! Get going. We streak down the street, tracked by the cam. The store is a bleak shed of light behind us. The other buildings along the street are blank. There is a tremendous whine and crash and Briggs's store vanishes in an incandescent burst! Both of us are thrown to the ground as shards of wood and glass shower down around us.

The cam is tight on us now with our heads down. I raise mine and look back at the store. It is gone. A moment ago it housed a little man and towering piles collected over who knows how long. Steam or smoke rises from the rubble strewn lot.

Matt, I say. Matt's in there! Anguish washes over me.

Matt! and I slump forward.

Jimmy turns to me and says, We can't be certain.

The same hushed VO intrudes again: We have this real-time report, but caution everyone that nothing has been confirmed. It appears that the hideout has been destroyed, but CentOp cannot confirm or deny the source of the incoming missile or pulsar or even that anything other than bad internal systems are the cause of the destruction, if destruction has, in fact, occurred. We will replay this sequence and provide updates as necessary. Everyone is urged to remain calm and not to respond to false information and rumors.

The girl and the boy begin walking down the nighttime street again. They pass beneath a cam and continue on. Ash sifts down.

I am heavy with grief. I feel as though I have failed myself. I continue to watch the screen. Stay away from that store! Do not go in the store! But it is no use. We will enter and re-enter. It will explode again and again. We will hit the street and feel sharp slivers rain down on us. Again and again.

Jimmy shifts to the P's info log.

Britt, he says, check these Sub50s coming from the P's guys. Weird stuff.

I look. Jimmy has locked onto the Producer Data Queue (PDQ). Thoughts are crunching in like junk food.

Gryph11: raise pikes now 4 capture

G: Hole in wall wrecked no D

M: Pee sez need no alarm

D: M gone, Britt on case

G: Britt, friend in wilds

D: Plan 2 move in fast

D: Implement plan B

G: If not B, C or D1

D: U R A O K

Why are we in their Sub50 feed? I say. Like they
have us on some kind of mission. This takes off from the
Zoneratti embed. Where did they get that video? How did
they destroy this place?

I look around at the still-teetering piles of disks,
the silent birds and creatures riveted on us it seems.
Briggs starts hollering.

Let me the hell out of here, he shouts. It's drier
than a tomb. I ain't some desiccating piece of paper.

There doesn't seem to be much point in keeping
him locked up now. His store just got blown up and we
are cut and hurting in the middle of the street. I pull the
bolt back and open up. Briggs is still sitting in the chair, a
smug look on his face.

No threats? he says, eyebrow cocked. Ha ha ha!

As he gets up, I turn away and slump onto the
counter. The six-shooter is on a shelf below. The street is
quiet. Jimmy is still zoned into his pad, reading the
Sub50s.

Britt, Jimmy says, we are okay. It seems there
was a threat in this area, best I can tell, and they cleared it
away when they blew up the store. We got out just in
time. Now we should be able to make it to the pits, that's
what I think, anyway, barring unforeseen circumstances.
Matt D has disappeared and all the P's men are on the
hunt. They are apparently banking on us. That's the line

they're putting out. They have woven a storyline around us somehow.

We are news, Britt. News!

Briggs listens closely.

News, he harrumphs. He reaches down and pulls up a box of Veet, the pure bottles. He's got bags of Plugettes, too – Nutri's luxury snacking line. He hands it all over and I take a long drink. Somehow the Veet is cold. Jimmy finishes off a bottle in a gulp and grabs a Paulette, the saucy kind in the middle.

You folks aren't news, says Briggs, looking at us, one to another and back. You're part of the distraction, same as Matt D. They're just cooking the zees.

What?

Managing the zeitgeist, he says. Ha ha ha. Me, I don't cotton to distractions; distractions don't cotton to me. That's why I'm here.

He rolls back and forth out of the office. You know, he says, they can focus on anyone they want. That's what they done to you. Now me, maybe I might see something different if I were to have a pad and open it up and check, that would be assuming they were on me, of course, and I was emitting, like some tenderfoot on the prairie.

Sure, says Jimmy, they hold you and drill down. That's the idea. But something this big? I don't know.

Briggs says, That's the point pardner. You never know. You may be Wally Simpson, or you may be the king's queen. Whatever they want. Whatever they think you want. Whatever they think your neighbor down the street wants. They give it all to you. You serve them for your own convenience. That's smooth-systeming. Don't cost nothing. Keeps most everyone in their own bunk. And keeps most everyone else all riled and anxious and striving. Yep.

Look Briggs, we know who we are, at least at the moment, and we know what we want, and they don't seem to like either, I say. Why go to the trouble, that's my question. I keep asking it. We're just a couple of people on the road.

That's all it takes, says Briggs. Gotta start somewhere. They like to, as you say, as your friend describes it, drill down. Doubters and travelers are big trouble. You can't have that, no siree. You folks are sowing doubt every step you take. Anyways, how you know who you are? Ever think of that? How you know who you are and what you think? Where's it all come from? Ha ha ha.

Jimmy has his pad shut now, reluctantly, it seems to me. I'm taken by Briggs simple question. It seems to contain its own answer if I could put my finger on it, if I could think after all this.

Where'd you get all this stuff, Jimmy says to Briggs, all these round thingies and the leather seats?

I just picked up what I fancied, like I said, Briggs says. Look, back in the day, people had all this tucked away. All these buildings around here? They were for peddling stuff – selling saddles, selling bridles, selling gizmos, selling pictures, dresses, belts, shoes. They dealt it all, and people would snap it up and lug it back to their rooms. Some stuff sure was popular. Take these discs here. People wanted them, I'm not sure why, but it doesn't matter. Wants are wants and who can account for what you want?

But isn't that what you said they knew all about? Wants? I interrupt.

That's a lesson to be learned and re-learned, I reckon, Briggs says. What makes you want? The corps and the P, they want you to want certain things, so they nudge you or push you one way or another. That's life, missy. Stuff, thoughts, actions – they nudge it all. So there's times you get, and there's times you get got.

For some reason I think of my mother, what she might have been if I could remember her or anything from way back. Maybe there's nothing to remember. Maybe she just dumped me in a camp and headed off to nowhere. Maybe she took a look at me and took off. Maybe they took her. Maybe not. I don't know. I don't know. What do we have?

We got got for sure.

Jimmy doesn't say anything. He's holding his pad and staring off beyond Briggs, back toward the rear of the store. I got to say he looks fucked up, like he woke and forgot where he was and where he's going.

Mrs. Petri, I say to Briggs, she ran our camp, you know, she'd say what we have now, the way it is now, is at a whole new level from what used to be. She'd say what's done is done; a new day's here. A new day is always here.

Be efficient, she'd say. Work together. Give to the screens and you give to everybody – and everybody gives back to you!

Briggs says, That's a lot of hooey, you know. You've got my dander up, missy.

He spits in another one of those damn brass buckets. Pi-tang!

People just take and that's a fact, he says. Nothing about giving.

The wildest critters live in the city, he says, that's what my mama taught me, god bless her. And that's what your history is – the story of wanting and taking and wild city critters. All that old stuff for sale in these here buildings, before all the collapses? All them people out on the street thinking their own thoughts, meeting each other, banging around? All that was once real. That's why I'm here and that's why I'm keeping all this right here now. You lose what I got here and you lose everything. Not just the critters, you lose the story of getting and spending, the march of brands, the niches, the stuff – all that came before the smooth flow of micros and your own sweet self, if you'll pardon me missy. You can't forget that, otherwise nothing has any meaning. Your mama never taught you that, I reckon.

I don't say anything. My mama's teaching's in her absence, I think.

It was the micros and the P and the pikes and piles that staved off the threat though, Jimmy ventures.

Briggs spits again into the brass bucket.

What threat? he says.

The threat of the collapses, says Jimmy. Everybody knows about that. How the big guys had to step in. How they had to prop it all up. You can see the story on the P's site somewhere.

You are one ignorant kid, pardner, says Briggs. Nobody propped anything up. Why do you think this is the way it is around here? You some kind of sugarfoot? Shit went down. They didn't care. One way or another they were gonna get their cut. Right about that too. No matter where you ride to, that's where you are. Look around.

Briggs hitches up his pants. We was already in trouble. Collapses? What did the P or the corps do about the collapse of the OrganBanc, he says.

The what? Jimmy says.

You heard me. The OrganBanc? How you gonna ride that one out?

I don't know, I say. Was it bad?

Briggs snorts. You are a couple of daisies in a barnyard, he says. We're talking the Big One, savaged the organ market. First sign was trouble in liver futures. Bad livers, bundled with good ones, started to fail. Brought people right down to their knees, and then pushed em face down into the mud. Markets started to slide soon as the bodies started to pile up in the Transplant Depots. Panic followed. Sellers, takers, buyers – all the trading houses went wild. A lot of houses bet heavy on futures but the markets went into free fall. Organ bundles went toxic. Never was supposed to happen, I hear tell.

I never heard anything like this, says Jimmy. Sounds completely made up, like a fairytale or something. OrganBanc?

Right, bud, says Briggs. You just got blown up in the street by pulses of light and you're talkin fairytale? Fine. Go ahead. But I'm talkin complete obliteration, decimation, destruction, defunctation. Buyers and sellers cut to shreds. Blood in the streets! OrganBanc collapse. A toxic, stinking world. Did the corps care? Hell no. They got their cut, like I said.

Geez, I say.

Jimmy stares, shakes his head, finishes another Veet in a long slug. I can't tell what he really thinks.

Bodies rode down the rapids up toward the Hood, back when the river run through it, Briggs goes on. Had to dam the whole shebang to stop the dumping. People just cleared out by then. They just hightailed it, you want to know. Then there was them Mercy Bugs, you know? The ones they couldn't do nothing about in the clinics and in the schools and camps except spread em? Took everybody out. That's what took my mama's mama's mama. Or maybe it was her mama, the one before or the one before that. Not too clear on that.

And all along, Excellon and them guys are extracting more and more until most everything is sucked out of the substrate and the ground begins to sink like a bad soufflé and it begins to crater. Sheesh! Don't get me started on that, pilgrim!

So here I am, Briggs says. I figure, this is good enough for me. My mama always said, when you get to the end of your rope, tie a knot and hang on. So I'm a-hanging here. I'm a-hanging and trying to keep what I can together for them what appreciates the finer things, the older things. Things.

Jimmy and I are quiet for a moment, trying to absorb Briggs's story.

Was this before they were marching the workers underground from the ships? I ask. I heard about that from Donny K. He heard it from some other guys. They're all dead now.

Briggs says, Nope, never heard tell of any underground marches. Don't ring a bell. Anyways, everybody's dead now. Ha ha ha.

It was back when the Hood was full, I say.

Must've been, must've been real way back in the day. One of our many losses, I'm sorry to say. Can't add em all up together and make a fit.

263

He looks at us with what strikes me, oddly, as sympathy.

It's the screens, ya know, says Briggs. It's all in the screens somewheres and you can't touch nothing no more or find it and bring it back.

What's with that?

He spits again – pi-tang! – and looks at us and says, Here, take this. He hands Jimmy a crumpled piece of square green paper with a picture of a guy with a curly wig on it. The guy has tight lips and a supercilious look. Matt in a wig? Whatever.

Take this, Briggs says again, take these Plugettes. Stuff em in your pockets and stay on this street. When you get to Ashington, jag right and then circle left. You'll find the pits at the end of the line there. Give this paper to Pluto. He'll do what needs to be done. Remember one thing.

What's that, says Jimmy.

You can't keep trouble from walkin in, but you don't gotta offer it a chair.

Chapter Ten

Our backs are slumped against a pointy brick wall as we sit, nibbling plugs – I am so hungry even a Plugette washed down with Vect is a blessing, a powdery gift of the gods.

Jimmy, I nudge him, what you said to Briggs – what did you mean that marauders never seemed like such a big deal? The P and everybody says be careful of them. There're armies out there. They deploy across the Hood, varmint bags empty and waiting. You said so, too. You told me. Sentry used to patrol until they pulled back to the Zone with all that belt-tightening stuff. So our flanks are exposed, just raw flesh surrounded by toothy, hungry gangs. That's what it seemed like, and that was when you really started to take off with your show. Remember? I armored up. You told me! But – it's true – I never had an issue.

Jimmy takes a swig and says, Yeah, well, they're out there. It's just I personally myself never saw many, or any, actually. But it's not like what you don't see won't hurt you. They move in when you let your guard down or when your back is turned, far as I can tell. They're an invisible army, shadow jihadis, okay? Looking for unprotected windows. Looking for vulnerabilities. That's why you got to be ready to zap with your setter plates. Everybody knows that. Everybody was telling me. Even the P talked about it in his shows.

But you never actually saw any, I say.

Nah. They stay away from legit workers and activity and stuff, I guess.

Maybe they aren't even there? I wonder out loud. Maybe the P's guys just spun them out, or the corps did? Made an army of marauders out of nothing, conjured vids from a couple of red-headers on a buzz? We know they're rats out there – we see them. We know there're geezers. Bless Jerry. Bless them all. Marauders, we don't know. Maybe that's what Briggs meant about the screens, too. He said it's all in the screens. But if everything's in the screens, what's left for us?

No, Britt, that's not it at all! What does that mean, like really? I heard a lot about marauders and threats. There was the guy, I think I told you, who was sleeping in his room, woke up and found some creepy little man sitting naked on a stool tying a rope into a noose to hang from a ceiling hook. He had a cam set up and was streaming vids of what he was doing. Didn't I tell you about this? So the guy wakes up and sees this going down in his room! Like some guy was turning himself into a dangling, bony ornament. Hello? No threat? Happy Holidays?

Grabbed a can of Freeze-It hair spray and chased the guy out of the house. It's all on this guy's site – Dwarf Flees Hairspray.

That guy, I point out, was dealing hairspray from his site: Freeze It! Or Lose It! I remember that too.

Then you remember Mealy, Jimmy goes on, how Brute sent her out on the street with the MealyCam and she wandered into some house in the middle of the night and started in with the baby? No locks on that house; we won't even mention plates or pikes. That's risky business to put out there. Who wants that?

Yeah, I say, But she's no pack of marauders. She was checking out the street, or at least that's what Brute

266

seemed to have in mind. She was verifying. Plus Mealy needed something herself on her insides; she didn't want to waste anybody. We said so at the time. Remember? She may have known that woman with the baby.

That's speculation. Rumor. We don't know that at all, Jimmy says. I'm sure that girl sleeping felt real friendly when she woke up and some weirdo with frizzy hair and blank eyes has snatched her baby and is standing right there with her tit hanging out. You saw that. You saw her.

No, that's not quite right, I say. There's a lot more to it. You want to know, I think Mealy's lost herself, kind of like Deb. She wanted something to hold, something that needed her. Somehow she lost herself or lost what she once was or thought she was. Brute manipulated her, you know? Mealy needed something and Brute sent her out on street searches. That's what the baby thing was all about. It touched something missing or forgotten or real.

Not only that, I go on, she didn't see anybody on the street and we didn't either. Just heard the storm-drain dude. The whole thing seems fracked up.

Mealy's on another planet, he says. What're you saying?

No. Mealy, as you pointed out to me, has disappeared, just like Brute, I say.

She's kind of a hermit anyway, Jimmy says. Never on the screens unless Brute tags her.

Briggs is a hermit too, I say.

Briggs is a loon, he says.

Everybody on the outside is nuts or a marauder? I say. I don't think so. Briggs's solitary, living off the edge. Listen! Listen! Listen! That store's something like an old trading post. Last chance for food and water for 1000 miles – that kind of thing.

(I'm excited I thought of this. Useful knowledge from the past found by me!)

There were stores ringing the wilderness back in the day, I say. They stocked up with essentials for travelers. The guys that ran them were like important. They had the food and stuff, the matches, pencils, you know, and they knew about the weather and where bad news was hiding out.

Oh? Jimmy says. Where'd that come from? That's really obscure.

I found out a lot of this when I realized I was all about Hip – but I didn't know what Hip was or where it came from or how one person's Hip seemed to be somebody else's Totally Pointless. I didn't want to make branding mistakes and I didn't want to elbow into somebody else's occupied territory. That's when I really got into Donny K's and rooted around for background, Hip tips, retro fashion – stuff about what used to be, or what was thought to be or heard to be. So there were these stores. Yeah. That's what Briggs is. He's like outside the Ville. An outpost store. On the edge. Off the screens.

Jimmy is looking at me a little askew. What's with that?

You know, I say, now that I think about it, I can't believe Brute didn't know Briggs. I bet he did. I bet Mealy did too. They're all looking for the outside, something that used to be, something from before your only home was the screens.

Jimmy looks more uncomfortable.

What's wrong, I ask.

Nothing, he says. Nobody cares about what happened way back or yesterday or anything like that. Why should they? Brute didn't care. Neither did Mealy.

How can you say that? How can you know?

Jimmy ruminates. He says, Brute and Mealy were an item and a show once, Boogling in the Hood with B & M, I think it was. Everywhere they went, they'd shoot each other and blast the vids out. Up in the morning, getting dressed, dinner, hanging, whatever. We got a continuous stream. It was kinda cool because they were funny, you know what I mean? Really popular too, drove all kinds of wannabes – Low Lights, Low Lives was one copycat. All in the Hood, Get It Up or Hang It Out, Granny's Geezer Bait, Sal & Val's Parmigianino – they all copied Brute. Peaked after a few weeks and everybody got bored and went after, like, High Class Games or Violins on the Draw or Ernest's Key Lime Sunday or Miss Diva – like more production value. Brute fell off the main screens with his stuff.

I say, What about Mealy? Looks to me like she couldn't just walk away.

It was a show, Jimmy says, and shrugs.

Yeah, but she was showing her life, I say. She was showing her world, like for real, and nobody cared.

It tanked and Brute wanted to start up the Geezer Academy and Training Center, Jimmy says. Ha! That was rich! One for the screens. Please. Mealy was just a prop like everything else.

A prop? I say. Didn't he care? Brute manipulated. He manipulated for himself. And then he cut her loose.

Maybe you're right, Jimmy says, dropping the subject. But you never know about anybody, you know?

269

Yeah, I say, that's true.

Jimmy leans his head back and closes his eyes. I am tired, I think. I don't know how much further to the pits. Could it be far? A light ash is still falling, and the street is dull and quiet. I doze off for a couple of minutes and when I wake up, Jimmy is hunched over his pad again, that cold glow washing his face. There's a shiv of brick jabbing my back and I move closer to him. He looks up, eyes bright. He has almost a flush.

Britt, he says, I'm on your site. I didn't know you were posting.

Huh? No way.

You just uploaded a piece.

Jimmy, you know that's not true. I've been next to you for hours.

Here, he says, take a look at this.

I take the pad and I see that there's an entry for Britt's Hip Bitts that just went up. Oh man.

THE HIP AND THE DEAD

Hey EB: I'm like out here with the gangs now. My main squeez JJJ just wasted a river of King Rats and we are on the move. I've got an MR-37, a hyperpulse, lots o flashbangz; JJJ packs a wallop with his collapsible rear-loader. You want to make it on the street, any street, these are what you gotta have. You wanna be hippest top dawg, you gotta walk with an MR-37. Get one today! You need a rear-loader that's super on top? Head on over to the nearest Excellon Street Depot for all your weaponry needs, maces to mace. You want to be Hip? Or you want to be dead?

Update: They may have taken out MATT, you can see us *here*. We're moving into a disguised marauder nest in that vid, just uploaded. They hit us hard and fast. We are plugged into CentOp now. Sats may PU Matt's blood type and cross check with his protein emissions. Will move south, now, see if we can nail these evil ones.

Remember: Evil's Hip when you're the evil; when they're the evil, they're just evil.

More later. luvya b

Jimmy, I say, who is this? What does it link to?

It links to that vid of us at Briggs's store, the one where the store blew away and we landed in the street in a shower of glass and rock. This here seems to be you, he says. If it's not you, how'd they access?

That's the least of it, I say. I'd never write that anyway. Whoever it is has wrecked my brand. Wrecked my brand. And what about me? Nobody knows the real deal. Nobody. And JJJ? Oh my god.

Yeah, and nobody's happy. Look.

I can see that people are going wild. The conversation on Zoneratti is out of control. They're talking about me? On Zoneratti?

@MattLoverXXX I told you she was gonna take a hike. Using all that shit to suck you in and then she goes lovey dovey with Matt D.AkcelRoads

271

@AkcelRoads No way. She just slit his throat. No luvy duvy. MD be daid.MarsUPPER1

@MarsUPPER1 Why don't you stuff it you can of labial shit.Anon

You guys really need 2 take a breather here. @MarsUPPER1 that means you, you sibilant twaddle. @AkcelRoads you are way behind curve, as usual. She lost it awhile ago. u c that back with the sandals and all that stuff re gretas and the p-pal shoutouts. move on mofo.CabinFever4

@CabinFever4 she worked w P 2 bring down hood. take out Matt. drew e/b in. we all n crowded theater & she threw bomb.AkcelRoads

@AkcelRoads I think u mean she yelled fire.CabinFever4

@ CabinFever4 she threw a frackin bomb. Who cares what she yelled?AkcelRoads.

@CabinFever4 now she bring down zone.Anon

Jimmy! They've got me taking down the Hood and throwing bombs and killing Matt. This is awful! I will never be a brand again. It is beyond belief.

@AkcelRoads u c new show i do btw? CabinFever4

@CabinFever4 wat chanel?AkcelRhoads

@AkcelRoads its ZoneDawgs N Hood streaming now.CabinFever4

@CabinFever4 That's a piece o shit. No wonder u r n it! lol MarsUPPER1

@MarsUPPER1 Not funny! Chk it out, or chk out when ur dune buggy sinks n 2 a mlm!!CabinFever4

This is what it's come to, I think. People just beating and hustling. You can't go out anymore without somebody laying some fantasy on you like jelly. You can't present. I give Jimmy his pad and close my eyes. Used to be just thug trolls. Now everybody is a thug or a punk if you don't buy their stuff or go along to get along.

What's that noise? Jimmy asks. You hear it?

I listen. You can definitely hear scuffling and scraping, but there's nothing on the street. I look up, back the way we came from Briggs's store. Nothing. But the sound is getting louder, like thousands of feet, scrabbling, shuffling. A thick and silent cloud of dust hovers in the distance beyond some building shells.

To hell with it, I say, and pull out my pad and begin a stream of the street. Jimmy inspires me. Or maybe Brute. O gawd.

Maybe we should move over behind that post, I say, nudging Jimmy. We pull ourselves up and over just as the first figures come into view, dragging legs, straggling along, their clothes like torn flags. I follow them with my lens as they trudge our way.

We are beyond the Ville, I narrate for the cam and fans, a real VO with a real scene. The streets have been empty. But this is happening now. You are seeing this as we do.

The figures move closer. Several of the guys are using old, splintery crutches. Their heads are wrapped

273

with bandages, dirty and bloodstained. They hobble down the street in line, in slow formation. No one says a word, they just limp along, gimpy soldiers in a losers retreat – right past us across the street. Nobody looks our way. Within moments they are gone. A limping band of brothers. The last guy, a battered cap on his head, a black patch covering his left eye, keeps looking back over his shoulder. They seem broken, defeated in the worst way. Seems like they've even lost their voices.

Those are not marauders, I say to Jimmy and the cam. We don't know who they are, where they came from or where they're going. This is just the street, the real street, on the outside.

There is a louder sound from the direction the figures came, a skittering, scratching sound, like a broadcast you can't quite tune in, and it grows, a ballooning static, until I see rats, thousands of them, a great frothy stream rolling over the cement. It's as though something has burst open and they're just pouring out, a rancid, spreading delta. Brown ones with the blackest eyes and points of needle teeth glistening in the half light; greys with emaciated legs and slithery tails, spittle splattering everywhere, hurrying past everything, little slimy missiles, a scavenging fleet with nothing to scavenge.

I pull my feet in and wrap my arms around myself and prop the cam forward, pointed out onto the heaving darkness. The rats fill the street, an undulating blanket, the earth disgorging its hungry little babies. They are a gale, a greasy nor'easter. We are rocks they crash over. We are bodies lost at sea. We are tied to their backs as they head deeper into bad weather. They are paying no attention to us. They brush my shins and hairs stand up all over my body, hedgehog spines. The rats just keep trotting along, eyes ahead, noses and faces twitching, crawling with bugs. Jimmy is frozen, a body lost to the dementia of fear.

This is our parade. This is our celebration – a spewing of rodents. Somehow I keep the cam steady. I close my eyes so tight. There are men and women I see in my head. They pick up their banjos and drums, their saxophones and xylophones, their trumpets, their basses, their clarinets. They are dressed all in swirling capes and feathers. Their faces are painted with the broadest smiles. The reddest lipstick smears from ear to ear. They dance in swirls – the tango, the rumba, the grand waltz. They hoe down and dive for the oyster. A real parade! On a rolling platform is a girl covered with glitter, a golden cape sweeping from her shoulders, black-red roses in her arms. She waves! Hello! Thank you! I love you! She flings a petal. It drifts to my lap as she passes by, a feathery kiss. The music is grand! The belle of the ball. O happy days! Lift me far above all this. I want to see everywhere!

No.

Not here. Not now. Maybe never.

This is for us. A man staggers by, laughing and shouting, and turns to me, pulls out his dick and pisses on my foot.

The rats have passed on. I can hear their gibbering receding.

Jimmy, let's go. They've stolen me. I will not exist anymore. I streamed that entire scene. Geez.

Jimmy looks at me. Morrie will have a fit, he says, putting his arm around my shoulder. We will get to the pits soon, I know. I need to check one thing. Let the rats move on. I've heard about those rat brigades. They move in giant regiments like that. Pluto told me about them, but I thought he was riffing.

What about those guys, the ones with the bandages?

I don't know.

He opens up his pad. I'm on your site now, he says. There's your stream! It's already looping. There are already hits. Look at those rats. Oh shit! He just stares for a minute. I think you need to see this.

Jimmy passes the pad over. There's my stream, I can see the hits coming very fast. But it vanishes as I watch. The stream just goes poof! Some kind of interference. But what grabs me is a Wabbit embed, a vid. It begins to play. Oh my god, there's Deb! She's wearing rags, what used to be that incredible velour vest? It looks like a garbage bag now. She's staring right into the cam.

Jimmy, where is this? This is Deb. Where is she? Deb! Where are you? I shout at her.

I can't tell, Jimmy says. It seems to be outside the Zone, though. Look at the light, all dead. Looks like she's got herself a street feed.

Deb just looks straight at me, her sad eyes red and swollen. Snot is dripping from her nose.

Britt, she says, Britt. I need you. Please. Help me. I don't want to be here. Britt. Britt. Britt.

And that's it. I start to cry. I just sob.

Jimmy. Jimmy. Help me, I say. She's desperate. I can't do this. I am so afraid. She's trapped.

Okay, he says, okay.

He pauses.

We have to move out now, he says.

I still have the pad in my hand. My stream opens up again. There is the street we're on.

Jimmy, the stream is back up on my site.

A rhythmic metallic sound begins faintly and grows louder. There's the cloud of dust rolling toward us, must be the gimpy soldiers. Do I want to watch this? Do I want to see all that again, the great rodent ocean?

We are beyond the Ville, I hear myself say, just as I said before, that's my VO! The cam is still focused down the street, in the direction of the sound.

The streets have been empty, I say. But this is happening now. You are seeing this as we do.

Far down the street on the screen I see small figures, sheathed in white, marching along, the gimpy, blood soaked guys with the white headbands? No, no gimpy guys. No band of brothers. They come closer and I see they are little ghosts from a children's tale, the diminutive white-sheeted dead. The front rows bear enormous banners uplifted on poles:

Triumph Over Occupation!

Then behind it:

Little Caesars Sporting Club

A third:

End of the Burning Season

And the last:

Victory!

I hear myself saying, Here comes the Victory Parade right now.

That is my voice!

We are reporting directly from the WHBS Studios, or I should say, the street, where these events are being beamed to you live. The Caesars have just come into view, right on schedule. Aren't they darling, James?

Indeed, says Jimmy's voice. This is one of my favorite moments in the celebration, he says. The Caesars have been presenting their colors for, what? As long as anyone can remember, that's for sure. And they are always a treat, Brittany. Here they are with their balloons, folks! Let's watch.

The ghastly little buggers glide by us like oil slicks, their white coverings completely concealing whatever might be inside, if anything. They could be little rat automatons for all we know. Their banners have precise lettering, as though stenciled in laser labs. The Caesars fill the street, a moving rectangle, a wavy white flag of twisted anonymity. The dead.

Jimmy's voice breaks in. The floats! he says. The Victory Floats are coming on. Now let's remember everyone that these floats are intricate in their symbolism. They represent not only the defeated, but serve as memorials for those who are no longer with us as well. A dual purpose that I always find moving, don't you, Brittany?

I do James. Look, there is the Grand Dragon, high in the air. If he were any more full of gas he'd float through the studio roof! What a marvel of vinyl construction, too. The Grand Dragon consists of some 800,000 square feet of plain reused mylar and good old-fashioned polymethyl methacrylate. He's decorated with ash and colorful wood dust collected by the Caesars themselves over the course of the burning season. Isn't he marvelous! So fierce! I think he's life size, too, James – that's what our reference notes say. The Caesars have outdone themselves this year.

Oh look, here come the Critters!

278

First into view, far down the street, is what seems to be a floating cow; a flock of chickens follow, enormous feathered bodies bobbing along.

Look, James! There's the brindle cow! And here come the bearded goats! Folks we are witnessing quite a magnificent sight here, all coming together right now! Are those, yes, I think we have the wolves now! Look at that fur, so grey and bristly. Grrrr! The beavers, too. Oh my goodness, I think I see the eagle! Yes! James, there he is! Look at the size of that bird! Wings a mile wide it seems. Not really, folks, just looks that way from here. A great spread of avian defeat. He took on the wrong guys when he took us on, right James.

You are certainly right, Brittany. It says here that these claw-based creatures once spanned the globe, ripping and tearing their way year in and year out. Not anymore! If you can't take the heat, stay out of the kitchen, right Brittany?

Ha ha ha, correct James.

Now this guy, wait a second, let me find it here, this guy was put together from some 90,000 Plugs® dyed with recycled Aqua Veet®. How they managed those vivid browns, greys, and taupes, I can't imagine, Brittany. And look at that beak! It's carved from Excellon DuneStone® by one of the Caesars' finest artists, L'il Wild Bill. Remarkable.

James, James: The Jungle Beasts are coming into view! Wait a minute, everyone, I have a correction to make, I'm told. The first float was not the brindle cow.

I didn't think so, Brittany, I was a little uncomfortable with that. What did we have first up with the Critters?

That was, I'm now told, a buffalo, and what a buffalo it was! Big and furry, just the way they used to be.

I feel completely satisfied just seeing him. Everyone, we made a mistake, plain and simple. And we apologize. This is the first year for the buffalo, standing in for the other range-based Critters. Over one million strands of Xytex® carefully woven into "fur" and "hair." What a marvel of our ingenuity! We are so sorry for the confusion.

I slam the pad shut.

No more! I can't stand it. Jimmy!

He blinks and looks up at me. What about the jungle Critters? We didn't see them all yet, he says. The monkeys and dart frogs and whatnot.

Jimmy's voice trails away. He looks at the closed pad and thinks for a moment. Shakes his head.

They drill into you, he says.

The road is quiet. No sign of rats or limping people. We begin to walk, well behind all of them. And my pad begins to buzz and vibrate. These people are relentless. I can't handle it, I can't open it. No no no! But I do.

Britt, that was not wise, that video you faked, not wise at all, Morrie says.

Faked? There's a lot more coming, you asshole. Get Deb and bring her in.

I'm pissed. I'm not going to show this guy any tears.

I've just about run out of patience, says Morrie. He's still in that control-room set up. Which makes sense, I guess.

I've just about had it.

You've run out of patience? I say. You've just about had it? None of this would've happened if you hadn't barged in. Everything was fine. Nothing couldn't be fixed. Nobody couldn't be found, or at least it looked that way. But then you stuck your face in, you and your bully partner, and now everything is falling apart.

The hell! Morrie says, cutting me off. Your friend skipped out on her own. She's the one who made that decision. She's the one who pulled out of town. She's the one who went wandering in the Zone. She's the one who got trampled in the mob. You're the ones who set the mobs going. You're the ones shooting subversive vids out into the sphere. I thought you had some sense. I thought you were the one who would be reasonable. I think I was wrong. That last stream you sent out – we've now intercepted it of course – was just ridiculous. We have you on the sats. We have your transmitting chip frequencies. We know where you are and where you're going. And I'm telling you now to stop. The P is anxious. The P is concerned about the Zone and about the corps and about the many franchises. Now listen to me, and listen very carefully.

You sound like an old vid, I say. Don't try and push me around. If you know where we are and where we're going, why don't you come on down and stop us? Why don't you just do that? You were a big deal in my rooms, playing with all my stuff, looking at this and looking at that. I even gave you a Mexicana glass for next to nothing. You don't care about any of that, do you? You could care less.

That's not true, Morrie says. The P gave you a huge shout out.

Jimmy has turned away from this and is looking up and down the road, like he doesn't want to be here.

And even if it is true, I can't allow this kind of disruption to continue, Morrie says. Your little chaos in the streets stream was already diverted before we could even get to it, by the way. We can't tell who has it, though we are working on that. In the meantime, we have dismantled your illusion, stripped it of its fantasies and put it back out there. So nice try, no cigar, as they said back in the day.

You are forcing us to take remedial action, he says. I have tried to avoid that. I argued that it was premature, that you would be back on board in no time, that you and Mr. Jones would be back on the tracks before you could say Jack Sprat. I said this is not a deliberate effort to muck up the system. Britt's not like that, I said.

Who did you say this to? I ask. Who's running your show?

Why, everyone, Morrie says, everyone who's a stakeholder. We've partnered with everyone you can imagine to keep this whole show on track, on the straight and narrow, afloat and on course.

Oh my god. Change who's running the show and we can talk. Or maybe just find someone who's running the show and we can talk. Get me a producer!

We should get going, Jimmy whispers in my ear.

Well, well, says Morrie. If it isn't Mr. James J. Jones, a fan. Mr. Jones, you're a reasonable fellow, I've always said so, and I've always treated you that way. I told Jewell, I said, Jewell this is a reasonable man.

Jewell said, Oh he has a snake inside him.

No, you are seriously mistaken, I said. We can talk with Mr. Jones. Progress depends on reasonable men.

What a load, I say.

Now, I'm asking you, Mr. Jones, can you please speak to Missy Britt? Talk to her. She is delusional at the moment, hysterical, broadcasting surreal videos which are causing great alarm to her other fans and to the Ville at large. It's the rumors, you know. They stir up things you can't imagine. We are facing a serious, serious disruption. Once you start disrupting, everything that had a comfortable niche rattles out and clatters to the ground. You've brought us all to a very bad place, as even you might imagine.

I really don't know what you're talking about, says Jimmy. We are out here in some place called the Flats. We haven't had anything to do with fans or the Zone or mobs. We've had nothing to do with any disruptions. We are on like a search, which you know. You know all this.

Jimmy has that glazy red look now. It begins with his ears and spreads across his cheeks as he stares at the screen.

Oh ho ho ho, says Morrie. Aren't we the jokester. That vid stream you fellas just broadcast was viewed with alarm by a lot of folks, even though we intercepted it. Where are you getting the morphing tools to create something like that? Those gimpy soldiers? That rat brigade? Please. Spare me the denials. You didn't pick those tools up in that store, did you? If you did, we'll have to take even more serious prophylactic action. Briggs has been a pain for years, waylaying outliers and what not. He drags people in, captures them and holds them. He entices them with treats and then he cooks and eats them. Sometimes he even uses force. He's about due, I'd argue.

That's it, I say. You are living on another planet, Morrie.

I'm right where I always am, he says.

283

I take my pad and slowly and carefully close it. Jimmy's face is flushed in the aftermath of the glow and he takes out his own screen and just holds it, like a doll.

Let's go, I say. Follow the rats.

We begin to shuffle along and I see that there are fewer and fewer buildings. It's not like stuff was built here and has collapsed. It looks as though there were fewer places to begin with. You can't see much because the half-light has grown even dimmer with the ashfall picking up. There must be some new fire out there somewhere, out beyond duneland. Dawn should be coming soon.

We walk along in silence. There are ribbons of crumbling cement paths and broken cement pylons or columns. Now and then there's a rusted clunker. Old maroon and grey pump housings with surfaces of dull polyethylene sit on splitting concrete pads. Brown grass knifes its way through every crack. Piles of vinyl form moraines that spread to the west and east. This is like some kind of prehistoric realm, a wilderness. Is this a wilderness? There are sure no coyotes or anything, except on the screens in the Victory Parade. Jimmy doesn't say anything.

Where is Papa's now? I wonder, looking around at the spreading decay. Where is the Deb who belted out Debrity? – Wanna be me! Wanna be me! Me! Me! Me! Thumpa thumpa thumpa thumpa! – Oh, so great! How she rode high up on the mountain with the P. – Life is no beach, we know! – What lyrics! She's vibrant, mutable, flexible, whatever you want to call it. Made for us.

Okay, you can say she's just a shell and we're all involved in a shell game. And that's true, I suppose. I mean, yes, it's true. But damn it! She's a hell of a shell, she holds oceans within. You can cup your ear to Deb and a whole universe opens up. You can hear multitudes. What didn't she contain? All there, all there in her secret garden.

Jimmy, when we find Deb, we have to heal her, like on the inside, where she really lives. She's given herself up to nothing. It's as though she's just emptied out. I know that feeling.

What, he asks. What feeling?

I never had any idea of Deb's secret place, I say, the place she wanted to protect from everyone, from her fans, from the screens, from all the grasping and gaping.

Jimmy stares. I look at him, his hair falling over his pale forehead, shoulders kind of hunching. Contained, tense. Being here, wandering the Flats, whatever the Flats are, has brought something back to me, something I don't remember, or maybe something latent, something hidden, something secret.

When I hold you, I say to Jimmy, it's a different kind of holding. When I look, it's a different kind of seeing. I never felt that before.

I reach out and touch his cheek and something invisible inside me wells up.

That's what Deb's been talking about, I say to him. The invisible stuff that makes us us, that puts us here, in the Flats, in the world. It's speaking to me, it's making itself known. I can see.

Jimmy looks uncomfortable. He looks away and around. He doesn't want to talk about this, about us, I don't think. Or what we could mean. I'm feeling a new ache. Jimmy.

What's making itself known is this empty place, he says, these streets. This isn't at all like the Westway

285

approach. This is all foreign. What a maze. They really know how to dislocate you.

Jimmy, you used to go to the pits a lot. You even knew the back way out of the Ville. What's with this that's so different?

Well, the locaters helped, you know, even when they were down or messed up. They showed you something about what was there. This is so broken up. So many angles. So many fronts and piles. It's more broken up, it seems, every day. Different languages, different customs like I told you. You can't even communicate sometimes anymore. I don't know. It's not what I'm used to.

Before he can continue, the rumbling begins, a grinding, cranking sound that seems to come from the very bones of the street. Please, no. Please, please, please.

What the hell, I say, and start to look around.

Jimmy says, Oh geez. I follow his gaze and I see them rolling toward us, dozens of Megas, maybe hundreds, all attended by little sweeper bots. They are coming right down the street, curb to curb, a cleansing phalanx.

What are they doing here? I say. There's nothing here but us and the rats and gimpy guys ahead somewhere.

I don't know, says Jimmy. He stares at the Megas.

Get over there, behind that broken pile of stone wall, I say.

We trot off the street into a deep lot, crouch behind the wall, and watch. The Megas and the little bots sweep by, whooshing and grinding. They are all crowned with orange wreaths of interlocking circles. Some kind of logo? I wonder. The Mega that cleaned up Jerry had one of those too. We wait several minutes for them to pass and then take to the street again, walking quickly. I can see the bots in the distance, but we are too far away for their sensors. The road curves around and they roll out of sight. But now I hear something else. The whoosh and grind has escalated. There is a crunch and bang, a chaotic whirr. Is that a shout?

Jimmy, are those shouts?

Sure seem to be, he says, and begins to slow down. I am caught between fear and concern. Jimmy says, It's getting a bit lighter, the sky is getting lighter, it must be close to dawn and we must be very near the pits.

But what about those awful noises? I ask. It sounds like somebody's in trouble. We should check that out, like now.

I begin to trot ahead as Jimmy slows. When I reach the bend in the road, I stop. It can't be.

Ahead is a wall, high and final. The road ends in a wall. No exit.

All the Megas are swarming in front of it. They've descended on something and are engorging, sucking it all in, every last bit. They're a mass of vacuuming, gnashing scrubbers. They'll continue until there is nothing left on the street, nothing at all. That's their nature.

Jimmy comes up. He sees the flock picking and scraping and sucking.

There's no other way to go on this road, he says.

The street's flanked by lowish, wrecked buildings. Piles of rubble form low bluffs running up to curbside. A cul-de-sac.

We have to back track and find an offshoot branching around this dead end, Jimmy says.

He turns abruptly and begins walking in the opposite direction.

Wait! Wait up! I run to his side.

We must have missed a turn, I say.

I hope so.

I'm sure we did.

He's walking faster now. We may be able to get around by going to that field with the stone wall, I say.

That's the wrong direction, he says. It's tricky down here.

We reach the lot and walk past the old stone pile. There is a narrow opening between some collapsed sheds or something, maybe they're cement; it's just wide enough to let us through. I was right!

Jimmy, what was going on with those Megas? I ask. What were they doing?

Cleaning, he says. That's what they do.

But what?

He doesn't answer. And I don't want to think about it. I don't even want to let my mind limp or float out into that territory. We have to stop for a moment while I take a few breaths.

It is getting noticeably lighter. I want to push those Megas out of my head, but I can't help but notice that there is nobody around, nothing moving, no signs of other life.

There, Jimmy says.

It's a small pathway threading between collapses and dank embankments. We move forward. The fit is tight and my arms are scratched from rock and splintery wood. My old khaki shirt with the ripped off arm patches is a mess, covered with dirt. And now there's cobwebs and stringy stuff hanging down on the narrowing path.

I don't know about this, Jimmy.

I stumble forward and grab on to his back. It is good just to feel another human being. A body. Our bodies. He stops and helps me up and over a couple of fallen timbers. He holds me for a moment. We move on.

As we come around a corner, the path opens up. We are on a low escarpment, a pile of dirt kicked up by construction or something, a little vista looking out over our land. And there they are, the pits.

Chapter Eleven

We are standing on a rise looking out over a prostrate landscape, flatness that seems to run forever in the dim early light, a tableland, a calm treeless sea of dirt reaching away in the rising sun. The brown endless crust is not yet shimmering in the dawn shadow, nor will it. The shifting dunes and collapsing piles and predatory winds are still, at least for now. This land is your land.

Its indifference is beautiful.

I have to say upfront that I expected shanties, a kitchen-sink mishmash of tin roofs and burlap and vinyl, a muddle of stick huts and boxes scattered in a confused tableau. Where are the people, black bags over their shoulders and boxes on their heads, stooping in their search for tidbits? Where the kids in rags – ragamuffins? – feet wrapped in tough plug packaging wound tight with wire, picking over mounds of trash in search of a treat? Where are the guys in the pre-pak area, muscled and sweating, carts stacked with desks and table chairs, broken lamps, cast-off screens, chipsets, carpeting fragments, old cloth stamped with a grinning President or a grieving Mizz? Where are the guys gathering every bit of scooped up nothing dropped off here, in the pits, at the tip of a blank dawn?

But no. None of that sentimental crap. No shanties, no vast piles of garbage, no swarms of broken people pecking at rancid stuff. Just a long loading dock platform fronted by waiting pallets, thousands of them it seems. Behind the dock, stretching its length way into the distance, a low flat building, elegant and ribbony, like an eel.

I don't see a single living thing.

There is a wide approach to the loading dock, a sweep of concrete, that extends far beyond our view to the right. Perhaps it runs forever, an impermeable open field leading to the last stop, here on the edge.

What's the story here, Jimmy? This isn't what I expected at all. Where're the pickers? Where's the junk? Where do we find Pluto? What about Aunt Rita? Where did those plugs crash down on her? Where was she trapped? Where did you go when you came down here? What is this place?

Jimmy is looking down, surveying the scene with an expression of relief, like he's just sighted a lost friend or found his way home after a heavy night carousing in the Zone.

Hold on, he says. This is the approach area, they take care of business behind the building, the long one there, that's the staging arena. But the setup has changed. I don't see pre-pak.

What about Pluto?

Lemme see.

Jimmy looks back and forth.

I think he would probably be in his usual spot out behind here, he says, pointing toward the back of the long building.

But I never actually went looking for him, Jimmy says. On a regular day, when you'd show up and head out back, you'd just run into people. There'd be people out here, too, of course. In back, that's where Pluto'd be. But they seem to have shifted pre-pak inside or something. Used to be out front here in the open. You could skim before everything moved inside the staging arena. But all the stuff in front is gone now, all the carts, dump corrals, chute mouths – all that stuff. Inside the building is where orchestration takes place.

Orchestration? The music of junk and castoffs?

What's that? I ask.

Sorting. Ordering. That's what they call it. Inside there. You can't get inside – too mechanical. Too dangerous. You'd be battered to bits.

I look back at the dock and building. It's amazing there's no security or anything. No fences. No Sentry. No signs or directions, no lights – nothing to indicate any kind of conscious activity or restrictions or anything forbidden. All is on auto-mode, no manual overrides. No intervention or supervision. But what the heck, it's all just waste.

The WRMS drones must be out back too. I don't want to dwell on them. They're nasty, bullying machines programmed to take what they can wherever they find it. I think for a moment of Aunt Rita, the Gurney Boy's lost limbs, Jerry. This is where Auntie Rita met her end, probably out back. This is where Jerry and the Gurney Boy lost arms and legs. All still now, a simple landscape.

I look down. There are no paths or trails from up here, not that we're all that high, but to descend we'll have to walk in switchbacks. I want to get down as fast as possible. I want to be down now.

Come on, I say, and begin walking. Small clumps of dirt tumble down from where I plant my feet. Jimmy stays for a moment, just savoring. I look up and he seems a captain on a ship casting his eye over the calm waters at the welcome sight of land.

Come on, I say again, it's getting lighter. He follows in my tracks. Back and forth, back and forth, we move lower and lower without difficulty until we are down.

The access area is enormous. It extends well beyond the rise we just descended. There is a rumbling and a humming coming from what must be the far end, beyond sight.

What's that? I ask after we are down. Doesn't sound good.

Drones, says Jimmy. Sweepers. They gather in some kind of set formation and then move forward for off-loading at the dock. Some just move directly inside, the big ones do, maybe some others. It's all programmed.

I can't see a thing other than the building and dock and the vast concrete access approach. The whole scene seems like a flat immobile canvas, empty, waiting for the first stroke. It is very clean. I shudder for some weird reason. It's so cold.

Jimmy, I say, what if we can't find Pluto? What if he's not here? What's the plan then? Do we have a plan?

He'll be here, says Jimmy. He's always here.

I reach over and touch his face. He looks down. We are together in this. It is our mission. It is our reason. We will find Deb and then we will find ourselves in some new situation. I don't know where it will be. I don't know what it will be. But what's done is done. It's over. We need to figure how to rebuild in our own way, for our own good, for our own lives. That's what I think. We'll take what we've discovered inside of our true selves and use it.

I just put my arms around Jimmy and hold him.

Don't move, I say, just stay for a sec.

He tenses and then slumps a bit, as though I am weighing on him.

We have to be ready, I say. We have to stay focused on finding Deb.

If we don't, Jimmy says, we have to move forward and consider what's next.

What's next is we find Deb, I say. That's next. Then we figure out the next thing and the next.

Think about it, Jimmy says. Outside the system? Well we've seen that. Geez, there is no outside the system, I'm telling you.

And it's true, I guess. Failure and collapse, what's abandoned, the geezers, the rodents, the sweepers, the empty streets and marauders, the P, the producers, Morrie, Mrs. Petri – the whole thing. It's all woven together. Like they need all the dysfunction and loss to keep it going. How else are they gonna to do what they want to do, whatever it is, if they don't have excuses? If nothing's screwed up, there's no need to fix it, you know? No need for us to all pull together. We're out here on the edge, and what I realize, what I just realized, is that they want us out here. They need us to stir up stuff so they can reconfigure. We're doing a job for them. We are their workers. All in for the screens. A show and a lesson.

But I don't care. What's more powerful is finding Deb. What's more important is my feeling for Jimmy. I never felt anything like this before. We should be together. I never needed another person before; I never knew I needed a person. And now I need two.

Jimmy, we should be together, I say. That's completely outside the system. They can't control that. That's you and me, that's what this is about – you and me searching for Deb. Why we're doing it is for us, not for the system, the P, Morrie, Jewell, Brute, the screens, or anything else. We are inside our selves.

Jimmy says, They know that too.

The rumbling is continuous and growing. The building and dock are still.

Okay, Jimmy says, we should get off to the side here and head for the rear pit area behind the building and the dock.

He walks over to the left. There are no trees or bushes or anything around here. It seems to be all cleared or all dead or something. The cement access area seems never-ending, and where we are, off to the side, is just as hard and desiccated – gravel laid down, asphalt spread over a slight rise, packed dirt on the berm we just descended.

This seems an ancient gathering area, I imagine, continental tarmac where machines from beyond settled in and disgorged their passengers and took on new ones. Or perhaps it was a vast approach for what might have been stores way back, a run up to shop fronts that might accommodate hoards of people in search of stuff. They'd need to get a running start. But there are no stores. No passenger vehicles. The low building worms off and disappears into the distance. The rumbling gets even louder, and closer. Jimmy picks up his pace.

We want to be around the side here when they hit the dock for discharge and off-loading, he says. We want to be beyond sensor range. In the back, you got to keep an eye out for WRMS drones, though they're usually not a hassle – they pick off stuff in the pre-pak area and the pits.

There is a tremor in the ground, a kind of nervous tremble, and when I look back out across the access area, I see a mechanical army, it extends beyond sight, rolling forward in what appears to be a series of perfect rhombi, lozenges maybe, followed by other trapezoids and squares. The geometry is difficult to see, although I can sense its perfection. The rumbles and whirls wrap us in cloaks of sound as sweepers and cleaners move slowly forward in a careful marching pattern of timed advances and idles.

This is the rhythm of work, the way the factories must have run back in the day, back maybe in the times when the tunnels were used and the workers stood at their spots moving and stopping in synch with some unseen master – a timer, a clock, a machine. On the screens, there is no rhythm, nothing but the nervous push of now, herky jerky, no pauses, no stops, no idles, and I realize I have now stopped myself just to watch this ancient dispassionate dance of the machines. The old patterns of making things mirrored in the march to the dump. I feel something in it.

Britt, Jimmy calls, and I have to trot to catch up with him. There are so many. How could there be so many? How could there be so much waste in one night? I see Jimmy is heading for a smallish metal boxy structure well off to what must be the southeast end of the building. He gets behind it and crouches down. I do the same.

Takes just a few minutes to reach the pit area in back, says Jimmy, watching the advance of the sweeper drones.

I see some are simply carriers – they have nets and platforms that hold large or awkwardly shaped items – there's one with part of an old motor, one with some kind of knobbed boxy screen device, one with a battered fridge. These sweepers seem like models moving down a runway, displaying the latest fashions. There is a tubey hat and there a gown of wires and cylinders; there a draped cape of netting with wooden pins and fishy looking critters dangling from it; there a corsage of crisscrossed yellow signs featuring black stick figures holding hands. What style! All headed for the pits. Oh my god.

They'll lock into the removal runway belts, Jimmy says, studying the mechanics at the front of the building. The belts pull most of them through orchestration and then out for dumping behind the building. You have to be really careful in back. There are dozens of Nutri-Waste chutes that funnel underground, beneath here where we are and then under the dock and building and out to the pits in back. That waste stuff comes in from the Ville real fast. Just blasts into the pits. They flush when necessary. Aunt Rita should have known that.

I don't say anything – I'm too caught up in watching this dance. It's almost like a carnival ride. Each machine approaches the building and attaches to a moving transit chuteway. One after another they move forward, lock in, and whip around into the inside, a funhouse ride of waste removal. Whee! Above the rumble I hear crashes from somewhere off, somewhere I can't see.

Jimmy says, They've started to dump out back. We'd better get moving. He rises and begins to trot around the building. I follow. I am wasted myself.

As we round the corner, I see the trench in the ground. It is huge, a broad shallow gully gouged into the earth, cleaving into the distance. It must run the entire length of the building. Machines are lined up along the edge of a platform above it disgorging packages from their guts. Their entire fronts swing open; square, compressed tumors, grown through the night's travels, are pushed forward and then propelled, sailing in earthbound arcs down into the long pit, gifts for the rising sun. Light glints off the drones, they gleam like shining works of art greeting the new day. What offerings they bear!

I am captured by this scene. Their front panels snap shut and the belts continue to whisk them around and back through the building. What a show! This has been running without missing a performance since I don't know when. Down in the trench I see one guy standing way back, looking at the first droppings.

Is that Pluto? I ask Jimmy.

No, I don't know who that is. They've changed the set up a little since I was last here. Pre-pak used to be open and there were pickers out front and more back here, like I said. Where is everybody? See those openings, the big round culverts right beneath the platform lip? Those are the Nutri chutes. All the Nutri-Waste runs from the Ville and spills out from there. You use your Nutri recycler in your room? This is where it ends up – all underground till it comes out here.

That's where Aunt Rita got nailed? I ask, looking down into the catchment area. She was down in that trench?

I guess, Jimmy says, wrinkling his forehead. Then over on the other side? That's where the WRMS drones funnel in for pick up of reusables, which is just about everything as far as they're concerned. We can snatch like individual things – old chipsets, motors, stuff like that, some edibles. The WRMS drones want that stuff – they take about everything. It's all reused, actually.

All?

Yeah.

I think about this for a second.

I don't know about this, Jimmy. I'm getting a kind of sick feeling again.

What?

Like all that stuff loops back to the Ville.

Yeah, but it's reprocessed. Nutri takes care of it. See those tankers over there?

He points to roller tanks lining a far edge of the pit.

Those are Nutri haulers for reusable collections.

He stops and says, Hold on, there's Pluto.

Oh yes! I say. Oh yes! Yes!

I see a thickish little guy coming toward us along the edge of the trench. He's wearing old denim overalls and work boots, a red bandana around his neck. Very retro, I think. He walks with a list and a roll.

Come on, Jimmy says. We get up. The little man sees us and stops, but then he seems to recognize Jimmy and continues walking.

I didn't know if you'd be here, Jimmy says to him.

Where else would I be? the little man says, looking at me.

This is Britt, Jimmy tells him.

I know who you are, Pluto says. I hear y'all've caused quite a ruckus. They've got the Zone locked down now tighter than usual, I've heard, and dragon choppers are everywhere over the Ville. Used to call them whirlybirds. Ha ha.

He cackles.

Haven't seen a heavy time like this since I don't know when, Pluto says. Gonna be kind of tough to move around for awhile. I were you, I'd go to ground.

We can't, I say. No frigging way. We have to find our friend – she's disappeared. That's what started this mess. She was lost, shed her brand, shed her image, her sites, and just went wandering. We have to find her. We have to! She's in danger of losing everything! Jimmy thought you may have heard something. You may have some idea where she is. Deb. Have you heard anything about Deb? The President's Girl? The Boy's Lost Girl? Deb. Debrity. Glamour – that kind of thing?

Pluto listens. Glamour? I'd go to ground, if I were you, he says again.

You've got to help us. There aren't any options, I say.

I look at him. He's taking my measure, he's heard of me, I think. What does that mean anymore? What does anything I have ever done in my whole sorry life mean to someone living on the edge of the pits, on the edge of where it all ends? Is he in the system with everything else, like Jimmy says?

Do I amuse him? Do I entertain? Am I a star? The sky is so full of stuff, you can't see the stars. Who is this Pluto, anyway? He's seems kind of like Briggs, whatever that means. Is he an enabler of travelers? An outlaw? A guardian and scavenger? Are outlaws part of the show? Do they even exist?

I shake it all away. The main thing is to get Deb. Find her, and extract her.

You're not gonna find her, least not in the current climate, Pluto says after looking me over. I heard of lots of disappearances in recent days; not a good sign. There was a guy down here – was it yesterday? – lost some gal. She went to bed at night; gone the next morning, just a smudge of plug on her pillow. That's mighty unusual. A gal in a bed, for gawd's sake. Another guy come by looking for his pal. Hey Jimmy, that'd be your friend Brutus11. Yeah, he was down here looking for his squeeze, Melinda. I had to say, he wasn't gonna find her. She's gone. He's probably gone now too. Said he come down through the Zone in the middle of them dislocations and disruptions. A tsunami, he calls em.

Jimmy says, Brute? Down here? What do you mean he wasn't going to find her? Melinda is around somewhere. Where's Brute now? What do you mean he was in the Zone? What disruptions? Where's he gone? What'd he say?

Settle down, says Pluto. Look, the plain fact is that once somebody gets to the point of checking down here, there's usually nothing left to find. You know that. Bad juju, they call it. Gone's gone. It's been happening long as I remember, my pappy too. When the system begins to really wobble, they take out more and more. Disappearances, yeah. Corrects the balance, eliminates the issues.

Pluto voices the word issues like a bad sneeze in a dusty room, and I don't want to hear this anyway. I say that. I tell him straight out that I don't want to hear it. Just because somebody gets lost in the Hood or the Zone doesn't mean they're lost to the world.

These are the pits, you know, he says. What are you gonna find here? Nobody disappears for seven years and then reawakens to the world with the kiss of the P, or something. Not down here.

He cackles some more, like Briggs.

Humph! he goes. Sorry honey. I'm saying there are no magic touches. People disappear for reasons that you can't figure and for no reason. Let me tell you, when the P's boys and the big dawgs or whomever get afeared they don't try to find the lost princess or go after the wicked witch, honey.

What does that mean? We are talking somebody lost like in the Hood or the Zone.

Pluto looks exasperated.

This is the way it works, he says. So they see something to fear in the Zone. Or in the Hood. Systems are dislocated or malfunctioning. Product isn't moving. They send somebody in to take a look and he runs out screaming, Oh my god! It's awful! And somebody else steps up and says, I can handle it. And heads into the Hood and sees whatever it is, flips out, and runs away. Another guy comes along and says, These guys are twits. I can take care of business. They send him in, he takes one look, and tries to work his magic, fails, flees. So then the P gets together with his pardners and they come up with a plan, Hey, nobody can deal with the problem? Here's a plan: We'll remove the issue, eliminate the question, burn down the Hood from the outside in. No more problem. And so they do. The end. That's the story. That's the story for all of us. There's an issue, it gets yanked like a tumor. Cauterized, burned out, like the fires in the west.

Oh come on, I say. That's ridiculous. Nobody's torched the Hood. We were just there. We walked out last night.

Suit yourself, says Pluto. Happens over and over. Lots of ways to torch the Hood without a general conflagration. You seen the screens. Although, now that you mention it, I've seen an awful lot of ash whirling around lately, haven't you? Kind of late in the season for that.

By the way, speaking of last night, there was a guy come round looking for you. I heard him talking to Serbs-R-Us, my bud. Serb didn't tell him nothing, kind of scared him, I think. Got the impression your friend – Deb, her name? – Deb was out of the Zone, but who knows where. Somewhere else in the forest. Of course, mind you, there is no forest. Just the dark.

I try to wrap my mind around this. I go, So like you think she may be out of the Zone?

Sure, he says. Leastwise, that would be good for you trying to find her whereabouts. The Zone is the realm of the impossible. In the Zone, forget it. The Ville is the realm of the maybe possible. Here? We just make do with what comes our way.

So how do we make do?

Stay away from the corps, he says. Stay away from the P. Stay away from the Hood. Stay away from showers of plugs. Stay away from everything. Be invisible. Go to ground. Wait for the rebalancing.

That's not helpful, I say. We will find Deb, with or without your help.

Pluto shrugs again.

Who was this guy who came round? Jimmy asks.

I already think I know, but I don't say anything.

I don't know, Pluto says. Some foreign guy? Maurice or something?

Morrie? I offer.

Yeah, that's the one. Nice guy, considering. Said he needed to find some folks, I believe. Serb told him that nobody stayed here, too calamitous nowadays. This Maurice fella? He'd be one of your fix-it guys for the P, I believe. Seemed to know the drones are going after everything in their Focused Activity Areas now. Didn't seem to bother him none. Didn't go running away, either. That's a fact. Those FAAs have become no-go zones too.

No, says Jimmy.

Yeah. Focused Activity Areas have become forbidden territory. You get scooped up in a nanosec and then that's it. Must have reprogrammed the bots. Waste is more generously defined nowadays then it used to be, if you can believe it. Ha ha ha.

That's awful, I say. Then I think of Jerry and think I don't know anything.

There is a particularly loud crash and we all look over at the sweepers. Larger ones are moving along the lip of the platform. They slide quickly, stop, snap open, disgorge their innards skyward and down into the pit – kaboom! – snap shut, move on. Repeat.

Jimmy watches. Where is everybody? he says.

Pluto shakes his head. There've been disruptions here too. That's what I'm saying. That's what Serb was telling this Maurice fellow. Anyway, they moved pre-pak inside. Last week was it? Last month? Awhile ago. They sent in extra regiments of WRMS drones, scared the bejaysus out of everybody. Ha ha. One morning these little buggers just appeared, swarms of them. We were all down the pit and they just swooped in like a pack of hyenas. Haven't scrambled so fast since they started flushing the plug shoots into the catchment pool. I think they got Ranse and maybe somebody else. Haven't seen him since. It was about as gross as it gets.

What do you mean, they got Ranse? I ask.

Pluto looks over at me and says, Oh, they just knocked him for a loop. Don't know what happened then, honey, cause I was climbing up the side faster than a speeding bullet. Ha ha. Don't want to get whacked by WRMS. All I can tell you is I haven't seen him since.

What about you? I say. What are you doing here? Who's that other guy down there? Would he have any info?

Where else am I gonna go? Pluto says. This is what I do. I stay around here. Pick up this and that. Live over beyond the approach runway. Me and Serb, we're about the only ones around last few days. People been coming in asking did you see this, did you hear that. Haven't heard nothing, really. They stay for a bit and go away. That guy down there, I don't know. Came around during the night and just looked over the pits, like some kind of mourner.

Jimmy reaches into his pocket.

I just remembered, he says. I have this for you. It comes from Briggs? At the store?

He hands Pluto the crumpled piece of green paper.

Pluto takes it with a look of surprise.

Well now, he says, I didn't know you'd been by Briggsy's. He puts the paper in the front pocket of his overalls.

This changes things a mite, he says. Come on, I gotta get something down here. Then we'll talk a little more.

There are more crashes. This has to be recorded, I realize. Maybe there's interest out there in what's happening at the end of the line. Hey, Aunt Rita thought so. I pull out my pad and begin to shoot the scene, like I did on the street with the forlorn gimpy soldiers and the river of rats.

Even bigger machines are moving above and disgorging. A great crash! Is that an explosion? Powerful jets of brackish liquid are erupting from the Nutri drains. Great arcing rainbows of plug waste, liquefied, viscous, spew out and splash into the catchment area. A slopping lake is forming down there, rippling with little Nutri waves. Barrel-like machines move forward, seemingly from nowhere, dip their plastic snouts into the trough and suck it dry. They roll to the back and shoot their loads into the waiting Nutri tankers. The catchment area is left boney white after just a few seconds. I follow the bots with the cam.

The march of sweepers has paused above and the first WRMS drones appear below.

Careful, says Pluto. They are nasty.

I add a little VO: WMRS cleanup bots have just appeared at the pits.

I watch and shoot as they swarm over the day's first piles, sweeping it all in, it seems. But no, they leave some larger items – too big, I guess. Another wave of hefty machines kicks in, moving out from the base of the building, these must be what Jimmy calls assemblers. They scoop up everything left behind. All goes into the waiting tankers.

Look, Jimmy shouts, and points to the lone figure at the far side, the guy we saw when we first looked out over the depression.

A lone picker, I say into the cam mic, is working the pits this morning.

The guy sees the drones and begins to scramble toward the back slope. A contingent is moving toward him. They form a semicircle and close in.

Holy shit, I hear from somewhere. The drones surround him, a constricting wall, vacuuming and sucking, and when they back away and move toward the tanks, the man is gone. There is nothing. They've swept him up like the rest of the reusables. I'm speechless. The cam just keeps recording the lifeless pit.

This is what's happening, says Pluto.

I begin to turn the cam on him. He pushes it away. He is grim now.

Reprogrammed for sure, Pluto says. There used to be a question about what was dropped off here – you used to wonder. Why they sweeping so much? Serb and me, we don't wonder anymore. Needs are great and growing. Everything gets swept up and everything gets sucked in.

What happens to all this, I ask Pluto. He is dead silent, his face a dark hole, a look that says he wants to go away somewhere.

Sheesh, he says, finally. There's beauty in it, honey. It all gets reprocessed and reused. You gotta admire it. There's an old saying, you can't get something from nothing. Wrong! Everything comes from nothing nowadays. Everything is coming from what has disappeared. That's the system.

Jimmy this can't be happening. We are not here. We did not see what we just saw.

Pluto says, Let's get down there while we can. See that chip pile? He points.

Before I can even say Deb, what about Deb, he's scampering down the sloping trench wall headed for a little pile the drones must have missed. Jimmy scrambles and slides after him, and without thinking, I'm moving down there too.

We are all three in the trench. I look up at the drones on the lip. They tower over us. I'm shooting, of course, as I thread my way through junk left by the first pass of WRMS bots. Lots of bricks and rocky rubble, actually, tons of it, fragments thrown off by the collapsing Ville. Most of the electronics and polymethyl is already gone; some device parts are scattered about.

I pan over this final landscape – the last landscape, you know? – showing the now-distant and waiting WRMS drones, and then up to the long line of towering sweepers, still paused for some reason on the lip. They seem like stout bollards, staunch at the edge of the cliff above.

Actually, looking up from below ground, they are tombstones, settled in, marking our descent.

Pluto reaches his coveted chipset and picks it up. Not bad, he says to Jimmy. Could use it to fashion a DBS platform.

You need another two, Jimmy says, looking around at the ground. Here and there are some wires tangled in the stony fragments.

It's a start, Pluto says. He pulls a thin sack out of his pocket, drops the chipset in and hangs the sack from a big button on the side of his overalls. I'm panning slowly across the line of paused bots above with my cam. I'm live streaming, I realize. I should tell people what this is, like more formally?

We are now in the pit area, I say. All is quiet. The morning dump has just begun. We have just witnessed

WRMS drones surround and sweep up a man seeking to climb out of the pit. He has been processed and removed. You heard right. Processed and removed and deposited.

Even as I say this, a new grinding whirr fills the trench.

There is some activity among the sweeper drones, I say, a VO for the few who may be seeing this vid. These sweepers are here to drop off their nighttime treasures, what they've captured in a night of cleaning under the P's Fragrant Streets Program (FSP). The night's waste all ends here. All the junk you guys toss has to go somewhere. Just don't come down here to take a look, you may be reprocessed yourselves.

I feel a tug on my arm and pause the stream.

Pluto is looking at me. You need to take a hard look at what we're dealing with, he says.

What do you mean?

Shoot it for what it is, he says. And don't shoot me.

I'm flummoxed by this.

Pluto sighs. Everything from the street comes here, he says. Everything. Everything is picked up, carted off and recycled. Waste doesn't exist. Junk doesn't exist. We call it the pits. They call it the Reusable Catchment Area (RCA).

Waste doesn't exist? I say.

No way.

The sweeper drones up above are moving again, and a new line stretching above us is rumbling in, big ones, Megas. I am shooting these behemoths above, their boxy bodies and domed caps. The changing of the guard.

This new regiment, I see, has those orange tiaras, a chain of three broken circles laid over a fourth, just like the one that swept up Jerry and the ones that moved past us toward the gimpy soldiers and parade of rats not too long ago. Now I realize, as they loom above me, that these are the real marauders, the ones who rule the nighttime streets, the ones who own the Hood, the Zone, the Ville, the Flats and every other place we are. We are cleaning up ourselves.

I am shooting them from below as they slam to a stop. Their fronts open.

Move back, Pluto shouts. Get as far back as you can.

He pushes me away, even though we are nowhere near the drop area. I stumble toward the rear wall and turn back, shooting all the time. The Megas are poised. Their front cabinets burst open and enormous compacted packages are cannonaded up and out, crashing down all about us, a pyroclasmic display the likes of which I have never seen.

At the same time, the Nutri chutes erupt again. We are under assault from the junk we've made. It is erupting from within us, I think. The pyroclasts crash down into the pits, some splash in the Nutri waste catchment area. The assault lasts only a few seconds. The Megas snap shut and move out. The barrel machines in the pit wheel up, their hardened proboscises distending for intake. I have been shooting this entire time, capturing these final moments of last night. I've caught the gummy Nutri fountain, its brown gook bubbling and glopping in the catchment area. I have the barrels sucking it all in, eager bugs gathering nourishment. I track them as they lurch to the waiting Nutri tanks to discharge their treasure, pollinating the tanks, insuring the continuation of the species – their species, and ours.

They withdraw, fading away until the next eruption.

I turn my attention to the packages, now settled on the ground. One has come to rest five or so meters from us. I aim the cam directly at this squarish discharge, a jumble of wire and unidentifiable junk. I zoom in closer. Is that a work boot, its sole facing out for inspection? There is a large round hole in the heelless sole. Is that a broken end of a crutch, its padding stripped, no comfort needed? I pan to another package. It appears to be full of red-splotched whitish rags. Tips of what seem to be rat tails stick out all over, hairs or the snap ends of whips, thorny rodent nipples offered for display in a dump.

I can't move. The camera is frozen in my hand. The hairs, the rags, the boot. Oh geez.

Get out! Pluto shouts, and I see the WRMS bots revved up and jostling across the rubble. Out of the pit. Go!

We are close to the side and far away from the machines. We are up above and safe in a moment. I turn back and shoot what I know is going to happen. They gather up the leavings, the dreck, the dross, they gather up the packages, Jerry and the rats and the gimpy soldiers, they gather up everything from the compressed night. I shoot it all, speechless. They move almost in synch to the tanks, a rolling parade over the rubble. They halt, offload, withdraw. We watch in silence.

That was last night's catch gathered up and deposited into the tanks, I VO finally. Whatever was on the street and couldn't move fast enough, whatever was out of place, whatever was moving in the night, and whatever was still, all now tanked up and ready for its return to the Zone, the Ville, the Hood, and all the other places under the P's umbrella. These are the Fragrant Streets delivered to your doorstep and your kitchen shelves.

311

I stop shooting and just stand there. This is the circle of life.

The pad buzzes, again. What's the use? What's the friggin use? I open it.

Britt, wrong move, says Morrie. Definitely the wrong move. Wrong, wrong, wrong. Why do you persist? We have intercepted that absurd stream. There's nothing more I can do. I have made the case that you and Mr. Jones are salvageable, reusable, but no one finds my arguments acceptable. The feeling here is that there is no more slack to cut. Mr. Jones may be able to return, but they are definitely unhappy with you and I have to say that I can't argue with them anymore.

I say nothing and close the pad.

Jimmy is standing beside me. I turn to him.

Why can you return? We're in this together.

Jimmy looks down and kicks a polymethyl blob with his clod.

They need me, I guess. There's always a reason. I give them something they don't have, or do something they need but can't do themselves. I don't know. What do I do? Maybe they see me as a safety valve. I give people stuff that satisfies them. You give them something that makes them unhappy or afraid or full of emptiness – and now doubt.

Why? I say. I was just living and dealing. That's all I did.

I don't know, says Jimmy.

I begin to sob again. This is just too much. Jimmy puts his arms around me. Oh I need him! I need him in some indefinable way I've never felt before, a way that reaches deep into my own struggling inside self. He is already letting go, though, already pulling away, already loosening his grasp before it is fully formed, a look of confusion on his face. It is at that moment, a moment of tentative certainty, that we hear the sound, the thwacka thwacka. We both look up.

To the northeast, I see them coming in, choppers low to the ground. Maybe half a dozen? They are moving fast.

Shit, Pluto says and begins to hurry away from the pits. He begins to run toward the building. He turns. Get away from there! Head for the building, they won't be able to detect you beneath the canopy.

Let's go, I say to Jimmy, and begin to run.

But he stands there in the open, just looking up, his face flushed.

Jimmy! Hurry! Snap out of it! He turns toward me and then looks back at the choppers, now alarmingly close. He looks back at me. He is unable to move.

Please! Get going!

He looks again at the machines swooping in and back to me, caught in what seems like indecision or fear or just plain crazy shit, and then he turns and runs toward me. He runs fast. He moves over the hard dirt. He is like a gazelle as the net drops over him and he is swept up, caught in the tangles of unbreakable polymer, lifted high up, high above the pits, high above the building, above me, above our land. He struggles and flails as he is sucked toward the innards of the chopper. Faintly, it reaches me on the receding winds, before he disappears through the black hull hole: Britt, Britt, I feel, like I ...

The machine veers north as I watch. No no no no no

Chapter Twelve

I am numb.

Jimmy! I watch the chopper hurtle through the gently falling ash toward the horizon. It dwindles and dwindles, a dying match, until there is nothing left but a smoky absence in the north, stitched with distance. Its emptiness reaches back and opens within me – a pitiless hole so close, so deep, nothing can sew it, nor salve it. Not even ash flurries can fill it.

Jimmy. Jimmy. I stand, arms dangling, lifeless things; they are dead wires connected to nothing.

Pluto grabs me. Forget him for now, he says. We have all these others, swarming.

I look and see the other machines circling over the pits. Pluto and I are flat against the long building, beneath a canopy and behind a post. We are invisible from above. Along the lip that runs the length of the gash of pit, the Megas continue their conga, a new line has just moved into place for discharge.

The choppers whack away in the air, their gyres widening.

Packages explode from the Megas. Their front flaps snap shut, and they move out. Another line moves in. The pit is swarming with drones. They bump and grind over to the tankers. The choppers circle and circle, hungry birds.

This is an unending loop.

Wait em out, says Pluto. Wait the choppers out.

I say nothing. I can wait forever, you know. I am not here. I am not here at all. I am in my room with Jimmy. We are sitting in the front, bottles of Veet half full. Deb is there. She's telling us that the P will rescue the Lost Girl. She says everyone will pick up on his generosity and concern. She says it is a perfect ending to the drama. She is excited and her usually sad eyes are full of light.

Where are you, Deb? Will you meet up with Jimmy? Are you sitting at my table? Are you waiting for me? Are you in the street? Are you one of those tumorous packages bursting into the pits?

Why, oh why didn't I say no. No, Deb, this is not the right move. This is going down a bad tunnel. No. I didn't. Why didn't I see?

There will be no more meetings around my table, I think. There is no generosity coming from the P. There is nothing.

I remember. I remember it all in my brain and in my body. My body! I remember my friends, their bodies, their minds, their talk:

Jimmy says, Are you sure you really want to go through with this? Do you have a plan B?

There's no need, Deb says. This is too perfect. It can't miss. This will be the ultimate brand, the brand that lasts forever. A brand you can live in and live on!

I remember. Oh, yes I do.

Tears are running down my cheeks. I've never sobbed so much in my life, my long, long life. I open my eyes. Pluto is there, watching the choppers from behind the post. They are like aerial spiders, or what aerial spiders might have looked like.

How can we wait them out? Why should we? What's the point? They will swoop in. They will wrap us in polymer winding cloth and loft us to wherever it is they've taken Jimmy. Some reprocessing facility, probably. Maybe they'll take pity and dip us in vats of resin, let us float in the pure muck of our salvation. There is no way out. I am full of the darkest space, all closed.

My pad is buzzing and buzzing now. I can feel its vibrations in my pocket. My body absorbs them until my whole self is a buzzing column of flesh. I am nothing beyond that buzz. It rasps through me, fills me, drains me, leaves only a rattle. I take my pad out and look at its black surface. It is calling me. It is my Miss Diva back from the early days at camp. It is my Mrs. Petri. It is my Morrie. It is my everything.

I throw it on the ground and smash it hard with my heel. I pick up a broken brick and bring it down with all my strength. The screen cracks into slivers that splatter out over the ground. There is the sliver of Zone, there the sliver of Hip, there the slivers of Plugs and Mizz and Zoneratti and Morrie and Jewell and, yes, the President and Me. They scatter across the cement, they spew away from me. They are shattered here at the edge of the pits.

Pluto watches me, a look of solemn approval and maybe alarm on his face. I bring the brick down again and again until there is nothing left but bits and pieces of glass and plastic and pseudo-metal. That's what I have – busted bits sprayed helter skelter.

Probably a good idea, says Pluto after a moment, although what a shame to lose those circuits. Serb and I could rig up something they couldn't track. How'd that be? You could track them, but they couldn't track you. No chip ID. No frequency ID. That's what you need.

317

I don't answer. I am on my hands and knees, head down, brick in my hand. The choppers are now lifting up and widening their surveillance circles.

See, says Pluto, you killed your signal. You killed your ID. You killed your world. They don't have anything to pick up on. You are your own frequency. You've disappeared yourself. Ha ha. He cackles.

I know, I say. That was the idea, if there was an idea. What's to link to anymore? It's all gone. There's nothing left.

I toss the brick aside and sit. I am crying, of course. Tears are streaming for all that's lost, all that's vanished, all that I'll never know. I'm crying for Jimmy and for Deb and for myself and for the pathetic nothingness of this run-up to now, a mass of nothingness.

Well, I wouldn't say that, says Pluto.

Is he trying to comfort me?

You're here, he says. You've just pulled out a bit, you might say. You've stepped outside the spotlight. You're off the stage. You know, Serb and me, we got non-trackers, he says.

He pulls a pad out and says, Take a look. One of these babies lets you follow them. Nothing goes out, though, to home in on. No tracks. As far as they're concerned, you don't exist.

He punches in and the screen lights up.

BREAKING! BREAKING! BREAKING!

See, says Pluto, they already shot your news all over. Ha ha.

BREAKING! HOT! HOT! HOT! SHOCKING!

A vid opens up – the pits with three figures on the edge watching WRMS drones salvage cabinets and electronic gear. It is a simple scene, pristine, bucolic even, with no pasture add-ons. There is no hopeful green stuff woven here. The drones move carefully over the rocky bottom carrying their prizes to waiting tankers. The three figures walk above, watching. A VO says, The P and Sentry have identified those responsible for the disappearance of Matt D.

Oh no. I don't want to see this. I don't want to see this.

Hey, there we are, says Pluto. Boy I need a makeover. What a mess! You look good though. He cackles again. Can't really see us, now that you mention. Ha. Could be anybody, actually.

I do not look good. I do not look.

I hear the VO though:

These three are responsible for Matt's disappearance. They are now all in custody. We are showing you raw footage of the first netting. Sentry dragon choppers are seen here moving in on the suspects. Watch carefully. One is netted. There! They have him! He is struggling to escape the polymer binding, but no can do! The dragon is reeling him in. There he goes! Inside the belly of the great air beast! What a show! We are told by highly placed sources in a position to know that he is now back in the Zone and is undergoing extensive scrutiny. He is under watch and the P himself is looking in. We may be able to present this individual for viewing in a few minutes. The President will also appear and make a statement. The netting of these unfortunates brings to a successful conclusion the efforts to locate and return Matt D. Matt himself, we are told by those same highly placed sources in various positions to know, may be joining the P for the briefing show. You can see here the captured individual said to be the mastermind behind this incredible story! His name, one second, his name is, I have it. No, I'm told we do not have a name yet. We will bring that to you as soon as it's edited and available. I can say, however, that the P and his close advisors are examining a supposed handyman seen in the Hood who may also be responsible for the conflagration raging there now.

Pluto says, Conflagration? Did I call it? Am I right? They are so predictable, honey. So predictable.

There's no conflagration, I say. We were just there not more than a few hours ago. There are a bunches of anxious Hoodies afraid of the night. That's it. They are talking about Jimmy. They are talking about us. What are they doing?

Who's to say there's no conflagration? He says. Look at all this ash sifting down. You gonna argue with the screens? Ha ha ha. Anyways, watch this, now.

He seems expectant. He seems to be poised. He is excited.

There's gonna be some action, Pluto says. I can feel it coming.

What is with this guy, I wonder. How can he be excited at this point? I can't think of anything worse than watching Jimmy paraded through angry, abusive crowds. They are spitting on him. He's dressed in a clown suit, topped with a dunce cap, badgered by mocking throngs brought out by the P's advance team, his producers, or something. Jimmy is being kicked. He is down. The sweepers are on his case. I don't want to be here!

The shots of choppers have dissolved, and Pluto's little screen displays an elegant room. Graceful wing chairs are arranged near a flickering gas fireplace. That must be the White-House-By-the-Sea, or one of the mock-ups in a bunker. Looks like the P's brand.

And yes, there is the P striding in, as the cam zooms back, signature grin slapped on his face. Right behind him is Matt D. And there is Jimmy! Jimmy! How could Jimmy be anywhere near there, wherever there is? Plus he is dressed in some kind of Aramid jumpsuit. This is all wrong. Jimmy never wears anything but retro chinos and leather whatever pulled from the pits or an old building collapse. Plus his hair is as neat as fresh laundry. He is buffed and shining and lighting up the room. He is positively glowing as he slaps Matt on the back and points him to a chair.

I want to die looking at this. It is so off, so wrong, it feels like I stepped on a mine.

I have to sit down, I tell Pluto. Shut that fracking thing off. Shut it off!

Hold on Honey, the best is yet to come, he says. They really hold nothing back.

That can't be Jimmy, I say.

Don't know, says Pluto, can't say myself, but I learned a long time ago, about the time I began balancing along the edges out here, that what pops up on a screen one day, may head into the trash the next. Ha ha. Maybe vice versa, too. Honey, I grab what once was but isn't anymore, though it might be again. Kinda like what you do, but I do it because nothing deserves to disappear, even bad stuff, you know? Need to hang on to what was, no matter what it was.

I have what you once saw but can't see now, he says. Then again, what you see may not be what you get. A fool sees not the same tree a wise man sees, that's what Grampa Pluto used to say.

What are you? I ask, a fool or a wise man?

Don't know, cackles Pluto, ain't no trees to tell by. Ha ha. But I'll tell you honey, I got a lot of what once was, a lot of it, back at the shack. Stuff'll go to an archive maybe, if there is an archive, which may or may not be the case. Ha ha.

Stop! Stop with that shit!

I'm sorry, says Pluto, suddenly contrite and considerate. One thing you realize after a nanosec out here is that everything dies away like the sound of a word, he says. I kinda want to keep the echoes going though. The unseen lasts forever if you handle it right, even if it's dilapidating.

I am weak in my bones, but I am drawn to Pluto's screen and its seductive blaze and Jimmy! Matt is thanking Jimmy, or something, or whomever, thanking him for the rescue.

If it weren't for you and the courageous Britt, I would not be here, Matt says.

Courageous Britt?

Jimmy turns red.

Folks, Matt continues, we are fortunate to have brave fans like Jimmy and Britt who are willing to risk comfort and a night of viewing and selling and all-around pleasure, to extricate their fellows, and in my own personal case, to go the extra mile and pull the Ville and the Zone from catastrophe, to keep the images flowing, to keep me on the screens. I don't know what would have happened if Britt and Jimmy had not appeared in the outlying districts somewhere in the hinterlands when they did. Dropped from the sky it seemed. I was dealing with a desperate gang of terrorists, street disruptors, an invasive species, I truly believe, who threatened me with cancellation if I did not accede to their demands and follow their direction.

What did they want? Matt says, in an overly earnest tone. (Where is the Mizz when you need her to grab him by the throat and pour the pills down? I still watch though.)

They wanted appearances in my show! he says to us. They wanted to muscle onto the stage, they wanted to become big wheels in all of our lives. They wanted to take over my platform. Can you imagine that? They were threatening my space, my performance, my future – all of our futures – to get their way and appear in my life and in all of our lives that are my lives. They were threatening to insert a wad of cyclonite in a Plug™ and force feed me! Those are the kinds of drama queens we're dealing with here. They intended to broadcast the dispersal of my body parts! They were going to shoot me up like a missile and watch me rain down on the Zone. And stream it out to you the whole way down!

The P interrupts at this point.

Matt, he says, we are still looking at this series of events and I'd appreciate it if you left the explication of any details and attendant speculation to the authorized production experts. We don't know what exactly happened, but one thing we do know: Everyone's a critic. So we are examining feeds and we are still seeking to reel in Britt who was given the hook, everybody, by some losers working the fringe. But we will all pull together and get back on the tracks very soon. Why? Because it speaks to our better nature, the satisfaction of now, and to the future we have shining brightly ahead.

Absolutely, says Matt. I know you will find my old friend Britt and return her to her own familiar rooms. We all want to see what's going on there!

Old friend? Old friend?

Matt moves right along.

But I want to give this final shout out to Jimmy, Matt says, the Wonder Man, the Man of a Thousand Faces, and let everyone know that I will be back in my own life as soon as I wrap up this outside appearance, although, I believe we are also streaming from within Zoneratti, which everyone should check out, right now. I know that Mizz is waiting. She will spread her arms and enwrap me. I can't wait! And I know you can't.

So this is how it ends? I say to Pluto, who shrugs.

How can I be the wicked witch and the good witch? I ask. How can I be a marauder and a savior at the same time? What about Jimmy? I don't want to go back there. I can't go back there! I want Jimmy, just Jimmy, the real Jimmy, here. We need to find someplace outside where what you touch is what you touch and who you talk to and hang with are the same ones you talk to and hang with tomorrow and tomorrow and tomorrow. You're here, you've been here, you should know.

Oh I've been here, all right, Pluto says. I've been here all my life, just like Pappy Pluto and Grampa Pluto and Great Grampa Pluto and his pappy going way back. We are here, I'm told – it's a family story, I guess you'd say – because there was some kind of altercation or floodification or eruption who knows when and it did not turn out well. So we come out here and staked a claim outside the screens, and been here ever since. The P – not the current P but the old P, the then P – kinda decided to just let sleeping dogs lie, I guess. Well, the corps did, actually, you know. What is the P without the corps? And vice versa?

I am not even listening to this.

Everything has a purpose, he says. That's what they say anyways.

We are in another wilderness, I think. Maybe somebody else has been in this wilderness before us, but it's wilderness just the same. Pluto is rattling on about wilderness now, wilderness and traveling, and finally staking a claim. He says this is the only place worthwhile. He says he guards it, sort of, from the screens. Keeps track. Everything has a purpose, he says. We shouldn't forget the purpose or the things, he says. He says. He says. He says.

It doesn't matter.

All I have is myself, or what I seem to be, and I want Jimmy! They've sucked all the blood from him and left a dried husk and a luminous glow. I want the arms and the boy. I want those chinos and those strands of falling hair. I want his angles of cheek. His expertise. His lips! Why didn't I understand this before? Was I so scraped out myself I didn't see a thing? But maybe the body remembers. Maybe it does. Maybe for all the scraping and scrubbing, something essential remains, like an underdrawing.

The predatory choppers are gone. I didn't even see them leave.

I need something real, I say to Pluto. I don't mean in the screens, I mean here. I think Jimmy is real.

Oh, he replies, looking out across the pits, out over the cracked ground beyond, this is real.

A rumble of Megas. Arcs of packages blasting into the air. The slosh of Nutri-Waste. Brown dirt stretching forever. Lethal sunlight. Oh let us love the real! I think to myself. Oh let us love it all, for god's sake.

You know where you stand when you're out here, Pluto says over the noise of whipping, grinding drones. I sure know it, and now you do too. This here dollar Briggsy gave you tells me you're okay. He pulls the crumpled old green paper from his pocket and shows it to me.

I'm not okay, I say, curling myself into a tight ball behind the post, out of the sunlight, away from the sky.

I just want to die.

Why would that be?

I've lost everything I knew I had and thought I wanted and now I've lost everything I've found and realize is worth something more than a micro.

But now you know where you stand, he says.

Great. I can't even stand. I'm tucked into a ball like something ill, hard by the feeding dump. That's just great. My best friends have vanished. I have nowhere to live. The P is on my case and I'm starving.

I glare at him.

I don't even know who I am, I scream. Who am I? Do you know? Tell me that. Who am I?

Why, you're just you.

I bury my face into my scrunched up legs. I wrap my arms tight around my shins. I'm me.

Pluto is silent a long time as the dumping continues. Look, he says, I don't know where your friend

Jimmy is or where your friend Deb might be. I don't know where anyone is, really, but I can give you some advice and a small token that may help you out.

I feel listless, but it's possible he may have something to say. I think of the glow on Jimmy's face when he was captivated by the screen last night and his disappearing self when he was bagged by polymer and drawn into the air just an hour or so ago. Those are bookends for life in the Ville and the Hood and the Zone and here at the pits too, no matter what Pluto says.

There are so many ways to be captivated and captured.

I can't go back to that. I can't go back to looking at myself in the mirror every day and bragging about it on my site. I can't keep rummaging around seeking something that's been said repeatedly so that I can say it again, but not the same. I can't live a series of riffs for sale. If everything is a possible sale, what's mine? What remains? What stays?

There's nothing here, either, nothing here in this wilderness – everything's been devoured already. Pluto's born to it; he's like some exotic critter, something that once ranged around here or maybe still ranges far up in the northern zones. They say there's all kinds of stuff up there, including camps.

Down here, where I am this very moment, nothing. Pluto's inured to the Megas and the dirt and the broken bricks. He's habituated to the rubble raining down every day. He's toughened up. This is his world, his and the invisible Serb – they rule the pits where everything does not end, but continues on in a dwindling circle of reuse.

How can I get out of this? I ask.

Well honey I was wondering when you was going to ask. Now you brought me that token from Briggsy, so that means a lot. He and I are sort of aligned. We help each other out and scout ropers, you know.

Ropers?

Yeah, the guys and dolls they send in to draw people like me and Briggsy out into the open where we're easy marks. See, honey, it's all a con, a grift, a scam. We're all marks, more or less. To the P. To the corps. Nothing but marks.

Chumps? I say.

Yep. So Briggsy and me, we have our ways of helping each other out and giving a hand to people who want to exit the game. Not easy, as you have noticed. Not easy to pick them out either. Some people think they want out, but don't really – they just want to make it all work better for them. Some people want to con us, I mean. So we're pretty careful, know what I'm saying?

No.

I am waiting for Pluto to get to the point here, so I just say, What's your point? It's a flim-flam? What else could it be? What difference does that make?

Sorry, he says, sometimes folks don't get it. They think they can beat it. They think it's real and working for them.

He pauses, rolling the thought around.

I've got something for you, Pluto says. He reaches into his pocket and pulls out a small silver key and hands it to me.

It's tarnished, of course. I look at it and then at him.

What's this? I say.

That's the key to the highway, he says. Ha ha.

And I laugh a little too. I know that one.

You don't hear much music around, but when I was little at Mrs. Petri's, Sally Kamaski taught me some old songs late at night, night songs during quiet time. Mrs. Petri didn't sing herself, although she liked the jingles we learned in our lessons – Every day in every way we're getting better and better; Plugs for the Plugged In; I feel happy, I feel healthy, I feel showy! She'd do these ta-das and hum-alongs with little Nutri tunes.

Sally knew some real songs, like old ones. I don't have any idea where she picked them up or why she sang them to me in those whispery late nights. She was just a kid. Shine on, shine on, largest moon, beyond the sky, da da da. Deb did great songs and incredible thumpa-thumpa-thumpa-thumpas! But that was all for the screens.

The gurncy boy and the Nighttime Echoes were something else again. Real music seems to do well on the edges of things, when songs get between spaces and can roll off walls and work their way into your blood arteries. Music, real music, makes your body visible. It reveals the world. It gives you yourself. That's what I think. What if Deb just made music of her own? What if she could just do that? What if she just broke into a song for the heck of it?

I'm not too young, I'm not too old
Not too timid, not too bold
Just the kind you'd like to hold
Just the kind for sport I'm told
Ta-ra-ra BOOM de-ay!

I can see Sally just standing in her room. She turns to me:

Ta-ra-ra BOOM! de-ay!

She'd yowl it out in a bumpy whisper and the whole room would bump along with her. But she stopped after awhile. And then she became Miss Diva, who only made music when it was worth her while. I sang Sally's song for Deb after President's Girl fell apart. She loved it and needed it. Songs are for the bad times, and even the good. They give you power to be. The key to the highway. Ta-ra-ra BOOM de-ay!

What's this key for? Why are you giving this to me? I say to Pluto. I turn it over in my hand.

Take that key and head up to the Orpheum, Pluto says.

The Orpheum? We were there. Heard what seemed like voices coming from it, but the building was all sealed and when we tried to get in and knocked and all that, nothing happened. Nobody let us in. I don't know if anyone was really there.

No, says Pluto. That's why you've got this key. It will get you in that front door. Maybe they're there and might be able to hook you into what you want, whatever that might be. Or maybe not.

Why are you giving this to me?

Why not? You seem to want the real. You can give it back, of course. Here, I'll take it.

No, I say. But I don't see the point, if you want to know the truth.

You might find something you're looking for, says Pluto.

But everything I'm looking for just disappears anyway, sometimes before I even know I'm looking for it.

Happens that way sometimes, he says. That's what we built for ourselves. Built and tore down. Been wrecking ourselves for a long, long time.

I hold the key in my hand. Where could I go with this? No doors offer anything for me. I put it in my pocket. I put it in my pocket and think that maybe I can find a way to get back to Jimmy. Maybe find out something about Deb. I need some time to like regroup. What else is there? I've got to regroup. I'm a fool for hoping.

The Megas have been still for some time now. No drones are moving about in the pits, although I can't really see all the way down. It's pretty quiet. This key may be useful. I will find Deb and Jimmy. I know I can. I have to. I close my eyes and see the Megas high over me preparing to launch. Here comes Jerry! Here comes the muddy Nutri fountain, full of last night's leavings. The Megas launch again and again and the catchment area fills with reeking waste liquids. Oh my god. You have disrupted the whole system! Mrs. Petri says, her pearl-like face right on top of me. You have built an empire of dissatisfaction and doubt! It is ugly! Angelina, you are not listening and we can't have that! Angelina! Angelina!

I open my eyes and it's just the pits, the pervasive echo of the pits. Pluto is dozing. I get up. Maybe I should head out now. It's not a good thing to travel in the daytime, but maybe I'll be better off. I can see around the post, out over the pits, out along the crusted dirt. There's nothing. Yes, I think I'll move out now. I look down at Pluto who starts and looks up.

I'm going back to the Orpheum, I say.

He stands up and takes out an unmarked bag from one of his pockets. Geez, he's carrying a lot of stuff!

Take this, he says. Serb and I eat em instead of plugs. Pappy Pluto got ahold of some seeds, I think it was pappy, and we still grow em over by the shack. They're real.

I look in and see some green things.

Thanks.

He says, If you're traveling out now, just head up that road over there. He points in a direction veering off from the way we came in. Ranklin Way.

Clear curving shot to the Orpheum, if that's where you're headed, he says.

That's where I'm headed.

Oh my god, I think – I'm going back.

If you find your friends, lemme know, Pluto says. Want to hear what y'all've got to tell. Watch out on the street. Weather should be fine, I hear.

Sure.

I pocket the key, pat his shoulder, turn away from the pits and begin walking. At the corner, I look back. Pluto's watching me. He gives a brief wave and then walks out from behind the post and heads back to the pits, his horseless kingdom.

I'm alone again now, but this is what I want to do. This is what I need to do, for me and for Deb and for Jimmy. The bot sweepers and Megas from the front of the orchestration building are gone. The concrete approach stretches off, empty now, the morning business done. I walk close to the building, alongside a row of pallets, until I see a small rise and Ranklin Way leading north. That's where I have to go. I have to go north.

I reach into my pocket and then realize I have no pad anymore. I've cut that cord. It would be useful to have something. Maybe I should wait until dark. Maybe I ought to just find some place, hang for a few hours, and then head to the Orpheum.

What would Jimmy do? He'd probably say wait, like he did back at my room. Wait for awhile. Okay, where do I wait, though? I look around. There's nothing. No buildings or walls. No tunnels. No caves or ditches. What flatness! It's hard to imagine anything built here, but there was at some point. Why else would you want to have all this concrete? You build stuff on it so it doesn't sink in, you know. They took it down, though, or something, or it fell down, and nobody ever bothered to build it back up. Why should they? Everything else is collapsing and sinking anyway, whether it's built on concrete or just plain old dirt. Who needs a building when you have a universe on a screen?

I walk up Ranklin. The sun is hot and its light is falling directly on me. Invisible light full of all the colors you can think of, invisible light that will sizzle you in a nanosec. I see a little gully with some spiky dead brush along its edges. A concrete block juts out over the top. That's where I'll maybe take a nap for a few hours and then head to the Orpheum. Sounds good. Yep, that's what I'll do. I jump in and settle under the stone, take out Pluto's bag and have some of the green things. They are long, like fingers, and crunch. A peculiar taste, too, like nothing I've ever had, kind of sweet though. I eat them all.

The rumbling must have awakened me. I can hear it coming from somewhere, but I don't know where. I don't know how long I slept on this stony dirt. I'm wedged into what is really a shallow crevice, dead branches reaching out over me beyond the cornice of concrete.

I listen closely. Yes, definitely a rumbling and a grinding. Sitting up, I look around. There's nothing to see, but I can tell I've been asleep for quite awhile. The sun is high and bright. There's nothing I can do about that though. I should head out. Are they still looking for Britt? Or have I made an appearance in Zoneratti already? What will they have me wearing? Will I be a hero? Or will I be somebody for Matt to trash? Maybe Jimmy will rescue me and then bed me or stick me in a bottle. Maybe I've just disappeared.

No. I am here. This is where I am. This fringy tableland.

There are fragments of foundations alongside the road now. I see them more frequently as I walk toward the Orpheum – cement pads or squares of blocks laid down in the dirt. Buildings were here once. What happened to them? Piles of rubble rise higher and higher the further I go.

The rumbling is growing louder. I must be nearing a sweeper area, but they don't usually operate outside the center of the Ville. Or at least I thought that until the rats and the gimpy soldiers ended up in the pits.

What else don't I know?

There! There's the first real building shell, off to the right. Several floors wrapped in dark red brick. No words on the side of that one, just the bulge that precedes collapse. There's another one, a smaller shell, it's fronted by a concrete approach. A fallen sign, most of it rusted and broken away, sits near the street. XX it says. X marks the spot. Of what?

The further I go, the closer I get to the Orpheum, the more signs and buildings lean and topple along the way. HELL and LUX teeter over the road. Warnings maybe or directions or signs of some kind of dual world to puzzle over. The HELL of the Ville, the LUX of the Zone. I don't have time for this now. I'm walking fast through the sun and I am definitely getting close, I think. I don't want to pause and puzzle over the ancient mysteries, the words from the past. I want to move and move quickly back into the present.

This is a much more direct route than the one we took last night when Jimmy seemed more foggy the further along we went. Out of the Hood, he just seemed to lose himself in some way. No surprise, really we've all lost ourselves.

What happens now at the Orpheum? I wonder. Are there really people in there? It seems bizarre, even though I heard the voices. I'm sure they were voices. Somebody definitely told us to go away. Somebody definitely was hostile in that place. I don't think I made that up in my head. I sure don't think it was a recording we activated somehow.

If there are people in there, who are they and what will they do? I get the feeling that they are like escapees or rejects. Pluto didn't say that, but it sort of sounded like that's what he was saying. There were voices all the way in the tunnel from my rooms, too. Or what sounded like voices. Murmurs and snorts, like there was life.

Maybe they will help me with Deb and Jimmy? I think about that for a moment. Pluto wouldn't have given me that key and told me to go to the Orpheum if there wasn't help there. Or would he? Maybe Pluto isn't who he seems to be. Maybe he's simply telling me to do something just for his own amusement. Or something that would make it easier for them to bag me. No, that couldn't be. Couldn't. There's no choice in the matter anyway. Here is where I am.

Pluto must be the genuine article, I decide, his bona fides are okay. Jimmy vouched for him. He talked about Brute. He talked about Melinda. Like they are real. No, Pluto is all right. But maybe he's wrong about this Orpheum. Definitely hostile vibes coming from that place, although not as hostile as what Jerry the MC had to deal with on the street outside. If there was somebody inside, they could've helped him. They could've. Maybe they couldn't. What's in that old pile could simply be sounds left over from what once was. A tape loop, really. Echoes.

Oh my god, I am so out of my depth here. I wasn't trained to be some kind of sleuth or subversive. I just want to be me. That's all. I just want to be left to myself and decide what to do and where to go and how to do it on my own. Using my own inner resources. All that's been stripped away. I don't know how to do anything except what I'm told. And I can break down a squeeze page and pull together a focus group and get it to say what I want it to say so I can move product and draw some ads. Really useful stuff.

The rumbling is now much louder. This is not good. I look around. There is nothing behind me. The buildings are more substantial now, more like the built-up Ville. Where is that sound coming from? I stop and listen, but the echoes off the building walls seem to come from all over. The light is beginning to die, too. I hurry up a bit. Uh-oh. I see cams on the next corner. Are the street feeds live? Probably. But I have no signal, so it most likely doesn't matter. Who am I? They may try to run an FR scan if these cams are operational.

Okay, there's nothing I can do about it but keep going. I pass beneath the first cam and see two more in the next block. If they scan me, they can run me through Fat Boy, shoot the data to the sats and track me that way, once they zero in on the protein emissions. Geez. Protein emissions. That is a revolting thought. We emit on a molecular level.

Ta-ra-ra BOOM de-ay! I shout it out. It comes from nowhere and everywhere.

Ta-ra-ra BOOM de-ay! Ta-ra-ra BOOM de-ay! Ta-ra-ra BOOM de-ay! Ta-ra-ra BOOM de-ay! Ta-ra-ra BOOM de-ay! Ta-ra-ra BOOM de-ay! Ta-ra-ra BOOM de-ay! Ta-ra-ra BOOM de-ay!

I shout it as loudly as I can. I can drown that rumbling. I can echo off the walls. I can smother it all. I am giddy. Maybe it's the sun. Ha!
It's me.

Ta-ra-ra BOOM de-ay!

And then I see them coming right at me, a whole squadron of Megas rolling along, bouncing right down the street with a coterie of little bots fanning out on both sides, little helpers. Oh shit. There is no way around them. Somehow I think these guys are not concerned with motion. They are not concerned with stillness or warmth. They aim to cleanse.

I am at the street corner, I cut to my right and run as fast as I can past some broken down old buildings and a corroded hulk, its insides spilled out and ravaged,

337

its polyresins degraded. Nothing left to take or use – it's all devoured already. I look back and see the Megas round the corner. Okay. I look to my right and see another line of Megas moving up this new street. Ahead is another. Definitely not good. A cam is above me.

I go left and just run. At each corner I look. The road behind me is now clogged with sweepers, and at each corner they begin the same announcement:

Your attention please. This area is now closed. Please do not proceed. Sanitization is about to commence. We are sorry for the inconvenience. Thank you. Attention. Sanitization is about to commence.

The rumbling is deafening. There must be hundreds of bot cleaners sweeping this useless area. They are all focused on me. They want to dissolve me for I have sinned. How far is the Orpheum? It can't be far. I am not going to end in the pits. No fucking way.

Ta-ra-ra BOOM de-ay!

I stop to rest. It really can't be far now. I am breathing hard. I am exhausted.

Ta-ra-ra BOOM de-ay! Ta-ra-ra BOOM de-ay!

I will find Deb! I will find Jimmy!

The Megas do not stop. They do not rest. I head left back to Ranklin and continue north toward the Orpheum. The rumbling is overwhelming now. It seems to billow through the whole street; the entire Ville is shaking with this monumental effort to purify itself by tracking down a failed clerk. I continue to trot, slower, but still okay, until over a slight rise I see the Orpheum, its brick façade quiet in the ebbing light. I can make it. I can make it. Maybe a block.

I look behind me. The machines are closer now.

They are an advancing posse, a mop up crew moving in after the fire fight. I hear the whoosh! of their vacuums.

Cleaning is about to commence. Attention!

I sprint the last block to the Orpheum and move toward its foyer. I see another line of Megas headed toward me from up the street and across the square. Where the hell is Pluto's key? I need it now!

It is a simple key, tarnished at the top. I am at the door. Megas are really quite close now. If this key is a phony, I'm sunk.

I insert it in the lock. It fits! I turn it. The lock clicks. I pull and the door opens.

I look back at the Megas, all topped by tiaras of orange circles. They are very close. I step over the threshold and slam the door shut. I lean back and just breathe for a moment. Through the door I hear that whiney metallic voice:

Attention! We apologize for any inconvenience. Sanitization is about to commence. Thank you.

It is dark inside, dark with a faint smell of must pierced by something sweet and cool and peculiar. My eyes are adjusting to the dimness. In front of me is a stairway leading down. Another set of stairs to the right leads up.

I hear voices coming from deep underneath somewhere. I'm sure. Talking, rustling, moving. The creak of chairs.

It all stops and there is nothing but the sound of simple motes drifting.

O dear god, I think. This is just one more dead end. One more con. I am done and gone. I take a step.

A voice calls up from below: Who's there?

I hold my breath.

Who's there? Account for yourself.

ACKNOWLEDGEMENTS

Many friends read this manuscript at various points and contributed often-astute, often funny observations. I want you to know how important those comments were to me. I am, of course, solely responsible for any screw-ups. A special thanks to Jennifer Baker, whose editorial judgment, sharp eye, sense of humor, and encouragement have been invaluable.

CPSIA information can be obtained
at www.ICGtesting.com
Printed in the USA
BVHW09s2251290818
525942BV00010B/329/P